PRAISE FO

"*Crystal Blue Murder* is an expertly crafted mystery that kept me guessing until the end. In addition, Oliver Parrott is the most charming detective to come along in quite some time. He and his family -- consisting of a hero wife struggling with PTSD and a cockatiel who steals every scene he's in -- elevate this into one of the best procedural series going. Satisfying in every way, *Crystal Blue Murder* is another wonderful installment in author Saralyn Richard's Detective Parrott series."— **Rick Treon**, award-winning author of *Deep Background* and *Let the Guilty Pay*

"Detective Parrott and his chatty cockatiel, Horace, are back in this delightfully entertaining and expertly crafted mystery. *Crystal Blue Murder* keeps you glued to the page from its explosive beginning to its suspenseful end. Saralyn Richard is a masterful storyteller!" —**Margaret Mizushima**, author of the award-winning Timber Creek K-9 Mysteries, including *Striking Range*

"We could talk about the intrigue and solving the mystery, but for me, relationships make the story. The tender, loving relationship between Detective Parrott and his wife, Tonya, was perhaps what I most enjoyed about *Crystal Blue Murder*." —**Sheila Lowe**, author of the Forensic Handwriting suspense series

"What's not to love about the tenacious Detective Parrott who sifts through the evidence of arson and murder, uncowed by self-entitled gentry. While dealing with his own issues, Parrott digs out long-hidden secrets, and, at great risk to his person, proves his worth to the people of Brandywine Valley." —**Susan P. Baker**, author of the Mavis Davis Mystery Series.

"In *Crystal Blue Murder,* readers will find Saralyn Richard's hallmark clear writing, vivid descriptions, and an assortment of complicated characters with deep secrets, stirring a plot so delicious one must keep reading. The tension, surprises, and sparks of humor as Detective Oliver Parrott unravels another Brandywine Valley mystery make this book another page-turner in the series."–**Ginny Fite,** award-winning author of the Detective Sam Lagarde mystery series

"When Claire Whitman, the owner of Sweetgrass, blasts into one of Detective Parrott's Brandywine Valley cases, he has to remind himself that nothing is as perfect as it seems." —**Phyllis H. Moore**, author of the Meg Miller Mystery Series

CRYSTAL BLUE MURDER

SARALYN RICHARD

PALM CIRCLE PRESS

GENRE: Police Procedural

Crystal Blue Murder is a work of fiction. Names, places, characters, and incidents are either the product of the author's imagination or are used fictitiously, and any resemblance to any actual persons, living or dead, businesses, organizations, events, or locales is entirely coincidental. All trademarks, service marks, registered trademarks, and registered service marks are the property of their respective owners and are used herein for identification purposes only. The publisher does not have any control over or assume any responsibility for author or third-party websites or their contents.

Also by Saralyn Richard

Bad Blood Sisters

A Murder of Principal

A Palette for Love and Murder: A Detective Parrott Mystery

Murder in the One Percent: A Detective Parrott Mystery

Naughty Nana

To Mamie and Scott
Third time the charm

CHAPTER ONE

B eing awakened at two a.m. was bad enough, but the word *explosion* yanked Detective Oliver Parrott out of bed in nothing flat. The barn on eighty-two-year-old celebrity hostess, Claire Whitman's fifty-acre farm was burning.

Grumbling, Chief Schrik elaborated. "Suspected meth lab. Whitman and her helper evacuated. Air quality testers from Philly're on the way. Fire chief asked for you by name."

The touch of flattery did little to diminish the adrenaline surge. Parrott threw on the shirt and pants left on the chair the night before, tiptoeing so as not to wake Tonya. He brushed the grit from his eyes and downed a glass of cold water. He needed to be alert. The only meth lab explosion he'd ever investigated was a simulation. His role would be secondary to the fire department's, but no less dangerous. If it was meth, laws had been broken, and people who cooked drugs could be unpredictable, desperate, or violent. Parrott sped to the scene, hoping to arrive before all evidence was reduced to ashes.

Driving on the winding country roads, windows down and with the summer breeze sweeping his face and neck, he had mixed feelings—dread of what might lie ahead, but also, he had to admit, excitement. Solving crimes was its own elixir, and that never got old. He barreled toward the dark, quiet countryside, the woodsy smells giving way to something more sinister.

When he turned off the road and onto the long driveway of the Whitman estate, the lack of streetlights didn't matter. The fire illuminated the area like a beacon. A third-of-a-mile away, and the noxious chemical odors and thick, warm air already wrapped him in toxic filth. Meth fires were no joke.

Parrott rolled up the car windows and turned on his flashers. A firefighter in a white hazmat suit waved him to the side of the roadway, a good five hundred yards before the gravel path to what might once have been a stately barn, set into a hillock. Jagged blackened edges of burning timber stood tentatively above a stone wall base, the spray from hoses jousting with the still-raging flames.

"Over here," the firefighter yelled, pointing toward a sprawling willow near the side of the road.

When Parrott stepped out of his car, the stocky fireman extended a gloved hand and a hearty welcome, despite the occasion. "Detective Parrott? Name's Skip. Heard a lot about ya, kid."

Parrott shook the offered hand, thinking this was no time for compliments. Parrott focused on the suit that hung over Skip's left forearm and boots on the ground next to him.

"Put this stuff on. The air's poison."

Grateful for the protective garb, Parrott stepped into a fire-resistant jumpsuit that covered his body, clothes, and all. He pulled the hood up over the top of his head, securing the drawstring. He traded his Nikes for thick, steel-reinforced boots.

Skip handed him a black gas mask, identical to the one he now pulled over his own face. Parrott donned the mask, glad he'd never been claustrophobic. Heavy rubber gloves completed the uniform. Eager to begin his search, Parrott headed toward the blaze, but Skip shook his head, blocking him. Talking through the gas masks was difficult, but Parrott understood. Everything about this scene was dangerous—the fire, the debris, the toxicity. There was even the possibility of another explosion if flames reached a new accelerant.

Parrott nodded, but he wasn't going to stand there watching while he waited for the firefighters to get the blaze under control. He moved his gloved index finger in a large circle. "Get a look around," he shouted.

Throwing his Nikes into the front seat of his car, he grabbed his tactical flashlight, cell phone, and an evidence kit, all of which he pocketed in the suit. He took off at a slow jog, the heavy boots dragging on him. He kept adequate distance between himself and the intense heat from the barn. The light from the flames illuminated the gravel path and the split-rail fence that separated this part of the property from the rest.

As he circled the perimeter of the barn, he looked for any signs of traffic, other than those of emergency vehicles--tracks of wheels, footprints, objects dropped on the gravel or grass. He didn't expect to find much from this distance, but he'd rather be moving than standing still.

On his second lap, he gazed in the opposite direction. The generations-old Whitman country mansion stood, tall and broad and neatly etched against the horizon to the east, quiet in contrast to the drama surrounding the barn. Where had the inhabitants gone in the middle of the night—to a nearby farm? Or somewhere closer to Philadelphia? A car or truck was parked on the circular drive, in front of the house. Parrott couldn't tell for sure with the smoke and distance. He saw no spectators anywhere on the property, not even wildlife—only firefighters, going at the fire like a flock of furious birds on attack.

Parrott stopped jogging. The flames were dying now, and with them, the illumination of his path. Spots of light shone from the headlamps and other high-intensity flashlights attached to fire equipment, but these were focused on the smoldering remains of the barn. Parrott was glad to have his own flashlight, even if he would have to decontaminate it later. As he paused to assess the disaster zone in front of him, the pungent acid-smell invaded his gas mask, and the air hung about him like a thick sooty curtain.

This scene was going to be a bear—a grizzly. As Skip or another white-suited firefighter waved him onto the main stage, Parrott sucked in a deep breath. He strode into the path of destruction with only one hope, a slim one—no dead bodies.

CHAPTER TWO

Barn conversions were fairly common in Brandywine Valley, and Claire Whitman's bank barn, built into a hill, so it had ground-level entrances on two floors, had probably been one of the simpler remodels. Based on the stone wall perimeter, the barn was about eight thousand square feet, four thousand on the ground floor and another four thousand in the converted loft. The exterior of the first floor was composed of large stones, still largely intact.

Skip materialized at Parrott's side again, apparently to welcome him into the still-smoldering debris. "Be careful. You can burn yourself on some of these surfaces, so test everything before touching." Skip tapped the top of a pile of timbers to illustrate.

"This stone stable?" Parrott shouted at Skip as they approached the structure.

"Can't count on it. Fire melts grout. One minute it looks solid, and the next minute it starts to crumble." The fireman shoved a gloved fist against the timbers at the top of the nearest boulder. A sheet of wall, covered in sparks and cinders, crashed to the ground, but the stone held. Can't take anything for granted in explosions like this."

Parrott recalled having read about a famous local explosion and fire in the early 1800s. "Wasn't the Dupont gunpowder factory a stone building?"

"Sure was. Over in Hagley Yards. And even so, it blew up in the direction of the river, and people were killed."

As they entered the stone perimeter, Parrott and Skip stopped shouting at each other through their masks. Other firefighters were moving about, some with hoses, some with hatchets and other equipment. There was no clear path to take. Debris littered the entire area, most objects barely recognizable after collapsing or burning to cinders.

Preserving the crime scene would be near to impossible under these circumstances. All the objects were either scattered in pieces or burned, some still too hot to touch. The roof had caved in, and timber fragments lay across objects that might have been toilets and cabinets and furniture. Parrott had investigated fire damage before, but nothing like this. At any moment, a wall could cave in, or another fire could break out. Everything in sight was coated with ash and chemical residue. The masks helped, but Parrott wondered whether they screened out all the poisons.

Parrott's initial excitement over the new case was tempered now by thoughts of what his wife would say if she knew he was here. Tonya suffered from PTSD. Anything could trigger an attack, and lately Tonya had been harping on the dangers of Parrott's job.

He couldn't dwell on Tonya's fears, though. Inside the hot protective suit, his heart pounded, and his breath came in staccato gulps. Parrott let the adrenaline do its job. He knew what to do--observe, note, question, hypothesize, and repeat. Whatever bad things had happened in this place, he would discover them. He might not be able to make them right, but he could make them better.

Skip had left Parrott's side to help another fireman clear a path into the interior of the barn. Parrott began a methodical trailblazing of his own, as he crouched, stretched, twisted, and leaped through the debris, the beam from his tactical flashlight leading the way. He would make this first pass as quick as possible, without sacrificing thoroughness of observation. He'd search more meticulously once he had daylight on his side.

In the dark wet muck, he could make out a few objects—a brass headboard, a broken sink, a fragment of countertop. It was hard to tell which items had fallen from the second floor, although, if he had to guess, the living quarters had been there. He swiped his gloved hand over his visor to clear it of ash and soot, and he shone his light on the ground in big arcs around him, looking for whatever interesting bits of information he could glean. Bits became pieces, and pieces became stories. He wouldn't leave until he had a picture of what had happened.

As he eased himself further into the center of the barn, Parrott hit paydirt. His flashlight caught the gleam of something shiny under what might've been a table. Parrott dropped to the ground and shone the light under the crushed furniture. The light illuminated a pile of hypodermic needles, maybe a gross of them, lying in a puddle of blackish-amber muck. Needles had been on the list of items most often found in meth labs in the manual Parrott had studied. So were colanders and metal strainers, both of which Parrott found next. Plastic soda bottles would have burned in the fire, but Parrott found a few bottle caps scattered among shards of glass. There was enough evidence that this barn had been a working meth lab. But who was running the operation, here in the yard of a proper dowager, and how and why had it blown up?

He wished he could take photos, but he couldn't use his cell phone without contaminating it. Instead, he dug red sticky flags from his evidence kit. His clumsy gloves slowed him down as he marked areas of potential evidence. Parrott continued his methodical examination of the barn's mystery, swinging his flashlight before him. In the next moment his light landed on something blue—a piece of fabric, part of a short-sleeved shirt. And inside the fabric was a man's arm, covered in soot and blood.

CHAPTER THREE

At eighty-two years of age, Claire Whitman had experienced a lot of highs and lows, and she'd learned anything could happen at any time. Life's events hadn't surprised her in at least two decades. She simply did not permit herself to engage in drama.

So, when her assistant Tammie woke her from a satisfactory sleep to say there had been an explosion in the barn, and they needed to evacuate, Claire didn't cry out in shock. She didn't panic. She insisted on brushing her teeth, combing her silver hair, and putting on a mauve pant suit.

"We need to hurry, Mrs. Whitman. The fumes, and the danger of the fire's spreading." Tammie's melodious voice was raised to its highest volume. Claire didn't bother to reply that her hearing was perfect. Just a little way of facilitating her eavesdropping when the caregivers thought she couldn't hear.

"Relax, Tammie. This time of night we only have the two of us to worry about. I'm practically ready." Claire smeared her lips with her favorite mauve lipstick and grabbed her collapsible cane. "Just in case I need it," she said, holding the implement aloft and dropping it into her handbag. She led the way down the hall to the elevator and down into the kitchen, where a door connected to the laundry room and garage. Claire's stride was purposeful, though slow, and her posture was as perfect as her hearing.

Once seated in the passenger seat of her Mercedes, Claire tapped Tammie on the arm. "By the way, where are we going?"

"We're evacuating. There's a fire in the barn."

"I know that. But what is our destination?" She consulted her wristwatch. "We can't just show up on the doorstep anywhere at two a.m. What's the plan?"

Tammie hesitated. "I thought we'd go to the Fairfield in Kennett Square. They'll probably have a vacant room where we can get a few more hours' sleep. We can eat breakfast there, too. The firefighter I spoke to said we'd be able to come back home by mid-morning if all goes well."

"That's fine, but perhaps we should go back and get a change of clothes and my makeup. I wouldn't want to be embarrassed having breakfast in yesterday's clothes."

"No need, Mrs. Whitman. I took the liberty of packing a few of your necessities in an overnight bag. It's in the trunk."

"That's wonderful." Claire patted her young assistant on the shoulder. "You thought of everything." Now that the most immediate concerns were apparently met, Claire turned her thoughts to the explosion in the converted barn. Many months had passed since she'd set foot inside. Maybe a year.

The barn had housed generations of European sport horses for as long as Claire could remember, up until her granddaughter moved to California to attend Stanford. Of all of them, Bonnie had been the horsewoman. So, in a rare, unified coalition, her daughters had persuaded Claire to sell the horses. "You don't need to worry about horses and stable hands at your age," they had said.

Claire hadn't really missed the horses. She hadn't ridden since her seventy-fifth birthday, when she'd decided that, after a few untoward incidents with orthopedic ramifications, bouncing around six feet off the ground wasn't her cup of tea anymore. The barn had stood empty until a couple of years ago, when her older daughter Jessica pushed converting it to living space. Many Brandywine homeowners had done so, and it had increased the value of their property substantially. Claire's financial planner had concurred with sinking over a million dollars into the structure, and the conversion had become Jessica's passion project. And now it had exploded.

"Tammie, did the fireman give any explanation about the explosion? I hope no one was hurt. Good thing no one was living there yet."

Tammie took her eyes from the country road and squinted at her employer. "Really? I've seen a truck there sometimes when I've been coming or going. I thought you might've rented it out."

"Not at all. I did agree to let Bonnie's boyfriend use it temporarily. Maybe that's whose truck you saw." A twinge tugged at Claire's memory. Bonnie was always coming up with oddball ideas for spending her grandmother's money. "Anyway, I hope nobody was harmed by the explosion. Did they say what caused it?"

Before answering, Tammie made a left turn into the hotel parking lot. She pulled into the circular drive and parked in front of the entrance. "I don't think they knew for sure, but they suspected it might have been a chemical explosion."

"Chemical? How on earth would chemicals get into my barn?"

"I don't know how to tell you this, Mrs. W., but the fireman thought it might be a meth explosion. Do you know what a meth lab is?"

The word, *meth*, hit Claire Whitman in her solar plexus, knocking a burst of air from her throat. After a few seconds, Claire took a deep breath and drew her upper body into a straight line. "Of course, I know what a meth lab is. I read the newspapers every day." She didn't say, though, how much this turn of events had actually surprised her.

CHAPTER FOUR

Finding human remains in the converted barn was a game changer for Parrott. Glad he could engage the radio and mic on his belt without opening the hazmat suit, he radioed for back-up, including the elected coroner and two forensics techs from Chesco, otherwise known as the Chester County governmental offices. Parrott's buddies, Jerry, who headed up the forensics department, and Maria, chief coroner, might still be snoozing at this hour, but Chesco was good about sending help 24/7.

While he waited, Parrott wrapped yellow crime scene tape around the obvious places where someone might enter the burned-out barn. There wasn't enough tape to string it around the entire perimeter—this would have to do.

Someone had set up a flimsy tent about fifty yards from what used to be the front entrance to the barn. Covering the ground underneath it, was a thick plastic tarp. Next to the tent was a large rectangular box for disposing of hazardous materials. This would be the area where everyone would decontaminate, shedding the single-use suits and equipment. A portable shower would be used as a preliminary washing station for non-disposable items.

Parrott made for the split-rail fence behind the tent. The top rail served as a perfect chair for his lanky frame. Now it was 4:15 a.m., and the sky was turning from charcoal to a light-tinged silver. Dawn wouldn't come for another ninety minutes. Chief Schrik would be up, though, and waiting. He punched the radio button again.

"You okay, Parrott?" Schrik's voice was strong, probably laced with a black coffee fix.

"Yep. Still at the scene. At least one body in the rubble. Male. Young. Right arm and leg dismembered. Head, trunk and left side intact."

"Shit. Bad enough to have a meth lab explode on a genteel lady's property, but a casualty, too. Spoils our stats for this year."

"I know." Schrik's concern for the county's published statistics was notorious. Brandywine Valley enjoyed a pristine reputation for safety and security, and Schrik liked keeping the taxpayers happy. Parrott didn't share that exact concern, but then his feet were on a different ground when it came to crime. Parrott was more attuned to picking up the rocks and examining the crawly creatures beneath them. Sometimes that caused friction with his boss. "The county guys are on the way. I'll update you when they've had a look." Parrott's stomach gurgled beneath the layers of clothing.

"You wearing a hazmat? I hate for you to be in that soupy air, but we need you to stick with the scene till Chesco's cleared it."

"I'm covered, like a chicken smothered in gravy." He couldn't wait to get out of the suit, which was becoming hotter and stickier by the minute. "And don't worry. I won't leave." Parrott wished he could fish in his glove compartment for something to mollify his stomach. Surely there were protein bars, but he couldn't contaminate his car, the food, or his insides. "I'll be itching to talk to Mrs. Whitman, though. What's her status?"

"She's stashed at the Fairfield in Kennett Square, a downgrade for her. Her caregiver, Tammie Caballero, has kept in touch with the fire department. They hope to send them back home later this morning."

Schrik's remark about Fairfield being a downgrade was a relatively new habit. Parrott didn't remember his boss's showing resentment of rich people before Parrott, himself, became rich. Maybe it was hard to accept. Schrik had worked hard practically all his sixty years, and Parrott came along and snagged a multi-million-dollar gift at the age of twenty-seven. And then there was the matter of race.

"I'll pay Mrs. Whitman a visit once I get the scene squared away." He stretched his back muscles against the fence. "Wonder how much she knows about what was going on in her barn."

"Two things before you interview her, Parrott. First, she's eighty-two. Who knows how reliable a witness she'll be. Secondly, you'd better put on your best clothes and company manners. Before you were born, Claire Whitman was a famous party hostess. She starred in a weekly TV show called, 'Entertaining with Elegance.' I suspect she's surrounded herself with people a lot different from you and me."

By now Parrott was used to interviewing people different from himself. Brandywine Valley residents were, with few exceptions, rich white people, many with aristocratic ties to the land for generations. Schrik had taken a chance to hire a young Black detective for a community like this, and, at first, Parrott had admittedly been intimidated by all the wealth and privilege. Now, not so much.

"No worries, Chief." Adrenaline notwithstanding, Parrott's hunger roared through his gut, and he pictured the elaborate breakfast he would have when he got out of there. "I know all about great parties. My mama threw the best parties in the neighborhood when I was growing up, and she insisted on perfect manners, too."

"In that case, you can practice the politest way to break it to the lady that you found a dismembered body in her burned-down barn."

CHAPTER FIVE

While waiting for the guys from Chesco to arrive, Parrott trudged back into the crime scene, trying to ignore the sweat rolling down his back inside the suit. The firemen were still at work, chopping into piles of debris with their axes, looking for possible errant flames. Nobody paid attention to Parrott, and, for his part, Parrott confined his search for evidence to the quieter areas.

So far, besides the body, he hadn't found much—just evidence this had been a working meth lab. He was looking for something more personal, something he could link to Claire Whitman, whoever had been living here, or the person whose arm he'd found under the debris. Gazing into what had been the loft, Parrott realized that the danger wasn't over. A jagged hole where the ceiling had been, offered glimpses into the former living quarters, but not much was left—just pipes and the skeleton of a staircase. What the fire hadn't incinerated, the jets of water had stripped away, but there was still a chance that what remained would collapse. The meth residue carried other risks.

Parrott tested a wooden spear that may have once been a bedpost. Through his thick gloves, the wood was cool, perfect for poking into piles of rubble. Using it, he scattered debris, trying to imagine where various fragments had come from. He dug around what might have been the face of a clock, the spigot of a faucet, the handle of a pitcher. Moving to another pile, he stabbed at what might have been a metal security box. Still hot to the touch, the rectangular box was melted, but it retained its hardware and locking mechanism. Parrott's brain buzzed at the possibility that someone had kept money or important documents inside. Unable to open it, he tagged the box. This might be an important find.

Before he could poke any further, he was greeted by three hazmat-suited professionals from the county, two men and a woman. Through the mask, Parrott recognized the coroner, his friend, Dr. Maria Rodriguez. She had helped him with his first case as a detective, the death of Preston Phillips. The four of them elbow-bumped, and, not wanting to waste any time in this hellhole, Parrott led them to the victim's body parts.

Maria got right to work. "You guys go ahead. I'm going to take measurements and photos and bag the hands for fingerprints. Let me know if you find anything else for me."

"Okay," one of the techs replied. "Let us know when you're ready to move the body."

By this time, most of the firefighters had finished putting out the blaze, and only a few remained inside the shell of the barn. Skip approached Parrott and the two evidence techs, a noticeable limp in his step that Parrott hadn't seen before.

Parrott offered the briefest of introductions. "You okay, man?"

"Yeah, nothing a day's rest won't take care of. We're wrapping up inside here. There's a detox station outside. Someone will stay there to help you with your suits and equipment. You don't want to hang around any longer than necessary."

"Thanks for all your help," Parrott said. "But I have a question. Who called in this fire? Someone from the big house?"

Skip threw back his masked and hooded head in the equivalent of an eye roll. "Nope. A neighbor who lives down this road was returning home after a transcontinental trip. Smelled the smoke and then saw flames. If he hadn't called when he did, this woulda been much worse."

"Pretty bad as is. We'll finish up as soon as possible." After all the activity, the barn soon took on the aspect of an ancient ruin, emptied of life. Patches of sky overhead had lightened enough to cast an early morning glow over the macabre piles of rubble, soot, and ash. Parrott walked the techs around to the spots he had marked. "Anything else you see of interest, let's grab it. We'll be lucky if much is left."

This stage of the investigation was important, and Parrott wanted to find the perfect balance between thoroughness and expedience. He was dying to get out of the sweltering suit, and he was itching to talk to Claire Whitman.

CHAPTER SIX

By the time Parrott finished with Maria and the guys from Chesco it was almost ten a.m. Glad to shed the hazmat suit, but hating the grubbiness left behind, he headed home to clean up and change clothes. More tired than hungry now, he ambled into the house, unsure whether Tonya would be there.

As he opened the door, he was greeted with a hearty, "Welcome, fella." Horace, the cockatiel, was in full-energy mode, spreading his wings and ringing the bell at the door to his cage.

Horace never failed to soothe Parrott's nerves. The little dude was always happy to see him. "Come to daddy, Horace." Parrott opened the cage, and the yellow and gray bird leaped onto Parrott's shoulder.

At the same time, Tonya appeared at the doorway, wearing a purple velour body wrap and a matching towel on her head, turban style. "I thought I heard you. Just took an online Pilates class."

"I thought you had art class today. It's Wednesday." Parrott moved in for a light kiss, inhaling the scent of citrus and vanilla, but all-too aware of his own odor.

"Not so fast," Horace squawked. He flapped his wings and landed on top of Tonya's toweled head. Tonya waved him away, and he flew to the top of his cage, king of the family room.

Tonya returned her husband's kiss with a deeper one. "I didn't even hear you when you left. What time was it?"

Parrott wanted nothing more than to unwrap this purple-garbed beauty and take her back to bed. "I must smell something awful." Planting a quick kiss on her throat, he dashed for the bathroom to remedy that.

Tonya followed, arms ready to receive his clothing as Parrott stripped it off.

"Let me handle the clothes. You're all clean, and who knows what residue might be on them." He carted the dirty clothes straight to the washing machine, while Tonya sat on the closed toilet seat.

While her husband splashed and soaped and scrubbed, she interrogated. "When did you leave, and where'd you go? You smell like smoke and sweat. A fire?"

"Schrik called after two. Not like you to sleep so soundly, but glad I didn't wake you." He hesitated before revealing more information. Sometimes Tonya would take violent events in stride, but other times they'd set off her PTSD something fierce. "Big fire in a converted bank barn. Meth explosion." The shower curtain and the sound of the spray prevented him from gauging her reaction.

A few long moments passed while Parrott shaved and washed his hair under the pulsing hot water. He pictured the ashes and rubble in the Whitman barn, and even though he'd been protected by the hazmat, he washed all over a second time.

When he turned off the water, Tonya said, "So, you home for the rest of the day? You already put in a full day."

Parrott slid the shower curtain aside and leaned over to take his wife's face in both his hands. "We'll see. I'm tired and hungry. Glad to spend some time with the queen of my heart. But—"

Tonya's lips parted into a resigned smile that showed the tiny space between her front teeth. "I know. You have to investigate while the case is fresh."

"Well-said, my love. But first things first." He grabbed the oversized towel from the hook on the wall, stretched it around his backside, and extended his arms and towel around her waist as she stood against him. "First, the extremely clean Mr. and Mrs. Parrott are going to make up for lost time in the nest."

As the towel-clad Parrott and Tonya waltzed to the bedroom, Horace rang his bell.

Later, Parrott ran his fingers through Tonya's damp hair. Only recently had she unbraided and straightened it to go for a more

Michelle-Obama-type look. "How come you didn't go to art class today? Not that I'm complaining."

"Elle canceled. She's quarantining since she was exposed to Covid. She gave us an assignment to do at home."

"Right thing to do." Elle Carmichael was the Parrotts' dear friend, art therapy instructor, and benefactor.

Tonya rolled out of bed with the smooth grace of a ballerina. "Wednesday just became my favorite afternoon. Now, what can I get you to eat for that growling stomach of yours?"

"Surprise me," he replied. He rifled his underwear drawer and then moved to his closet. Much as he hated to go back to work, he had people to see and papers to fill out. Dressed in a pair of casual slacks, an open-collared shirt, and a light-weight sport jacket, he reported to the table.

While Parrott demolished two grilled cheese and tomato sandwiches, Tonya sipped an iced tea and nibbled on a Chips Ahoy cookie. "I forgot to tell you. Your mother called this morning. She wants you to call her. Something about a new financial planner Herman wants her to hire."

"What's wrong with the financial planner we all have? He's done an excellent job of managing our money so far."

"I know, but you know Herman. He puts a bug in your mother's ear, and she's ready to buzz. Haven't you noticed she's not coming around as much, and when she does, all she talks about is Herman-this and Herman-that?"

"Well, I'm happy she's got somebody to put a little pep in her step. Nobody should be alone, and she spent too many years raising me all by herself. I'd like to cut her some slack, but your perceptions are usually right."

"It's just—" Tonya bit her bottom lip and looked away.

Parrott wiped his mouth and moustache with a paper napkin and started to clear his dish from the table. "What? Something worrying you?"

"Well, Cora didn't start this relationship with Herman until after we set her up in her catering business, after she had a good nest egg. I hope he's not after her for her money."

"I don't think so. Herman's not poor by any means. Mom says his construction firm is extremely reputable, and he does lot of jobs in the whole Philly area."

"Well, you never know. Your mother's a good-looking lady with a lovely home, an up-and-coming business, and a very rich son and daughter-in-law. I think he bears watching."

"Point taken. Let's keep an eye on Herman." Parrott rinsed his plate and put it in the dishwasher. "And now for someone else who bears watching, I need to go see a very rich lady with a beautiful mansion and a blown-up barn."

CHAPTER SEVEN

P arrott's mother had raised him to be tough when toughness was required, but she'd also taught him how to behave like a gentleman. Polite manners had served him well in the Brandywine community, where almost everyone was a native or a relative, and outsiders were suspect from the get-go.

Standing on the doorstep at Sweetgrass, the home of Claire Whitman, sniffing the still-smoke-tinged air enveloping the manicured lawn, Parrott rang the doorbell. He brushed the sides of his head with his hands, neatened the creases in his trousers, and put on his best professional smile—pleasant, but not overly friendly.

A petite Asian woman wearing black slacks and shirt and a frilly white apron answered the door. "You must be Detective Parrott," she said, before looking at his identification. "Mrs. Whitman is expecting you." She ushered him into the largest entry hall he had ever seen, and he'd seen many large ones in Brandywine. The checkerboard marble floor went on forever from the doorway and down a long, wide hallway lined with oil paintings on either side of a winding staircase.

The woman led him through an archway to the right of the staircase, into a cozy study that may have once been a parlor. The walls were covered in peach-colored suede, and billowy curtains dressed the two west-facing windows.

Seated at an ornate curvy-legged desk was a slim, silver-haired lady in a powder-blue pant suit. Her eyes sparkled with a blue-green clarity that gave her face a vibrancy rare for an octogenarian.

"Come in," Mrs. Whitman said, rising from her chair and extending a bony hand for a firm handshake. "Please have a seat.

Can I have Aiko bring you something to eat or drink? Some lemon squares, perhaps?"

"No, thank you. I just ate." Parrott settled into the chair opposite the desk, surprised it accommodated his long legs comfortably. "I've been investigating the scene of the explosion in your barn. Sorry you've had this trouble."

Mrs. Whitman dismissed Aiko with a nod and turned her turquoise eyes onto Parrott. "I'm happy to be back in my undamaged home. Apparently, the explosion has caused you considerable trouble, too. Though you don't look as though you've been toiling amid ashes and rubble."

"No, ma'am. I cleaned up before coming to talk with you. And it's no trouble. It's my job." His witness reminded him of his second-grade teacher, Mrs. Avery. That lady didn't miss a trick, either. He removed his cell phone from his jacket pocket and set it on the chair next to him, in case he needed to take notes. "Mrs. Whitman, I'd like to ask you a few questions about the barn."

"Go ahead, but you probably know more about my barn than I do at this point. Maybe I should be asking you questions. Oh, and please call me Claire." She folded her hands and sighed, her eyes traveling in the direction of a formal family portrait, hanging on the wall near Parrott.

Momentarily distracted, Parrott had a feeling he'd be getting to know this family in the days and weeks to come, and there would be more to learn than smiles and pretty poses. He cleared his throat. "Let's start by talking about the barn itself. What can you tell me about its history?"

"W-e-l-l," Claire said. "That barn is original to Sweetgrass. Built the same year as this house, 1878. Same style, same stone-and-wood construction. Used for generations to house horses and farm equipment. Maybe other livestock at some point in time."

"Looks like it was converted to living space. When did that happen?"

"A little more than three years ago." Claire glanced at the family portrait again. "My husband and daughters arranged for me to sell the remaining horses and rehab the barn. It was a big project."

Her tone gave Parrott the distinct impression that Claire hadn't been entirely happy with the idea, but she was too genteel to complain. "What was the reason?"

"That depends on whom you ask. Our financial planner felt it would add substantially to the value of the property. I'd stopped riding horses, and it was costing me a lot to keep the five horses I had left—their food and vet bills, the stable hands to keep them in shape. Jessica convinced my husband I could put that money into the barn rehab and end up with an asset, instead of a liability. My other daughter agreed, although she doesn't live in the area. I doubt it mattered much to her."

"What about you? Were you in agreement?"

A close-lipped smile said maybe not. "I'm rarely persuaded to do anything I don't want to do, Detective Parrott. My motivation was slightly different. I planned to use the converted barn to entertain."

"For parties?" Parrott couldn't imagine why the big house wouldn't be suitable for entertaining, but he tried to keep the incredulity from his voice.

"Yes, of course. Parties are what I'm best at—or was." She studied her hands as if she couldn't believe they belonged to her. "You may not know I've written books about entertaining. I had a television show, too. *Entertaining with Elegance.*"

"Yes, ma'am. I knew that. So have you been entertaining in the barn?"

Claire drew herself into a pillar, her eyes shooting an expression of—what? Outrage, irony, sadness? "How can anyone entertain these days with that horrible virus going around? By the time the barn was ready for company, Covid was shutting down social gatherings faster than you could say *R.S.V.P.*"

"I understand that. Was there a security alarm on the barn?"

"We installed one once the renovation was complete and furnishings had been delivered. We didn't use it much, however. People in Brandywine are generally honest, and who would care about breaking into a renovated barn?"

Apparently someone did. "Who monitors your alarm? I'd like to check the usage record." Claire supplied him with the name and phone number of the alarm company. "The only person I can think of who would go in and out of the barn is my groundskeeper, Charlie Wukitsch. I assure you he'd never allow my property to be used as a meth lab."

"When was the last time you were in the barn?"

"I was trying to remember last night, when I was talking with my assistant, Tammie. When the project was completed, I took a tour with Jessica. I loved what she had done with it." Claire paused to take a sip from a teacup that had been sitting on the desk. "Jessica's daughter Bonnie, my granddaughter, asked me if her boyfriend could stay there when he was in town, just until this Covid business was over. I couldn't see a good reason why not. The building was sitting there. Might as well get some use."

"What is Bonnie's boyfriend's name, and when did he start staying there?"

"That's the funny thing. I'm not sure if he ever did. No one mentioned it to me, and I never followed up to find out. Bonnie has a busy job at Bryn Mawr College, so I don't talk to her much, unless it's a holiday, a birthday, or she needs something." She compressed her lips and waved a hand. "Her boyfriend's name is Ray something. He's connected somehow to my financial planner."

"The one who encouraged you to convert the barn?"

"Yes. A charming young man who moved here from another state. His people have a home in Newport, Rhode Island. Very well-connected." Claire folded her hands on her desk and smiled.

"Can you tell me what Ray looks like?" Parrott asked. He glanced at the family portrait in case one of the people pictured might be Ray.

"That portrait is about four years old, and, no, Ray wasn't even around then. Here's a photo of Bonnie and Ray. This was taken in the past year." Claire handed a three-by-five frame to Parrott. Inside a blonde, curly-haired woman gazed into the eyes of a dark-haired man with a square jaw and scruffy facial hair. There was no way for Parrott to tell whether this was the same young man blown to bits in the barn.

"Looks like they are serious about each other." He hoped not, if Ray did happen to be the victim in the barn.

"Don't let appearances deceive you, detective. I call photographs 'status reports.' People come and go in an ever-changing landscape. Even this portrait." She pointed to the family grouping on the wall. "Taken a few years ago, before my husband died. Lots of things have changed since then." Claire rose from her chair and leaned forward, fists on her desk. "Now, let me ask *you* a question, detective. Do you believe someone was running a meth lab in my bank barn?"

Now comes the hard part, Parrott thought. *No point in sugar-coating the bad news. This lady's a straight-talker, and she deserves to hear the truth.* "I do. There was evidence of equipment used to cook meth inside the barn. The fumes were strong, even though we were all wearing protective equipment." Parrott rose and peered into Claire Whitman's face. "There's something else you need to know. We found a body in the debris—a young man. His face and body are badly disfigured. We need to identify him and notify his next of kin."

Claire didn't flinch or utter a sound. She held the picture of Bonnie and Ray to her chest. "And you think the young man might be Ray?"

"Is there anyone else you can think of who might have been inside the barn when it exploded?"

She shook her head and sat. "Hard to think that such a terrible thing happened on my property, and I had no idea—no idea at all. A meth lab? A person killed? I need some time to wrap my head around all this."

"Another question—who takes—took care of the barn? Someone go in to clean it, keep the plumbing flowing?"

Claire pushed her chair away from the desk but remained sitting. "That would be Charlie Wukitsch, same one I mentioned regarding the alarm. He oversees all the property. He lives in the small brick bungalow at the east edge of my land."

Parrott didn't want to overwhelm this lady, and he feared he had already questioned her too long. "Why don't you give me names and contact information for your daughter and granddaughter and Mr. Wukitsch, and I'll give you time to process what's happened. We can talk again tomorrow or the next day, as things develop."

Claire tore a page of monogrammed stationery from a pad on her desk. She wrote the names, Jessica Abramson and Bonnie Warner and their phone numbers and email addresses. Below those she wrote the maintenance man's name and phone number. As she handed the paper to Parrott, she said, "I want to be kept informed, no matter how bad the news. I've lived through many joys and tragedies. Whatever happens, you can count on my full cooperation."

The steady gaze from those turquoise eyes touched Parrott even more than Mrs. Whitman's words. This lady was one tough cookie.

CHAPTER EIGHT

Leaving the circular driveway in front of Sweetgrass, Parrott doubled back past the remains of the barn. Afternoon shadows were beginning to cast magic over the police-taped area, though the stench remained. The landscape looked more like a TV show set than the gruesome crime scene of earlier. All the emergency vehicles were gone now, and there'd be no sense in stopping to investigate further, especially in the waning light. The tent and portable shower were gone, too, and the pile of hazmat suits.

The absence of vehicles triggered something in Parrott's mind. If the dead man in the barn had been living there, where was his vehicle? How did he get to and from wherever he had to go, way out here in the country? Had there been a truck or automobile at the site, identifying the body would have been simpler. But that wasn't the only thing. If the deceased hadn't driven himself here, then someone else had to have driven him, and that other person brought up another whole set of questions.

Part of his brain was telling him to drive to the station, where he could document his activities and his interview with Mrs. Whitman and get started on researching her relatives. The other part of him was aching to go home. The grilled cheese sandwiches from earlier were a distant memory, and his eyes still stung.

Chief Schrik might not be in his office, and he wouldn't expect Parrott to come in after working so many hours already. When he'd spent the night at the station after solving the Allmond art theft case, Schrik had lectured him on taking better care of himself. At the last moment before turning onto Lafayette Road, he swung his car in the direction of the highway and home. Tomorrow would be another day.

Fifteen minutes later he stepped into his front room and was enveloped by the sounds of Tonya, starting on dinner.

"Shoo-shoo. Get yourself on out of here. Dinner is a surprise." Parrott held his hands loosely over his eyes and marched to the bedroom. "Okay, I'll grab a nap."

He was awakened by smells of pineapple chicken and warm Hawaiian rolls, one of his favorite meals. His mouth watered as if every cell were screaming to be fed. He hurried into the kitchen to confirm. "Mmm, I could eat ten plates full."

"Here," Tonya said, popping half a buttered roll into his mouth. "I knew you'd be hungry, so wash up and sit yourself down. I made enough for four, just in case."

"Don't have to ask twice." Parrott did as instructed, patting Horace on the head through the birdcage on the way to the washroom. He called over his shoulder, "You've been a busy woman."

When he returned and sat at the table, Tonya set a bowl of sauteed green beans and a casserole dish with aromatic pineapple chicken in front of him. "That's what happens when I don't have art class. I have to find another way to be creative."

"You ask me, this is one luscious work of art, on its way to my stomach." The first bite was heaven-on-earth delicious, with the sweet, tangy sauce cloaking the juicy chicken and soaking into the tender grains of rice beneath. Parrott shoveled bite after bite into his mouth.

Tonya's lips curled. "I love watching you attack your food when you're hungry. You might be named after a bird, but you eat like the king of the jungle." She picked up her own fork and knife and began eating at a more leisurely pace. "When you come up for air, I'd love to hear how your afternoon went. If you can talk about it, that is."

Still enjoying his food, Parrott said, "Why don't you tell me about yours first?" He was stalling while he decided how much of his day he could share with his wife. He wasn't overly concerned about confidentiality. Tonya, as a former Navy SEAL, knew how to keep information private, and at this point, he didn't have much information to share, anyway. He was more concerned about which details might fire up her PTSD. She had made a lot of progress with counseling and therapy, but setbacks could happen at any time. He'd learned that the hard way.

Tonya's eyes met his in a look that said, "I know why you're delaying," but she went ahead as if they were an ordinary couple having an ordinary conversation. "I washed your clothes, cooked the chicken, fed Horace, and read a couple of chapters in a historical novel. Oh, I googled Herman's construction business. He's got a neat website, lots of testimonials."

Parrott raised his eyebrows. "Glad to hear it, but you can't trust everything you learn from Google."

"I know. I thought of asking Elle's nephew Alexander if he's ever heard of Herman or his company. Construction people talk about each other, and he may have an ear to the ground. There's also Dunn and Bradstreet and the Better Business Bureau."

"I admire your tenacity, but I'd stay away from asking people we know. We don't want it getting back to Mama that we're suspicious of her boyfriend." Parrott pulled apart a roll and used a piece to sop up the pineapple sauce from his plate. "Bad manners, I know, but I can't let a drop of this good sauce go to waste. Good thing I'm here at home and not at Claire Whitman's house."

"Claire Whitman, the party lady?" Tonya set her utensils on the side of her plate and took a long drink of water.

Parrott stared at his wife, amazed that Whitman's fame had extended to someone like Tonya, who was raised in a totally different environment. "Long-ago party lady. She had a TV show."

"I know. My grandmother watched it while she was ironing. Granny thought Mrs. Whitman was the perfect lady. She used her name as an example of good manners for us, growing up." She began stacking the dishes at the table. "How do you know her?"

"That's whose barn burned this morning. Where I was this afternoon—at her house in Brandywine Valley." Parrott rose and patted his stomach. "Thank you for this outstanding meal. I feel like a new man. Let me clean up the dishes."

"Really? America's Miss Manners lives in Brandywine? My granny would be so excited." Tonya jumped in, as Parrott took the dishes to the sink. "I'll take over from here. You've had a long day. Besides, you're going to need your strength in dealing with

Claire Whitman. As Granny would say, 'You'd better mind your p's and q's with her.'"

Parrott wrapped his arms around his wife and gave her a hug. "If you're sure about cleaning up, there's something else I want to do tonight."

"I'm sure. Hardly any left-overs to put away, no big deal. What're you going to do now?"

Parrott pulled back and wiggled his eyebrows at his wife. "Follow your lead, Mrs. Parrott. I'm going to make friends with Mr. Google."

CHAPTER NINE

Early the next morning at his office, a thermos of scalding black coffee kept Parrott company while he waited until seven-thirty to call the coroner. He'd already swung by Whitman's alarm company, who staffed their office twenty-four hours per day. Unfortunately, the alarm in the bank barn hadn't been set for months.

At the stroke of seven-thirty, he called Maria Rodriguez, the county's chief coroner. Having caught her on the one time per month that she had the midnight shift was pure serendipity. She would have performed all the preliminary procedures on the dismembered body in the past few hours, and she'd be getting ready to go home. Maybe she'd have something to tell him.

He opened his office window to catch the summer breeze, and he reviewed the information he had printed off at home the night before. At work he had access to much more specific information than provided by Google, but for an initial foray into Claire Whitman's family, he had learned a lot.

Sweetgrass and the Whitman name belonged to Claire's family by birth—she hadn't changed her name when she'd married Scott Abramson in 1960. Abramson was Jewish, a fact that may have caused Claire's family and the Brandywine community some consternation. Parrott chuckled when he'd read that. The eighty-two-year-old Claire must have been spunky even when she was young. An only child, she'd been indulged with horses, the best education, and lots of parties. She met Abramson while he was at Harvard Law and she at Radcliffe. They married just after both graduations.

Photographs showed the good-looking couple to be active in the New York social scene, as well as in the Brandywine community, for decades. Her television show had earned high ratings for six seasons, and she had written several "how to" books on entertaining, the most famous of which was *Parties Perfect: What Every Hostess Must Know.*

A car door slammed outside Parrott's second-floor office window. Distracted, Parrott stepped to the window and gazed at the vacant children's playground. When he'd first come to work at West Brandywine, he'd thought the juxtaposition of a playground and a police station strange, but recently, he'd appreciated the irony of innocent play and heinous crime being just a few yards apart. The former often relieved the stress of the latter.

A minute later, footfalls on the stairs announced the arrival of Chief Schrik, who often bragged that this bit of exercise would counteract the extra pounds he'd picked up from quitting smoking. He had to walk past Parrott's office to get to his own. "'Morning, Parrott. Didn't expect to see you here so early after the long day yesterday."

Parrott pointed to his coffee thermos. "I'm okay. You know me. This case has already got me jumpin'. Hoping to catch Maria before she goes off duty, see what she's been able to figure out so far."

Schrik looked at his watch. "Don't let me stop you. It's already after seven. Tell me what you find out." He waved a two-finger salute and trudged off toward his office.

Parrott had the coroner's direct number on speed dial. He hoped Maria would answer. None of the assistants were as thorough. While the line rang, Parrott thought about the person who had lost his life. The best part about working with Maria was that on top of being both the coroner and a pathologist, she shared his view that victims weren't cold objects on a table. They were human beings who had stories to tell, even though their voices had been silenced. With Maria's help, Parrott would piece together this man's story.

After three rings, he figured he might have missed her, talking so briefly with Schrik, but on the fourth, she picked up, her voice breathless. "Hey, Parrott. Thought it might be you, so I ran back in to answer. I was in the next room, cleaning up.

Parrott had seen Maria after an autopsy, so he could picture the cleaning up part. "I'm sure you must be tired—"

"—And I'm sure you must be curious. I was going to call you on my way home. I won't have the report until late tomorrow, and you know toxicology is going to take a week or more, but I'll give you some highlights." She paused, and Parrott could hear the rustle of paper. "I have eight fairly good fingerprints for you to run through the files. Teeth are intact, too. Seven, eight, and nine are implants. A lot of trauma to the body, but it's safe to say his height is just over six feet, weight around two hundred. Age between thirty-five and forty-five."

"Good information," Parrott said. He jotted facts as fast as Maria gave them. Doing the math, Claire Whitman's granddaughter might be around thirty, so the victim could be an age-appropriate boyfriend. "Anything else?"

"Yes. You'll love this. There's a tattoo lateral to the umbilicus, the Greek letters, *sigma alpha epsilon*. Should be helpful, right?"

"A gift from heaven above. Any other identifiers?"

"C'mon, Parrott. Don't be greedy. You looking for his name tattooed on his butt?" Maria typically teased him about her findings, but Parrott made sure she knew how much he appreciated her, too. Without her meticulous attention to detail, he would have been severely handicapped in solving some difficult cases.

"It's all your fault. You've spoiled me rotten. How about cause of death?"

"Okay. Here's where it gets really interesting." Parrott could picture Maria's dark eyes shining. "Let me put on my pathology hat. No sign of disease, which is to be expected at the victim's age. Trauma from explosion and fire would lead to an obvious determination of accidental death, but—"

"But you don't think so?" Parrott was ready to jump out of his skin.

"I think that would be hasty. Hard to tell how long the victim had been dead. The fire destroyed tissue and accelerated decomposition. The stomach was full, so the victim died within an hour of eating a meal. Not impossible, but I doubt anyone would eat a full meal after midnight." Another rustle of papers filled the next few seconds. "But I ran some preliminary tests on my own, and here's the *piece de resistance*—there was no soot in the victim's airway, and less than two percent carbon monoxide in his blood."

"Amazing," Parrott said, scribbling the information and dropping his pen on the desk. "The guy didn't die in the explosion. When the barn blew up, he was already dead."

CHAPTER TEN

After learning that the body in the barn had died before the explosion, Parrott had his work cut out for him, but top priority was figuring out who the victim was. The only lead so far was Claire's granddaughter's boyfriend, Ray, who supposedly lived there. Since no one had said that the granddaughter, Bonnie Warner, lived there too, apparently the couple didn't live together. All Parrott knew about their relationship was what he had seen in the photograph, two people gazing into each other's eyes. His next step was to visit Bonnie Warner.

This being Thursday, Ms. Warner might be at work. Claire had told him Bonnie worked in an office at Bryn Mawr, Calling the college, Parrott was referred to the Center for Community Development and Inclusion. When he tapped in that extension, the call went to voicemail. A message that said the office hours were nine to four-thirty on weekdays.

If Parrott left now, he could be on campus by nine a.m. Abhorring a messy office, he filed the few documents on his desk, locked the desk drawer, cleaned the desktop and computer screen, and slung his jacket over his shoulder on the way out. He stopped by Schrik's office to fill him in on the autopsy news. "I'm off to Bryn Mawr to interview Whitman's granddaughter. Hopefully we'll get a bead on identifying this body soon."

Schrik removed the paper clip from between his clenched teeth. "Good for *you*, Parrott. We'll run the guy's fingerprints when they arrive from Chesco. Maybe we'll get a hit before you get back."

What was with the chief's sarcastic tone? Parrott would likely be back in the office within a couple of hours, and the coroner's report might take another day to come in. Schrik had hired Parrott, mentored him, and supported him 24/7, even when the feds or other entities had threatened to take over their cases. Remarks that insinuated that Parrott's work wasn't all that important were kind of a new thing. Parrott tried not to let them get under his skin, but he couldn't help being annoyed.

At nine o'clock on the dot, Parrott strode into the Pensby Center and found his way to the Center for Community Development and Inclusion. Inside the open door, a curly-haired blonde wearing tight gray jeans, a light-yellow button-down blouse, and a black rhinestone-studded mask was intently arranging a stack of fold-over brochures on a coffee table. Despite the mask, he recognized the face from the picture in her grandmother's home office.

"Bonnie Warner?" Parrott asked, through his own mask. A sign on the exterior door had stated that masks were preferred.

The woman startled and turned around, dropping a few brochures on the floor. Wide hazel eyes met Parrott's darker ones. "Yes?" She stooped to pick up the papers from the low-pile charcoal-colored carpet. "May I help you?"

"Sorry to have surprised you. I guess you didn't see me come in." He glanced at the brochures in her hand, featuring the school seal on the front and several tabs in colors matching Bonnie's outfit. "Detective Oliver Parrott of the West Brandywine Police Department. May I speak with you for a few minutes?"

Light eyebrows shaded her squinty eyes. "Brandywine? Is my grandmother okay?"

No mention of the explosion in the barn or her boyfriend, possibly a good sign, or was this family so out of communication with one another that news hadn't traveled that fast? "She was, as of yesterday, when I met with her." He pointed to the wide chrome and vinyl chairs circling the coffee table. "Can we sit?"

"Oh, sure." Bonnie plopped down in a chair, crossed one leg over the other, and pumped the crossed leg. "What's going on with Gran?"

"Your grandmother seems fine. I'm here to talk to you about her barn." Parrott's eyes locked on Bonnie's, searching for a tell. Did she know about the meth lab, or not?

"Her barn?" Nothing but a flicker of bewilderment, one eyebrow raised.

"Is it true your boyfriend has been living in your grandmother's barn?" Something was off here. The words *barn* and *boyfriend* should have triggered more of an emotional response.

Bonnie's leg stopped pumping. "My boyfriend? Who told you that?"

"Let's back up. Your grandmother remodeled the bank barn on her property. Are you familiar with that?"

"Yes, of course. And since it was sitting empty during Covid, I asked if Ray could stay there. Why is any of this of interest to the police?"

"I'll explain, but first, what is Ray's last name? Did he move into your grandmother's property?"

Bonnie ran her hand through her thick hair, curling one lock behind an ear, where it remained for less than a second. Apparently, her ears had all they could handle with supporting the mask, a pair of large gold hoops, and two pair of sparkly studs. She hesitated a few seconds, and then nodded.

"Okay," she said, "I know this is going to sound weird." Her leg started bouncing double-time. "Ray—his last name is Plummer—is a music engineer. Do you know what that is?"

Parrott thought he might, but he wanted to keep Bonnie talking. "Tell me."

"He works with musicians and their producers and equipment to optimize the sound in recordings and live performances. He knows everything there is to know about tone and pitch and tempo, but also about how live sounds are transferred. He's basically a genius, and he knows all the famous people in the industry. He's worked for Lady Gaga, Rihanna, The Weeknd, you name 'em."

"Sounds like an exciting career."

"It is. He gets to know the celebs. He flies all over the world for special gigs."

Parrott thought of Claire Whitman and wondered how she felt about her granddaughter's choice of boyfriend. "How did you meet each other?"

Bonnie's eyes and cheekbones crinkled into a smile. "Gran got me backstage after a Billy Joel concert at Madison Square Garden on my birthday. Billy Joel is a distant cousin on my grandfather's side. Ray was taking down the sound equipment, and I tripped on a cord and fell. He came over to help me, and that was it. Instant attraction."

Noticing she hadn't said *love*, Parrott pressed on. "Sounds like his job might keep him pretty busy." Musicians weren't known for stable, full-time relationships.

"Oh, yeah. He works all the time, all over the world. I got to go with him to Japan just before Covid."

"Probably not much call for a music engineer in Brandywine Valley, is there? Is Ray living in your grandmother's barn?"

"Huh," Bonnie said, a syllable that could have been mirth or disgust. Impossible to tell through the mask. "Ray doesn't really live anywhere. Except for the months when the pandemic stalled out concerts, he was in New York or on the road eleven months out of the year. It wouldn't pay for him to own a place, although he could well afford it. He doesn't have the time to maintain a home. You might call him a vagabond. Turns out his close friend is Gran's financial planner. That's who first suggested Ray stay at Gran's barn whenever he's in town visiting me. I only live about twenty minutes away from there."

"Did Ray stay in the barn during the pandemic, then?"

"A few weeks here and there. Even when the performances were shut down, he had work. Recordings. Small, private venues. The music business thrives one way or another."

"Forgive me for asking something personal, but why doesn't Ray stay with you when he's in town?"

Bonnie closed her eyes and took a breath before answering. "That *is* a personal question. I wish you'd tell me what's going on."

"Okay, do you know whether Ray was in town and staying at the barn on Tuesday night?"

Another crinkling of the eyes. "That's a question, not a statement, detective. But no—Ray wasn't there. I don't think he'll be back until next month sometime." She fired up her cell phone and showed Parrott a string of text messages. "See? Here are some texts from Ray that came in late Tuesday night. He's in London." She uncrossed her leg and sat forward. "Now what's got the Brandywine police so interested in my grandmother's barn?"

Parrott mirrored the woman's body language, leaning forward until his elbows met his knees. The information he had to impart had just become much less personal, easier to convey. "Early Wednesday morning the bank barn exploded."

Bonnie squealed something unintelligible and shot out of her seat, hands pressing the sides of her face.

Parrott rose, too, mostly so he could watch the expression on Bonnie's face. "Someone had been cooking meth in the barn."

"Meth? In Gran's barn? I don't believe it." If she wasn't truly surprised, she had missed her calling as an actress.

"There's something else," Parrott said, gazing at Bonnie's eyes. "We found a young man's dead body in the barn. Now you can understand the reason for my questions."

"Oh, no-o-o. This is awful. How's Gran taking it?"

"She's doing remarkably well under the circumstances. I'm surprised she didn't call to tell you, herself."

"Gran wouldn't do that. She'd be worried that I'd freak out over Ray. In case you haven't noticed, my grandmother is the epitome of control. Sometimes I'm way too much for her."

"Well, I'm glad your friend is safe. I'd like to have your contact information and his, too, in case I need to talk with you further." Parrott readied his cell phone to take the numbers. "Do you have any idea who else might have been in the barn?"

"I haven't the faintest idea. I'm still in shock about a meth lab in Gran's barn." Bonnie twirled a lock of hair around her index finger.

"Oh, and one more thing. You didn't answer my question about why Ray doesn't stay with you."

Bonnie huffed, but now that she knew the reason for Parrott's visit, she seemed more relaxed. "Because, Detective Parrott, I live with another man--my four-year-old son, Scotty."

CHAPTER ELEVEN

Driving back to the station after meeting with Bonnie Warner, windows down, so the summer breeze swept over him, Parrott thought about what he'd learned from the interview. Factually speaking, not much. Bonnie had filled him in on her father, who had divorced her mother and moved to California, and her ex-husband, who had divorced her and done the same. But he was no closer to learning who the victim in the barn was or why a meth lab had been there.

But sometimes the absence of information is information, and he was beginning to get a picture of the why. Whitman's barn was isolated, uninhabited except occasionally, a believable setting for a meth lab. The fact that neither Claire nor her granddaughter showed overwhelming angst over the anonymous young man's death or the destruction of property on the grounds of Sweetgrass said something, too. Either the family's wealth and privilege enveloped the women with dispassion, or they were acting. Were they protecting someone or something?

If an explosion and fire revealed a dead body in the garage of someone in Parrott's family, everybody would be hooting and hollering at one another, trying to figure out every last detail of who, what, when, where, why, and how.

Bonnie's comment about her grandmother's being in control was certainly apt. Maybe Bonnie didn't realize it, but she was a lot like her grandmother. Claire had most likely bucked her family to marry Abramson. Whatever the circumstances of Bonnie's relationship with her son's father had been, possibly Bonnie's parents hadn't approved. And now, she was hooked up with a music engineer whose availability was practically nil.

Despite Bonnie's nervous tic of kicking her leg, she had a certain reserve about her. She was more in control than she might think. There was plenty of room for digging, and Parrott could be a strong shovel when he needed to.

As he steered off the highway into West Brandywine, Parrott's cell phone rang. His mother. He picked up on Bluetooth. "Hey, Mama. How're you doing?" His mother rarely called during the workday.

"Good morning, Ollie. I hate to bother you while you're working. Is this a bad time?" Her voice had that little snip that told Parrott she was on some kind of mission.

"Not at all. I'm on my way to the station, taking in the smell of sweet grass and the sound of my mama's sweet voice." Parrott checked the time, mostly out of habit. Chief Schrik hadn't ever put him on a time clock, but he also never took advantage of his freedom to come and go as needed. "What's up?"

"I'm just gonna say this straight out. Does Tonya have a problem with Herman?"

Whatever he was expecting, he wasn't expecting this, the very subject he and Tonya had spoken about. "Why do you ask, Ma?" Was his mother clairvoyant? He couldn't imagine Tonya's sharing those concerns directly with her mother-in-law.

"I just hung up from talking to her. When I first called, your wife was all nice and friendly-like. But then I invited the two of you to have dinner with Herman and me this weekend, and she got that—I don't know—evasive tone of voice. Told me she'd have to ask you and get back to me. I'm not imagining this. Every time I mention Herman, she goes cold on me, and I'm plumb perplexed. What seems to be her problem?"

Caught between protecting his mother and protecting his wife, Parrott punted. "I don't think you need to worry about Tonya, Ma. It's natural to have a period of adjustment when a new person comes on the scene with a tight little family like ours. If Herman makes you happy, we're happy for you. Maybe we just need to spend more quality time together, get to know Herman better."

"That's exactly what I was trying to do, inviting you to have dinner with us. But, no. Tonya had to get all tentative with me, like spending an evening with Herman and me was pure torture."

"I'm sure that's wrong, Ma. I'll talk to Tonya when I get home. Maybe you caught her at a bad time or something. When do you want us over for dinner? Pretty sure we'll be there, and we'll bring dessert."

Apparently mollified, Cora Parrott let out a long sigh and a sniff. "All right, son. Saturday night at seven. No need to bring dessert. Herman is making his special Kentucky bourbon butter cake. It's to die for."

"Sounds delicious. I didn't know Herman could bake."

"Hmmph, there are a lot of things you don't know about Herman. He's really a fine gentleman, and I'm flattered that he enjoys my company."

Despite having told Tonya to cut his mother some slack with this new relationship, Parrott shook his head. He'd been the man of the Parrott household for a long time. Hearing his mother fawning over Herman caused a twinge of emotion he wasn't proud of.

"You've always been a good judge of character, so I don't doubt Herman is worthy of your time, but I'll say one thing as your only son who loves you. There's no man, Herman included, who's any better than you. So don't go 'round being flattered by his attentions. He's the one who's lucky to be hanging with you."

"Thank you, son. You always know the right thing to say. You're exactly like your daddy in that way. I'll see you on Saturday, and see if you can sweet-talk a smile onto Tonya's face, too."

Parrott shrugged as he disconnected and pulled into the station's parking lot. Fulfilling his mother's request might be a problem.

CHAPTER TWELVE

After Parrott's visit to Sweetgrass, Claire Whitman had sat at her desk and put in a call from her landline to her younger daughter Rebecca, who lived in Chicago. Of the two daughters, Rebecca was more like Claire, the least excitable. Claire was hoping to pre-empt Jessica by notifying Rebecca of the barn explosion first.

"Hi, Mom. How's everything going?" Rebecca's breathy voice meant she was probably on the Peloton.

"Am I interrupting your workout, dear?" Claire arranged the pens and pencils in her desk drawer, so they all pointed in the same direction. "I can call back later."

"Not at all, Mom. My Peloton class just ended, so a good time to break. What's up?"

Obviously, Jessica hadn't conveyed the news yet. Rebecca didn't have a clue. "There's been a big explosion in the bank barn. I wanted to tell you before you heard it from someone else. The fire was contained to the barn, and everything is fine here in the house."

"Oh, no. I'm so sorry to hear that. How did it happen? Was anyone hurt?" A cat meowed in the background, one of Rebecca's menagerie. "Wait a minute, Mom. I've got to feed Pearl."

Claire's lips curled in amusement. If she'd notified Jessica that the barn had exploded, her elder daughter would have shrieked that Claire wasn't safe and demanded she leave the house immediately, but Rebecca? She paused to feed the cat. What sounded like cabinet doors slamming and the clatter of something hitting metal filled the background.

"Okay, I'm back. Now tell me about the explosion."

Claire could picture her daughter, perched on a bar stool at her kitchen counter, running fingers through her long brown hair, and giving full attention to the phone. When Rebecca was in, she was all in. "I don't know too much about it yet. There was an explosion, a fire, and a casualty. The police seem to think someone had a meth lab in the barn."

"A casualty? A meth lab? You've got to be kidding."

"I wish I were. It's quite disconcerting to think something illegal may have been going on right under my nose. I hadn't set foot in the barn in ages. Presumably, Charlie's been checking regularly when he makes his rounds, but we haven't talked yet. Tammie and I spent the night in Kennett Square. We just returned home this morning, and I met with a very nice detective, and now I'm calling you."

"Glad to hear Tammie's okay, too. You said there was a casualty? Who died?"

"I have no idea, dear. An unidentified male. Hoping it's not Bonnie's boyfriend, Ray. I doubt that, though. If it were, Bonnie would have surfaced by now, and she hasn't."

"Does Jessica know about this? I'm surprised she hasn't called me."

"I'm sure she does, but I haven't talked to her yet. You know how tight she and my housekeeper Aiko are. I'm sure Aiko considers it a sacred duty to report everything to Jess."

"Mom—"

"I know. At my age, it's important to have people keeping close tabs on me. I'm not complaining. And I'm lucky to have Jess living nearby to help if I need it. Anyway, I'm fine."

Rebecca chuckled. "Only you, Mom. You're the only person I know who'd remain unruffled after a sudden, violent tragedy practically at her doorstep. You're going to be surrounded by police activity for the foreseeable future, you know."

"I don't mind that as much as having your sister pushing me to move out of my home. 'For your own safety,' she'll say." Claire rearranged the photo frames on her desk into a single line. "Can I count on you to support me in staying here?"

"Sure, but maybe you'd better get your granddaughter Bonnie on your side, too. Otherwise, we could be outvoted." Another phone rang in the background, and Rebecca said, "That's Matt. Do you want me to stay on with you and call him back?" "No, darling. See what your husband wants. I'm fine." As she hung up the phone, she realized she really was.

Five minutes after disconnecting with Rebecca, Claire received a call from her elder daughter, Jessica. "Mom. Why didn't you call me? Aiko told me the barn exploded. Do you want me to come bring you to my place?"

"'Course not. I'm perfectly fine. I was just getting ready to call you. Tammie and I stayed in Kennett Square, just as a precaution. The fire department was concerned about fumes, I think. But the fire is out, and the house is not affected." Claire stood and stretched her back, pressing one hand against her L5 vertebra. "Have you talked to Bonnie about any of this? I need to call her, too."

"No, Mom. The only people I've talked to are from the police department. They didn't want to tell me anything at first, but I pressed them. Did you know they think it was a meth explosion? Meth in your bank barn!"

Leave it to Jessica to squeeze every drop of information from the police. She probably said she was my advocate or power of attorney. "I know, dear. I can't imagine how methamphetamines got into my renovated barn. Can you?"

"Have you asked the groundskeeper? Maybe he knows something. And a man was killed. I'm frantic over this. Brings back bad vibes about Dad's death."

"I know you miss your father, dear. I miss him, too. But it's been three years, and he died of natural causes, so I don't see the connection. And, no, I haven't talked to Charlie yet. But I will soon. I promise. That nice young Detective Parrott is probably interviewing him as we speak."

"I want you to know I intend to follow up on this. I'm not comfortable knowing a man was killed on your property. Even if it's someone we don't know, why *your* barn? Have you notified your insurance company? Do you want me to do that?"

"I'll take care of it, sweetheart. First, I want to talk to my financial planner. He'll find a way to smooth out all the details for me."

"Are you sure I can't bring you to my house for a few days? I'd feel so much better, knowing you're out of the way of whatever's going on at Sweetgrass."

Claire sat on the edge of her desk and wrapped the phone cord around her hand several times. Jessica's house would be the last place she'd want to stay, but she didn't want to hurt her daughter's feelings. "Thanks for the offer. I appreciate it so much. But, to tell you the truth, your place is way too quiet for me. While I'm appalled that such a serious and devastating crime has transpired in my barn, I must admit I rather like the excitement. Kind of like being at a bizarre party, you know. Waiting to see what's going to happen next."

Claire had another call to make before she contacted her financial planner. She needed privacy for this one, so she'd asked Aiko to go into town to pick up her dry cleaning and some banana cinnamon swirl bread from the Evergreen Café. She tiptoed on the parquet floor to the double doors leading to the main hallway, where the weekly cleaning service was doing routine tasks. A vacuum cleaner whirred, and dishes clattered in the kitchen. No one paid attention to her.

She retreated to the comfortable chenille-upholstered chair overlooking the side rose garden. Pulling her cell phone from her pocket, she scrolled to the contact listed merely as R. She tapped the initial and waited, while the phone rang. Anticipation fizzed inside, as if she were a girl of twenty-eight instead of a woman of eighty-two.

When the golden warmth of a man's voice answered, Claire's heart overflowed with all the emotion she'd suppressed thus far. "Oh, Robert," she said, as wetness stung her eyes, "something horrible's happened at Sweetgrass."

CHAPTER THIRTEEN

Parrott trudged into the station Thursday morning, discouraged that his visit with Bonnie Warner hadn't produced a better lead on the identity of the bank barn victim, and a little peeved over the friction between Tonya and his mother. The day stretched ahead like an unmarked country road. Which turns would lead to the best information?

He waved to Lucretia through the plate glass that separated the public entrance from the hallway leading to the upstairs offices. The desk clerk jumped from her chair, jiggling an envelope in the air and pointing. Parrott reversed direction and re-entered the building through the other entrance, where Madame Lucretia held court most days.

"Got something for me?" he asked. Maybe this wouldn't be such a dull day, after all.

Lucretia tapped the white envelope against her palm. A grin lit up her whole face. "Yessiree. Special delivery for Detective Parrott. A skinny lady, fiftyish, with auburn hair and freckles. She didn't even ask to see you, just asked me to give you this letter. I asked for her name, but she waved me off. Said her name and contact info was inside." She handed the envelope over with a flourish.

"Thanks a lot." In this age of texts and emails, an old-fashioned letter usually meant something. Often letters were the preferred means of communication among the well-bred rich.

"Just my opinion from the looks of the person who brought it, Mrs. Parrott don't have to worry. It ain't no love letter."

Parrott held his arms in a semi-circle, and Lucretia returned the gesture. The virtual hug had started as a joke between them during Covid but hung on. "Have a great day, Lucretia." He was almost at the threshold when he turned back. "Anyway, Mrs. Parrott never needs to worry about that."

Parrott climbed the stairs two at a time to get to his office. The door was closed, but not locked. Anything important was secured in cabinets or in his desk, and there had never been a problem. Daylight brightened the office, not as much as it would in the afternoon, but enough to show that nothing was out of place. Still, Parrott sensed something unusual. He turned on the fluorescent overhead lights and circled the desk and guest chairs. Sniffing the air, he caught a whiff of aftershave, something with sandalwood. That was what Chief Schrik had been wearing that morning. Could the smell be left over from the brief interaction he'd had when Schrik stood at the door to the office earlier? He didn't think so. But why would Schrik have come into Parrott's office when Parrott was gone?

Parrott set the letter on his desk and pulled his chair out, preparing to sit. The fragrance was undeniable. Someone wearing cologne had been near his desk while he'd been out. Parrott unlocked his desk and pulled out a pair of disposable gloves and a letter opener. The outer envelope had been handled, but presumably the insides had only been touched by the person who wrote the letter. He might want fingerprints later.

Inside the envelope was a single sheet of stationery, embossed in a fancy script with the initials JA. His eyes flew to the signature first, Jessica Abramson, Claire Whitman's daughter and Bonnie's mother. Jessica would have been Parrott's next person to interview, but with the letter, she had come to him. He wondered why.

Leaning back in his chair, he held the stationery at eye level, processing the words slowly. He knew enough about handwriting analysis to think that the letter had been written in haste and with emotion. Her letters were large and strongly slanted to the right, running closer to the right margin than to the left.

"Detective Parrott," it began. "You don't know me. I'm one of the two daughters of Claire Whitman and Scott Abramson. I'm the one who lives locally—in Philadelphia, that is.

"My mother told me you are investigating the explosion in the bank barn. My sister Rebecca, who lives in Chicago, and I are absolutely shocked at the thought of a meth lab there. That the barn is destroyed, and that there was a fatality in the explosion are distasteful to our mother, but they are extremely upsetting to my sister and me—although not for the same reasons."

Parrott set the letter down for a moment. As he did, he noticed a fine white hair on his desk. Okay, the hair hadn't come from his head, and the only person with whitish hair in this department was the chief. Parrott had wiped his desk clean before leaving this morning, as always. He would need to get to the bottom of why Schrik had been in his office. He put the hair in an empty envelope for safekeeping and returned to Jessica's letter.

"I speak only for myself when I say that I'm very concerned for my mother's safety. You have met my mother, and you have likely been impressed by her intelligence and wit. She prides herself on these characteristics, and they are indeed admirable. But, while my mother is a strong and relatively healthy woman, considering her age, she is more vulnerable than she appears.

"I may be the only one in the family who thinks so, but I believe something is very wrong at Sweetgrass and has been since before my father died three years ago. I've begged my mother to sell the farm and move to a place where she would be safer and not so isolated, but Sweetgrass is in her blood, and Covid added new fears about assisted living facilities.

"I ask you to pay particular attention to Tammie Caballero, my mother's lead caregiver. My mother thinks Tammie hung the moon, but I'm not so sure. All I know is before Tammie started working for my parents, nothing untoward ever happened in their home. Since Tammie's arrival, there have been accidents, mix-ups, illnesses, and even death. I'm not accusing Ms. Caballero, or anyone else, of killing my father. He was, after all, eighty-three when he died. But he was a young and healthy eighty-three. I never could accept that he died so suddenly.

"Now there's an explosion and a fatality on the grounds of Sweetgrass, and I'm terrified that something is going to happen to my mother. Here is my contact information in case you want to talk to me further. I've heard good things about you, Detective. I trust that you will do your best to uncover the evil that threatens my mother's safety and serenity."

There was no closing, just the signature and an address with the zip code 19103, a fancy area of Philly, a phone number, and an email address. Parrott had no reason to doubt that the letter had been written and delivered by Jessica Abramson. He folded it and put it back in its envelope and stripped the gloves from his hands. He wanted to think about the contents for a while before he acted.

He locked his desk, picked up the letter, and strode to Chief Schrik's office, many questions floating in his mind.

CHAPTER FOURTEEN

Chief Paul Schrik was opening a double-sized take-out container of buffalo wings and blue cheese dressing from Mr. E's, a favorite local restaurant. The pungent aromas caused Parrott's mouth to water. Mr. E's wings were the absolute best.

Parrott stopped short at the doorway. "Oh, sorry. I didn't mean to disturb your lunch. I'll come back later."

Schrik closed the box and shoved it back into the paper bag on his desk. "Don't be silly. I can eat anytime. C'mon in and sit down." The smile on Schrik's face seemed genuine enough. "I had a hankering for wings that I couldn't resist. Not the best for my diet, though."

Parrott perched on the guest chair and crossed his leg, thinking about the best way to broach this unsavory subject. *Just stick to the truth*, his mother always said, and that had proven to be good advice up until now. "Chief, there's something on my mind that's been there for quite a while now. It has to do with our relationship."

Schrik broke eye contact and fiddled with the take-out bag on his desk. "What do you mean by that? Don't we have a good relationship?"

"I always thought we did. You've always supported and encouraged me—until a few months ago. After the Allmond case closed, seems like things are different. I've tried to tell myself it was all in my head, that you still trusted me and valued my work. But lately—"

"I *do* value your work, Parrott. What would make you think otherwise?" Schrik held his arms out, hands up.

"Little put-downs here and there. Maybe I've been too sensitive, but you never used to talk that way to me. And—"

"—can't imagine what you're thinking of. I don't recall any put-downs. If there were, they were unintentional."

"—I could overlook little remarks, Chief, but I believe this morning, while I was out at Bryn Mawr talking to Claire Whitman's granddaughter, you went into my office and sat at my desk. Am I right?"

Staring at his hands, Schrik took a few seconds. "I guess I'm not surprised by your detection skills. I thought I'd covered my tracks pretty well."

Parrott pressed his lips together in something less than a smile. "All except for the cologne traces and a single hair you left behind. But why, Chief? Why not just ask me anything you need to know? This feels like you don't trust me."

Schrik sighed, pushing his chair back from his desk and standing. He walked to the large window and stared outside. "I didn't think it would come to this with you. When I hired you I hoped you would grow in the job, maybe replace me as chief someday. You started out so brilliantly."

"So, you *are* unhappy with my work. Is that what you're saying?" Parrott tried, but couldn't think of a single time when he'd been reprimanded or failed to complete a task on time.

"Not at all. Quite the opposite, in fact." Schrik paced, fingers interlocked behind his back, a pose Parrott had seen many times.

"I don't understand then."

"Look," Schrik said, taking his seat again and meeting Parrott's eyes. "First you become independently wealthy through a gift from a community member—"

Heat rose from Parrott's gut to his face. "You and I talked about that before I accepted the money, and you told me it was not a conflict, that the gift had no relationship to the art theft, which was our case. You *told* me to accept it."

"I know I did. And that's still true. I was pretty sure you wouldn't want to keep working here after that. Why take on all the stress when you don't have to work another day in your life? But you decided to stay on, and I was glad."

The more Schrik talked, the more confused Parrott became. "My career means a lot to me. I don't want to give it up." He spoke through clenched teeth then. "So, *is* it the money, or what?"

Schrik's squinty eyes peered into Parrott's. "Let me ask you a question. Are you planning to move to Galveston, Texas, to work for the PD down there?"

A light flashed in Parrott's brain. He and Tonya had met the Chief of Police in Galveston when they were there on their honeymoon. Parrott had helped out on a case, and there had been some chatter about how great it would be for the Parrotts to move there. Parrott had forgotten all about it.

"Is that what's got you all upset? The answer is no. I don't have any intention of leaving. Chief Gonzalez was grateful when I helped him interpret some evidence, and he might have mentioned having me apply for a job, but that was a year ago, and I didn't think anything of it. How did you even hear about that?"

"Gonzalez called me. Asked what I thought of your performance. Hinted around that a guy like you'd be better off in a more lively environment with better climate. Yada, yada. I was chafed that you would apply for another job without telling me about it. Thought you were going to leave us high and dry."

"I'm as surprised as you that Gonzalez would call. I never had a single serious discussion with him. Besides, I wouldn't want to leave my family, and Tonya wouldn't want to leave Elle. Sorry to put you through any worry." Parrott gave his boss what he hoped was a convincing smile. "Why didn't you just ask me? You could've saved us both a lot of stress."

Schrik returned the smile with a sheepish look. "Guess I felt it was your place to come to me, not the other way around. Prideful of me."

Remembering the hair on his desk, Parrott asked, "So what were you doing at my desk?"

"Looking for correspondence, notes, anything that might reveal what was going on with you and Galveston. I know it seems I didn't trust you, and maybe I didn't. I'm sorry. The kind of detective you are, I should've known you'd find me out."

A huge weight that had been sitting on Parrott's shoulders for many weeks began to shuffle off into the stratosphere. "There's a lesson here about communication. I'm sorry it took so much time to straighten out this misunderstanding. I'd never apply for another job without talking to you first. I guess I'd better call Chief Gonzalez and set him straight, too."

"All right, then," Schrik said. "How about I warm up these wings for both of us? You can tell me what's going on with the Whitman case while we eat."

As if on cue, Parrott's stomach gurgled, and both men laughed.

CHAPTER FIFTEEN

After lunch, Parrott paid a visit to the county coroner's office. Something wasn't sitting right regarding the dead man in the barn. Maria, whose pathological investigative skills were always spot-on, hadn't been able to determine a cause of death, based on external or internal examination, only that the explosion and fire had occurred post-mortem. The toxicology would take several days, even though Maria had put a rush on it.

Without knowing the identity and cause of death of the unfortunate victim, Parrott was unable to organize his investigation plan in his usual fashion. There were people he could interview, like Claire's daughters and the barn's caretaker, Charlie, but, as in the meeting with Bonnie Warner, he wouldn't be able to home in on the questions he most needed to ask, until he had an idea of who and what he was dealing with—and why.

He'd printed off the autopsy report. It was neatly folded in his jacket pocket. He'd stopped at the nearest Starbuck's to pick up two coffees, a venti hot for himself, and a venti cold for Maria. Assuming she was available for a quick visit, he was ready for a coffee klatch. If not, he would at least be able to conduct another viewing of the dead body for himself.

Parrott opened the glass door to the coroner's office and set the coffees down on the counter. "Maria in?" A young male sat behind the fake-granite, talking into a Bluetooth device. Parrott didn't recognize the clerk—maybe a summer intern?

"Never mind." Parrott mumbled as he badged himself in through the latched gateway. He finger-saluted the youngster and carried the coffees down the hallway to Maria's office.

The always-professional Dr. Rodriguez was standing behind her desk, her navy shirtsleeves peeking through the armholes of a white smock. Her ponytailed head poked through the top, and she stepped backward. "Oh, I didn't know I had a visitor."

"Bad timing?" Parrott asked. "Brought you an iced coffee."

Maria's smile showed in her eyes. "I was just wishing I had one of these. Are you clairvoyant?"

"Maybe. I need one, myself. Got a minute to chat about the victim?"

"Sure. I've told you pretty much everything I know, though. Undetermined COD. No smoke in the lungs. Toxicology may yield more." Maria dropped into her chair and reached for the coffee. "Have a seat."

Parrott folded his frame into the metal chair. He opened the mouth-hole on the lid of his drink and took a swig. Patting the front of his jacket where the autopsy report was secreted, he said, "I read your report. White male, age between thirty-four and forty-four, approximate height six-one, approximate weight one-ninety. That could fit a million people. I really need to find out who this guy is."

"I told you about the frat tat on his stomach. And fingerprints." Ice rustled as Maria shook her coffee cup. "I wish there'd been more, but the explosion and fire shut down most of the typical lines of inquiry. Heat and smoke damage."

"I understand. Mind if I examine the body?"

"Be my guest. I have a few minutes before I need to get started on the next one." Maria ushered Parrott downstairs into what Parrott thought was the coldest room in the county. The rows of bright fluorescent lights obliterated the shadows and bathed the metal tables and a single long row of body-drawers with intensity. "Here you go," Maria said, crossing to the drawer in the middle of the room. With one hard jerk, she rolled the drawer open. A gush of even colder air came with it.

"Here's our victim, poor guy. Burns over forty per cent of his body, but I cleaned him up best as I could. I sent you prints."

"Already being run."

"Okay, then. Do your magic, Parrott. Make him talk to you."

Maria retreated to a corner, giving Parrott the sense of being alone with his silent witness. Pulling his cellphone from his pocket, Parrott scrolled to the magnifier accessory. Tapping it on, he opened the sheet that shrouded the unknown body and moved the camera app all around, from the disfigured face to the torso. The sigma alpha epsilon tattoo took up a good three inches in the middle of the stomach in purple and gold. Parrott had researched the fraternity, whose motto was, "Together we rise above." He wondered whether this marking had been part of an initiation rite, where it had been done and by whom. The colors looked neither fresh nor worn.

"Talk to me, fella." Parrott scanned the man's bluish-white body, looking for moles, scars, identifying marks. Finding nothing on the torso or legs, he opened the sheet wider. The detached right arm and leg were badly damaged. There was no point in wasting time there. He turned to the left side and ran the magnifying app along the man's shoulder, upper arm, elbow, and forearm. The shirt he'd seen covering this arm in the barn was now gone, part of the marked evidence he might study later. Now all that covered the arm was a sprinkling of freckles and hairs. The skin from upper arm to fingertips was darker than the skin on his shoulder, remnants of a suntan.

The dead man's skin was cold and still hard as stone. Parrott thought of how sculptors worked to bring life to stone. He was witnessing the opposite, stone coming from what had been alive. As he passed the magnifier over the man's left hand, he observed several faint marks, white on white. Fine straight lines on the side of the forefinger crossed a curved line that ended in a tiny depression, a pit. A similar curved line with a hole appeared on the palm.

Parrott recognized these injuries. He and his cousin Bo had spent many summers fishing from the Schuylkill banks, and Bo, having been older and more serious, had sustained many cuts from lines and hooks. Whoever this guy in the morgue had been, he had been a fisherman. Parrott was sure of it.

A fraternity-fisherman wasn't much to go on, but it was something. Parrott wrapped the sheet back around the corpse with a respectful tenderness. "Somebody's got to be missing you by now, Mr. Fisherman. Whoever you are, wherever you come from, I'm gonna find out. And then I'll figure out how you ended up in a rich lady's barn."

CHAPTER SIXTEEN

Thursday was Claire's favorite day of the week. There was always a flurry of activity in the house, because Aiko wrapped up the week's housekeeping tasks and prepared enough dishes to last the weekend. The cleaning staff was too busy to hover around Claire. Except for checking on her and bringing her meals or tea and biscuits, they generally left her alone in her study. She used the time to read, review financial matters, make phone calls, or watch the occasional show she'd recorded. All of these she did with a light heart, because Thursday evening was the start of her weekend.

This Thursday, the barn explosion weighed on Claire's mind. She needed to talk to Charlie, the groundskeeper, to see what he might know. In fact, she was surprised that Charlie hadn't called or stopped by yet today, or for that matter, when the barn was blazing. It wasn't like Charlie not to be right on top of things.

Claire called Charlie's cell phone. Four rings, and it went to voicemail. "Charlie, it's Claire Whitman. I'm sure you know about the explosion and fire in the bank barn. I trust you've not been affected, but I do want to talk to you." She glanced at the antique grandfather clock in the corner of the room. It was already four p.m. "Please give me a call or stop by."

A chill flashed up Claire's spine, as she pictured Charlie's squarish face, his bowl-cut hair style, and his wide, toothy smile. Ridiculous to think that something had happened to him, but he always answered his cell phone. Maybe Detective Parrott had stopped to interview him and taken him to the station. The unknown dead man in the barn couldn't have been Charlie, could it?

Claire needed to get out of the house, and a visit to Charlie's cottage seemed just the thing. Though she had stopped driving this past year, she still had her Mercedes in the garage, and there was usually someone around to drive her wherever she needed to go. She also had an enclosed Rover golf cart, perfect for getting around on her fifty acres. Sometimes, when she felt like a change of scenery, she'd buckle herself in and take the Rover down the road to visit a neighbor. Jessica would have a fit if she knew, but Claire cherished this little bit of independence and dreaded the day she might have to give it up.

If she rang for Aiko to drive her to Charlie's cottage, the housekeeper would drop everything to take her, but Aiko usually left by five, and Claire didn't want to slow her down. She could slip out of the study and into the garage without disturbing anyone. In case she failed to return before the staff came in to say goodbye, she left a note on her desk. "Gone to check on groundskeeper. Be back soon."

Turning on the golf cart's ignition, Claire recalled her young self, sneaking out of the same house, sometimes on horseback. Here she was at eighty-two years of age, acting like a teenager. If she weren't concerned about Charlie, flooring the accelerator would be exhilarating.

Several minutes later, Claire turned off the road onto the gravel that led to Charlie's. His Jeep Cherokee was parked outside the garage. Claire eased the cart onto the gravel, until she was close enough to hear and see Charlie's black Labrador, howling and turning in circles on the other side of the front room window.

Something's wrong. Claire had never seen Radar so upset. She parked the cart and climbed down onto the gravel as fast as possible without being foolhardy. Glad she was wearing her fitness shoes, she rushed up the path to Charlie's front door.

Radar's barking drowned out Claire's thoughts as she opened the screen door and started to knock. Her knuckles met with no resistance, though. The door was unlatched. The dog was at the door now, his nose and breath practically touching Claire's pantleg. She pushed the door open. "Calm down, Radar. Where's your master?"

Radar darted outside to water a bush, but, not wanting to wait, Claire stepped inside, leaving the door open behind her. "Charlie? Are you home?" The smell of feces overwhelmed her.

Claire couldn't recall the last time she'd been inside the groundskeeper's cottage. Radar, apparently finished with his business, returned to lead her to the kitchen, from which faint groaning sounds and acrid smells were emanating.

Claire stopped short, her orthopedic gym shoes seemingly glued to the carpet bordering the linoleum of the kitchen floor. There on the floor, blindfolded and gagged and tied to a tipped-over chair, lay Charlie Wukitsch. The dog leaped around the chair, barking and pausing to lick his master's hands.

Suppressing a groan, she searched for a cutting tool. There were knives, flimsy ones and huge ones, too big to slide in between Charlie's skin and the plastic cable ties that bound his wrists and ankles. "Charlie, it's Claire Whitman. You're going to be okay." She squatted on the floor next to Charlie and used her fingernails to loosen the knotted blindfold and then the gag, eventually removing both.

Charlie blinked at her, and when he spoke, his voice was little more than a croak. "Thanks."

"Where can I find some sharp scissors to cut these cable ties?" Claire asked. She pulled herself up from the floor, using a kitchen cabinet door.

"Drawer by the sink." Charlie pointed toward the drawer with his chin. "What day is it?"

Claire rifled through the drawer, finding the sharp point of the scissors. "Thursday, late afternoon. How long have you been like this?" She bent over, easing the scissors blades between Charlie's chafed and oozing wrist, the plastic tie, and the back of the chair. After a few slips of the blades, the razor-edge bit into the plastic enough to snip it loose, one wrist and then the other. Charlie flexed his wrists and squeezed both hands into fists. "Gimme those scissors. I'll do the rest."

"Not a good idea. Let's get your feet free from the chair legs, and then you can get up and walk around. It'll only take me a minute." Claire repeated the procedure with the scissors on the cable-tied ankles. "What happened here? Who tied you up this way? We need to call the police."

Charlie stretched his arms over his head and behind his back and exercised his legs. "No idea who tied me up or why. Sleepin' in m'bed, and somebody put a blindfold and a gag on me. Never saw a thing, but afterwards, I heard a huge explosion and fire engines. I hope it wasn't Sweetgrass."

Claire opened a cabinet and removed a tall glass. Filling it with tap water, she said, "You must be dehydrated. Here."

She handed Charlie the glass of water, which he guzzled down. "The explosion you heard was our bank barn. You've been lying on the floor on this chair for almost forty hours."

"I'm the one turned the chair over, tryin' to get free. Hurt my back doin' that, too." Charlie held up his pajama top in the back, revealing deep bruises.

"I'm calling the police. Detective Parrott wanted to talk to you, anyway. Now he'll have many more questions to ask."

"I don't know much of anything to tell a detective," Charlie said, backing up toward the bedroom. "I must smell to high heaven. Gotta get outta these dirty clothes. 'Scuse me."

Claire had already picked up the receiver of the kitchen phone and was dialing 911.

"Maybe you'd better wait," she said over her shoulder. "The police may want to examine your clothes."

"I'll save the clothes for them, but I need to use the bathroom. I must smell terrible."

Claire spoke to the dispatcher at the West Brandywine PD and gave her directions to Charlie's house.

While waiting for the police to arrive, Claire shouted over the sound of the shower. "I'll give you some privacy." She went outside to her Rover, where she had left her cell phone.

By the time the police interviewed Charlie, it would be late. She'd better make some phone calls. Her Thursday night "weekend" was crumbling before her eyes. After calling to dismiss Aiko, she walked further away from the brick cottage, while she tapped in the "R" contact.

"Robert?" she said, when the mellifluous baritone answered the line. "We'd better cancel tonight. I'm going to be tied up with the police and my groundskeeper. I'll call you as soon as I can."

CHAPTER SEVENTEEN

B y the time he left the coroner's office, Parrott was ready to head for home. Though dusk hadn't begun to draw its curtain over the Brandywine landscape yet, Parrott yawned, and his stomach rumbled, as empty as his investigation so far. The shared lunch with the Chief and the coffee with Maria seemed like yesterday, and the lack of sleep was catching up with him.

He resisted putting down the windows of his Camry, turning the a/c on low instead. The drive home from Chesco would take about half an hour in the afternoon traffic, enough time to check with the station to see if his guy's fingerprints had returned any hits. When he called, his buddy, Barton, picked up.

"Hey, Parrott. Heard you landed a tough one." The patrolman's smoker's voice was sympathetic.

"Yep. I wouldn't wish meth dust on my worst enemy. That stuff is nasty. Listen, do we have a report on the bank barn victim's fingerprints yet?"

"Let me open the computer file—hold on."

The tapping of keys on the computer caused Parrott's stomach to flip. *Let there be a match.*

Barton's huff wasn't a good sign. "Sorry, man. Looks like you only had partials to work with—nothing matched."

"Okay." Parrott sighed, rubbing the back of his neck with one hand, as he steered with the other. "Looks like nothing about this case is gonna be easy." He thought of the fraternity tattoo and the fish-hook scars. "Guess I'll have to resort to the missing persons' report." The MPR was Parrott's next best hope for identifying the victim, and it would be a long shot.

"Why don't you wait till tomorrow to start up with that? It could take all day, and you sound like you need to take the rest of today and tonight off."

"No, I'll catch my second wind after I get something to eat. We need to ID this victim, the sooner the better. I'm crossing my fingers that we won't need to resort to DNA. The backup is months."

After disconnecting, Parrott pictured his evening. The MP report would make for good after-dinner reading, and now that the fingerprints were useless, it was the best lead he had. For now, though, he needed to focus on Tonya. With only two days before their dinner with his mother and her boyfriend, he'd better do some assessing and preparing. It wouldn't do to have the two most important women in his life at odds with one another.

At six o'clock on the nose, he strolled into the house. The aromas of pot roast and fresh bread set his mouth watering. Tonya was nowhere to be seen. "Where's your mama?" Parrott asked the bird, as he poked a finger into the cage to smooth a feather. "I may need to smooth her feathers, too."

Horace chirped, "Mama, mama, mama," one of his favorite words. He tucked his crested head under a wing, one eye peering out in a debonair expression.

"Too cute, Horace. I'll be back to let you out of the cage." Parrott strode to the bedroom, calling Tonya's name, but there was no answer. "Honey?" He listened for any sounds of life coming from the bathroom. Finally, he returned to the front room, puzzled.

Then he noticed the door leading from the kitchen to the back yard was open beyond the screen door. He rushed toward the door, his detective's mind sorting thoughts of what might have gone wrong.

He flung open the screen door, yelling, "Tonya."

"Over here." Tonya called from the back corner of the fenced yard. She had on white shorts and a gray tank top. A navy headband corralled her long tresses from her face, as she pulled her body weight up and down from the branch of a sycamore tree. A shoulder pulley with weights and two handles swung from the branch next to her.

Tonya dropped to the ground and met Parrott for a long kiss. He loved the way she smelled—sweet shampoo mixed with salty perspiration. More than a year since she'd left the Navy, but she still worked out every day, even last year, when she broke her shoulder in a car accident with a deer.

"Quite an outdoor gym you've got here." Parrott grabbed the ends of the shoulder pulley and stretched his own limbs. As tired as he was, moving those muscles felt good.

"I decided to move it outside today since it's so nice, but we really should go in. Dinner's ready." She picked up a hand towel from the ground and threw it around her neck.

Parrott removed the pulley from the branch with one hand and wrapped his other arm around his wife's slim waist. The couple walked toward the house in perfect synchrony. "Was that pot roast I smelled?"

"Yes, and mashed potatoes. Baby carrots and peas. I thought you might want comfort food after all that meth business." Tonya hooked her fingertips inside the waistband of her husband's trousers in the back, a gesture that dated back to their college days at Syracuse.

"Can't wait. And we've got a lot to talk about tonight, too."

"If you're referring to having dinner with your mom and Herman, that's on my agenda, too."

Parrott should have known. When Tonya used the word "agenda," dinner might be more business meeting than meal. No wonder she'd cooked pot roast. She was softening him up for something. "What else is on your agenda, my love?"

Tonya released her grip on his waistband and raised her arm over her face in a move that reminded Parrott of Horace's sly head-in-wing expression. Apparently sly looks were trending in the Parrott household. "Let's eat first. Then we'll talk."

After filling up on melt-in-your-mouth beef and vegetables, Parrott was a new man. "I'll do the dishes," he said, jumping out of his chair to carry them to the sink.

"Let's do them together. Goes much better with two." Tonya started putting away the leftovers, while Parrott tossed the scraps into the garbage and ran the water on hot.

Horace piped up. "Better with me. Mama mama mama."

"Did you say 'me,' little fella?" Parrott turned off the water. "C'mon out of the cage, while Daddy gets your dinner ready."

Horace flew to the alcove, where he had a perch and a few cloth-covered toys. He squawked and chattered, amusing himself in his freedom, but when Parrott finished serving the birdseed mixture in the cockatiel's cage and returned to the sink, Horace flew onto Parrott's shoulder.

Parrott washed, Tonya dried, and Horace sang. When the dishes were done, Parrott set Horace back in his cage to eat, and he turned to his wife. "What all's on your agenda?"

"Let's sit on the sofa." Tonya led the way to the three-seater opposite the dining table. "You sit first."

Once Parrott was seated in the corner, Tonya sat on his lap. "Uh-oh. Lap conversations tend to be serious." He kept his tone light, but his instincts were on alert.

"No worries, Ollie. I thought you like for me to sit on your lap." She shifted so he could see her profile, and he couldn't resist touching her soft cheek, her perfect nose, her full lips. "Don't distract me. In a minute I won't be able to talk at all." She slid off his lap and moved to the ottoman, facing him.

"Okay, let's talk about my mother. She called me after she talked to you today."

"I knew she would," Tonya said. "I'm sorry, but I just couldn't get excited about having dinner with Herman. You know how I feel about him, and I can't lie."

"Mama could tell, and it bothers her. She thinks if we spend some quality time together, the four of us, we'll grow to like Herman. Maybe she's right." Parrott reached for Tonya's hand and squeezed. "Anyway, I'd like us to try. Maybe we can find out why Herman makes Mama so happy, and we can appreciate him for that."

Tonya's gaze was fixed on their entwined hands. "I'll try, Ollie. For Cora's sake and for yours, but if that man starts trying to tell her what to do with her money, or if he starts bossing us around, I can't be responsible for what I might say. That's none of his business."

Truthfully, Parrott agreed, but he didn't want to add fuel to his wife's opinions. Knowing how his mom dug in when confronted with opposition, he thought it best to soften, rather than support, Tonya's argument. "I'll bet Ma is lecturing Herman right now, making him promise not to be bossy. Let's just give them a chance."

"Okay, but if he starts in—"

"I'll try to head him off. I promise." Parrott leaned forward until his lips met Tonya's forehead. "So, what else is on the agenda?"

Tonya rose from the ottoman and ambled across the room to the desk. She lifted her laptop and brought it with her to the sofa. Snuggling next to Parrott's long frame, she took a deep breath and showed him the page she'd been on. "I've been thinking we should buy a bigger house. I've spent most of the afternoon looking online. Want to see what I've found?"

Parrott couldn't hide his surprise. "A bigger house?" Where he came from, and Tonya, too, people didn't buy big houses for no good reason. To his way of thinking, their little bungalow was just perfect for the two of them. "What brought this up?" He was pretty sure there wasn't a baby in the picture yet.

"I don't know. Ever since we decided not to move to Galveston, I've been thinking we could use a bigger place. A better kitchen. A bigger laundry room. An office. Maybe an art studio. We've got the money. Why shouldn't we have more space and conveniences?" She sat cross-legged on the sofa and turned the screen so Parrott could see. "Here's a beautiful house in Malvern. Five bedrooms, four baths. And a beautiful, wooded lot."

Parrott stared at the listing on the screen. The house was beautiful, for sure, but so was the price tag—one million seven hundred thousand. He shook his head in disbelief.

"Don't shake your head until you take a better look. This house could be the best investment you've ever made." Tonya's fingernails started tap-dancing with a practiced rhythm on the twenty-two exterior and interior photos.

"I don't know, honey. You're hitting me with this out of the blue. I need time to think about it, ask some questions."

"What type of questions? Maybe I can answer them. I've been studying these listings all day."

"Well, what are the neighbors like, to start with? There aren't many Black families in Malvern. Or law officers. What would we have in common with the folks who live there?" An itch took over his insides as he thought of how uncomfortable he would be, living in such a grand community. His wife's shining eyes told him she had already made the move in her mind, and there'd be no going back.

"Those are good questions to ask the real estate saleswoman." Tonya shifted her hips away from him. "I'm sure she'll be able to tell us. Meanwhile, look at this backyard swimming pool. I can picture you swimming in the mornings before you go into the station. And here's the kitchen—the countertops are works of art by themselves. All the appliances are brand new." She flipped through the pictures like a child opening gifts on Christmas morning. "This master bath has a sauna and a tub big enough for both of us. And there's a gym in the basement. No more exercising on a tree branch in the back yard."

Parrott wanted to cover his ears and eyes and shout at her to stop, but the adult in him chose a different voice. He took Tonya's hand from the computer's mouse and his eyes sought hers. "I thought we agreed we weren't going to let the money from Elle change us. That we were happy the way we were."

Tonya removed her hand and stood, plopping the laptop on the ottoman where she'd been sitting. She began pacing around the sofa, and Parrott realized how small this room had become.

"You're right," Tonya said. "We did say those things last year. Except for helping your mom start a business, we haven't made any big expenditures, and that money has been growing and growing. This house was fine for you before we were married, and we're managing okay here, but why shouldn't we invest in a bigger house, now that we can afford it? Elle didn't give us that money so it could sit in the bank, earning interest. She wanted us to enjoy it.

"Anyway, don't you see, Ollie? The money *did* change us." She walked to the window and gazed out. "Look at the neighborhood we live in. Do you see any other multi-millionaires? Are there any rich people at the police station or at the local Walmart where I shop? When I talk to anyone in this community, I'm self-conscious and wary of saying anything that might mark me as different. I know the neighbors gossip about us. Even if they don't know about the money, they think we're standoffish. We don't fit in here in this house any more than we would in Malvern."

The truth of Tonya's argument gut-punched Parrott. He recalled the winsome, idealistic Tonya he had known in college, the girl who was hungry for knowledge, not material things. Like him, she had wanted to contribute to causes that mattered. Maybe the ten-million-dollar gift from Elle had been more of a curse than a blessing.

The comfort food in his stomach wasn't doing its job, and fatigue leeched any desire to counter-argue. "I'll tell you what. You've given me a lot to think about, and in the spirit of compromise, I'll say this. You agreed to give Herman a chance, and I'll give the new house idea a chance. I'll go with you to look at the house, but right now I've got some work to do, and then I need to hit the sack. It's been a long, long day."

"No problem. I've got a good book to read, so work as late as you'd like." Tonya's voice held no trace of pique or malice.

Tonya left for the bedroom, and Parrott sat at the dining table, wrought-up and bleary-eyed, though it was still early. He was determined to identify the body in the bank barn. Before he could pull up the database on his department-issued computer, his cell phone rang.

"Parrott?" Officer Barton's voice boomed into the room. "Can you meet me over at Sweetgrass right away? You need to interview Claire Whitman's groundskeeper. Somebody bound and gagged him. Made sure he was out of the way when the meth lab exploded."

The corpse's identity would have to stay on the back burner for now. A live witness would trump a dead one any day. Parrott gave Tonya a hurried kiss, petted the top of Horace's head, stuffed a stick of spearmint gum in his mouth to wake himself up, and rushed out into the gathering darkness.

CHAPTER EIGHTEEN

When Parrott arrived at Sweetgrass, he was greeted at the front door by Tammie Caballero, who had just come on duty. The words in Jessica Abramson's letter echoed in his mind. So, this tall, thirty-ish woman with bobbed brown hair was the object of Claire's daughter's suspicions. She would bear watching.

The assistant's small hand cooled his large one, but her voice was warm and musical. "Nice to meet you, Detective. Ms. Whitman asked me to take you to the groundskeeper's cottage. Officer Barton is already there. Please follow me." She pivoted, military style, and headed toward a hallway, low heels clicking on the marble floor.

"No need. I'll drive myself, if you'll point me in the right direction."

"That might have worked if you'd arrived earlier, as Officer Barton did. Now it's getting dark, and if you don't know where you're going on these winding paths, it's easy to lose your way."

Tammie kept walking, and Parrott followed. Sometimes he found it best to go with the flow. Besides, this would give him a chance to talk to the personal assistant without having anyone else around.

The hallway led to the three-car garage, where a new model Mercedes sat in the center berth next to two empty spaces. Tammie slapped the garage door mechanism with her palm, and the motorized door creaked open.

"We could've taken my car," Parrott said, as he slid into the passenger seat.

"That's okay. It's getting dark, Besides, I need to drop you and come back. I'd just be in the way out there." Tammie started the Mercedes and backed it out without having to adjust the seat or mirrors. Parrott guessed she drove this car often, perhaps daily.

"How will I get back then?" The narrow road twisted in the growing darkness, past the remains of the barn and beyond a copse of leafy sycamores. If Charlie were the only groundskeeper, he certainly had a lot of grounds to keep.

"Oh, Ms. Whitman took her golf cart there. She doesn't drive the car anymore, but she's a wiz of a driver in that cart, even at night. It has headlights, of course."

"A golf cart? With all this contamination in the air?"

"The cart has a thick plastic enclosure, so she's not exactly out in the elements."

"How long have you worked for Mrs. Whitman, and what do you do for her?" Parrott looked out the car windows, attempting a casual air.

"Is this an interrogation or conversation?" Tammie's warm tone had an undercurrent of flippancy that Parrott recognized as fear.

"Just making conversation." The road curved around, and the cottage came into view.

Tammie gripped the steering wheel and pressed her lips together. After a few seconds she said, "I've worked for Ms. Whitman for five years. I'm kind of an everything-helper. I take care of clothes, handle the mail, help with special projects. I work mostly at night. Better for me, better for everyone."

The car was moving at about twenty-five miles per hour, but on the one-lane curves, without streetlights, that speed was more than adequate. Parrott kept his eyes on the road, except for sneaking sideways glances at the driver.

"So, in the interest of conversation, how's your investigation going?" Tammie turned toward Parrott, taking a hand from the steering wheel.

"Look out!" Parrott pointed to a pair of deer leaping onto the left side of the road.

Tammie jammed on the brakes. The Mercedes obeyed, gluing tires to pavement, and flinging its seat-belted passengers' upper bodies forward as far as the restraints would allow. The deer dashed past without injury, perhaps oblivious to how close they'd come to mortality.

Not so with the humans. Tammie shook, and Parrott's heart raced like a Brandywine horse after taking a stone fence. After a few moments of breath-catching silence, Tammie said, "Thanks for the warning. That could've been disastrous. I never saw them coming, and I drive around here at night all the time. I should've paid better attention."

Parrott put his head in his hands, thinking of Tonya's collision with a deer last year. No point in lecturing this woman about the hazards of driving in Brandywine Valley. She'd already learned the lesson. "Glad I saw them."

"So sorry for the scare." She took a deep breath and began easing the car forward. "We're almost there now."

Parrott followed Tammie's gesture to a driveway ahead on the right. As they drew closer, a brick house appeared, dotted with a cluster of vehicles, a truck, some farm equipment, a golf cart, and a West Brandywine police squad car. Barton had beaten him there, but wouldn't have begun questioning without him. A dog with a wolf-like howl provided wild forewarning of their presence.

Parrott thanked Tammie for the ride and hustled toward the open door, from which a triangle of yellowish light spilled onto the pavement, backlighting the big, black dog, and illuminating Parrott's way. The air still held a faint acrid smell, a souvenir from the meth explosion. A dull headache was taking up residence above his eyes. He'd need to find a reserve of energy to push through this interview.

Before he reached the door, Barton stepped into the light, peering out. "There you are. C'mon in. Ms. Whitman's groundskeeper is ready to talk."

"Thanks, man." Parrott shook hands and gestured for Barton to lead the way. After sniffing the backs of Parrott's hands and the cuffs of his trousers, the dog slipped ahead of them and lodged himself next to a chair at the kitchen table. Seated there were Claire Whitman and a middle-aged man, wearing jeans and a short-sleeved plaid shirt. His hair was wet, and his expression was worn and pained. Three cups of coffee sat on the table, possibly cold. If it weren't for the chair lying on its side, and evidence of plastic bonds and a gag on the floor, Parrott might have thought he'd interrupted an evening get-together.

Barton spoke first. "Detective Parrott, I believe you know Claire Whitman. And this's Charles Wukitsch, the groundskeeper here at Sweetgrass." Parrott nodded but didn't offer a hand. Technically, Wukitsch should have had his hands bagged, and he shouldn't have had anything to drink.

"Mr. Wukitsch had already had some water and taken a shower before I got here," Barton said. "We've tried to preserve the scene, otherwise, but between Radar, here, and Mr. Wukitsch's desire to clean himself up, I'm afraid it's been compromised."

Disappointed, Parrott sat at the only empty seat, probably Barton's. "We can work around it. More important to get information from Mr. Wukitsch himself than from his clothes." That wasn't necessarily true, but Parrott didn't need to beat up on the witness for taking a shower.

"Call me Charlie. We don't need to be so formal." Charlie petted Radar's head, and Parrott noticed the chafe marks on his wrist. He looked for, but didn't see, needle tracks on the groundskeeper's arms.

Claire stood. "Can I get you a cup of coffee, Detective? Officer Barton, why don't you take my chair? I don't need a place at the table."

Parrott agreed to the coffee, thinking it would help rejuvenate him. The clock on the wall said eight, but his body said past midnight.

"Actually," Officer Barton said, "I need to get back to the station. Now that Detective Parrott is here, you're in good hands. I'll let you get to it." He nodded at everyone in the room, including Radar, whose rambunctiousness had morphed into snuggling against his master's leg and occasional thumping of his tail.

After Claire deposited the coffee mug in front of Parrott, she looked from Parrott to Charlie. "Maybe I'd better give you two some privacy. I have some phone calls to make, and a good book on my phone. I'll stick around to drive you back to the house whenever you're ready."

Parrott nodded. "Thanks, and thanks for the coffee, too." As soon as she'd left the room, and he was alone with Charlie and his dog, Parrott began questioning the groundskeeper. He learned Wukitsch was fifty-two, had been working at Sweetgrass for thirty years, was divorced, and had a son and a daughter living in New York City. "Kind of a solitary job, way out here in rural Pennsylvania. I don't guess you get much time to socialize." Parrott felt for the guy, living alone like this.

"Yeah, it's lonely sometimes, but I've got Radar to keep me company, and this job has a lot of advantages."

"Such as?"

"I get to work outside in the fresh air, enjoy the seasons. I'm pretty much my own boss. I set my own schedule each day, and no two days are the same. These days with covid, it's not a bad thing to be isolated from people. And Ms. Whitman is a wonderful woman to work for. She grew up out here, understands what it takes to maintain the property. She treats the staff like family. Whatever I need, all I need to do is ask." Charlie took a swig of his coffee and made a face. "Cold coffee don't cut it for me. Want a warm-up?" He tossed the remains of his cup in the sink and poured a fresh cup from the pot.

"Mine's still warm," Parrott said. "Why don't you tell me what your job as groundskeeper entails?"

Charlie sat with his coffee and drank. "Shouldn't have too much of this, or I won't sleep tonight. Hard to say what my job is. I take care of everything outside of the main house. The land, of course—trees, shrubs, grass. Sometimes we grow crops. Even though we don't keep horses anymore, we maintain the ground for neighbors who ride. We allow access year 'round."

"Everything outside of the main house. Does that include the bank barn?"

"Yeah. Gorgeous place it was. I didn't have much to do with the renovation, but I watched it every step o'th' way, and Ms. Whitman spared no expense. A dirty shame it never got to be used, and now I hear it's gone." He fidgeted with the salt and pepper shakers on the table.

"What was your responsibility with the barn?"

"Would've been mostly outside stuff, if the barn had been used like it was s'posed to be. The inside staff would have kept up the inside, and I would've taken care of maintenance and grounds. But, because of the pandemic, the place was shuttered. No need to clean the inside that much, and not a good time to find reliable staff to clean it. I volunteered to check on it and report back if anything was out of order."

Parrott had a lot more questions, and the bump of energy from the coffee wasn't enough to keep him alert. He didn't want to rush this interview, but he needed to accelerate it. "Did that include checking on the inside? Do you have a key? How often did you check on it?"

"Yeah, I opened the place up a couple times a week. Flushed the toilets, got the air circulating. Being closed up can cause problems, like termites and other critters. It wasn't a problem for me to help out." Charlie's stomach gurgled. "Sorry. I guess I need to eat something. I haven't had a proper meal in two days."

Another delay wasn't welcome, but common decency required Parrott to wait. "Go ahead and grab something. Mind if I keep questioning you while you eat?"

Charlie went to the refrigerator and pulled out a tub of smoked ham. He set it on the table and started eating with his fingers, straight out of the package. "Want some?"

"No, thanks." Parrott drained his coffee cup and set it in the sink, giving Charlie a few seconds to scarf the meat down. "Let's talk about Tuesday. Tell me everything you did from start to finish. Don't leave anything out, even if you think it's unimportant."

In a monotone, Charlie catalogued his activities, with nothing remarkable throughout the morning and afternoon. He'd tractor-mowed the grass around the main house, fixed a bad rail in the fence, changed the oil in one of the trucks. "Around three I swung by the bank barn. I didn't go inside, but I checked the doors. Everything was locked up tight."

Impatient, and wondering at the man's lack of emotion, Parrott interrupted the narrative. "Were you aware of a meth lab inside?"

"Absolutely not! I would've told Ms. Whitman and called the police immediately. I never saw any sign of that. In fact, I never saw any sign of traffic in or out of the place, except when Ms. Bonnie's boyfriend was in town. To me, it was just a very beautiful place waiting to be appreciated and used."

Parrott thought of the needles and equipment he had seen in the barn after the explosion. Was Charlie lying, or was the evidence planted to substantiate the theory of a meth lab explosion? The meth was real, for sure. No one could fake that toxic smell or the chemical dust that covered everything.

"Okay, let's move on. What happened when you returned home? Give me a blow-by-blow account."

Charlie tossed the container of ham back into the refrigerator. Before returning to the table, he peeked into the next room. "How're you doing, Ms. Whitman? Can I get you anything?"

"I'm just fine, Charlie. Thanks for asking." Again, Parrott was struck by Claire Whitman's resilience and good nature. She seemed as comfortable, entertaining herself in the small space of her employee's home, as she did in her own opulent mansion. He was similarly curious about Charlie's lack of affect. Most people who'd been tied up would be a lot more distressed.

Charlie sat down and began to recount the events running up to his being assaulted. "I wasn't hungry. Sometimes in the summertime I skip dinner and have a snack and a couple of beers. That's what happened Tuesday night. Radar and I watched "Turner and Hooch" on Disney, but I was so tired, I fell asleep on the bed before it was over, maybe around nine. I still had my work clothes on.

I was in a deep sleep when Radar started barking and jumping around. I put my hand out to pet his head, and I lifted myself off the bed, aiming to see what had him all riled up. Usually, it's a deer or fox or something. Before I could open my eyes good, somebody hit me on my head, and I went out."

"Did you get a look at the person?"

"No. By the time I came to, I was blindfolded and restrained."

"How about his voice? Or any smell you remember?"

"Definitely a male. Sort of a fake voice, like he was trying to sound like a woman. Radar's barking was coming from outside, as if the person had lured him out."

"Wouldn't Radar have attacked this guy?" Parrott couldn't see a big dog like that being lured away from his master without a fight.

"Nah. I've trained Radar to go after animal predators, but to leave humans alone. Radar scratched on the door and whined, while the guy tied my ankles to the kitchen chair. My hands were already tied. I can't remember any smells, except maybe my own breath."

"How did this guy get in the house?"

"We don't lock doors out here. No need to. He didn't talk much. Gagged me at the end. The whole thing took less than ten or fifteen minutes. Last thing before he left, he let Radar back in. I couldn't see or talk, but I could hear Radar, barking up a storm and dancing all around me. Between Radar's trying to help, and my own struggling to free myself, I toppled over in the chair. I might've blacked out for a while."

"Then what happened?" Parrott was piecing together a chronology. If Charlie had fallen asleep during the movie, the intruder might have tied him up before eleven. That would have given him a couple of hours to wreak havoc in the bank barn before the explosion.

"Sometime later, I heard the fire engines and thought I smelled smoke. Radar was clearly upset, but I couldn't do anything except lie there. I stayed there on my side, tied to the chair, all this time, until Ms. Whitman came and rescued me."

The man had survived an ordeal, and Parrott thought it best to wrap up the interview. He'd send out a forensics team to collect whatever evidence might be left on the scene, but he wasn't optimistic.

Claire was ready to leave, after making sure Charlie didn't need anything. Parrott left his card in case Charlie thought of anything else. He shook Charlie's hand and patted Radar on the head.

As he was preparing to leave, Parrott thought of one more thing. "Charlie, you didn't answer my question about the key. I assume you have a key to the bank barn."

"Sure, I do. It's on the big key ring I keep by the front door." He walked to the tiny entry hall at the front of the house. "Right here." He pointed to the first peg on a wooden rack, a peg that was empty. "Omigod," he said, his voice a whisper. "Somebody took my keys."

CHAPTER NINETEEN

By the time Parrott returned home after questioning Charlie Wukitsch, it was late, and he was running on fumes. He kissed his wife and fell onto the bed, clothes and all.

The next morning, he decided to sleep late and work from home. The paperwork to document last night's interview and the use of the Missing Persons List could be done from anywhere, and he had logged so many hours in the field the past few nights, no one would be looking for him at the station. He phoned in to let Lucretia know, and he lay back on the bed a few more minutes.

Tonya had fixed plates of orange French toast for both of them, but she'd eaten hers and left his in a warming oven. Friday mornings were her therapy sessions at the veterans' hospital.

Having the house to himself was a luxury, especially since he wasn't in the mood for conversation—about his mother's boyfriend, a bigger house, or anything. He put new food in Horace's dish, replaced the soiled papers at the bottom of the cage, and then retired to the bathroom for a shower and shave before breakfast.

The French toast surpassed his expectations. The perfect combination of tangy and sweet making him glad for a wife who knew her way around a kitchen. He thought about the photos of the kitchen in the Malvern house and a twinge of guilt stabbed him. Maybe Tonya deserved a spectacular kitchen.

Horace interrupted his thoughts. Having eaten and eliminated, he fluttered around the cage, calling, "Go to work. Go to work." Parrott opened the cage door and motioned the cockatiel toward the small play area in the alcove of the den, but Horace wouldn't have it. Instead, he flew to the dining table, where Parrott's computer sat.

"Okay, Horace. You can go to work with me." Parrott opened his police-issued laptop and started writing up the report of his interview. Then he turned to figuring out the identity of the body in the bank barn. Parrott had never had much occasion to use the Missing Persons List before. The list contained photos and physical details about people who had been reported missing by relatives in all fifty states of the United States. Many times, the missing persons were people who didn't want to be found, people who went missing intentionally. It wasn't a crime to be missing, so most people listed weren't the kind police officers looked for. That was why many law enforcement officers regarded the MPL as something akin to chasing rabbits down holes. If Parrott had had any other avenue for identifying the body in the barn, he would have taken it, but right now, this was the best prospect.

Apparently having tired of walking the perimeter of the table, Horace leaped onto Parrott's shoulder, gazing at the computer screen. More than seventeen thousand thumbprint photos with names, categorized by state, filled the screen, all reported missing this year.

"So many missing," Parrott said aloud. The number seemed gargantuan, even though back in the days before cell phones and other tracking devices, the numbers of missing persons had been double that.

"No lie, Sherlock." Horace jumped back onto the table and gazed into Parrott's eyes.

Parrott petted the bird on the head. "I've got to get to work now, Horace. Go on now."

"Go to work. Go to work." Horace strutted around the table, puffing his chest out, as if Parrott couldn't do this work without him.

Turning back to the listings, Parrott read through the numerous identifiers that he could use to search for matches to the body in the morgue at Chesco.

On a notepad, he jotted down what he knew about the body—
Height – six-one
Weight – two hundred
Race – Caucasian
Gender – male

Age –thirty-five

Identifying marks – Sigma Alpha Epsilon fraternity tattoo on stomach, fishhook scars on hands

The fact that his victim's face had been disfigured by the explosion would be a big deterrent to a successful match, since facial photos were primary in the listings. Also, if he were lucky enough to find a viable match, the next step would be to send a photo of his victim's face to the listing police department, a useless photo, in this case.

The way he entered the identifiers into the computer would be tricky, as well. The broader the categories, the more "matches" the computer would give him, and the longer it would take to read through them. On the other hand, if his search was too narrow, and he asked for exact matches, he might miss out on the right guy, because he might have had different wording or spelling from the way it was listed. Parrott resigned himself to accessing the long list of possible victims based on a search for *x, y, z, and anything close to x, y, z.*

He decided to go with *male, Caucasian,* and *tattoo,* even though he knew he would have to dig a lot deeper for a second sort. While he waited for the search to run, he rummaged through the kitchen cabinet for an antacid. By this time, Horace had tired of helping with police work. He'd flown to his play area, where he ran on a treadmill, rang a bell, and squawked like a child on the first day of summer vacation.

Returning to the computer, Parrott found the fruits of his search, a total of eleven thousand. The listing was broken down by state, with over two thousand in California. Parrott was confident he could eliminate the West coast cases as being too far from home, but he wouldn't be smart to limit himself solely to the more than three hundred missing males in Pennsylvania. Before he sorted by geography, he ran a search with a new x, y, and z on this eleven thousand. This time he inputted *age twenty to forty, location of tattoo on torso,* and *height five-eleven to six-two.*

By now, it was past nine-thirty, and Tonya would probably be back soon. Determined to find out something this morning, he stretched and poured himself a second cup of coffee. Horace flew into the kitchen, landing on Parrott's shoulder. "Time to go back home," Parrott said, holding out his finger. The bird leaped from shoulder to finger to cage, sputtering, "Go back home."

Parrott returned to the table, where the second sort had turned up a little more than thirty-five hundred, with just under two hundred in Pennsylvania. He did one more sort, narrowing the list *to people missing within the last three months.* That brought the numbers down considerably, to one hundred ninety in the country, sixteen in Pennsylvania.

Tonya breezed in at nine-forty, a hardback book sticking out of her handbag, with the book's title obscured. *She must be enjoying that book if she took it with her to therapy.*

"What are you reading?" Parrott asked. He wondered if she was miffed at him.

"Historical fiction—about a Black woman from Chicago who ends up in the South Dakota Badlands. You getting some work done?"

Not a trace of bad feeling. That was one great thing about his wife. She rarely held grudges. When a difference of opinion was expressed, she moved right on. That didn't mean the topic of buying a new house was off the table. Not by a long shot. Parrott bent to kiss the top of her head before answering. "Trying. Thought I'd go in later today. I'm working on a missing persons report."

"Okay, I'll stay out of your way. I've only got two chapters left, and I'm hooked on Rachel DuPree."

Parrott returned to the dining table, somewhat refreshed and relieved. Picking up his pen, he added some assumptions to the list of characteristics of his victim—

Found in a meth lab—probably narcotics involvement? An addict?

Fraternity tattoo—college student at a school where SAE on campus?

Fisherman's scars—comes from a coastal town?

Parrott opened a new box in his browser and searched for Sigma Alpha Epsilon chapters. There were two hundred thirty. He scanned the list, looking for universities located on the East Coast, but decided it might take too much time to highlight those right now. Instead, he went back to the MPR search and narrowed it to *fraternity tattoo.* Searching for *SAE* or *ΣAE tattoo* might be too specific and eliminate viable possibilities.

The resulting list was way more manageable—ten in the country, one in Pennsylvania. Parrott's heart raced, as he clicked on the picture of a light-haired man wearing a white collared shirt and a blank look. The man's name was Thomas Proctor. Height and weight fit. Tatt on stomach. Definitely a possibility. Under "details," it said, "Thomas Proctor was last seen in Pittsburgh, leaving his office at Brown, Hughes, and Brown law firm on May 21."

As delighted as he was to find this Proctor guy, Parrott's instincts told him that it was unlikely an attorney or paralegal would be messing with a meth lab, and Pittsburgh was at least a four-hour drive from Philadelphia. On the other hand, the three rivers that joined at Pittsburgh might make for good fishing. Parrott jotted Proctor's name and city on his sheet of paper.

Next, he opened each of the nine other missing males who matched his search, noting names and locations beneath Proctor's.

Miles Marcus, Tucson.

Benjamin Warren, Houston

Aaron Leipzig, San Francisco

Reginald Ratliff, Chicago

Tucker Anderson, III, Raleigh

Jeremy Curry, Los Angeles

Boris Brown, Cincinnati

Bobby Baker, Memphis

Charles "Chuck" Winston, New York

Just for the heck of it, he ran another search for *SAE* or *ΣAE tattoo* on this list of nine. As expected, it turned up no matches.

He then brought up the list of SAE chapters and tallied how many were in each of the states represented by his ten MPs. California had the most chapters at twenty-eight, and Arizona had the fewest at three. He might have to go back to the chapter lists later.

Parrott would have to narrow the list the old-fashioned way, by studying each listing and eliminating the ones that didn't match. He might have to contact the individual listing police departments to find out more specific information. All of them might be rabbits in holes, but Parrott didn't think so. His top prospects were diamonds in the rough. He intended to mine each one and assess its potential. He wouldn't do it now, though. His legs needed stretching, and he wanted to spend some quality time with Tonya in the next room, assuming she was finished reading.

Parrott shut down his computer program and folded his page of notes into a rectangle the size of a dollar bill, and then slid it into his wallet. He set his coffee mug in the sink and turned toward the sofa, just as Tonya closed her book and squealed. "Wow, what a great ending."

CHAPTER TWENTY

Parrott left for the station after eleven a.m., but not before promising he'd go look at that house in Malvern on Saturday afternoon, before dinner at his mother's. The thought of spending more than a million dollars on a house still brought on gut-clenching, and he wondered what new problems this promise might lead to.

He laughed at the irony. Chasing armed suspects in the dead of night alarmed him less than buying a new home in a lovely neighborhood. Perhaps a matter of training—or comfort zone. Anyway, he had a lot of work to do on this bank barn case, and he didn't want to waste time or energy thinking about personal matters.

Lucretia greeted him with a message from Maria. Preliminary toxicology was in, and please call. This was a super-quick turnaround, even for a preliminary report. Parrott's heart beat faster, and he flew to his second-floor office, his feet touching every other step.

He picked up the office phone and speed-dialed the coroner's office. After greeting Chesco's version of Lucretia, he was put through to Maria's extension.

"Got my message?" Maria's voice had a sing-song quality that Parrott liked, especially when he thought she might have good news for him.

"Crossing my fingers. We need something good on this case."

"How about this? Stomach at time of death was full—food, alcohol, and poison."

Poison was a game changer. "You don't mean meth poison, do you?"

"No, this guy ate a meal shortly before he died—maybe thirty minutes. He ingested plenty of alcohol, and a deadly portion of aconitine."

"What's that?"

"Plant toxins that come from monkshood."

"The purple poison?" Parrott remembered monkshood from a book on poisons he had read when studying for his license. "Sometimes people use monkshood as a therapy for arthritis, but there's a risk for overdose."

"This guy likely ate the leaves or root in a salad or soup. Numbness and tingling upon swallowing, followed by nausea and vomiting, paralysis. Not an easy death." Maria paused to gulp down something, and Parrott marveled at how she could eat while talking about poison. "Anyway, I forwarded the report to you. There'll be further analysis that takes more time, but this is something for you to chew on—pardon the pun."

"Sounds more and more like our victim was killed elsewhere and the meth explosion was staged to cover up the killing." The pieces of information he had from Charlie, who'd seen no evidence of a meth lab in the barn, who'd been tied up to prevent his interfering in the meth explosion, and whose key to the barn were missing, all pointed to this conclusion, even without the contents of the victim's stomach. "Thanks for getting this to me so quickly. It's great."

"No problem. Always glad to help."

After disconnecting with Maria, Parrott turned to what he lovingly referred to as grunt work. He wanted to narrow down the list of ten missing persons from this morning's search, and, the only way he knew to do this was to create an Excel document with the ten names and the locations from which they were reported missing. He then spent a half hour researching whether there was fishing there, and whether each of those cities had a college or university. If there was a college, was there a Sigma Alpha Epsilon chapter on campus? The tedious nature of this research, plus the knowledge that there were many ways this information would be worthless, caused Parrott to shake his leg with impatience, but the need to identify the body overrode the temptation to skip this step.

The fishing column was the easiest to fill out, because every one of the ten cities had fishing of one type or another. Ten yeses meant zero information to go on. Next, Parrott targeted the colleges or universities. Nothing guaranteed that the victim had actually gone to school in the same city from which he was reported missing, but Parrott pressed on, nonetheless.

Each of the cities had some form of higher education, with Tucson being the smallest, and having no Greek life on campus. Houston, Chicago, and New York had multiple prestigious institutions, giving Parrott pause as to which ones to search, but again he pushed forward, glad for his own college experiences at Syracuse that made him familiar with other schools and their fraternities, both black, like his, and white, like SAE.

At the end of the exercise, he found Sigma Alpha Epsilon chapters at Carnegie Mellon in Pittsburgh, Northwestern in Chicago, UCLA in Los Angeles, and at University of Cincinnati in Ohio. These corresponded to the names Thomas Proctor, Reginald Ratliff, Jeremy Curry, and Boris Brown.

The next step was the grim task of sending photos of his victim to each of the police departments listing those missing persons. Now that he suspected the meth lab was a cover for murder by poisoning, he would send these photos to the general police station, rather than to narcotics. Disfigurement of his victim would make it hard for the listing department to identify it as their missing person, but his note explaining where and how the body was found might trigger something.

The fishhook scars on his victim's hand reminded Parrott of how like a fishing expedition police work could be. Sometimes the best weather, the best bait, the best equipment, and the best casting might bring in the best catch, but other times, the smallest input would yield the best output. *You never can tell.*

If he didn't hear something affirmative from any of the four police departments, he could always send photos to the other six, or revisit the missing persons list to do a different kind of sort. He might also resort to social media to check out the names and locations on his list. Seeing the last dates of posting for each of the names might prove useful.

For now, he felt good about what he'd learned today, and he wanted to push on with interviews. Because of the letter Jessica Abramson had sent him after the explosion, Claire's elder daughter was high on his priority list, although he had some more questions for *her* daughter Bonnie, too, now that the possibilities from the MPL were on his mind. Bonnie was closer to the age of his victim and might have some insight.

While he debated about which one, mother or daughter, to approach first, his desk phone rang. When the caller identified herself, he wondered whether Bonnie Warner had extra-sensory perception.

"You asked me to call you if I could think of anything else about Gran's bank barn." Her voice was strained, and spurts of laughter from a TV in the background suggested she wasn't calling from work at the college.

"Yes, thanks for remembering. I have more questions for you. How about if I drive over there, so we can talk in person?"

"Well, that would be okay, I guess, but I'm not at work today, and I'm not at home, either. Scotty's got a bad cold, so I brought him to my mom's house in Philadelphia."

Parrott couldn't believe his luck. He might be able to get both of his desired interviews from one trip. "If it's okay with your mother, I can zoom on over from my office now."

"Just a minute. Let me ask." Bonnie left Parrott on hold, listening to afternoon cartoons. When she returned, she said, "Come on over, assuming you don't mind being around Scotty. And if you like chicken soup, my mom's is the best on the planet."

CHAPTER TWENTY-ONE

Claire appreciated all her employees, but the one she trusted the most was Tammie. The head caregiver at thirty-seven was younger than Claire's daughters and older than Claire's granddaughter, but Tammie had a unique ability to understand Claire, to anticipate her needs, to make her feel safe and comfortable.

Tammie had begun working at Sweetgrass more than four years ago, when Claire's husband was still alive. A few years older than Claire, Scott had begun having sporadic dizzy spells and headaches. Claire had advertised for a "companion" to assist her husband with daily activities, and Tammie had applied. What had impressed Claire most from the interview was Tammie's clear blue gaze, her utter sincerity. Finding loyal employees, who wouldn't mind the long commute to Brandywine Valley, and who were interested in their employers as people, rather than as sources of income, was rare, and Tammie was a treasure.

After Scott died, Claire hadn't wanted to lose Tammie, so she asked her to stay on as her own personal assistant. Claire was in perfect health, not yet eighty years old, but her daughters had begun making noise about her moving to an assisted living place. "Not my style," she said with the firmness of generations of Whitman land and finances behind her. "I don't need any care, and if I do, Tammie is here to provide it."

Tammie's current work schedule included the night shift on Wednesdays and Thursdays, and all weekend. After all the drama at Charlie's house last night, Claire was glad to have Tammie around to make sure she had a good dinner, a soothing bath, and a new bestseller to read. All of this was a poor substitute for her Thursday evening with Robert, but so be it. There was always next Thursday.

Now it was Friday morning, and Claire wanted to swim laps in her outdoor pool. "I'm assuming the air quality is safe by now," she said to Tammie, who had delivered a poached egg and rye toast to Claire at her desk.

"I'm not sure. Yesterday he fireman told me no one should go near the bank barn until further notice, that meth contamination lasts a long time, but he didn't say anything about other outdoor areas." Tammie opened the French doors between the office and the backyard swimming pool area. She sniffed the air. "Still has a hint of chemical smell, like paint or nail polish. Maybe I should call the fire department before I go off duty."

Claire broke off pieces of toast and dropped them into the wet, jiggly egg yolk. This was how she preferred to eat poached egg, even though good manners prohibited "playing with one's food." She had taught her daughters proper table manners, and she never would have done this in front of them—another reason she enjoyed being around Tammie.

"—yes, Mrs. Whitman's caregiver. Wondering whether it's safe—" Tammie paced around the large room, her steps taking her in and out of earshot for Claire.

Claire imagined the day ahead. Her habit of exercising in the mornings dated back to her childhood, when early mornings meant visiting the horses in the bank barn, and sometimes riding before school. Exercising the horses had contributed to Claire's slimness, her tight quads and hamstrings. Summer mornings like this one, she might've ridden one horse after another, each ride different, even though the path was the same.

Afternoons might've been spent at the pool, swimming and splashing with friends or visiting cousins. Now there were no horses, no out-of-town relatives, but Claire was not one to focus on what was missing. She still had a pool to swim in, girlfriends who, until the pandemic, had met weekly for yoga class and at a restaurant in Kennett Square afterwards, but who met now by Zoom. And she had Robert. Handsome, intelligent, well-bred, married Robert.

Tammie disconnected from her call and returned to sit across from Claire at the desk. "Not advisable right now. No one has done an air quality test today, but until we get some rain, the pollutants may still be hanging around in the air."

Disappointed, Claire considered indoor options for exercise, but the tolling of the grandfather clock interrupted her. "Tammie, you've done enough for me today. Thanks for checking, and I'll see you tonight when you're back on duty."

"I don't think Aiko's arrived yet. I can stay until she gets here."

"Don't be ridiculous. I'm perfectly fine. You go now, and I'll do these few dishes myself. I'm not handicapped, you know." Claire punctuated her remarks by shooing Tammie out of the room and out of the house. She carried her breakfast dishes to the kitchen, where she rinsed and put them in the dishwasher. A bowl of fragrant peaches sat on the cobalt granite countertop, tempting her. A peach would be the perfect finish to a delicious morning meal.

Claire cut the peach into juicy eighths and arranged the pieces on a bone china dessert plate. She carried the dish and a linen napkin with her into the office. Before eating, she called to check on Charlie, who was doing fine, and to warn him not to be out in the toxic air. "At least until after we get a good rain," she said.

"Thoughtful of you. I can work in the storage shed behind my house today. I need to sharpen the tools and change the oil in the big mower. Always plenty to do inside and out."

Claire hung up in time to answer another call on the first ring. "Hello, Aiko." She glanced at the clock on her desk. "What's the matter?"

"I'm so sorry, Mrs. Whitman. I should have called sooner, but I was on my way to your house when I got a phone call from my son-in-law. He and my grandson have tested positive, and I've been exposed." She sucked in a breath, a whoo-whoo-whoo sound filled with emotion. "I called my doctor, and she told me to self-isolate for a few days, so I turned around. I'm on the way back home."

"I understand." The girl sounded frightened, so Claire put on her mildest voice. "In fact, I'm grateful to you for checking with the doctor before coming here."

"But I hate to leave you unattended. Fridays it's just you and me. Do you want me to try to get another one of the girls to come in my place?"

"That's not necessary, Aiko. Just take care of yourself. I hope you don't come down with the virus. I'll be fine. Only a few hours until Tammie comes back for the evening, and I've got plenty to eat, wear, and do until then." A cheery chuckle meant to convince Aiko of that truth, but a delicious plan was working in Claire's brain.

An hour later, Claire lifted her champagne from the ledge of her indoor Jacuzzi for two in a toast to her neighbor, one-time boss, and most intimate friend, M. Robert Pennington, chairman emeritus of ModCom Broadcasting. "Here's to fabulous Friday spent with fabulous you. Proof that not everything about covid is bad."

Robert clinked her glass with his own. His eyes twinkled, and his mouth formed that brilliant, movie-star pucker that Claire wished she didn't adore so much. "Sorry for your housekeeper and her family, but I can't remember the last time we had a whole day together. Feels like two kids ditching school." He took a sip and scooted closer, draping an arm behind Claire's shoulders. "Mmm, that's good."

"Krug Grande Cuvee' Brut, your favorite. I've had it on ice for a long time."

"*We've* been on ice for a long time, too. Tell me about this meth explosion. Who was killed, and who might have done such a thing?"

Claire tasted the champagne, appreciating the iciness in her mouth in contrast to the dizzying warmth of the hot tub. "I haven't the slightest idea. It's horrifying, though, a dead man, and my groundskeeper tied up. Nor can I fathom why someone would choose *my* barn as the setting for such violence. Why, I don't even know a single person who uses meth. At least I don't think I do."

"I did some noodling on one of the ModCom sites and learned there are meth labs scattered throughout Brandywine. Our farms are perfect 'hiding-in-plain-sight' spots, because the population density is so low. No one expects an old barn to be anything but an old barn. And since covid, hardly anybody comes or goes much." Robert drained his glass and poured another from the ice-sheathed bottle.

"I had such high hopes for entertaining in that remodeled barn. There wasn't another structure like it anywhere out here." Claire leaned her head against Robert's chest and closed her eyes, wishing she could hold her ambivalent feelings at bay forever. "Now it's in ruins, and everything around it is contaminated. Someone was killed there. And what of his family? I'll never be able to look in that direction without remembering this."

"Have you contacted your insurance company? Hopefully everything will be covered, and you can rebuild your dream barn." Robert nuzzled her neck the way he knew she loved best. Robert was a man of contradictions. He could talk about business matters with perfect precision, while simultaneously sending passionate prickles through Claire's body and mind. He could be as comfortable as an old porch swing or as exciting as a Spanish toreador.

Claire paddled out of Robert's embrace to refill her glass and top off his. When she returned, she perched herself on his lap. Somehow the thought of insurance reparations and all the stolen moments with champagne left a bitter aftertaste in Claire's mouth. Nothing would be able to restore the barn's victim to life. "Everything's out of my hands right now. The police and fire department are involved. The insurance company knows. I put in a call to Brock Thornton, but he never called me back."

"You know these financial guys. They control your money from wherever in the world they happen to be, but they don't always return phone calls. I tried to reach him on another matter, myself, with no luck, but somebody told me he's off at some polo match or other."

The fizzing from the champagne mingled in Claire's mind with the bubbles in the Jacuzzi and the light-headed emotion she experienced every time she was alone with Robert. Theirs was not the giddy love of teenagers or the planning-for-a-future-together love of young marrieds. They had been neighbors and close friends all their lives, and theirs was an intimacy born of shared upbringing, lifelong experiences in the same world, similar expectations. Sometimes those were enough.

"The alcohol's definitely gone to my head. Right now, I couldn't care less about meth labs, insurance companies, or financial planners. I just care about you."

The words rang false to her ears, even as she said them, the kind of platitude Bette Davis might have delivered in a dramatic moment. Claire cared about many things in her life—her family, her dead husband's memory, her heritage, her home, and the fact that something had gone very wrong at Sweetgrass.

But for right now, she played the actress, leaning into this wonderful man's embrace and giving him a long, heartfelt kiss. As always, Jacqueline's image hovered in the corner of Claire's mind, watching. "How's Jacqueline today?"

"Always the same, or worse. Dementia never gets better, you know." He rubbed Claire's cheek with his index finger. "At least she's well cared for. That's a solace."

"I wonder if she'd mind terribly about us. If she knew."

Robert moved away and splashed his chest and arms with water. "I think Jacqueline stopped caring a long, long time ago. We never had the relationship that you and Scott had. I envied you for decades."

Claire pulled him back into a silent embrace. The two sat on the ledge of the hot tub, entwined in each other's arms, until long after the bubbles had stopped, and the champagne was gone. "I wish we could stay like this forever," Claire said, her voice a whisper.

"Me, too. But soon Tammie will be here, and I must go home to Jacqueline. She won't know the difference whether I'm there or not, but I'll know, and the servants will know. My kids will know." His face was a mask of resolve as he stood, pulling Claire by the hand, leading her to the steps and the plush Turkish towels awaiting them.

The familiar sadness twisted in Claire's chest like the tail of a kite that, flying high one moment, had impaled itself on a tree branch the next. Saying goodbye was not Claire's strong suit. But goodbyes were a constant part of this relationship, and Claire reminded herself that goodbye was the price to pay for the stolen moments of joy.

"Next Thursday evening at my place?" Robert had already towel-dried his hair and slipped into his sandals and bathing suit cover-up.

"Of course." She stood on tiptoes for a wobbly kiss. "Assuming nothing else explodes between now and then."

CHAPTER TWENTY-TWO

Parrott couldn't believe his luck in being able to interview Claire's daughter and granddaughter at the same time. That way, he could observe the relationship between Jessica and Bonnie while comparing their answers to his questions.

Normally, investigative protocols recommended single-person interviews, and Parrott preferred these, too, especially if the interviewee was a serious suspect in the crime. In this case, he doubted either or both women fit the profile to pull off a meth explosion at Sweetgrass, unless they had help.

His previous encounter with Bonnie at the college had given him the impression that she was straightforward. Despite having been raised with money, she had a responsible job and took her role as a single parent seriously. That Bonnie had contacted *him* this time was another check in the plus column. People with something to hide rarely called detectives to set up meetings.

The mother, Jessica Abramson, might be a different story. Having met her only through the handwritten letter she delivered to the police station, he wondered about her motivations. Casting suspicion on Claire's assistant, Tammie Caballero, to the point of hinting that she may have been responsible for Claire's husband's death, presented a red flag. He didn't think Jessica would have blown up the bank barn, but she might be stirring up trouble for some reason. He looked forward to meeting her in person.

As he pulled up to the three-story limestone mansion in the Chestnut Hill neighborhood, he shook his head at the immensity of the gray-brick home, maybe eight thousand square feet, and inhabited by one person. Maybe it wasn't as big as her mother's single-resident home in Brandywine, but it did give him pause to think of people in his old neighborhood, some of whom crammed a dozen people into two-bedrooms. Then a jolt struck him. If he and Tonya bought that house in Malvern, they would be guilty of the same.

He climbed the marble stairs, bordered by hydrangeas and gardenias in full bloom. Even the scent was rich. He rang the doorbell and slipped on his mask, expecting a servant to open the door. Instead, a woman's voice came over a speaker to the right of the door. After he identified himself, the voice told him to wait. Within a minute, a red-haired woman who fit the description Lucretia had given him of Jessica Abramson opened the door, herself. She wore black capris, a yellow and white tank top, and orange glasses on a cord around her neck. The colors reminded him of Horace.

"Come on in, detective. I'm Jessica. Bonnie's in the kitchen, so we can talk in there. You can remove your mask if you'd like. We're vaccinated and boosted, and Scotty's sleeping upstairs." She led him down a polished marble hallway to where the smell of chicken soup set Parrott's mouth watering. One of the largest kitchens and dining areas he'd ever seen, the space was decorated in blue and white with flashes of silver. He was sure his entire cottage would fit within the expanse of countertop and cabinets.

Bonnie, wearing denim shorts, a white t-shirt, a red headband, and a pair of sandals, stood at the stove, stirring a huge pot of soup. As he entered the room, she put down the wooden spoon and covered the pot. She met him at the edge of the kitchen island, her hand outstretched in greeting. Perspiration beaded on her forehead and upper lip.

"Thanks for coming on such short notice. Why don't we sit here in the casual dining room? Can I get you a bowl of Mom's soup?"

Parrott shook Bonnie's hand, wondering that the old-fashioned gesture was made by the younger woman, rather than the older. Of course, these days, handshakes, fist bumps, and elbow touches were all unpredictable. As tempting as the smell of the soup was, Parrott couldn't envision himself eating while conducting a police interview. "No, thanks, but I appreciate the offer."

Jessica was already seated at the table, a manila folder in front of her. "Sit right here." She tapped the tabletop at the place next to her, a gesture that, like the rest of her, came off as frenetic.

Parrott was having trouble picturing this woman as having come from Claire Whitman's gene pool. Wary that Jessica was apparently ready to lead a meeting, when Bonnie was the one who had called to set it up, he stood at the table without sitting. "Bonnie needs to be here for this interview."

Bonnie washed and dried her hands and scooted to the table, where Parrott remained standing until she sat. He looked from mother to daughter before clearing his throat.

Before he could utter a syllable, Jessica opened her folder and slapped the table near Parrott's seat. "I'm sure you've read my letter, detective, so you know how concerned we are about my mother's welfare and property."

"Yes, of course you are, and we are doing our best to solve this case." He made eye contact with Bonnie. "You said you have some information for me." He patted his jacket, reassured by the crinkle of pages from the missing persons report.

Bonnie twirled a blonde curl around an index finger, the casual movement belying the serious expression that drew her eyebrows into a valley. "I do. Two things. And my mother does, too." She stared at Jessica, who motioned for her to go on. "I've been so upset over the idea of a meth lab in Gran's barn. I'd never imagine meth and Gran in the same sentence, much less on the same property."

"Gran is so isolated out there. It's hard to believe anyone she associates with would be cooking meth. But then I got to thinking." She dropped the springy curl and clutched one hand in the other on the table. "Gran's groundskeeper, Charlie Wukitsch, has worked at Sweetgrass as long as I can remember. He's a good guy, and Gran likes him a whole lot."

Parrott kept his face neutral, wondering where this was going to go. Bonnie's knuckles had turned white.

"Charlie's got a son, Wyatt, who's been in trouble with drugs. He lives on the East Coast somewhere, maybe New York. I hung out with him a couple of summers when we were kids, but I haven't seen him in years. Gran told me he'd been in trouble with the law and spent some time in jail."

Parrott's suspect radar sent tingles down his arms and legs. "How old's this Wyatt?"

"About my age, I think."

Jessica had crossed one leg over the other and was tapping the foot on the floor. "He's actually a few years older—thirty-five or six maybe. Part of the reason we didn't like your spending time with him back then."

Parrott leaned forward. "Do you have any idea whether Wyatt went to college anywhere?" *If Charlie's son is the body in the barn, that adds a whole new dimension to this case.*

Jessica and her daughter shrugged in tandem, and Bonnie spoke. "I have no idea. I haven't seen Wyatt since I was about eleven years old."

"We made sure of that," Jessica said. She slapped the table again. "I never thought much of Charlie's kids, either one of them, and your dad and I weren't going to allow you to be unsupervised with that boy once he hit puberty."

Parrott wondered whether Jessica's protectiveness of her daughter continued to this day. He searched Bonnie's face for an expression that might tell, but she was back to twirling her hair, and her eyebrows had formed a straight line.

Extracting the missing persons sort list from his jacket, Parrott said, "I'd appreciate your looking over this list of ten men around the same age as Wyatt. Do any of them resemble him, or do you recognize any of the faces?" He handed the pages to Jessica, who donned the glasses hanging around her neck. Bonnie looked over her mother's shoulder.

As they perused the list, Parrott watched their expressions, hoping for a glimmer. A long minute of watching yielded nothing. "Definitely not Wyatt," Jessica said, and Bonnie agreed. "Hard to tell whether any of the photos are familiar. They're kind of grainy."

"The names aren't ringing a bell either," Jessica said. "Are these people you're thinking might have been killed in the explosion?"

Hating when witnesses asked questions, instead of answering them, Parrott mumbled a reply. "Possible victims or perpetrators, we don't know at this point." He was disappointed but took back the papers and returned them to his jacket pocket. Addressing Bonnie, he said, "You said you had two things to tell me."

Bonnie returned to her seat. "I do. I thought you'd want to know about Wyatt first. But I was telling my boyfriend Ray what happened to the barn. We were saying how thankful we are that he wasn't there when it exploded, and we were wondering who might have had access. I asked him if he had his key. When he's leaving the country, he sometimes gives it to me for safekeeping.

"He told me to hold on a minute, while he checked. He came back to the phone, saying, 'Nope, I don't have it. Did I give it to you?'" Bonnie squeezed her hands together again. "But I didn't have it either. So, Ray told me to check with Brock Thornton."

"Who's Brock Thornton?" Parrott asked.

Jessica piped in. "The guy who invests my mom's money."

"He and Ray are good buddies, and they get together sometimes when Ray's in town. Brock is the one who suggested to Gran to allow Ray to stay in the barn. Anyway, Ray said maybe he gave the key to Brock this last time. I was at work when he left, and Brock took him to the airport."

Another set of tingles traveled through Parrott's body. He'd never expected his casual comment to Bonnie to bring any promising leads, although sometimes that's how things happened. He wanted to high-five Bonnie and make her an honorary cop. Instead, he said, "Thanks for reporting these things. I appreciate the information."

He'd all but forgotten Jessica's folder, when a thin voice came over the intercom. "Mommy, can you come here?"

Bonnie jumped from her chair and muttered an apology as she headed for the foyer staircase. Parrott must have jumped, too, because the next thing he knew, Jessica's manicured hand was pressing on his forearm. "Let her take care of my grandson. You still haven't heard what I want to tell you."

Parrott sat back, unsure what to expect. He wanted to trust her, but her eagerness raised doubts. He held both her mother and her daughter in high regard. So he reclined in his chair and attempted an interested expression.

Jessica opened her folder. "I mentioned in my letter that I wanted you to check out my mother's assistant, Tammie Caballero."

Parrott's first impression of Caballero when she had driven him to the groundskeeper's cottage was one of efficiency, but he was open to learning more, and evidently he was about to hear a folder-full.

"I've taken the liberty of putting together this folder of information about Ms. Caballero. It includes the job application, her W9, her references, her Social Security number, and various other documents. She was hired almost five years ago as a companion to my father. I was the one who screened the applicants." She pushed the folder across the table to Parrott. "To say that I regret encouraging my parents to hire her is an understatement."

"Why is that?" Parrott opened the folder and flipped through the pages, about fifteen of them.

"One bad thing after another has happened since she started working at Sweetgrass. Nothing that I can exactly pin on her, but she always seems to be around when bad things happen."

"For instance?"

"My father died in her care, for one. He'd been ill but was stable. He was only in his early eighties, and his death came as a shock. But there were other little things—one of the horses died suddenly, and a stable hand saw Tammie in the barn the day before. We got rid of the horses and converted the barn, but Tammie was seen making out with one of the construction workers. Highly improper."

Jessica stood and began pacing around the table, a tornado building in force. "Of course, Mom doesn't know anything about these things. I've tried over the years to persuade her to replace Tammie, but Mom thinks Tammie hung the moon and won't hear a word of criticism."

"Your mother doesn't seem to me to be naïve or lacking in judgment. There must be a reason she's so devoted to Tammie."

"If there is, Mom hasn't shared the reason with me." Sitting back down, Jessica leaned on her elbows, her face inches away from Parrott's. "You know there are a lot of illegitimate children in Brandywine, right?"

Taken aback, Parrott struggled to keep from reacting. "Not sure what you mean."

Jessica reduced her voice to a whisper. "It's really no secret, but I don't like to talk about this around Bonnie. Many people from the old families have fathered or mothered babies out of wedlock, sometimes through adulterous relationships. You'd think that would make for bad blood and intrigue, but, for some reason, people in Brandywine tolerate each other's indiscretions, sometimes even celebrating them."

Parrott tried to follow the revelation and its purpose. "Are you saying Tammie Caballero is one of those illegitimate children?"

"Yes. Her biological father is extremely wealthy and well-connected. But she was raised by her mother, a seamstress in West Chester. I'm sure she feels deprived of the life she might have lived if the circumstances of her birth had been different. And my instincts tell me she fantasizes that, being so close to my mother, she will eventually inherit enough money to take her rightful place in society."

"So, you don't trust her." Parrott was sure that was an understatement. "I'll keep an eye on her, and I thank you for this information." He didn't say that he would also be keeping an eye on Jessica. He thumped the folder and stood to leave. "Here's my card, in case you think of anything else I should know."

"Are you sure you don't want some soup to take with you?"

"No, thanks. It would spoil my appetite for dinner." The food for thought that Bonnie and Jessica had provided had been even better than chicken soup. "Oh, by the way, who is Tammie Caballero's biological father?"

"You've probably heard of him. He was the chairman of ModCom for many years. His name is M. Robert Pennington. He's my mother's closest neighbor."

CHAPTER TWENTY-THREE

Disappointed that neither Bonnie nor Jessica recognized any of the missing persons, Parrott headed for home. The aroma of chicken soup had awakened his appetite, and he was looking forward to Tonya's cooking. The sun hadn't set yet, but as he drove west, piercing light glared through windshield, visor, and sunglasses, making it difficult to appreciate the blazing backdrops for the verdant trees and neighborhoods.

The case dominated his thoughts. He'd done a lot of work since the explosion, and he was no closer to identifying the body. Not being a "glass half empty" kind of guy, he re-framed that thought. A lot of work since the explosion, and he had numerous leads to work on—the ten missing persons, Charlie Wukitsch's son Wyatt, Claire's money manager Brock Thornton, and Tammie Caballero. Oh, and M. Robert Pennington, too. He had a good feeling that at least one of them would lead to some quality answers.

Saturdays and Sundays were Parrott's purported days off, but when he had a case like this, he worked all the time. That was why comp time was a joke—there was never any time to take it. On the other hand, tomorrow he had promised Tonya he'd go with her to look at that Malvern house, and tomorrow night they'd have dinner with his mother and Herman. Maybe he'd carve out some time tonight and Sunday to do some people research.

When he arrived at the cottage, the smell of barbecued chicken greeted him. Horace screeched from his cage, "Wel-l-l-come." Otherwise, the house was quiet. Was Tonya exercising in the back yard again?

Parrott opened the door to the back, but before he could unlatch the screen door, he heard a barely audible call from behind the closed door to the bedroom. "Ollie, I'm back here." The weakness of the voice, combined with its location, struck fear in his heart, and he sprinted into the bedroom. Something was wrong if Tonya had retreated to the bedroom before dinner. He fumbled with the doorknob, then pushed the door open. The shades had been drawn and the lights turned off. Lavender-scented candles emitted a soothing aroma. The bed was a lumpy jumble of covers and pillows, assembled to surround his wife with protection, isolation, comfort—whatever might help. The scene was all-too-familiar. Something had triggered a PTSD response in Tonya.

"What happened?" Parrott sat on the edge of the bed, careful not to touch the lump that was his wife. He knew better than to say, "Are you okay?" She clearly wasn't.

Tonya rolled over without exposing her face or limbs. "I ran out to the store to get something to go with tonight's chicken. Didn't even get to the store...trapped between two cars...road rage." A guttural cry emanated from under the covers, and Parrott knew there would be no more explanation. Tonya's PTSD had presented this way before.

Parrott exhaled, holding back on the deep sigh that might have expressed how much these episodes hurt his heart. Tonya's therapist had explained the coping strategies to use in these cases. Perhaps in time the episodes would wane in frequency and intensity.

"Let me gut this out...get some sleep."

Wanting to reach out and hug the bad feelings away, Parrott restrained himself. He was the one who needed the hug. What Tonya needed, sadly for him, was to be left alone. "Okay, my love. I'll be in the next room if you need me." He tiptoed out of the room and closed the door as softly as possible.

Parrott petted Horace's feathers and let him out of the cage, while he changed the newspapers and put out fresh food. "Wel-l-l-come," Horace said, landing on Parrott's shoulder. Remembering many evenings when he and Horace had kept each other company while Tonya was in Afghanistan, Parrott was glad to have these tasks to do.

When he finished, he put Horace back in his cage to eat. His own stomach rumbled, so he took the chicken out of the warm oven and stabbed a couple of pieces onto a plate for his dinner. Looking around for something to go with it, he settled on a couple of crackers and a half-eaten jar of dry-roasted peanuts. He found a bottle of beer in the back of the refrigerator to round out the meal. After he ate, he set up his laptop at the dining table, making sure to turn the volume to zero. He started with Wyatt Wukitsch. Knowing that the young man had been involved with drugs made Parrott hopeful that there might be a police record, and within seconds he found it. Age thirty-five, last known address in South Philly, arrested for possessing controlled substances, seventh degree, sent to Willard Drug Treatment campus for eight months last year. Wyatt's photo showed the same square jaw as Charlie, a distinctive feature not shared by any of the ten missing persons. In addition, Wyatt's height and weight put him shorter and squatter than the victim in the bank barn. While that eliminated him from consideration as the victim, it didn't exonerate him from suspicion in the poisoning

Having this information about Charlie's son made Parrott wonder about Charlie. Claire appeared to trust her groundskeeper, and he'd served Sweetgrass for decades, but something about Charlie's story worried Parrott. While he understood Charlie's desire to shower, his having done so ruined an opportunity to gather evidence on whomever had restrained him. Also, as attached as Radar was to his master, Parrott couldn't imagine Radar's failing to alert Charlie to an intruder. Finally, Charlie didn't seem as upset as one might expect about having been tied up. What if the person who had done this was Wyatt? Parrott printed out the police record information and moved on to the next person of interest.

Brock Thornton, Claire's money manager, was next, but before he started researching him, Parrott cleaned up his dinner dish and foraged in the pantry for a snack. He grabbed a couple of Chips Ahoy cookies and poured himself a glass of milk. The evening reminded him of his first year in Brandywine, when Tonya was on active duty, a million miles away. But now, although in the next room, his wife was two million miles away, and that thought filled Parrott with an emptiness bordering on despair.

Chewing on a cookie that tasted like dust, he did what he could to block out his worries about Tonya. Tomorrow she'd probably be better, and they'd go on as if this episode hadn't happened. Meanwhile, he had work to do.

Unsure whether Thornton was a local, he started by looking up Brock Thornton in the county residential directory. Bingo. Thornton, age fifty-two, lived in Unionville with a wife. No children, occupation, phone number, or business address was given. Parrott jotted down the address and started looking for an associated business entity. Thornton was a relatively common name, but Brock wasn't. Surprised not to find anything, Parrott made a note to ask Claire how to get in touch with him.

Next, he did a search for Tammie Caballero and West Chester. There were three of them, aged nineteen, thirty-seven, and fifty-seven. Assuming that Claire's personal assistant lived in a townhouse in West Chester, the thirty-seven year-old would be the one he was looking for. According to his information, she was related to Felicity Caballero, aged sixty-six. Felicity lived in a three-bedroom house on Troon Lane, where the average home price was $525,000, a hefty amount for a seamstress to shoulder. Perhaps they were subsidized by Tammie's father, assuming that Jessica Abramson's information had been accurate.

Parrott checked out arrest records and driving record, but Tammie was clean on both fronts. No marriage licenses, and her job wasn't conducive to an active social life. He wondered why a nice-enough-looking woman of Tammie's age would choose to work nights and weekends, taking care of an elderly woman. As sharp as Claire Whitman was, her company couldn't provide enough social stimulation for a single woman of marriageable age. And what about Tammie's biological clock? Some women in their thirties were fast-tracking their lives toward having a family. This speculation might have nothing to do with the explosion in the bank barn, and therefore was none of Parrott's business, but he would keep his eye on Tammie Caballero, just the same.

Parrott stood and stretched. The computer clock said nine forty-five, but his eyes were heavy-lidded, and he was ready for bed. There was one more person he wanted to look up, communications magnate, M. Robert Pennington. Parrott needed to invigorate himself. Instead of brewing coffee, he dropped to the floor in front of the sofa and did fifty pushups. Those were enough to get his heart pumping and his brain in gear. He returned to the computer and hit the search button.

Pages of information came up for Mr. Pennington, perhaps one of the wealthiest and most well-known residents of Brandywine Valley. The chairman emeritus of ModCom Communications Network lived in Brandywine Valley with his wife, Jacqueline. His age was listed as eighty-five, his wife's as eighty-six. If he had fathered thirty-seven-year-old Tammie Caballero, he was almost fifty at the time, and Tammie's mother was twenty-nine. Quite an age difference, but not unheard of. How a seamstress and a businessman had crossed paths, though, might have made for interesting gossip. Perhaps Felicity had been Mrs. Pennington's seamstress.

Parrott found a site with photos. Pennington had been tall and fit with rugged good looks that reminded Parrott of Gerard Butler. Not that Gerard Butler did much for Parrott, but Tonya thought he was cute. Pennington's wife and sons appeared in a few early photos, but the vast majority showed Pennington surrounded by celebrities and colleagues from ModCom. Parrott peered at a close-up, assessing whether Tammie Caballero resembled him, and deciding it was possible.

In addition to his work, Pennington had been active in the Brandywine Conservancy, the Brandywine River Fine Arts Museum, and the fox hunting and polo set. Whatever his connection to this case, if there was one, Pennington would have to be treated with care. Parrott had dealt with other such citizens in the past, so he knew how to tread softly. He also knew better than to assume that wealth and power equaled morality. If Pennington had anything to do with the meth explosion, Parrott would find out.

The surge of energy from the pushups was waning, and Parrott was ready to call it a night. He covered Horace's cage, turned off the lights, brushed his teeth, undressed, and sneaked into the bedroom, wishing for a sign that his wife was feeling better, that she wanted him here. He eased back the covers on his side of the bed, barely making out the outline of Tonya's face and body. He folded his long frame into place, trying not to jostle or startle his wife in any way.

Parrott pulled up the covers and rolled on his side, away from her, not wanting to see or hear her breathing and not be able to touch her. His eyes burned, so he closed them, willing himself to sleep. He was on the precipice between thinking and dreaming when a warm hand found its way around his back and waist, and the body it was attached to nestled against him.

CHAPTER TWENTY-FOUR

Claire's yoga class helped divert her mind from meth explosions and tied-up groundskeepers. She and a group of local senior former-equestrians had been meeting weekly in a gym in town, but now they'd gone virtual. Every Saturday morning, Claire practiced her breathing and poses on a sunlit mat in her in-home gym. Tammie had set up Claire's iPad, so it projected onto a large screen. The experience was as close to being in the real class as one could manage.

Before class, the eight ladies, all residents of Brandywine Valley, greeted one another in the rectangular screen space. Everyone had heard about the meth explosion, so the entire pre-class visit was taken up with offering condolences to Claire, and gratitude that she wasn't hurt. No one asked questions. The ladies were much too genteel for that.

After ten minutes or so, their yoga instructor, Sandy, called the class to order, and set the stage for the cleansing of mind and body. Soft background music played by stringed instruments created atmosphere, and Sandy's high, sweet voice took over.

Wearing her navy, loose-fitting yoga pants and shirt, Claire assumed the lotus position on the blue mat, stretching her piriformis muscles until she achieved the welcome pull in her lower back. Sandy began leading the ladies through deep breathing exercises. "Inhale the joy and light. Exhale the day gone by." Claire exhaled with enthusiasm, imagining her mind and body, releasing whatever toxins lingered.

Next, Sandy led the ladies through the numerous poses designed to increase energy, improve balance, build strength, and relieve stress. None of these were too complicated, and Claire had been doing them for years—the tree, the sun, the warrior. After the cool down, Sandy read from Walt Whitman's *Leaves of Grass*, a beautiful passage about patience:

"Have patience and indulgence toward the people,... read these leaves in the open air every season of every year of your life, re-examine all you have been told at school or church or in any book, dismiss whatever insults your own soul, and your very flesh shall be a great poem and have the richest fluency not only in its words but in the silent lines of its lips and face and between the lashes of your eyes and in every motion and joint of your body..."

The class ended with everyone's repeating Sandy's teacher's mantra, "My mind is brilliant. My body is healthy. My spirit is tranquil," followed by three "oms."

In the after-class, Claire's friend Monica commented on the passage from *Leaves of Grass*. "I've always wondered whether you're a descendant of Walt Whitman, and whether Sweetgrass is named after *Leaves of Grass*."

Before Claire could respond, Harriet's rectangle lighted up. "I thought Claire was related to the Whitman Candy Company, and *that's* where Sweetgrass came from."

Claire laughed, a throaty laugh that came from the irony of having answered these questions for as long as she could remember. She'd have thought Monica and Harriet knew. "No, yes, no, yes." She waggled her manicured index finger at the screen as she spoke. "As far as I know, my family is related neither to Walt Whitman, nor the Philadelphia candy Whitmans. But I couldn't swear to it. Maybe someday I'll do one of those ancestry tests.

"On the other hand, Sweetgrass was named after both—the candy and *Leaves of Grass*. My grandfather or great-grandfather probably thought he was being clever, but the name stuck, and it's been Sweetgrass ever since."

Angela, a relative newcomer to the group, having only lived in Brandywine for the past five years, cleared her throat, lighting up her rectangle. "Huh. I thought Sweetgrass was a reference to marijuana. Guess that tells you what generation I grew up in."

Angela was a good ten years younger than Claire, but, still, her comment stung. Claire was quite sure her forebears wouldn't have cared for the association between the Whitman family farm and drugs. She hoped the meth explosion wouldn't add fuel to that fire.

As soon as the yoga class was over, Tammie brought the morning's mail and a strawberry-yogurt smoothie to the gym's sitting area. "How was your class?"

"Lovely, as always. Thanks." She sipped the smoothie, enjoying the tart thickness. "I love my yoga class. It's quite relaxing."

"It does look fun. One of these days I might try it."

"When you're an older lady like me, you mean." Claire leaned back into the upholstered chair and put her bare feet on the ottoman. "Come, sit here for a minute." She pointed to the matching chair across from her.

"What I meant about taking yoga was, I might take it when I have time in my schedule." Tammie sat and crossed her legs at the ankles. Her black capris and white blouse flattered her figure, and her hair was freshly cut.

Claire thought, not for the first time, how surprising it was that Tammie was still single. "I'm not trying to be nosy, but what ever happened to that nice young man you were going with, the one who worked on my barn renovation?

Flinching, Tammie directed her gaze at the opposite wall, and Claire acted quickly to withdraw the question. But before she could do so, the house phone rang, and Tammie jumped to answer the extension on the bar.

"Whitman residence." Her voice had the professional crispness of a nurse or a lawyer, addressing a jury. "Just a moment, Detective Parrott. I'll see if Mrs. Whitman is available."

Claire strolled to the bar and perched on one of the leather barstools before putting the receiver to her ear. "Hello, detective. How may I help you today?"

Parrott explained he'd like to come over this morning for a few minutes. He had some questions for Claire, and also for Tammie.

Glancing across the room, where Tammie was cleaning the yoga mat with sanitizing wipes and rolling it up to place it behind the weights, Claire agreed. Parrott's request was a formality, anyway. In the process of investigating a crime, police detectives had free reign.

"What time do you think you'll be here?" she asked, wondering whether she had time to shower and change from her yoga outfit. The pink numbers of the digital clock on the wall flashed ten-fifteen.

"I'll be there in a half hour, if that's okay. I have another appointment in Malvern at noon."

Whatever calming Claire had achieved from the yoga was now completely gone. Parrott's visit and his potential questions were enough to raise her level of concern, especially since he wanted to question Tammie. Thirty minutes wasn't much time, but it was long enough to change clothes, put on makeup, and prepare her young assistant for Parrott's visit.

She wondered how much the detective already knew.

CHAPTER TWENTY-FIVE

Parrott arrived at Sweetgrass on the dot of ten-forty-five, eager to talk to Claire and Tammie. He'd arranged to meet Tonya at the Malvern house at noon, an appointment which had apparently helped her to suppress yesterday's PTSD episode. Tammie welcomed Parrott into Claire's study. "Have a seat. Mrs. Whitman will be here shortly." In the morning light from the window, the young woman's dark hair and startling blue eyes drew Parrott's attention more than they had two evenings before. Now that he'd been told about Tammie's biological connection to the chairman of ModCom, he could see the resemblance to M. Robert Pennington.

"I don't know whether Ms. Whitman told you, but I have some questions for both her *and* you." The ticking of the grandfather clock kept him on edge, aware that his time here was limited. "Separately. What I mean is, I'd like to speak with Ms. Whitman first, alone, and afterwards, with you alone."

A grimace clouded Tammie's expression. "You sound like a TV detective. Divide and conquer, or something."

"Not at all," Parrott said. "Just gathering information. Single-person interviews are standard procedure. They help paint a whole picture, often from different perspectives."

Before Tammie could comment, Claire breezed into the room, dressed in an aqua pantsuit, smelling of mint, and carrying a plate of *petit fours*, which she set down on her desk. "Hello, detective." He stood, and she took Parrott's hand in both of hers. "I'm so sorry to keep you waiting. Inconsiderate of me, as you said you have another appointment."

Parrott glanced at his watch. "No worries. We have enough time." Claire sat across from him at her desk, reminding Parrott of one of his strictest teachers. As much as he admired her, he couldn't take her goodwill for granted. "I was just telling Ms. Caballero that I'd like to speak with each of you, separately."

Claire nodded, apparently unruffled. "Shall we start with me?" She waved to Tammie, and the young woman tilted her head and left the room, closing the door behind her.

This was the first time Parrott had seen these two together, and he was impressed by how they communicated without words. He leaned forward, hoping to banish the teacher-pupil image in his head. "Mrs. Whitman—"

"Claire. I know I'm old enough to be your grandmother, but you need not stand on ceremony with me." She pointed at the *petit fours*. "Please take some."

Not wanting to disappoint, Parrott popped a dainty cake into his mouth and chewed. *Delicious.* "Okay, Claire. What can you tell me about Charlie Wukitsch's son Wyatt?"

Claire's eyebrows rose, and her blue-green eyes opened wider. "Wyatt? I haven't seen him in a long time. Maybe since the pandemic started. He and Charlie are close, even though Wyatt's been a challenge at times." She lowered her voice to a whisper. "Drugs, you know. I think he's done time in jail."

A second later her mouth dropped open, and her hand flew to her mouth. "Do you think Wyatt was cooking meth in my barn?"

"What do you think?" Even if the coroner had been right, that the meth explosion was staged to cover up the murder, the perpetrator had to possess the knowledge, ingredients, and equipment to cook meth.

Claire stood and stared at Parrott, as if wishing he would leave and take his suspicions with him. "I sincerely hope not. I've known Wyatt all his life, and Charlie even longer." She began pacing in the space between her desk and the bookshelves behind it. "I'm not a person to get all riled up over things. Bad things happen sometimes, and we must deal with them. That said, the horror of this explosion is just starting to hit me. Someone committed this violence, and you'll undoubtedly discover who. Somehow, I hope that the criminal is a total stranger. I'd not like to deal with the reality that someone I care about and trust is involved."

Parrott preferred having the advantage of height over the people he questioned, but in this case, he remained seated. "You mentioned Wyatt's trouble with drugs. Despite that, he's a person you care about and trust?"

Returning to her chair, Claire sighed. "I trust and care about *Charlie*. He's a good man, and he's had a rough go with his divorce and Wyatt's problems. Charlie has had access to these grounds, the barn, even this house, for years. He's never given me a moment's concern about his honesty and reliability." She rolled the pen on her desk. "Wyatt is an extension of Charlie. If he were charged with arson and murder, it would finish Charlie. I don't want to think that's possible."

Parrott questioned Claire at length about when she had seen Wyatt last, what Charlie had told her about Wyatt in the past year, and whether Wyatt had ever asked Claire for money or other support.

Replying in the negative to both questions, Claire folded her hands on the desk. "I assume that takes care of Wyatt. What other questions do you have for me?"

It was Parrott's turn to stand. "Who, besides Charlie and Brock Thornton, has a key to your barn?

"*Brock Thornton*? Why would my money manager have a key to my barn?"

"Bonnie, told me that her boyfriend Ray gave Thornton his key the last time he stayed in the barn."

"Hmph. No one bothers to tell me who's got keys to my property." Claire opened a desk drawer and fished out a purple file folder. Inside were a dozen zippered sandwich bags, labeled and stapled to the folder. "Here's *my* key to the barn. Far as I know, the only others who have a key are Charlie, Tammie, and, now, as you say, Brock Thornton."

Parrott's antennae elevated. "Why would Tammie need a key?"

Storm clouds passed over Claire's turquoise eyes, and her voice took on a lower pitch than Parrott had ever heard. "Now, listen, detective. A few moments ago, I told you I couldn't bear to think of anyone I care about as a criminal. That certainly applies to Tammie. Tammie is more than a personal assistant. She is an extension of me, just like Wyatt is an extension of Charlie. I trust Tammie with all my worldly goods, all my keys. You told me you want to question her, and I wonder why. She was with me the entire evening of the explosion. She never left my side."

"Whoa, wait a minute. I never said Tammie was a suspect. I merely wondered why she would need a key to the barn, when her time with you, I assume, is spent here in this house."

Red spots dotted Claire's cheeks. "I guess I'm a little overprotective when it comes to Tammie. She is very special to me, and I don't want her subjected to a distressing interrogation if I can help it." She closed the key folder and put it back in the file drawer. "As for having a key, when the barn was being renovated, Tammie ran back and forth to the barn for me all the time. She was an intermediary between the construction people and me. Rather than give her my key, I had her make a copy for herself."

Claire's passionate response was a tip-off for Parrott. He respected the older woman, but sometimes his duty required him to undo a witness's composure. Considering Claire's age, he intended to unzip slowly. "I understand about the key, but I do wonder about your being so overprotective of an employee. Do your feelings for Tammie have anything to do with her parentage?"

The spots on Claire's cheeks burst into flames, and her pupils widened. "What do you mean by that?"

"Only that I believe Tammie is the daughter of M. Robert Pennington, your neighbor and head of ModCom. Perhaps that gives her more status in these parts than an ordinary secretary."

The tiniest shift of her eyes betrayed surprise, but Claire recovered quickly. "Tammie is certainly not alone in being connected to a well-known Brandywine resident in such a way. I think that should bring her neither special privileges, nor undue scrutiny." Claire stood and planted her fists on the desk, leaning forward. "If you're finished questioning me, why don't we let Tammie speak for herself, shall we?"

"One more thing before we do that," Parrott said, removing his missing persons list from the inside of his jacket. "I'd like you to look at these photos to see if you recognize any of the young men." He set the pages on the desk, facing Claire, smoothing the crease.

Claire removed a pair of readers from her desk drawer and put them on. She lifted the pages and perused them, her mouth drawn into a dot, as if she were sucking air. After a few moments, she removed the readers and set the papers down. "I can't say that any of them look familiar. I wish I could be more helpful. Let me call for Tammie. Maybe she will recognize one of them." She handed the pages back to Parrott before opening a drawer and pushing a button.

"Oh, one more thing," Parrott said, as Tammie arrived at the doorway. "Can you give me contact information for Brock Thornton?"

"Certainly," Claire said, as she scrolled through the contacts on her cell phone. "I must warn you, though. Brock is hard to get in touch with. He travels a lot. Makes you wonder when he has time to work, but he sends monthly reports, so I can't complain. If I ever have a question, I have to leave a message, and he gets back to me eventually." She scrawled Thornton's phone number and email address on a slip of ecru paper. "Come on in, Tammie. Detective Parrott has a few questions for you. He's promised to keep it short, as he has another meeting to attend. Why don't you sit here at my desk?"

Claire glided toward the door, switching places with Tammie. Again, Parrott marveled at the casual, close relationship between employer and employee. The grandfather clock struck the half hour. Parrott would have to leave in about fifteen minutes to meet Tonya in Malvern.

"I'll try to make this short and sweet." Parrott had folded the missing persons pages and slipped them back in his jacket pocket. "First let's talk about your key to the barn. When is the last time you used it?"

Tammie hesitated for a second. "I honestly can't remember the last time I was in the barn. When it was being remodeled, I went over there a lot—to check on things, to carry messages back and forth. Since the reconstruction, and the pandemic, I haven't really been there. It's probably been at least ten months to a year."

"Do you remember seeing any signs of drugs of any kind inside?"

"Absolutely not. I would have called the police if I had. Ms. Whitman wouldn't put up with drugs anywhere on the premises of Sweetgrass. Employees aren't even allowed to smoke cigarettes in this house."

"Have you seen any activity at the barn in the last several months, maybe when you were coming or going?"

"As a matter of fact, I told Ms. Whitman the night of the explosion, I've seen a white pickup truck there on several occasions. I knew Bonnie's boyfriend stayed there sometimes, so I never thought much about it."

"Who would clean up after Bonnie's boyfriend was there?"

"That would be Charlie's responsibility. He takes care of the grounds and outbuildings. The barn is considered an outbuilding."

Parrott piggybacked on Tammie's mention of Charlie to ask about Wyatt. She claimed not to know him, except by sight, and not to have seen him in more than two years.

The clock ticked, reminding Parrott to wrap up this interview. He could always come back another time. He withdrew the missing persons list from his pocket again. "I'd like you to look closely at the names and photos of these ten young men." He positioned the pages in front of her, as he had done for Claire.

Tammie studied the photos, one-by-one, her eyebrows ruffling into a squint. When she got to the middle of the list, she dropped the page onto the desk, as if it burned her hand. "Oh, no. Tripp." She held a hand over her heart and stared at Parrott as if she'd seen an obituary. "What does this mean, being on this list? Are these people in trouble?"

Parrott wanted to leap out of his skin at Tammie's recognition. He leaned over the desk, trying to identify which photo Tammie had recognized. He explained about the missing persons list, that he was trying to make a connection between any of these people and Brandywine Valley. "Tell me which photo looks familiar."

Tammie pointed to the photo of Tucker Anderson III from Raleigh, North Carolina. "This one. This is one of the construction workers who remodeled the bank barn. I know him very well."

"When's the last time you saw or heard from him?" Parrott asked.

Tammie pulled out her cell phone and checked the last text she'd received. "Ten days ago. Do you think something's happened to him?"

Tammie's reactions put her squarely in the dear friend or more category with relationship to Tucker Anderson. Parrott looked for a noncommittal response to her question. "That's what we are trying to find out."

As she processed this information, Parrott watched various emotions playing out upon Tammie's face—concern, bewilderment, distress, and, finally, understanding. "Omigod," she said, covering her eyes with both hands. "Tripp might be the body found in the barn."

CHAPTER TWENTY-SIX

Parrott would have preferred to stay at Claire's to question Tammie more, but he'd promised to meet Tonya and the realtor at the house in Malvern, and this was one of those times that his personal life had to take priority. He arranged to meet with Tammie again the next morning, before she left Sweetgrass at the end of her overnight stint.

Technically, Parrott was off duty on weekends, but an active case made it hard to take any time off. Even if he stayed away physically, his head remained on the case.

Driving along the narrow roads and verdant landscape between towns, he tried to shift focus. He wasn't looking forward to traipsing through a multi-million-dollar house that he didn't need or want. Tonya had fixed his favorite corned beef hash with fried eggs for breakfast, and she'd hummed a melody as she served it. She was fired up about the house, and he didn't want to disappoint her with his lack of enthusiasm.

Malvern was the next town over from the Whitman property, which allowed only a few minutes of thinking time. As he pulled into the long, curving driveway and parked behind Tonya's Camry and another car, presumably the real estate agent's, his stomach roiled. The three-story house looked like something out of *The Hunt* magazine, one of those too-stunning-to-live-in mansions that people like him never owned.

The Campbells and the Bakers popped into his mind, people with old money whose Brandywine homes had graced the countryside for generations. The Malvern homes had similar sprawling appearances, sitting on huge lots that had been carved out of farms, but this one was newer. He'd read the listing a couple of times. The brick-and-frame home of 5,725 square feet had five bedrooms, four baths, and nestled on an almost-two-acre lot that had been part of the Schaper Farm. He never imagined himself living in a place like this. He gulped and hiked up the steps to the wide verandah.

The left half of the double front door opened just before Parrott touched the doorbell. A willowy light-skinned Black woman in a tight-fitting cream-colored suit and black-patent heels waved him in. Tonya, dressed in denim and silver, peeked from behind her in the vast entry hall.

"I'm Faith Hightower. Very nice to meet you, Mr. Parrott." The real estate agent placed her cool hand into Parrott's. "I've heard a lot about you."

Since receiving the multi-million-dollar gift from Elle, that frequent comment never failed to start a vague itch in Parrott's throat. Whatever Ms. Hightower had heard, the itch interfered with forming a proper reply, so he mumbled, "Likewise."

Once ushered across the threshold, Parrott greeted his wife by putting his arm around her shoulder, careful not to press too hard where she'd been injured. Tonya covered his hand with her slightly damp one. If she'd spoken, he was sure she'd have sung.

The lag of conversation was remedied by Ms. Hightower, who glided from one open space to another, pointing out amenities with every fling of an arm. "Just look at the twelve-foot ceilings in this light and airy living room. The current owners installed these silk-upholstered window seats in the bay window. Such a lovely touch, don't you think? And what a view—a private meadow surrounded by flowering peach trees. Malvern is so lovely at this time of year."

Parrott imagined what might happen if Horace strutted about on the silk upholstery. The vision kicked up the itch in his throat. Before he could clear it, he and Tonya were swept into the restaurant-sized kitchen, redolent with the aroma of baked apples. Glass and wood cabinets gleamed white, and chrome appliances blended into the dove-gray tile. His mother's catering kitchen wasn't as spacious or well-appointed as this one. Clearly in her element, Tonya peered inside the two double ovens, the Thermidor refrigerator and freezer, the built-in microwave, and two dishwashers, all top of the line, according to the realtor. The countertops were chisel-cut granite with a leather finish, full of swirls and mineral deposits. Tonya's fingertips danced over the counters and cabinets, as if she were the star of a culinary ballet. "Beautiful," she murmured over and over, and her smile was nothing short of a benediction.

The kitchen opened into a casual dining room and a family room with two fireplaces. All were surrounded by large glass panels that offered views of the outdoor swimming pool, flagstone patio, and large grouping of outdoor furniture. Not a speck of dust, nary a leaf to mar the outdoor splendor—Parrott wondered what it must cost to maintain this residence. At the same time, he indulged himself in imagining an early-morning or late-night swim in his own private pool.

Without lingering in any one lavish area for too long, Ms. Hightower led them on a whirlwind tour around hallways, bedrooms, bathrooms, a fully-equipped gymnasium, wine cellar, and theater in the basement, a sauna and hot tub in the master bathroom. One of the bedrooms had been dedicated as an office, another as a library. Tonya declared a third bedroom as perfect for her art studio.

"As you can see, the house is spotless, in move-in condition," the realtor said. "And the owners have reduced the price by fifty thousand dollars as of this Sunday." She waved her open arms to encompass the expansive master bedroom suite, including his and hers dressing rooms and walk-in closets the size of their present bedroom. "I can show you other homes in this area, but none will be as sleek and modern as this one, or as affordable."

Tonya grabbed Parrott's hand and squeezed. "This house is a dream come true, isn't it?"

Parrott winced but managed to squeeze back. He turned to the realtor and said, "Before we jump into a decision, I have a lot of questions." He glanced at his watch and a stab of hunger shot through him. It had been hours since the corned beef hash. "Why don't we talk it over and get back to you? I'm sure Tonya is as hungry as I am, and we also have a dinner date to get ready for tonight."

Ms. Hightower didn't skip a beat. "Of course. Shall we meet at my office tomorrow morning? You don't want to wait too long. Somebody is going to snap this beauty right up."

Parrott's hunger turned sour as he remembered his appointment with Tammie. He let go of Tonya's hand and looked into her eyes, aiming for sincerity. "I'm sorry, but I have an important witness interview in the morning."

"Oh, Ollie." Tonya whispered under her breath and turned away. A second later, though, she turned back, mumbling. "I understand. Work comes first."

"But maybe we could meet at your office at one o'clock. What do you think, Tonya?"

His wife turned back, her moist eyes betraying the intensity of her desire for this house. "That would be wonderful. Is one o'clock okay with you, Ms. Hightower?"

The attractive woman's lips curled into a semblance of a smile, and she placed her manicured hand on Parrott's forearm in a too-familiar gesture. "One o'clock would be per-fect." She extracted a business card from the pocket of her suit jacket. "Here's my personal cell phone number. Feel free to call me if you'll be delayed. Or if I can answer any questions for you. I pride myself on service to my customers."

CHAPTER TWENTY-SEVEN

A few hours later, the Parrotts were *en route* to Cora Parrott's home in Exton. By the time they'd arrived home in their separate cars from the house showing, they had barely had time to grab some snacks and get ready for their dinner date. The sixteen-minute ride gave them time to talk more about the house, but, truthfully, Tonya's thoughts had percolated over it all afternoon, so much that if her thoughts had been coffee grounds, they'd be soggy by now.

"It *is* a magnificent house, Ollie. Do you agree?"

"No question." He steered around a slow-moving car in the left lane. "I wonder, though. If you want to live in a better neighborhood, maybe we should look at homes in Exton, near Ma's. They're a lot more modest."

Tonya's insides squeezed. Her heart was set on that big, beautiful dream house. "Modest? Sure. There's nothing wrong with your mom's house, but it sure doesn't have the space or amenities of that house in Malvern. I can't stop thinking about cooking in that kitchen. Enough cabinet space for dozens of pots and pans and bowls and dishes and—"

"Hey, can I change the subject for a minute?" Parrott was nearing his mother's street. "I hope Herman doesn't get on your last nerve like before, but if he does, give me a signal, and I'll change the subject, maybe go into another room with him, and you can stay with Ma."

"Thanks. I'm dreading being cooped up with him for a whole evening. I'll rub my bad shoulder if I can't take it anymore."

Cora's dining room table was nothing short of a work of art. A white, lacy tablecloth and white napkins played canvas to plates of pale yellow and robin's egg blue. Blue and green and white hydrangeas filled a glass bowl in the center.

Tonya busied herself, helping her mother-in-law in the kitchen, where the savory aromas of chicken piccata, angel hair pasta with pesto, and grilled zucchini caused her to salivate. She cut up the vegetables for a salad, while Cora took care of the other dishes.

Ollie and Herman had sequestered themselves in the study, where the Phillies were battling the Braves, and occasional yells signaled that some male bonding was going on.

"The guys sound like they're getting along fine," Cora said, a smile lighting up her eyes. "That makes me happier than the hen that laid the golden egg. Herman is such a fine gentleman. I think Ollie and he might enjoy each other's company for a long time to come."

Tonya tried not to huff or roll her eyes. Cora had gone to a lot of trouble to make this evening cordial. So far Tonya hadn't seen any evidence that Herman was such a fine gentleman. Then again, he hadn't shown his bossy self either. She'd have to reserve judgment until after the four of them spent a whole dinner time together. "Are we ready to fill the water glasses? I'd be glad to do that."

"Go ahead. I'll call the men to the table." Cora left the room, and Tonya said a little prayer that the rest of the evening would go smoothly.

Once everyone else was seated, Cora rolled the hot dishes to the table on a food trolley. As she took her seat, she began lifting the lid on each dish and describing its contents before passing it around.

"I love the way you introduce the food," Herman said. "My grandmother used to do that at family gatherings, and I swear it made the food taste better."

Parrott served himself a large portion of chicken piccata. "My mama's food needs no fancy introduction to taste good. She's a superb cook, just like Tonya." He exchanged the platter of piccata for the platter of zucchini.

Herman closed his eyes, breathing in and smacking his lips. "You're right about that. I don't know a better cook anywhere." He winked at Cora, and her whole face glowed. Witnessing this, Tonya understood how intimate these two had become. She wondered whether Ollie noticed and how it made him feel.

"You've always had an aptitude for culinary arts, haven't you, Cora?" This had been one of Tonya's concerns about marrying the son of an accomplished chef.

"I s'pose you might say that," Cora replied. "I've spent many of my waking hours in kitchens, learning." She dabbed her mouth with her napkin. "Maybe this is odd, but when I'm preparing food for the catering business, I'm all into quality control, and I enjoy the process, but when I'm cooking for my own people—it's a whole 'nother task. I guess I'm folding love and joy into every dish."

Herman replied by waving a fork full of pasta in the air. "This right here. I can taste the love in it."

Ollie's eyes sought Tonya's, and the two of them burst out laughing. "No disrespect, but this is a dinner, not a love fest." Ollie turned to Herman. "Let's have some normal dinner conversation. How're things in the construction business?"

Tonya choked back more laughter, glad for the change in subject, but worried it might provoke Herman to meddle in other people's finances. If he did, she might start clearing the dishes.

Apparently, the construction business was booming. Herman had three shopping centers being built at once. "Stretching my crews, but everyone appreciates the opportunity for overtime, and these have been rolling twenty-four/seven."

Cora put down her fork and sipped from her wine glass. "One of the shopping centers is in a great location. Herman thinks I should expand my catering business—rent space there."

Goosebumps tingled on Tonya's forearms and the back of her neck. "Is that something you'd want to do? Double your business?"

"Oh, I don't know. It's fun to think about, but I'd need a lot of reassurances from someone in the know. And a specific business plan. Before I'd commit to that, I'd have to talk to my financial planner, and I haven't done that."

Herman encircled Cora's wrist with his thumb and index finger and gave a nod to Ollie. "My client for this shopping center invests his money with a fancy Brandywine money manager. Name's Brock Thornton. Have you ever heard of him?"

Ollie sat straighter and put down his fork. "Brock Thornton? Yes, I've heard of him. What does your client have to say about him?"

Herman set Cora's hand down on the table and leaned back, puffing out his chest. "Nothing much, but I hear Thornton's clients are getting a twenty per cent return on investment. In this economy, that's miraculous." He flicked at a spot on his shirt. "He won't take you as a client unless you have ten million or more to invest. I was telling your mother we ought to pool our savings— you, me, and her—and see if we can get in on this action. Twenty per cent is nothing to sneeze at."

Irritation boiled inside Tonya's belly. She'd expected the conversation to lead to this path. She looked at everyone's plates, gauging whether she could get away with clearing the table now, but Cora was still eating. Instead, she took a big swallow of wine. She hated people who wanted to tell you what to do with your money.

Ollie, on the other hand, was glomming onto every word. She hoped he wasn't buying into the idea of switching financial planners. He put down his napkin and leaned forward on his elbows. "Twenty per cent? That's unheard of. I wouldn't mind hearing more about this guy."

Wanting to divert the conversation, Tonya turned to Cora. "Did Ollie tell you we looked at a house in Malvern today?"

Cora's eyebrows shot up on her forehead. "Malvern? I've catered a few parties for clients who live there—very fancy." She glanced around the table, where everyone's plates were empty. "I hope you've saved room for dessert. Herman's Kentucky bourbon cake is scrumptious." She motioned to Tonya. "Let's clear the table and leave the guys to talk about boring financial matters. I want to hear about this house."

Thrilled for an excuse to get away from Herman's opinions, Tonya leapt from her chair and headed for the kitchen, carrying an armload of dishes with her. "How 'bout I make the coffee?" she asked. Cora had one of those restaurant-quality cappuccino-latte-espresso machines, so much fun to play with.

"I didn't know you and Ollie were looking at houses." Cora put the leftovers in plastic containers and made room for them in the refrigerator. "Is there a particular reason?" Her eyes slid to Tonya's middle.

"Nothing like *that*, and I think Ollie hasn't bought into the idea as I have. There's nothing wrong with our house, exactly. Sometimes the tiny rooms suffocate me. I can't explain it. We share the only decent closet in the house, and sometimes Ollie has to climb over me to dress for work in the morning. The kitchen is too small for appliances, like this awesome coffee maker or a standing mixer."

Cora patted her daughter-in-law on the back, as she returned to the sink to load the dishwasher. "I understand, dear, and I know you and Ollie will make the best decision for the two of you."

Tonya should have been gratified by Cora's supportive comment, but she was beginning to think that the desire for such an expensive house was greedy and selfish on her part. Maybe they should do as Herman suggested and invest the money for a twenty per cent return. They could always buy a bigger house once they started a family.

When Cora carried the cake, and Tonya carried the coffee cups back into the dining room, the men were also talking about the house in Malvern. Ollie was describing the massive kitchen and the outdoor pool, and Tonya cringed at the thought of what Herman would say about the extravagances.

The older man's eyebrows wove into a thick valance that shaded his expression. "This must be a difficult decision for you kids—a house with a price tag bigger than anything you've ever seen in your lives. 'Course it's none of my business to tell you what to do, but here's what I think—"

Oh, here it comes. Tonya steeled herself for Herman's proclamation from on high, hating the man already for having so much power over her emotions.

Herman stood and leaned back, arms crossed over his chest. "You could do a lot worse than buying a nice home in Malvern. You have the money. Give Tonya the kitchen of her dreams and do it while you're young and have a lot of years to enjoy it. Home values are only going to go up, and that's a very desirable area. You want me to check it out, construction-wise, I'll be glad to do it."

Cora sidled over and kissed Herman on the cheek. "Isn't this just the most wonderful man?"

Ollie and Tonya exchanged glances, and for the first time, Tonya had to agree. A warmth suffused her then, sweeter than anything, even sweeter than Kentucky bourbon cake.

CHAPTER TWENTY-EIGHT

D riving home from his mother's house in Exton, Parrott's
thoughts were weighted with the ironies of his life. The
car windows were down, and the breeze created in the
summer darkness lifted strands of Tonya's hair from her pensive
face. Who would ever have dreamed that he and Tonya would
be able to buy an almost-two-million-dollar house? Or that they
would disagree on the practicality of such a purchase? Or that his
mother's boyfriend would jump in the middle of that?

Perhaps the most fascinating irony was the fact that Herman
had a connection to Brock Thornton, Claire Whitman's elusive
financial planner, whose name kept cropping up in the meth
explosion case. This was not the first time Parrott's personal and
professional lives had collided, but it was chilling, nonetheless.

"I've been thinking," Tonya said, shifting in her seat and
placing her hand on her husband's knee. "You were right."

Parrott grasped her hand. "About what?"

"About giving Herman a chance."

"Changed your opinion of him, have you?" Parrott startled
at his wife's sudden shift. Tonya was anything but naïve, and he
couldn't see where Herman had said or done anything to earn
her trust.

"Yeah, sort of. And I know what you're thinking. It's not just
because he approved of us buying the house in Malvern."

Parrott's gut flipped at yet another irony. Herman's blessing of
their house-hunting was Parrott's least favorite part of the evening.
"What, then?"

"He seems genuinely fond of your mother, for one thing. I
thought he might be a gold digger, but his proposition to invest
his own money with hers and ours makes him seem more legit."

"Ah, and I thought you were going to say you were impressed by his culinary talents. That cake was superb." Parrott didn't want to get too deeply involved in a discussion about Herman now. Some ideas for exploring Herman's connections to the Brandywine financial planner were brewing in his mind.

"I agree. I wonder if he shares recipes." Tonya picked at a fingernail. "Ollie, I've been thinking about the Malvern house. I don't think we should pursue it."

Bubbly waves of surprise flowed through Parrott's thoughts, and he pulled the car onto a promontory about a mile from home, where he could focus on what Tonya was saying. The chirping of insects and the brilliance of the stars in the black velvet sky offered a perfect backdrop for their conversation. "Where is this coming from? I thought you loved the house."

"I did. I mean I do. But something bothers me about Faith Hightower's snobbishness. What if all the people in that neighborhood are as snooty as she is?" She picked at a spot on the knee of her pants. "And truthfully, what do we need with all that space, just two of us and Horace?"

Parrott thought he had mentioned that earlier, but hearing this argument from Tonya's lips was fresh honey from the hive. He reached over and cupped her chin in his hand. "What about having a bigger kitchen, and a pool and all that?"

"What really convinced me was your mother's house. She has spacious rooms and a fabulous kitchen. I'll bet there are homes with pools and basement gyms in Exton, and we wouldn't have to mess with all those over-the-top issues. Besides, I don't want to be cleaning almost six thousand square feet of house."

Parrott could hardly believe what he was hearing. "Okay, then. I'll call Ms. Hightower tomorrow and see if she has any leads on houses in Exton."

Tonya dropped his hand and gave his arm a slap. "Oh, no you don't. I'll take care of Ms. Hightower. I've decided I'm in the market for a male real estate agent from here on out."

"Fine with me," Parrott said, "but I do have one request."

"What's that, my love?"

"Let's not share any of this with Ma or Herman. Let them continue to think we're interested in the Malvern house for now."

"Can I ask why?" Tonya asked. "I doubt they'd be surprised or upset."

Parrott started the motor and turned to wink at Tonya. "Let's just say I have my reasons."

CHAPTER TWENTY-NINE

F irst thing Sunday morning, Parrott returned to Sweetgrass, having arranged to meet with Tammie at the end of her overnight shift. Her recognition of the missing person, Tucker Anderson III, Tripp, as she'd called him, might be a major break in identifying the body in the barn.

He knocked on the door of the Whitman home at six-fifteen, the blood pumping in his brain to the beat of his eagerness. Tammie opened the door, dressed in jeans and a t-shirt, her bob haircut combed, but her face unadorned with makeup. She put a finger to her lips and ushered him into the formal living room at the front of the house.

Her usual melodious voice was subdued. "Ms. Whitman likes to sleep late on Sundays. She says, growing up, her parents never let her miss church, so she's been making that up to herself for years." Tammie pointed Parrott toward a sofa covered in aqua-colored silk, and she sat in the peach and lavender wing chair, cater-corner. The plush area rug beneath their feet swirled with these colors, giving the room the ambience of an Easter basket full of eggs.

Parrott had no desire to wake Ms. Whitman. He removed the missing persons list from his jacket pocket. "Yesterday you thought you recognized this man. Now that you've had some time to think about it, I'd like you to look at the page again."

Tammie stared at the photo of Tucker Anderson, her eyes filling with tears and her hands shaking. "I'm sure it's him—the photo, the fact that he's from Raleigh, the fact that I haven't heard from him."

Parrott leaned forward, elbows on his thighs. A lot depended on this interview. "Can you explain how Tripp, as you call him, might be connected to Sweetgrass and/or the barn?"

Tammie brushed a tear from her cheek and took a deliberate breath. "Tripp works construction. His family owns a big construction firm in Raleigh, Anderson & Sons, and he's planning—uh, *was* planning—to take it over when his father retires. He came here to supervise the barn renovation project. That's how we met."

Something didn't add up. "Why would he leave his company in North Carolina to work on an out-of-town project like this?"

"All I know is that Tripp was coming off a bad break-up. He wasn't married, but he'd been living with a woman who was threatening to sue him for palimony. His lawyer suggested he take an extended vacation out-of-state, and someone hooked him up with this job."

"How did you two connect, and what was your relationship?"

Tammie curled a lock of hair behind her ear, and her face brightened. "Ms. Whitman hosted a get-together before they started on the renovation. The architect and the construction company owner were invited, and they brought Tripp along—to introduce him to Ms. Whitman."

The distinctive lilt had returned to Tammie's voice. By that detail alone, Parrott could tell she had strong feelings for this man. "And you were at the gathering?"

"Oh, yes. It was on a Thursday evening, so I was on duty, but Ms. Whitman typically schedules her social meetings when I am going to be present. Mr. Abramson did, too, when he was alive." Tammie scooted back and crossed one leg over the other. "Tripp sat right there where you are sitting when I first saw him. He was blond and tanned and strong-looking. He was wearing a short-sleeved shirt, and I noticed the muscles in his forearms. Ms. Whitman introduced us, and when our eyes met, I knew."

"What did you know?" Parrott didn't want to be lost in a maze of soap opera cliches, but he sensed this was a story worth his patience.

"The way he looked at me, so pleased, as if he'd won the ultimate prize in an amusement park game, quite by accident. No one ever looked at me like that—before or since."

Parrott remembered the first time he'd laid eyes on Tonya. He understood that magic. "So, you started seeing each other?"

"Yes. Whenever I was on duty, he'd find an excuse to come by the house, or, more often, I'd find an excuse to stop by the barn. We talked and eventually started meeting when we were off duty. After six months or so, we decided to live together."

Parrott thought Tammie lived with her mother in West Chester. "Where did you live?"

"A townhouse in West Chester. I'd just purchased it before I met him.."

"What happened to the palimony case?"

"It settled out of court. The day that happened, Tripp started talking about marrying me."

"Were you engaged, then?" Tammie wore no rings, but that didn't necessarily mean anything.

"Not officially. He planned to return to Raleigh as soon as the barn renovation was over, and I—well, I didn't want to leave Brandywine Valley just yet."

Parrott wondered whether Tammie's motives for staying had anything to do with being the daughter of M. Robert Pennington. Otherwise, she might have done well to marry Tucker Anderson, III, but that was irrelevant to the explosion case at the moment. "But you remained close, even after he finished the job and went back to his company in North Carolina?"

"Yes. We'd FaceTime several times a week, depending on our schedules, and we got together about once every six weeks, here or there." A cloudy expression passed over her face, and she covered her eyes with her hands.

Parrott made his baritone voice as gentle as possible. "Can you tell me about the last time you talked to Tripp?"

Tammie sucked in a breath, and when she replied, her voice carried a nasal twang. "It was on a Wednesday night, almost two weeks ago. Tripp told me he was coming to town soon. He sounded excited to have another project that would keep him here for a while. He asked to move back into the townhouse. He was always polite like that—never took me for granted."

"When you didn't hear from Tripp for so long, what did you think?"

"I wasn't overly concerned at first. The end of the week and into the weekend is my busy time here at Sweetgrass, and Tripp texted me a few times. I can show you the messages. I tried to call him on Monday and again on Tuesday. I left voicemails and texts, but then the explosion happened. Everything's been crazy since."

Parrott would get phone records to substantiate Tammie's story, but right now he was humming like a tricked-out sports car. "Couple more questions—did Tripp have any moles, tattoos, or other identifying marks on his body?"

Tammie blushed. "He had freckles on his nose and forehead. Really all over—his arms and legs and back. His hands were rough from handling construction materials, and he had scars on his left hand."

"What kind of scars?" Parrott's pulse increased, as he remembered the scars on the corpse.

"He told me they were from fishing. Tripp had fished his whole life."

Wanting to high-five Tammie, Parrott opted for a neutral demeanor. "Anything else?"

"Yeah, he had a tattoo on his stomach. His college fraternity at Chapel Hill."

Parrott had to restrain himself from jumping into the air with a whoop. Tammie had hit on all the criteria he was looking for. Now he had legitimate reasons for pushing forward with identifying the victim as Tucker Anderson, III. "One more thing, and I'll let you go. Do you have anything of Tripp's in your possession that might have his DNA on it? A hairbrush, a toothbrush, an article of clothing that hasn't been washed since he wore it?"

All color drained from Tammie's face, and when she responded, her voice was a monotone. "I was afraid you'd ask. You're looking for DNA to match with the meth explosion victim." She closed her eyes, inhaled, and let it out. "Unfortunately, I've got plenty of it."

CHAPTER THIRTY

When Parrott arrived at the station, he had to maneuver around several bike riders to get to his parking spot. Sundays in the summer attracted families to the park and playground adjacent to his building. He paused to watch a trio of giggly children sliding down the slide together. Two women were pushing little ones on the swings. The squeals and scrunching of footsteps on the rubber padding were sounds foreign to him. He barely remembered playing in parks when he was a kid. If he and Tonya ever had children, he wanted them to have this kind of fun.

Using his passkey, he entered the door leading past the station lobby, where the weekend clerk manned the phones and dispatch. He waved through the glass wall that separated the lobby from the stairwell going to his and Chief Schrik's offices, then darted up the stairs, two at a time.

The office was stuffy and smelled of the piney disinfectant used to mop the floors. Parrott lowered the air conditioning thermostat before sitting at his desk and flicking on his computer. He wanted to make notes about what Tammie had told him. Then he called Schrik at home.

"Working on Sunday, Parrott? Can't say I'm surprised—or unhappy." Schrik's booming voice sounded a little more relaxed than normal, but that didn't mean much. "Assuming you're calling to update me on the Whitman case. I have something to share with you, too. You first."

Parrott told his boss about the possible ID of the body, giving him details. "Whitman's personal assistant was a wealth of information. She confirmed all the points of identification on the victim's body. She's offered some of Anderson's personal items to run DNA on. I'll pick them up later today. Okay by you to send them to the lab?" The question was rhetorical. He knew Schrik would support the DNA tests, even though they were costly and time-consuming.

"Tell Jerry to put a rush on them. This case is turning into a heater, no pun intended."

All Parrott's cases had been heaters, but the urgency in Schrik's voice gave him pause, and the hairs on his arms stood at attention. "What did you want to tell me?"

"A question—do you know anything about Claire Whitman's daughter, Rebecca?"

"You mean the daughter who lives in Chicago? No. I've only met the daughter who lives in Philly, Jessica Abramson. Why?"

"You'll never guess who her husband, Matt Simmons, is related to."

Simmons? Parrott could only think of one Simmons, and that was Dave Simmons, the Zone Leader of the Democratic Party in Brandywine Valley. "Wouldn't be Dave Simmons, would it?"

"One and the same. The guy's chief platform is attacking the police, and now he's grabbed onto the fact that we aren't making enough progress in solving the tragic meth lab explosion in his sister-in-law's family."

"Give me a break. It's been less than five days since the explosion—and we've had so little to go on until today." Parrott could almost feel the indignation seeping from his pores.

"I know, Parrott, and you've been busting your ass. Assuming this victim checks out as Tucker Anderson, what are your theories about why he cooked meth in a fancy lady's barn?"

Had it really been so long since Parrott had updated Schrik on the case? Parrott thought back to the lunch they had shared on Thursday. Usually, Parrott was more communicative with his boss, but this week had apparently gotten away from him. "Actually, Chief, I don't think the victim was cooking meth. In fact, the autopsy didn't show any meth in the victim's lungs. My working theory is someone killed the victim, dragged him to the bank barn, and blew up the meth as a cover."

Schrik didn't skip a beat. Then again, Schrik rarely seemed surprised. Schrik was a bottom-line kind of guy. "Got any suspects?"

"Several names, nothing concrete yet. Whitman's daughter distrusts her mother's personal assistant, the one who may have ID'd the victim. Whitman's groundskeeper was gagged and tied up throughout the time of the explosion. He's got a son with a drug record. The boyfriend of Whitman's granddaughter, a music engineer, had been living in the barn off and on. He was in England at the time of the explosion, but he'd given his key to Brock Thornton, Whitman's financial advisor. No apparent motive for anybody to blow up a newly remodeled bank barn. Nobody benefits financially—unless the meth lab was a money-making operation, and the explosion was an accident."

"But your gut says otherwise." Even over the phone, Schrik could read Parrott well. "What's next?"

"We need to confirm the DNA match, but I'll proceed on the assumption that Tucker Anderson is our victim. From here out, it's about finding the details about his death. I'll email you the "cast of characters" I'm interested in. If Sylvester can do his magic and provide us with deep background on each of them, it would really help."

"Sheriff called me, trolling for business for Sylvester. Apparently, it's been a slow month, and this will put a smile on Sylvester's face. His wife's about to have their first baby, so they're going down to one income for a while."

"Always a silver lining, my grandmother used to say. Wish a young man hadn't had to lose his life to bring it on."

When Parrott hung up the phone, he prepared several evidence bags and started the chain of custody paperwork, so he could take Tripp's items back to Chesco for processing, once he obtained it. With the pressure of the Democratic zone leader on his back, he would do everything by the book and plus some. Then he made a list of people important to the case. Assigning deep background research to Sylvester would be expensive and time-consuming, so Parrott wanted to be judicious. After some thought, he typed five names into the email. Tucker Anderson, III; Charlie Wukitsch; Wyatt Wukitsch; Brock Thornton; Tammie Caballero. At the last minute, he decided to add a sixth name—M. Robert Pennington. Like the lifelong fisherman, Tucker Anderson, Parrott hoped he'd cast his net wide enough.

CHAPTER THIRTY-ONE

Working on Sunday had advantages. Distractions and interruptions were practically non-existent. But when it came to food, the station break room didn't exactly offer a smorgasbord. Normally, Parrott carried power bars in the glove compartment of his car, but he'd eaten the last one and forgotten to replace it.

Parrott brewed a pot of strong coffee, his beverage of choice when he was working a case. The vending machine boasted a wide array of junk foods, the most nutritious of which might have been salted peanuts. Parrott purchased two packages. He could do worse than coffee and peanuts.

While Sylvester worked on deep background, Parrott would re-focus on the meth explosion. That investigation remained primarily in the hands of the Po-Mar-Lin Volunteer Fire Department, but police and fire departments often conferred when they had cross-over cases like this one.

Parrott searched on the Po-Mar-Lin website's list of active crew until he found Skip, the firefighter he'd worked the scene with. Skip's last name was Oppermann, and he'd been on the force since 1974. Parrott called the fire station, assuming he would have to leave a message, but the scratchy-voiced dispatcher who answered surprised him twice.

"Detective Parrott? Yes, I know who you are. You worked the scene at the meth lab explosion at the Whitman place. You're in luck. Oppermann is off most Sundays, but he's subbing for another guy today. Let me put you through."

Parrott thanked the dispatcher and waited. He finished his peanuts and downed the rest of his coffee. He was eager to hear what Oppermann had to share.

Parrott identified himself, and the fireman replied with a friendly voice, "Hey, kid. Glad to hear from ya. You at work? This case must have your balls in an uproar, eh?"

Parrott smiled at the colloquialism. "You might say so. I hope I'm not interrupting anything important."

"Not at all, kid. You at the station right now?"

"Yes, sir."

"No need to call me 'sir.' Skip is just fine. But listen, how 'bout comin' over. We can sit outside in the back and talk about this crazy case. Much better than talkin' on the phone."

The fire station was only a few minutes away. The prospect of an in-person meeting outdoors on a beautiful summer day held a great appeal. Depending on when they finished, he might be able to pick up the evidence from Tammie's.

He parked at the curb, so as not to block any of the four vehicles, two full-size engines and two smaller trucks. A man stood on the long sidewalk, leading to the station's front door. As Parrott climbed out of the car, the man strode down the walkway to meet him.

Parrott accepted Skip's outstretched hand and shook, saying, "You look a little different outside of your hazmat suit." Skip's suntanned and deeply wrinkled face showed the firefighter's maturity and experience. Parrott guessed his age at late-sixty-something. Though not as tall as Parrott, he seemed lean and fit, and his gait was easy.

"Those suits. Till you've worn one, you have no idea how hot and uncomfortable they are, eh? Come on around back. We've got a table and a couple of benches. Can I give you a bottle of cold water?"

"No thanks." The two men sat, facing each other. Parrott admired a guy like Oppermann, a volunteer fireman who put his life on the line in the interest of public safety. "I was hoping to hear what you know about the meth explosion."

Skip nodded and showed overlapping teeth in a smile that crinkled the lines around his eyes. "We've learned a few things, and I'll bet you have, too. Want me to go first?" Skip leaned forward on his elbows.

"We did a thorough sifting through the fire debris. Our mission, of course, was to find evidence of arson, and, if so, what accelerants were used. The more meth-related evidence we found, the more we homed in on what products and method had been used in making the meth, whether this was a full-fledged meth production lab or something more amateurish."

"There wasn't much to go on when I was there."

The fireman fidgeted, scraping a fingernail against the ridges in the table. "True, but you'd be surprised what we can tell from the tiniest fragments."

"So, what did you find out?"

"Well, we found millions of glass fragments, and no fragments from plastic two-liter bottles, which told some of the story. Fragments of lithium battery. Residue analysis from the lab showed anhydrous ammonia."

Parrott knew enough from a workshop he'd taken a few years ago to understand where this was leading. "You think the cook was using the Nazi method."

"Exactly. Not the most convenient for a small-time meth cooker, but easier for us to trace, if we want to track the person who purchased these supplies." Skip clasped his hands together and rolled his thumbs around in a gesture that reminded Parrott of his grandmother. "The modern home meth cooker typically uses over-the-counter drugs. Almost anyone has or can get those. They're generally unsophisticated."

"So, are you thinking this was a big-time meth operation?" Parrott's gut told him that wasn't the case, but he needed to ask.

Skip cleared his throat. "The method would indicate that, but, no. We don't think so. Mostly, it's a matter of volume." He took swung his legs over the bench and stood. "If there had been a big meth production lab there, we would have seen way more glass, way more battery fragments."

"Well, let me say this." Parrott took a deep breath. "The coroner says the victim died before the explosion. There was no meth in his lungs."

Skip nodded. He'd probably seen the autopsy report, too. Parrott asked, "So, if someone wanted to stage a meth explosion to cover up a murder, how easy would it have been for him or her to do so?"

"It wouldn't be all that hard. Basically, gather up all the necessary ingredients. He might have had a glass full of solvent on a hot plate. Turned on the hot plate and left. Maybe left a burning cigarette or candle nearby for insurance. The solvent would heat up slowly and volatilize until it reached an explosive level, and boom. The resulting explosion would make it hard to figure out exactly how it happened, but if all the components were there, it would look like an accidental meth lab explosion."

This was the kind of information Parrott needed. Thoughts about next steps rolled around in Parrott's mind. "I've spent the past several days trying to ID the victim, and I think we've got a bead on that, but I wish I'd been able to analyze the debris with you. Maybe with more eyes at the site, we would have found more."

"Your time was better spent on the victim. Besides, the fewer people messing with the toxic materials, the better."

"Speaking of that," Parrott said. "I've got what looks to be a metal strongbox, found in the debris, partially melted. Wonder if you could help me open it."

"Bring it on over, and I'll take a look. Don't get your hopes up, though. Exposed to intense heat, whatever was inside's most likely turned to dust. Anyway, I have something else I think you'll be interested in."

Disappointed, but not surprised, about the metal box, Parrott glommed onto Oppermann's words. "Tell me."

"It might come to nothing, but we found several little pieces of plastic in the mess." Skip pulled out his cell phone and tapped on his photos. "Here. Take a look."

Tiny chills raised the hairs on the back of Parrott's neck as he peered at Skip's phone. Bar code fragments stared back at him, universal product codes from objects purchased in a store. At least seven of them. "If you want, we can transfer custody of these babies to you. I trust you know what to do with them."

Parrott high-fived the volunteer firefighter. If the bar codes matched the meth-making supplies, they might provide good evidence.

After leaving Skip, Parrott met Tammie at her West Chester townhouse. She gave him a hairbrush and a well-worn hoodie of Tripp's. Finally, some puzzle pieces were starting to fit together.

CHAPTER THIRTY-TWO

C laire had just finished her watercress salad with seared ahi tuna, and Aiko had brought in a thin slice of whipped-cream-layered pound cake topped with fresh peaches from the backyard tree. As much as Claire appreciated Tammie, she also cherished the lack of structure on days when Tammie was not on duty. This afternoon she planned to binge-watch a few episodes of that new mystery series on Netflix, starring Jake Gyllenhaal, who always reminded her of her husband Scott.

Her plans were derailed, though, when Jessica showed up without calling. "Hi, Mom. I brought you some homemade chicken soup. I gave it to Aiko to put in the fridge."

Jessica's magenta outfit clashed with her unruly red curls, but Claire had long since given up playing fashion police to her daughters, especially this one. "Chicken soup? On a warm summer day? I'm not sick."

"I know, but Scotty has some kind of bug, and I made a big pot. I thought you could use some cheering up after what happened to your bank barn. Anyway, you know what Grandma Abramson used to say about chicken soup."

"'The only thing sweeter than sugar is chicken soup.' I'd forgotten about that old saying." Claire gave her daughter a hug, catching a whiff of her fruity cologne. "Are you planning to stay a while?"

"Of course. I promised Rebecca I'd check on you, and I wanted to see the barn for myself. It's sad—such a beautiful old structure. Are you thinking to rebuild it?"

That question had been plaguing Claire. The charm of the historic bank barn had come from its outside structure, its weather-beaten, but sturdy materials, its rural charm. The renovated insides could always be replaced—all it took was money, and surely her insurance would cover a good part of that. But the exterior that blended timelessly into the landscape—that could never be replaced.

"I can't answer that question until I learn more about what's involved. I haven't even been able to assess the damage, because of the dangerous air quality. Why don't we take a ride over there in the golf cart? It's been enough time now. The air should be safe."

Claire won the argument over who would drive the golf cart, and the two ladies headed across the road to the site where the bank barn had stood for almost a century and a half. As they approached, the lingering smell of charred wood and burned flesh grew stronger.

She parked the cart on the pavement at the base of the hillock, where the foundation of the barn stood, unsurrendered, but stripped of its glory. Despite the warmth of the July sunshine, chills covered her arms and middle. All her life she had counted on the barn, which had sheltered her beloved horses. She had looked forward to entertaining in the elegant and spacious interior. Reduced to an eyesore, it pained her to look at the rubble.

Jessica put an arm around her mother's shoulders. "It's sad for me. I can't imagine how much sadder it is for you. I can't help wanting to strangle the person responsible for this. It's a travesty."

"More than that, Jessie. A man lost his life here. Whoever he was, there are family and friends whose lives will be affected. I hope Detective Parrott has made progress on identifying the victim, and then maybe we can find out who caused all this destruction and why." Claire walked around the soot-covered remains, bending here or there to examine a fragment of something that might be familiar, but between the fire and the dousing by the fire department, there wasn't much to look at. She kicked at a pink triangle of glass that might have come from a picture frame—or maybe that mosaic tray that she'd kept in the bar.

"Looks like any rebuilding will have to be done from scratch." Jessica swept her foot across the debris, forming a swath that showed the concrete foundation. "Rebecca and Matt offered to fly in to help."

Claire hugged her arms to her waist. She was capable of handling this herself. "There's very little any of us can do right now. I'll be glad to learn exactly what happened here. That's all."

The look that Jessica shot her way gave Claire a moment's pause. "Be careful what you wish for, Mom."

Claire and Jessica no sooner had returned to the house and asked Tammie to bring them tea and cookies, when the doorbell chimes rang. Claire was seated at her desk, but Jessica called out that she would go to the door.

A man's muffled voice alternated with Jessie's, and Claire recognized it as Charlie Wukitsch's. Footsteps approached the office. Claire rose from her chair as her ragged-voiced groundskeeper filled the doorway. He was neatly dressed, his hair slicked-back and face shaven, but the expression in his eyes was grim.

"Ms. Whitman, I came to ask for the next couple of days off. I've got some business in Wilmington I've got to take care of. It relates to Wyatt, and in a way, it relates to you."

"Sit down, Charlie. Tell me what's going on." Claire asked Jessica to excuse them, and Jessica left the room, closing the door behind her.

Charlie sat across from Claire, his legs sprawled wide, and his hands clasped in his lap. "You know Wyatt's been involved with drugs for quite some time. He's hit rock bottom before, and I thought he'd learned his lesson, but after a successful detox, he fell back in his old ways." Charlie wrung his hands and stared at the floor.

"He lost a couple of jobs, came to me for money, and I told him no. A year ago I probably would have bailed him out, but I've had counseling, and I didn't want to enable him. Something terrible happened, and it shook him up badly. He asked me to help him do it right this time." Charlie's voice cracked, and he took a deep breath. "He's going to sign himself in to detox for a week, then in-patient treatment for a month, and then, hopefully, he'll be admitted to a six-month residential facility, where he'll have daily AA meetings and psychotherapy sessions. A lot of hurdles to overcome, and he knows how hard it's going to be, but his motivation is strong, and that gives me faith."

Claire's memories of Wyatt as a child and the happy little family that the Wukitsches were before divorce and drugs took over brought a wave of sorrow, but it wouldn't do for her to add emotional weight to the conversation.

"Of course, you may go. Take as many days as you need and keep me posted if there is anything I can do to help."

"Very gracious of you," Charlie said, making no move to leave.

Claire didn't want to pry, but something Charlie had said about Wyatt's decision's relating to her echoed in her mind. "You said something about this relates to me. Do you care to explain?"

"That terrible thing that happened, that thing that scared Wyatt into sobering up. It has to do with the explosion in the bank barn—and with me being blindfolded and tied up."

Claire sat motionless in her chair, a person turned to stone. She whispered. "What happened, Charlie?"

"I wondered why Radar hadn't raised a bigger ruckus. How someone slipped into my bedroom to put me out of commission before the barn exploded. Well, I found out. The person who disabled me and took the key to the bank barn off-my key rack—it was Wyatt." He uttered a small sob. "It was my own son."

CHAPTER THIRTY-THREE

By the time Parrott logged the plastic bar code fragments and DNA-testing items into evidence, it was late afternoon. He hadn't intended to put in a whole day's work on this warm, sunny Sunday, but that's how things happened when he had a hot case.

Driving home with the windows down, he imagined walking into the house and savoring the aromas of whatever culinary creations Tonya had prepared. Peanuts, and coffee notwithstanding, his stomach was moaning for food. If Tonya hadn't cooked, he would take her out, maybe to the steak and ribs joint they both loved. Either way, he was looking forward to spending quality time with her.

Five minutes from home, his cell phone rang, flashing Claire Whitman's name as the caller.

"Detective Parrott, I hope I'm not disturbing your Sunday. There's something I think you need to know."

Parrott's rumbling stomach took a back seat to his racing heart. Another break in the case? "No worries. You can call me anytime. What have you got for me?"

"It's about Charlie Wukitsch's son, Wyatt." In a calm and unemotional voice, she summarized what Charlie had told her about Wyatt's entering detox and his confession that he had been the one to restrain and blindfold his father before the meth explosion. "Frankly, I'm surprised. I've known Wyatt his whole life, and, although he's had a drug problem for quite some time, he's always been close to Charlie and respectful to me."

Parrott's mind was ten paces ahead. "Do you know where Wyatt is? Do you have contact information for him?"

"Charlie's asked for a few days off to check Wyatt into detox in Wilmington."

'I'll touch base with Charlie." Parrott pulled into his driveway and cut his motor off.

"I hope this confession doesn't jeopardize Wyatt's recovery. Charlie is so hopeful. I almost didn't call you for that reason. But then I thought of that poor young man who was killed in the meth explosion, and I knew I had to tell you."

"You did the right thing. I'll need to interview Charlie and Wyatt." Parrott raised the car windows. "And thanks."

Parrott strode into his cottage, Wyatt Wukitsch, plastic bar codes, and DNA on his mind. He was greeted by the pungent aroma of barbecue sauce, followed by a full-body hug from his sweet-smelling wife. Tonya wore a pair of blue jean shorts and a white off-the-shoulder knit top that ended an inch above her waist. His hands massaged the warm, bony knobs of her spine, as he buried his face in her neck and shoulder.

Horace chirped from his cage. "Wowee. Wowee." Parrott lifted Tonya and swung her around, laughing at the bird's commentary.

"Welcome home, detective," Tonya said. Your bird and I have missed the heck out of you." She broke from the hug, leading Parrott by the hand to the oven, where a rack of ribs simmered in a thick, homemade sauce. Two strip steaks covered in marinade, rested in a dish on the counter, and two fresh ears of corn on the cob sat next to a pot of steaming water on the stove. "I hope you're hungry."

Parrott burst into a loud chuckle. "Funny. I imagined steak or ribs for dinner, even thought we could go to Isabelle's if you didn't feel like cooking. And here you have both. You read my mind."

"I figured you probably didn't eat all day. Also, I wanted to celebrate."

Parrott took her back into his arms and gave her a long kiss. "What are we celebrating?"

"Let me put the meat on the grill, and you go get cleaned up. I'll reveal all at dinner."

Parrott was so delighted to be home, he didn't know what to do first, shower, eat dinner, or do something more intimate, but he consoled himself with the fact that he could do all three in due time, and that made him a happy man.

After his shower, Parrott finished up the grilling, and the two sat down across from each other. Before he dove into his serving of ribs, Parrott poured two glasses of wine and lifted his glass. "A toast to the chef and whatever she wants to celebrate."

"I don't believe in distracting a hungry man from his food. Go ahead and start eating." She put her napkin in her lap and sipped her wine for a few minutes.

After three ribs, four bites of steak, and a whole row of buttery sweet corn kernels, Parrott came up for air. "Delicious. Aren't you going to eat?"

"Absolutely. I didn't want to miss a second of watching your greedy self." Tonya picked up a rib and slid the moist, tangy meat between her teeth and chewed. "Now, I suppose you want to know what three things we're celebrating."

"Three things? Tell me now."

"Number one. We're no longer represented by Ms. Hightower. I told her we've changed our mind about Malvern, and we're going to step back and regroup with another realtor more in line with our revised goals. I'm glad we never signed a contract with her."

Parrott muttered between bites. "How'd she take it?"

"She wasn't happy. Asked me if that was my decision or yours. I told her we shared the same concerns. Once she realized I really meant it, she got huffy and ended the call without even saying goodbye."

"She hung up on you?"

"Yeah, but no big deal." She took a bite of steak. "That led to celebration number two. I searched the Sunday home ads and found a couple of houses in Exton. The same realtor listed several of them. I called him up and he told me he could show them right away. So, we have a new realtor, Thom Thayer, and I've already seen three listings that I really like."

"That's great. You'll have to show me the listings after dinner." Parrott washed down his last bite of ribs with wine. "What's the third thing?"

"Third one might surprise you. I've been thinking about how busy you are with this case, and how much you love your work, even on a Sunday. Even though I don't need to work for the money, what with my pension and the gift from Elle, I'd like to be doing something valuable, something interesting. I don't want anything full-time. I need to keep time in my schedule for physical therapy and PTSD counseling—and my art—and house hunting." She grinned as if she'd told a funny joke. "So, I applied for and found a new job."

"You're kidding me—all in one day? What's the job?"

"Don't laugh. I'm going to work on Tuesdays and Thursdays at Elle's Don Guanella campus at Manderley. Elle has hired me to assist her with art therapy with the higher-functioning students. I've already reviewed the lesson plan for this Tuesday."

Parrott took both of Tonya's hands in his and squeezed. "I think that's wonderful—for you, for Elle, and for the people whose lives you will impact. Truly worth celebrating." He stood and began clearing the table. "Let me put everything away and clean up the dishes. Then can we call it a night? I'm bushed."

"Tell you what. I'll help clean up. That way we can get to bed sooner."

Within ten minutes the dishes were done, Horace was fed, and Mr. and Mrs. Parrott were on their way to bed. As Parrott stroked his wife's side from her neck to her thigh, he remembered the houses. "Don't you want to show me those house listings?"

Her voice had already thickened into that dreamy quality that reminded him of honey. "Maybe tomorrow. Some things are way more important than a new house."

Parrott couldn't have agreed more.

CHAPTER THIRTY-FOUR

Early Monday morning, the station was quiet as Parrott hunched over his desk, a thermos of black coffee nearby, and a printed-out list of items representing the status of the case. Tucker Anderson's DNA; the bar code fragments found by the fire department; and Wyatt Wukitsch's alleged "confession" to his father. Sylvester's deep computer search into Anderson, Wukitsch, Tammie, M. Robert Pennington, and Brock Thornton, not yet completed, simmered on the back burner.

First, Parrott did a search for stores in Pennsylvania that carried lithium batteries, UPC code **080926851771**. He listed the stores—Walmart, Cabela's, O'Reilly Auto Parts, Walgreen's, CVS Pharmacy. He'd taken photos of the bar code fragments, and he was elated to find one with 268 and one with 71. It would be helpful to find out which store used bar code labels with a kelly-green background. On the other hand, it would take tedious footwork to match the sticker material to the store, find the exact store where the meth cooker purchased the batteries, and see if any of the employees would remember the purchaser. A lot of time and effort with little chance of payoff. Solving cases sometimes came down to this type of unglamorous work, however, and Parrott would try anything, especially if other leads ran dry.

For now, his time would be better spent learning more about Tripp Anderson. Every victim had a story, and every story had the potential to lead to a perpetrator. Raleigh, North Carolina shared the Eastern time zone with Brandywine. Parrott took a chance that another early riser would be available to talk at the Raleigh police station. He searched for the number in the online directory of police stations. He let it ring three times before a dispatcher with a drawling accent answered.

"This is Detective Oliver Parrott from the West Brandywine Police Department in Pennsylvania. I'd like to speak to one of your officers about a missing person, Tucker Anderson, III. I may have information about his whereabouts."

The dispatcher's voice sharpened. "I'll connect you with Officer Sydney Kasman. Just a moment, please."

Another two rings, and then a woman with a smoky voice answered. "Officer Kasman. How may I help?"

Parrott introduced himself and stated that he might have information about Tucker Anderson, III. "We're trying to identify the deceased body of a man involved in a meth lab explosion. The body was severely disfigured, the face gone. The Sigma Alpha Epsilon tattoo on his stomach is a match, however, and a person who works nearby recognized Anderson's photo on the MP register. She states he's been coming here off and on for the past several years. We've sent DNA samples for testing. No results yet. "

"Oh. Obviously sorry to hear about the body. That was a quick turnaround. We just posted that MPR last week. Let me get your info, but we won't do anything until we hear back from you."

Parrott hung up, unable to shake the feeling that Tripp Anderson might have been more good guy than bad, that he might have gotten involved in something way over his head, and it had cost him his life.

Remembering what Tammie had told him about Tripp's family construction business, Parrott wondered again how Tripp had found his way to working in a sleepy little community like Brandywine Valley, and what kind of big project might have brought him back once the bank barn renovation had been completed. Maybe he was drawn back by love for Tammie and wanting to spend time with her, but he didn't need a "big project" to do that. The two of them had been visiting back and forth already.

Parrott needed to familiarize himself more with the construction industry. The only two people he knew well enough to call on were Alexander Vargas, his friend Elle's nephew, who had just started his business a year ago, and his mother's boyfriend,

Herman Powell, who had decades of experience running a very successful company. He opted for the latter.

"Hey, Ollie. You calling to have me check out that house in Malvern?"

Parrott smiled at the irony. How things had turned around in two days. "Not yet. Tonya wants to investigate that neighborhood first."

"Nothing wrong with a woman's thinking hard about a big thing like that—long as she does it before signing a contract. Good for Tonya." Parrott liked the way Herman's early morning voice sprang out of the phone and into his ear. He sounded lively and hearty and ready to take on whatever the day might throw at him. "So, what can I do for ya?"

"I was wondering if I could pick your brain about the construction business. I've got a case involving an out-of-state contractor." Parrott hesitated. This would be the first time he'd be around Herman without his mother present. Maybe he was assuming too much in expecting Herman's help.

"Don't know how much I can help with anything out of Pennsylvania, but sure. I'll be in Kennett Square late this morning. Want to meet for a quick lunch around one?"

Friendly enough. Parrott exhaled. "Okay, Portabello's at one. My treat."

Herman's laughter reverberated through the phone. "We'll have to see about that when the check comes, son. See you soon."

As Parrott hung up the phone, the word, "son," echoed in his ear. He couldn't remember the last time another man had called him that.

CHAPTER THIRTY-FIVE

P arrott sauntered to the break room to refill his thermos of coffee and start a new pot, the cast of characters flipping through his mind as if a slide projector were advancing them beyond his control. Tripp—Tammie—Claire—Jessica—Bonnie—Charlie—Wyatt—Pennington—Thornton. Who were the good guys and who, the bad? Or was there really any such thing as a good guy or bad guy in this crazy world, where nobody seemed all good, and nobody seemed all bad. Herman, for example. Tonya had been sure he was a gold-digger, but now he was in her good graces. As a policeman, Parrott had reservations about everyone, sometimes a benefit, sometimes a liability.

Still, someone had assaulted Charlie Wukitsch. Someone had killed the man who might be Tucker Anderson. Someone had set off a meth explosion in Claire Whitman's bank barn. And it was up to Parrott to find out who.

Looking forward to a lunch at Portabello, Parrott tried to ignore the roiling in his stomach. *Man doesn't live by coffee alone,* it seemed to be saying. "All right, all right," Parrott said, peering into the vending machine. A package of peanut butter and cheese crackers peeked back at him.

Returning to his desk with food and drink, he located his file on local drug detox centers. There were eleven of them in Wilmington, one designated for women. One by one, he started calling the other ten, identifying himself as a police officer and giving his badge number. Once he found the one where Wyatt Wukitsch was, he would make an in-person call.

In between phone calls, Parrott munched on his peanut butter crackers. He was on his third phone call when Schrik tapped on his door, asking to come in. The chief looked as if he'd overslept and dressed in a hurry. While Schrik wasn't known for sartorial perfection, he usually looked clean, neat, and, as Cora Parrott would say, "adequately put-together." Today his thinning hair was frizzy, and a rivulet of perspiration rolled down the side of his face.

"Did you see the op-ed piece in the Unionville *Times* today?" He dropped into the chair across from Parrott and wiped his face and the back of his neck. "The headline's *Are All Our Bank Barns at Risk?*"

"Oh, no." Parrott hated those kinds of articles. They invited trouble.

"Oh, yes. Our friend Dave Simmons says, 'The remoteness of large farm tracts and quiet country roads create the perfect storm for meth labs.' To make things worse, Lucretia got two anonymous tips about meth labs in barns. Officer Barton's checking them out now." Schrik's face had turned the color of boiled shrimp, and all the lines spoke of frustration. "And that asshole Simmons opines, 'Our police department is ill-equipped for cases involving meth-production.'"

Parrott grunted. "If Simmons gets his way, reducing the police budget, how would we be equipped to do anything?" He might have said more, but, given Schrik's body language, it'd be best not to pour accelerant on the fire.

Schrik slapped at the buttons on his shirt and straightened his collar. "Where are we with this Whitman case? Anything new to report?"

"Actually, yes." Parrott filled the chief in on where they stood with identifying the body as that of Tucker Anderson. "I'm interviewing a construction company owner, who happens to be dating my mother. He also has a connection to Brock Thornton that I want to explore." Next, he shared what Claire had told him about Charlie Wukitsch and Wyatt. "Hearsay at this point, but I'm trying to locate the detox in Wilmington, and I'll head over there to interview him, assuming I'm cleared through HIPAA."

"Well, that's a twist. Tying up his own father. What's your take on that?"

Parrott appreciated the way Schrik withheld his own opinions until after absorbing Parrott's. Once Parrott had asked him about this, and he had explained, "You're the one closest to the players and the evidence. I don't even form opinions until after I process yours."

Parrott remembered the scene at Charlie's cottage—the loyal dog, the overturned chair, Charlie's showering and changing clothes before the police could get there. "Certainly explains some things but raises questions about others. If the confession bears out, was Charlie complicit? How does the incident at the cottage tie into the meth explosion? Wyatt's history with drugs makes him an obvious suspect, but we can't jump to conclusions. A case like this has more levels than a Philadelphia skyscraper."

Schrik walked over to Parrott's chair and patted him on the shoulder. "So glad you aren't going to Galveston. We need your talent right here in West Brandywine. Carry on, son."

Parrott's ear reverberated, and he muttered. "Twice in one morning."

CHAPTER THIRTY-SIX

Claire chose to take her breakfast and today's Unionville *Times* out on the flagstone patio on the north side of her house. The summer garden adjacent to the patio was in full glory, serving up the fragrances of geraniums, cloud honeysuckle, clematis, and more. Charlie had outdone himself this season, and, judging by the butterflies, birds, and bees hovering, Claire wasn't the only one who thought so.

The vista from this patio was one of Claire's favorites, partly because of the broad expanse of land and sky, partly because her husband Scott had adored reading out here in the open air, and partly because Robert's property was just over the horizon. She could imagine him, having breakfast on his patio, reading the same newspaper, and looking out toward her.

She dipped her spoon into the yogurt parfait and took a bite, enjoying the way cool and creamy met sweet and crunchy. She opened the Unionville newspaper and folded it, so the op-ed page fit on the immediate right of her place setting. The teaser headline, *Are All Our Bank Barns at Risk?* drew her eyes and pointed her to page three. Skimming the guest column by Dave Simmons, she tried to dismiss the clenching in her stomach. She hated that the tragedy in her bank barn had been generalized to the entire community with one swath of the pen, and she didn't believe for one minute that Brandywine Valley was more at risk for meth labs than anywhere else. Rebecca's brother-in-law was a frequent contributor to the newspaper, and many of his columns raised good points, but lately Claire had wanted to shake him by the shoulders. Going after the police was just plain ignorant, and his using her bank barn to do that annoyed her more than she cared to admit.

She continued to read, moving from back to front, where an article about Longwood Gardens' renovated orchid house captured her interest. As she swallowed the last bite of breakfast, Claire's cell phone rang. It was Rebecca.

"Hi, Mom. I'm calling to check on you. How's everything going with the barn investigation?"

"I'm fine, dear. Contrary to what your brother-in-law Dave says in the Unionville newspaper, all of Brandywine isn't falling prey to illegal drug operations. Maybe you can have Matt reign him in."

Rebecca's musical laugh gave Claire a twinge of longing. She missed this daughter. "Matt and Dave made a pact long ago never to get in each other's way. They don't always agree, but they still get along. I guess you could say the same thing about Jessie and me."

"Yes, your father had a lot to do with that. It was very important to him that the two of you get along."

"Matt asked me if you were planning to rebuild the bank barn. Are you?"

The question caused a bit of acid to rise in her throat. She hadn't even thought about rebuilding. It had only been a few days. "That decision is a long way off, I'm afraid. The fire department has cautioned me to be careful of fumes in the air, and also of toxic material in the ground. I don't know how long we would have to wait to raze the ruins and do the necessary site work, but there are other considerations, too."

"Like money?"

"Well, yes. I've put in several calls to my financial planner, but he hasn't called me back."

"Matt says a financial planner should be available any time you need him. Even if he's on vacation, he should have someone you can call. Do you want Matt to try to contact him on your behalf?"

"No." Why must her daughters treat her as if her brains had leaked from her head with each birthday? "Maybe I can track him down through one of my neighbors who also uses him. I'll let you know if I'm unsuccessful." Robert had mentioned trying to locate Brock Thornton. She wondered whether he'd had any luck. "Anyway, at the moment I'm not inclined to rebuild. The beauty of the Brandywine bank barns is their history. New construction could never capture the simple elegance of the antique structure. Also, I'm out of the habit of entertaining. I'm older. My friends aren't as interested in large, fancy social affairs anymore."

Rebecca huffed. "That doesn't sound at all like you. Don't tell me you're going to retire from your social life."

"No, but I've been thinking about purchasing some more acreage and using it to enhance Sweetgrass in some way. You know I'm active in the Brandywine Conservancy, and my neighbors to the east want to sell their farm. I'd hate to see it fall into the wrong hands. Too many scalawags out there who want to grab up this land and turn it into condos."

"Now *that* sounds more like the mom I know. Any specific ideas?"

"One thing I've tossed around in my mind is an orchid farm, like the one James Duke set up in New Jersey. Or better yet, a wildlife sanctuary. I wouldn't want to block neighbors on horseback, though. I'll have to think about it more. And, of course, I'll need to talk to Brock Thornton. That would require me to withdraw money from the accounts I have with him."

"I like the way you're thinking, Mom. Let me know if Matt or I can help."

Claire smiled at her daughter's approval. "Maybe you'd better not share this with Jessica just yet. She might not be as open to my progressive ideas."

"Don't worry about Jessie. She's just like dad. Even if she hates your ideas, she loves *you*. She won't create problems."

CHAPTER THIRTY-SEVEN

When Parrott arrived at Portabello's in Kennett Square, Herman had already claimed the table. The aromas of lemon, basil, oregano, and garlic gave off a mouth-watering vibe that was all about the food—Italian cuisine.

A cheerful hostess in a black-and-white uniform led Parrott to the occupied table, past a sleek bar, comfortable group seating arrangements, and a baby grand piano. "Enjoy your lunch," she said, as she motioned to the round table with a mushroom-colored cloth, and Herman set down his menu and rose to greet Parrott.

The men shook hands and sat. "Nice place," Parrott said, taking in the framed oil paintings on the rust-colored walls, the antique tables and mirrors at both ends of the room. He was glad he had on his best sport jacket and soft leather shoes.

"You've never been here before?" Herman straightened the open collar of his shirt and patted his jacket lapels. "When we have a job in the area, I like to come here. Great place to meet with clients. You have to try the grilled mango."

"I guess I never thought of construction work as taking you to such a dress-up place. No offense."

Herman laughed, a rumbling, warm sound like brandy poured over ice cream. "I could say the same about police work, right? Maybe you could say we both clean up well." Herman opened his menu and motioned for Parrott to do the same. "Let's get our order in, and then we can talk."

Everything on the menu looked good to Parrott, but the beef stroganoff jumped off the page at him. He also ordered the grilled mango as a starter.

Herman followed with crab cakes and veal madeira. "Do you want an alcoholic drink? The selection here is excellent."

"Never drink on the job," Parrott said. "I'll have the iced tea."

The waiter repeated the order and scooted off, returning with the drinks and a basket of artisan breads and a mushroom gorgonzola hummus. Parrott dug in.

Herman waited while Parrott loaded his bread-and-butter plate with hummus and a yeast roll. "I'm sure you noticed so many of the dishes have mushrooms in the ingredients. I happen to love locally grown mushrooms. Looks like you do, too."

"*I* love them, but Tonya won't touch a mushroom if her life depends on it. She would definitely not appreciate this place."

Herman chuckled again. "We won't bring her here, then. This can be our man-to-man lunch place." His eyes shone, as if he'd just discovered the last piece to a jigsaw puzzle. "Now, tell me, Ollie, what do you want to talk about?"

Parrott finished his roll and wiped his mouth with his napkin. "Actually, there are two topics—one professional, one personal. But first I should explain that I'm investigating an active case. I can't answer questions or provide you with confidential information. Mostly, I need to pick your brain, but I can't let you pick mine, if that makes sense."

"I get it," Herman said. "Something about the construction business, you said?"

"Yes." Parrott took a deep breath. "Are you familiar with the Whitman bank barn that blew up last week?"

"Sure. It was in all the local news outlets. Such a shame."

"Were you aware that the bank barn had recently been renovated into living space?"

Herman leaned back, placing his elbows on the arm rests behind him and puffing his chest forward. "Y-e-e-s-s. My company actually bid on that job. Didn't get it, though."

This was going better than Parrott had expected. "Do you know which company did get the job?"

"Yes. The J.W. Sterling company had it. Old, established company with lots of experience in Brandywine Valley. Nobody was surprised they got the contract."

At this moment, the waiter arrived with their appetizers. Parrott's grilled mango was served on a chilled plate, and Herman's crab cakes were steaming. As the son of Cora Parrott, he paid attention to such things, and his estimation of the restaurant increased.

Herman dug into his first. "These are the best crab cakes I've ever eaten, except maybe the ones your mother fixes. I don't mind sharing."

"No, thanks. You were right about the mango. Cool and delicious." Parrott had never tasted cooked mango before. The piquant seasoning blended with the juice of the fruit to yield a perfect sweetness. "Let me continue, if you don't mind talking and eating at the same time."

Herman waved his fingers in a "come on" gesture and continued to eat.

"Are you familiar with a large construction company in Raleigh, North Carolina named Anderson & Sons?"

Nodding, Herman set down his fork. "I've heard of 'em, sure. Another one of those big-name companies who've been in business for generations. Those guys don't have to hustle business like the rest of us. People seek *them* out to do their projects. Not that I'm complaining."

Parrott's thoughts flew to the body of Tucker Anderson, III. No wonder someone would sue him for palimony. He was evidently part of a well-to-do family. A catch for Tammie Caballero, whether she realized it or not. "Are you aware of any link between J.W. Sterling and Anderson & Sons?"

Herman's eyebrows shot up. "You mean, like a son from one married a daughter from the other? Nah, I wouldn't know about anything like that. But that shouldn't be too hard to find out. Typically, construction companies don't pair up on jobs or anything."

Parrott finished his mango and washed it down with tea. "Well, how likely would it be that someone from Anderson & Sons would be in charge of the crew on a project of J.W. Sterling's?"

"Hmm, that question gets my curiosity up, but I won't ask. That would be pretty unusual. Sounds like someone with a lot of influence did a big favor—"

"—Sorry to interrupt. How were your appetizers?" The waiter appeared with a busboy, who cleared the plates and refilled the drinks. Immediately, the waiter served piping hot platters of stroganoff and veal.

"Really delicious," Herman said, rubbing his hands together in anticipation of the next course. "Excellent service, as always, too."

Parrott took a bite of his beef stroganoff. "This is stupendous."

Laughing, Herman said, "That's the exact word your mother used to describe the stroganoff when we were here last."

"I wondered if Ma had ever been here. Much as she loves mushrooms, I'll bet this is one of her favorite spots."

"We've been here about a half dozen times."

Herman returned to his veal with gusto, and Parrott did the same with his beef. Once both dishes had been mostly consumed, Herman sat back and took a deep breath. "Great meal. Can't eat another bite. Any more to talk about? You mentioned something personal."

Parrott scooted his chair back a few inches. A twinge of guilt shot through him as he approached this topic. He was about to be less than honest with his mother's companion. "Yeah. The other night, you mentioned investing with the financial planner, Brock Thornton. Can you tell me some more about him? I'm curious how he can offer a twenty percent return on investment."

A smile crinkled the older man's eyes. "I think a lot of people would like to know Thornton's secret. I once heard him say it's all about volume, and maybe that's why he only takes on clients with deep pockets."

"Well, I'm interested, but I want to be cautious. How did you meet him?"

Herman looked at the table, as if he were trying to remember. "Thornton and his wife moved here from out-of-state, maybe six or years ago. I did a project in Brandywine for a couple named Baker. Pretty sure they're the ones who introduced me."

Weird prickles ran up Parrott's arms and behind his neck. "Stan and Andrea Baker?"

"Yeah. You know them?"

"Small world, especially here in Brandywine. I met them on a case a couple of years ago." Parrott didn't say how Andrea's work as a true crime writer had helped him. "Do they invest with him?"

"I don't know. One of Thornton's selling points is that he never divulges who his clients are. Somehow that appeals to the high-roller mentality around here."

The waiter appeared at the table asking if either gentleman would like dessert. Parrott shook his head, and Herman said, "No, just the check."

Parrott took out his wallet, and Herman brushed his arm. "My treat this time. I hope we can do this again soon."

The guilty twinge reappeared, but Parrott decided it would be better to say thank you, rather than to start an argument. "Are you serious about getting together a little investment group with this guy, Thornton?"

"Of course. Why shouldn't we get in on the hottest financial action in town? Just say the word, and I'll see if we can set up a meeting."

Parrott hated having to deceive Herman in order to find out more about Brock Thornton, but sometimes his job required him to forge a path through a thorny thicket. "Okay, I'm interested." And who knew? If this guy was the real deal, maybe he and Tonya *would* invest with this guy.

CHAPTER THIRTY-EIGHT

When Parrott returned to the station after lunch, he had four things to follow up on: the DNA, the UPC label fragments, setting up an interview with Wyatt Wukitsch, and asking Andrea Baker about Brock Thornton. These were the times he almost wished he were working in a larger police department, where several officers could share what Parrott referred to as "the morsels" of the case.

More support and bigger cases were what had tempted him to apply for a job in Galveston last year, but there was no point in revisiting that decision—at least for now. None of these morsels were difficult, just time-consuming.

With a full belly, Parrott perched on the edge of his chair and dialed his buddy, Jerry's number at Chesco.

"Hey, Parrott. Bet you're calling about that rush job we did on DNA from Anderson. Report just came in ten minutes ago. I was about to call *you*."

"You're so efficient. What's the word?"

"Good testing samples at both ends. Ninety-seven per cent matching."

If this confirmation hadn't proven that Tammie Caballero's boyfriend was dead, Parrott's heart might have sung an aria, but his elation at taking a big step forward in the case was tempered by the sadness this would bring to people who cared about Tucker Anderson, III. The next of kin in Raleigh would need to be notified, and eventually, he would be the one to tell Claire, and most likely, Tammie. "You'll send me the report?"

"Check your email. It's already sent."

"Can't thank you enough," Parrott said. His mind was already spinning with possibilities of who might have had the motivation to kill the out-of-town construction supervisor.

Parrott opened his email to verify the DNA report before calling Officer Kasman from the Raleigh PD.

When he got through to Kasman, he said, "We spoke earlier. Regarding your missing person, Tucker Anderson, III, whom we've ID'd by DNA as the victim in a meth explosion. Unionville, PA, West Brandywine PD."

"Can you send me the particulars, so we can notify the next of kin and make arrangements?"

Not a chink in her emotional armor. Parrott hadn't met many cops that stoic. "Absolutely. You should know, however, that toxicology suggests death by poisoning. Meth explosion occurred post-mortem."

"Sounds like a complicated case. I wish you luck."

"Thanks." Parrott couldn't imagine what had made Officer Kasman so dismissive. "Please let me know when you've met with NOK. I won't proceed with related interviews until that's happened."

Next, he called Sergeant Dexter Wilcox of the Wilmington P.D., a guy he'd worked with last year on an armed robbery case. The borderline between Brandywine and Wilmington interactions was practically invisible, except in cases like these, where jurisdiction issues stuck out, like thorns on rosebushes.

Happy to catch Wilcox in, Parrott said, "Hope you can help me with another 'cross-the-state-line' issue. A guy I'm chasing, Wyatt Wukitsch, is in detox at Delaware Rehab. Can you get me in to interview him?"

Wilcox's deep, hearty voice reminded Parrott of a preacher he'd known, quite a contrast to Officer Kasman's. "I don't know. How long's he been in?"

Parrott said, "Twenty-four hours, maybe thirty-six. I know it's soon, but he's a key witness in a meth lab explosion."

"That explosion in the bank barn? Saw it on the local news." Wilcox had always impressed Parrott as a savvy cop, and he did a lot of volunteering in the Wilmington community, too. "Witness or suspect?"

Parrott hesitated. "Can't say for sure at this point. I'll know better once I talk to him."

"Can't make any promises. You know the first week of detox is rough, and we try to leave patients alone as much as possible. Your best chance is if the guy *wants* to talk. You know, as part of his recovery. Is he the remorseful type?"

"Might be. Supposedly told his father he's done bad things and needs help." The thought of waiting a week to interview Wukitsch made Parrott itch, but he knew from experience how firm detox centers could be at the beginning of treatment.

"I'll do what I can and get back to you."

That was all Parrott could ask. "'Ppreciate it. Much."

Wilcox huffed into the phone. "Believe me, I know. Sometimes the best thing we have going for us is us."

Satisfied he had done all he could do regarding Tucker Anderson and Wyatt Wukitsch, Parrott took a short walk to the break room and made himself a pot of coffee. Even in mid-afternoon, coffee gave him a sharp edge without jeopardizing his rest at the end of the day.

When he returned to the office, he called Andrea Baker, the crime writer, who lived near Caro and John E. Campbell. He had met the Campbells and the Bakers during his first big case in Brandywine Valley. Since then, Andrea had proven invaluable in offering inside information. Maybe she wouldn't mind his stopping by for a few minutes to talk about Brock Thornton. Afterwards, he would run by several stores to check out their UPC tags, and head for home.

"Right now?" Andrea asked. "Sure, why not? I've got a plot point for my work in progress that's driving me nuts. That'll give *me* a chance to pick *your* brain."

Driving to the Baker mansion, Parrott thought about how much his work was enriched by associations he'd made along the way. He felt sorry for anyone in the criminal justice system who didn't have those connections. Maybe Officer Kasman in Raleigh was one of those. Or maybe she was brand new and hadn't learned that lesson yet.

Andrea answered the door, wearing blue jeans and a studded red-and-white button-down shirt. A riding helmet sat on a table in the entry hall, and boots rested beneath the table. Clogs made a tapping sound on the marble floor as she led Parrott to the peach-colored living room with a spectacular garden view.

"How about a cup of tea or a glass of lemonade?"

"No, thanks." Parrott sat on the sofa, facing the wall of windows. "I don't want to take up too much of your time or hospitality." He remembered a time in the not-so-distant past when he had sat in this same room, not as comfortable as he was today. "Do you remember Herman Powell, owner of Powell Construction Company?"

Andrea paused. "Sure. He put in the enclosed patio, slash alternative kitchen, behind the garage. Nice gentleman with silver hair. He's not in any trouble, is he?"

"Nothing like that," Parrott said. "He and my mother are seeing each other."

"Seemed like a stand-up guy. Why are you asking about him?"

Parrott looked around the room, suddenly feeling dwarfed by the massive fireplace and huge oil painting over the mantle. "Herman told me about a financial planner whose clients earn twenty percent on their investments, a guy named Brock Thornton. Herman said you're the one who put him onto the guy. Is he your financial planner?"

"Mine?" Andrea's raspy laugh echoed in the high-ceilinged room. "Stan and I do our own investing. You remember that Stan taught economics and finance, and he's a wiz at these things. I think Herman might have asked me if I knew any financial planners in the area with a good return on investment. Some of my friends use Brock Thornton, so I might've mentioned him."

"You wouldn't happen to know anything about Thornton's background, would you? I know he's a relative newcomer, but nobody seems to know him well, considering that he's entrusted with a lot of money."

Andrea's right eyebrow lifted a quarter inch and stayed there. "Is this a business or a personal question, if I may ask?"

Andrea was one person Parrott hated to be less than honest with, but she also understood his limitations in discussing cases. "A little bit of both, maybe. Herman wants to put together a family investment group and see what he can do for us." That, at least, was true.

"Fair enough. I met Brock Thornton at my friend Missy Johnson's gathering last year. He's about fifty, a bodybuilder physique, speaks with a well-modulated voice, rather formal. His wife is blonde, wears a lot of makeup, sort of shy—Mavis, I think her name is. They have a reputation for being jet-setters. I love horses, but they take it to extremes. Polo games all over the world."

"They have kids?"

"I don't think so. I didn't get the impression that they've ever stayed home long enough to raise a family." She examined a spot on the fabric of her jeans. "I don't really know much about them, since they're part of a younger crowd. He did give me his card, however. He seemed to know quite a bit about Stan and me, and he wanted to make an appointment to visit with us."

"But you didn't want to meet with him." Now that Parrott was reminded about Stan Baker's background, that made perfect sense. When he'd first met the Bakers, he was investigating a case involving a group of party guests, all in the financial industry.

"Not at all. I think I may have given Thornton's card to Herman Powell."

Parrott enjoyed interviewing Andrea. She was always frank and objective in responding to his questions. If she felt distaste for the likes of Brock Thornton, she would never show it, but if she knew something factual that was positive or negative, she would share it. "Do the people you know who invest with Mr. Thornton seem satisfied with his competence?"

Andrea murmured what might have been a laugh. "You might not believe this, detective, but the people I know rarely, if ever, share info about their investments or the people they invest with. If they're losing money, they're too embarrassed to talk about it. If they're making money, they don't want to jinx it. Money is somewhat of a taboo subject in these parts."

Parrott shifted focus. "Do you have any idea why Brock Thornton's financial planning business would not be listed on the internet?"

"I wouldn't know for sure, but if I had to guess, I'd say that Thornton isn't looking for 'walk-in' business. The people I know who work with him—they didn't seek him out. He sought *them* out."

If Parrott needed to know who those clients of Thornton's were, he could always ask Andrea later. Right now, he thought he had asked enough questions, and he trusted he would have an in-person meeting with Thornton soon through Herman.

Before departing, Parrott remembered what Andrea had said to him on the phone. "You wanted to ask me some questions?"

"Oh, yes," Andrea said, repositioning herself on the sofa. "I'm writing about last year's murder-suicide that took place in the Wintergarden Hotel in Philly. I doubt you were involved in that case, but I have a couple of procedural questions."

Only too glad to cooperate, Parrott shared his expertise with his friend, the true crime author. When he left, a half hour later, he didn't have that much more information on his case, but, as always when talking with Andrea, he knew his time had been well-spent.

CHAPTER THIRTY-NINE

By the time Parrott left Andrea Baker's, it was past four o'clock. Armed with photos of the fragmented plastic UPC codes given to him by Skip Oppermann, Parrott swung by the closest of the stores in the area who sold large lithium batteries, Cabela's.

The parking lot was more than half full, most likely from customers stopping for a needed item on their way home from work. Parrott didn't mind parking at the end of the lot and sprinting into the store. His long legs covered a lot of ground with each stride, and he enjoyed moving.

Entering the store, he breezed past the crowded checkout counters, and he scanned the banners above the aisles, looking for the truck and auto section. He walked past interior accessories to exterior, finally spotting the large lithium battery he'd seen online. This one had a different UPC number, 100897402. A sign on the shelf said, "Deep Cycle Marine Battery, $499.99."

Eager to check out the UPC sticker, Parrott lifted the product and peered underneath. The sticker was not kelly green to match his fragments. He turned over several other products on the shelf—a GPS navigator, a radar detector, a power invertor—none had kelly green stickers.

Trekking back to his car, Parrott decided to put aside his search for the green stickers until he had a better handle on a potential perpetrator. Finding the store probably wouldn't lead to the person, but finding the person might lead to the store. As in most things in life, timing was everything, and right now, Parrott's stomach told him it was time to go home for dinner.

When he opened the door to the house, Horace swooped across the room and landed on his shoulder. "Pretty bird?" he asked. Parrott petted Horace's feathers and sniffed the air. "Roast beef and mashed potatoes?"

Tonya was at the table with her laptop, taking notes. She grinned at his question and stuck her pen above her right ear. "Actually, we're experimenting tonight." She jumped up to give him a hug, and Horace flew to his perch.

"Uh-oh. Experimenting how?" He looked around, but nothing looked new except the notes Tonya had made from the computer.

"Did you know there's a PTSD diet?" She dragged him by the hand to the oven. "Roast beef has been replaced by turkey breast, and mashed potatoes by brown rice casserole." She opened the oven, and a cloud of steam puffed around them, as she lifted the aluminum foil from the two dishes. "The rice also has walnuts, edamame, and red pepper in it."

Parrott thought of the delicious stroganoff he'd eaten at lunch time, and a guilty mantle settled over him. Maybe he wouldn't talk about what he'd ordered at Portabello's. "Smells delicious. Is turkey better for PTSD than roast beef?"

"Tryptophan, my love. A superpower for the brain. And while potatoes are on the diet, whole grain pastas and rice are even better. They help form glycogen." She flipped off the oven. "Ready to eat?"

Roast beef and mashed potatoes would have had him salivating more than turkey and brown rice, but Parrott would never say so. If a diet of bird feathers would help Tonya heal, he would eat that every night without complaint. "Sure. Let me wash up first."

When he returned to the living area, Tonya had put away her laptop and set the table. She was carving the turkey breast and placing thin slices on a platter. "How about carrying the rice and gravy to the table?" she asked. "I'm excited to try this new diet. Better nutrients help form better pathways in the brain, and better pathways make other therapies work."

"How'd you hear about this?" Having carried the food to the table, Parrott held his wife's chair for her to sit.

"I was researching therapy strategies in preparation for working with the mentally challenged adults at Elle's, and I stumbled onto brain research, pathways, and nutrition. Somehow, PTSD popped up. A great article with lots of tips." Tonya served herself rice, while Parrott put turkey on his plate. Then they switched.

Taking his first bite of turkey, Parrott said, "Delicious. What were the other tips mentioned?"

"Things like drinking water to hydrate the brain throughout the day, getting adequate sleep, exercise, getting out in the sun. Oh, and get this one—reducing the amount of time watching TV."

"That's easy for you. You'd rather read than watch TV any day."

"True. The article says these same suggestions work for alcoholics, drug addicts, abuse victims—anyone who has nightmares or flashbacks."

Parrott wondered whether Wyatt Wukitsch was sitting in the rehab facility, eating turkey and brown rice, the same as he and Tonya were. As he washed a bite of rice with edamame down, he said, "If this scrumptious meal is good for the brain, I'm all in."

"I'm glad to hear that, Ollie. I'm happy you don't mind changing the way we eat." She drank from her tall glass of water. "I know it's a sacrifice, but I'm determined to overcome this PTSD and have a normal life—even if it kills me."

CHAPTER FORTY

Tuesday morning, Tonya bounced out of bed even earlier than Parrott. On her first day to work with the good children of Don Guanella, she was raring to go. "I'm fixing a yogurt parfait with berries, nuts, and chia seeds. Do you want the same?"

Parrott rubbed his eyes and rolled out of bed. The alarm clock on his nightstand said six-ten. "That brain food must be working." He plodded to the bathroom, where Tonya was already flat-ironing her hair. "I'll get my own breakfast. You just take care of you."

Within twenty minutes, Tonya was fed, dressed, and headed for Elle's. The vacuum created by her departure created an odd, tingly feeling in the pit of Parrott's stomach. He uncovered Horace's cage and placed food, water, and newspaper inside, while the bird chirped a morning refrain.

Since Tonya's return from duty in Afghanistan and their wedding, she hadn't left him alone in the morning even once. It felt strange. On the other hand, Parrott had survived just fine, he and Horace, for two and a half years. He didn't mind getting his own breakfast.

He could get used to having a working wife. He especially liked that wide-eyed energy she'd displayed this morning. That was one of the things he'd always loved about her.

Parrott showered and brushed his teeth. He dressed in a charcoal suit, a white shirt, and a maroon tie. Unlike Tonya, he expected his day to be somewhat somber. He poured himself a bowl of Cheerios, adding milk and a handful of blueberries. He put a half dozen power bars in his pants pocket in case he needed a pick-me-up later in the day.

By six forty-five, he was in his car, headed for the station. The sun had already begun pouring its golden goodness over the treetops at the horizon, but the breeze coming through the open car windows was still cool. His cell phone rang as he parked in his spot.

"Officer Kasman of the Raleigh Police Department. Hope it's not too early. We've notified the NOK of Tucker Anderson, III, known here as Tripp. The father, also named Tucker Anderson, is on his way to the airport, as we speak. He's been in touch with the Chester County coroner's office. He'll claim the body, of course, and I gave him your contact info. I'm sure you want to speak with him."

"I sure do, thanks. What's his contact information? I'll try to get hold of him before he boards the plane."

Parrott scribbled Anderson's cell phone number on the back of a business card. He thanked the Raleigh officer again and disconnected. Maybe he'd misjudged her the last time they'd talked.

He punched in the phone number she'd given him and waited while it rang. After several rings, a brusque voice answered. "Yes?" Background voices and echoes indicated he was already at the airport, and a public address announcement confirmed that.

"Mr. Tucker Anderson?" Parrott waited for an answer, but all he got was a grunt. "Detective Oliver Parrott of the West Brandywine Police Department. Very sorry for your loss, sir, and I know you're in a hurry."

"Yes. Go on."

"I'd like to meet with you to share what we know so far. I'm sure you can add to that. Hopefully, together we can bring some closure to you and your son's family and friends." Parrott hated making this speech. There was no good way to approach a victim's NOK at a time like this, when the grief was raw.

"I'll meet with you, sure. When do you have in mind? I'm flying into Philadelphia on Frontier. Leaves at eight, gets in around nine-thirty."

"I can meet your plane, if that helps. Or I can meet you wherever you'd like. The sooner the better."

"No need to meet the plane. I've got a rental car reserved. How about meeting me at the coroner's office? Can we talk there?"

"That'll work. What time?"

"Soon as I can get there. I don't have to wait for bags, but the rental car might take a few minutes, and traffic. If all goes well, I'll be there around eleven."

It would take Parrott a good forty minutes to get to Chesco, but eleven was good. That would give him time to notify Claire that the body had been identified. He agreed to the plan, but before hanging up, he felt obligated to warn the father about the condition of his son's body.

If Anderson reacted with emotion, Parrott couldn't hear it with all the background noise. They were two strangers about to meet under the worst possible circumstances.

When Parrott hustled into the police station, Lucretia was at the front desk, waving as he passed the glass wall separating them. He ran up the stairs, two at a time, heading straight for the break room for his coffee fix. While filling his thermos with strong, black brew, he wondered whether coffee would count as hydrating the brain for a PTSD patient. *Probably not. Nothing calming about caffeine.*

Working backwards from his appointment at Chesco at eleven, Parrott thought he should meet with Claire no later than nine o'clock. He was unsure of Tammie's schedule. As most likely the local person closest to Tripp Anderson, Tammie would need to be notified, but Parrott's first obligation was to Claire, as the victim of the loss of the barn.

He didn't want to call Claire before eight, so he had about fifteen minutes to do a little research on J.W. Sterling, the construction company in charge of the bank barn renovation. Hoping to find the owner, and perhaps a connection between this company and Anderson and Sons in Raleigh, he was disappointed to find that J.W. Sterling was a limited liability corporation with numerous offices all over the country. The Philadelphia company showed a photograph of a young man, standing in front of a panel truck, but nowhere was there a name of an owner or group of owners. Photos, testimonials from satisfied customers, and links to social media pages were aplenty. If Parrott were in the market for a contractor, he might have been impressed.

Parrott opened his desk drawer and pulled out the booklet published by the Chester County Chamber of Business & Industry.

Flipping through the pages, he located the list of building and construction companies. J.W. Sterling was listed, and its president was Sean Guillemette. Parrott took down the name, address, and phone number.

It was now eight o'clock, so he drank some more coffee and punched up Claire's phone number on his cell. If she were amenable, he could be at Sweetgrass by eight-thirty.

"Good morning, detective. You're up and running quite early today." She sounded like she was doing the same.

"Yes, ma'am. I'd like to come talk with you this morning, if it's not too early."

"Not at all. Tuesday mornings, I usually ride the property with Charlie, but he's with Wyatt today. Come on over whenever you'd like."

Parrott liked it that she didn't ask what the purpose of his visit would be. Not all the people he worked with were that patient. "Thanks. I'll be there shortly."

When Parrott arrived at Sweetgrass, Claire was sitting on the front porch, wearing white slacks and an aqua cotton sweater, and reading the newspaper. She could have been the poster girl for senior living—that's how put together she was. The meth smell was completely gone now, a sign of how quickly nature repaired itself.

Parrott sat on an adjacent chair without being invited. Claire seemed in no hurry to go inside, and the outdoor temperature was so pleasant. Butterflies darted around the lavender-and-crimson-flowered bushes.

"Shall we talk out here?" he asked.

"That was my thought. Unless you're uncomfortable in that good-looking suit you're wearing."

Parrott smiled. His grandmother used to talk that way about his clothes when he was dressed up. "I'm fine. I came to tell you we've identified the body found in your barn."

"Oh, my. Who is the poor man?"

"He's one of the workers from the barn's renovation, a guy from Raleigh, North Carolina. His name's Tripp Anderson."

The color drained from Claire's face, and her blue-green eyes flew wide. "Oh, no. I never---never expected that." She clutched her chest near her throat. "My poor, dear Tammie." Claire paced up and down the porch space, apparently gathering her thoughts, and Parrott didn't interrupt. "What on earth was Tripp doing in my barn anyway? The renovation was completed long ago."

"One of many questions I have, as well. How well did you know this young man?"

"It's been about four years since I met him. He was the supervisor of the renovation, so I spoke with him often. I was always impressed by his knowledge, and he was easy to talk to. He was never impatient or snippy with me like some of the others. I had the idea that he came from good people with good manners. Oh, his family must be heartsick. Does Tammie know this?"

"I don't believe so, not with certainty. However, Tammie is the one who helped me identify him. I don't think she'll be completely surprised."

Claire returned to her chair. Reaching out to tap Parrott's forearm, she said, "Tammie is due here soon. Someone needs to tell her. Will you do that?"

Parrott nodded. "I have a few questions to ask you. Were you aware of Tripp's having used drugs of any kind?"

"No-o-o. I'd be very surprised if he was a drug user. Wyatt, yes. Bonnie's boyfriend, Ray, maybe. But Tripp? I just don't see it. He was so clean-cut. This is simply dreadful."

Parrott worded his next question carefully. "Did you get the impression that Tripp was well-to-do, or came from a family that was wealthy?"

"Hah. That is a trick question, detective, since wealth is quite a relative concept. But, yes, Tripp's family owns a big construction firm in North Carolina. I'm sure he was financially secure."

Parrott leaned back in the wrought-iron chair. "One thing I'm curious about is how a guy from North Carolina came to supervise a job in Pennsylvania. J.W. Sterling must have had their own supervisors."

"I don't think I ever questioned that. I didn't even know Tripp was from out-of-state until Tammie told me. All I know is he did a great job for me, and I think he got along well with the rest of the renovation team."

Parrott inhaled the outdoor sweetness. "I've observed how close you are to Tammie and vice versa. I wonder if you know why, after four years, Tammie and Tripp didn't get married."

The words hadn't left Parrott's mouth before Claire's face turned the colors of the bushes. She rose and turned away from him, her shoulders slightly bowed. When she turned back, her fists were clenched, but her voice was calm and even. "I believe I've told you everything I know about Tripp Anderson, detective. If you need to ask personal questions like that one, I suggest you ask Tammie—not me."

A soft mechanical sound drew their attention, and soon Tammie's blue MINI Cooper appeared on the driveway and parked on the side of the house, near the garage.

Claire descended the two steps from the porch to the driveway. In a clear, matter-of-fact voice, she called to her personal assistant. "You've arrived at the perfect time, my dear. Detective Parrott needs to speak with you."

CHAPTER FORTY-ONE

Tammie stared at Parrott with the dread of a convict about to be sentenced. She set her carry-on bag on the top step of the porch and asked if she should sit down.

Parrott nodded, and she collapsed into the wrought-iron chair Parrott had just vacated. "I've hardly slept or eaten since I gave you those DNA samples. Praying they wouldn't match."

Claire rushed to stand behind Tammie's chair, her hands on the younger woman's shoulders, and Parrott delivered the news.

Tammie clasped Claire's hand in her own, as tears spilled onto her cheeks. "I knew Tripp wouldn't go this many days without communicating. He said he'd keep me posted."

"I know it's not a good time right now, but I need to ask you some questions."

"You're right. It's not a good time. I'm grieving, and I need to help Mrs. Whitman get her day started." Tammie stood and picked up her bag. "Why don't we go inside?"

Claire exchanged looks with Tammie. "I can get my own breakfast. You really need to cooperate with the detective now. Do you want me to stay here with you?"

Tammie sighed and squared her shoulders. "All right. You go on inside, and I'll stay out here. It might be easier to be surrounded by nature."

Claire tapped Tammie's shoulder and headed for the door, her carriage perfectly straight.

Parrott motioned for Tammie to sit, and he sat, too. "I'm sorry for your loss. I want you to know our department will do everything in our power to find and bring to justice the person or persons who killed Mr. Anderson." He sat forward and made eye contact. "While that won't bring him back, it may help you and his family to know that whoever killed him won't go unpunished."

Sniffling, Tammie sat back in her chair. "Tell me how I can help."

That was the A-plus response. While everyone at this point could be considered a suspect, Parrott appreciated Tammie's cooperation. Indeed, he wouldn't have had the DNA samples if she hadn't provided them. "Before we get started, let me tell you that Tripp's father is on his way to Pennsylvania. Has he contacted you?"

Tammie shook her head. "I know Mr. Anderson, but we don't have the kind of relationship where he would call me for a meet-up. I doubt he'd even have my cell phone number."

"If he asks to speak with you while he's here, would you be amenable?"

"Yes, of course. I'd like the opportunity to tell him and Mrs. Anderson how much I cared for Tripp. I can't imagine their heartache—to lose a son. Mr. Anderson, especially, had big plans for Tripp."

Parrott's time with Tammie was limited, so he changed focus. "You've told me Tripp was coming back to town and might be here a while. He had a project to do. Is that right?"

When Tammie nodded, Parrott said, "I'm curious why his plans were so indefinite."

"He told me he was being picked up at the airport. He might be tied up for a day or two with business, but he would see me as soon as he could break free. We were used to working around scheduling conflicts."

"It sounds like the two of you were devoted to each other. Why didn't you make the relationship official? You told me earlier you had some things you needed to do here first. Can you tell me now what those things were?"

Tammie rose and turned her back on Parrott, walking to the end of the porch and back. "I would tell you if I thought they had any bearing on your case, but they don't."

"Let me be the judge of that," Parrott said. "Many times the most important evidence comes from someone who thought it was irrelevant."

Gripping her hands together, Tammie hesitated. "Let's just say that I'm attached to Mrs. Whitman, and before that, I was attached to her husband, Mr. Abramson. I want to stay here at Sweetgrass as long as Mrs. Whitman needs me."

"You were prepared to sacrifice your romantic relationship in favor of your professional one? That seems unusual. I'm sure Mrs. Whitman would have understood your choosing marriage over working for her. She could have found someone else to be her personal assistant."

Tammie's knuckles were white as she squeezed her hands together. "You don't understand. Mrs. Whitman is like a second mother to me, and I'm like a third daughter to her. In fact, her daughter Jessica would like nothing more than to put her mother in an assisted living facility. Rebecca, maybe not, but, living in Chicago, she isn't involved as much. I'm important in helping Mrs. Whitman stay as independent as she can."

"Are you saying Mrs. Whitman was opposed to your relationship with Tripp Anderson? That she didn't want you to leave her?"

"Not in so many words. Mrs. Whitman tells me all the time she wants me to be happy—and she'll do whatever it takes to keep me happy. Who could ask for a better employer than that? Anyway, I should be going inside now. Aiko won't leave until I come inside. Do you have more questions?"

When Parrott thanked her and said he'd be in touch, Tammie started walking toward the garage, instead of the front door. "I need to get something from my car."

Parrott followed her and watched while she got a plastic bag full of something and used an electronic garage door opener. Before he waved goodbye and headed for his car, his eyes snagged on a row of items lined up against the garage's right wall, including a large green lithium battery.

CHAPTER FORTY-TWO

O n his way to Chesco to meet Tucker Anderson, Parrott's thoughts twirled like a pinwheel on a windy day. Claire and Tammie. No wonder Jessica was so jealous of the relationship. The letter Jessica had sent to Parrott had said as much.

Tammie had said Claire was like another mother to her, and she was like a third daughter. That might have been presumptuous, except that Claire also appeared to take a motherly interest in Tammie. He wondered whether Tammie's being the biological daughter of M. Robert Pennington had anything to do with the relationship. Or, for that matter, with Tammie's wanting to stay in Brandywine Valley.

There had to be something missing in his information about Tammie. No offense to Claire, but no thirty-something unmarried woman he'd ever known would choose an eighty-two-year-old woman over a man she was in love with. And if she hadn't been in love with Tripp Anderson, why had she allowed him to live with her? Why had she been so distraught over his death?

So much of solving a case was posing questions. Parrott let these questions spin slowly, as he arrived at the coroner's office. When he walked in, he found Tucker Anderson already there, speaking with the coroner.

"C'mon in, detective," Maria said, extending her hand. "This is Mr. Tucker Anderson, who's arrived from North Carolina. We've just sat down to talk. I've explained my involvement with the case and my role as coroner."

Parrott shook hands with Maria and Mr. Anderson before taking the third seat. "I'm sorry to meet under these circumstances, sir. As I told you earlier, we are all committed to finding out what happened to your son."

Anderson's features hardened, and he bit off his next words. "Apparently, we know what happened to my son. What we don't know is who made it happen, or why. My son did not use drugs."

Maria and Parrott exchanged glances. "You're right, of course," Parrott said. "We know your son's body was found in a barn after a meth explosion. We also know that the meth explosion is not what killed him."

Anderson sat upright and looked from one to the other of them. "What do you mean?"

Parrott nodded to Maria, and she explained the tests she had done at autopsy. "What Detective Parrott means, sir, is that your son wasn't killed by the explosion. When the barn exploded, Tripp was already dead. He was poisoned." She went on to explain about the monkshood found in Tripp's digestive tract.

Anderson's eyebrows rose, and he held a hand over his mouth for a few seconds. "Can you elaborate on this poison? How does it work? How long does it take? What did my son feel when it took effect?"

Parrott mirrored the man's gesture, covering his own mouth. Explaining poisons was Maria's bailiwick, but Parrott was also interested in her answers—from the standpoint of the murderer.

"Monkshood is also known as wolfbane. Its scientific name is *aconitum napellus*. It's prevalent in the wild in these parts. The whole plant is poisonous, but the leaves and roots are especially so." She paused to slide a book from the shelf behind her desk and open it to show Anderson a picture of the plant. "Since I found aconitine in your son's stomach, I believe he ingested it. He would have felt immediate burning and tingling, numbness in the tongue and throat, nausea, blurred vision. As the drug spread throughout his body, he would have felt very cold, and his muscles would have been paralyzed."

Anderson's hand moved from his mouth to his eyes. "Would he have felt pain?"

The coroner nodded. At the very end, there would have been pain. The entire process might have lasted ten minutes to an hour or so."

Parrott offered the only consolation he could think of. "That sounds a lot better than having to endure an explosion and fire."

"Let me get this straight. You think someone poisoned my son and dragged his body to the barn, where the explosion occurred?"

"Yes, sir, I do," Parrott said. "If the poisoning had been accidental, Tripp would most likely have been found at the location where he ate the poison. He might have called for help. It's extraordinarily unlikely that he ate the poison at the bank barn, and then experienced a post-mortem meth explosion."

"Have you got any leads?"

Parrott had expected this question. Next of kin always wanted to know the status of the case. "Before I answer, I'd like to let you and Ms. Rodriguez finish talking, so she can return to her work. She doesn't need to be present while we talk about the case."

Maria's mouth widened into a line, the corners upturned slightly. "There is something else important. Besides finding the poison in your son's stomach, we found an absence of meth in his lungs. If he had been alive when the meth exploded, he would have breathed in those toxins. This tells us that his body was brought into the barn prior to the explosion, but after he stopped breathing."

Anderson stood and wiped his forehead with a handkerchief. "I see what you're saying. Will I be able to see him?"

"Yes, of course, but I must warn you," Maria said. "The explosion has disfigured his body and his face."

A flicker of something, perhaps hope, shone in his eyes. "But you're sure that it's Tripp?"

Parrott said, "Unfortunately, we're sure. DNA doesn't lie."

Anderson asked a few more questions of Maria, and then she left the two men alone in her office. Parrott opened his arms in a gesture of hospitality. "Would you like to have a change of scenery? Maybe sit outside on a park bench? We can talk just as well there as here."

"Nah. I appreciate the offer, but I'm okay staying here. I would like to hear about any progress you've made with the case, though."

Parrott sat on the corner of Maria's desk, his hands gripping the edges. "To be honest, Mr. Anderson, it's been less than a week since the explosion, and it's taken most of that time to identify the body. That's why this conversation with you is so important."

"How can I help?"

"You can start by telling me whatever details about your son you think might be important."

The father leaned forward and ran his hands through his neatly combed hair, mussing it. "Where do I start? Tripp was a great kid, smart, kind, happy. He wanted to study medicine, be a veterinarian, but I persuaded him to stick with the family business. He would've been the fourth generation." A small groan pierced the air between them.

Parrott continued. "Who were his friends or enemies?"

"Tripp had a lot of buddies. He made friends easily and kept them. He kept in touch with friends from elementary school, high school, college. No enemies that I know of. He studied architecture and construction, took to it well. And he had a good head for business, too."

"How did Tripp end up working for J.W. Sterling on this bank barn project four years ago?"

Anderson recounted the story about the palimony case, the reason Tripp needed to leave town for a while. "The owner of J.W. Sterling, Arnie Aranoff, is a friend of mine. He agreed to have Tripp work for him on this job. I was grateful, and Tripp didn't protest much. We all thought it was a good opportunity, and it worked out pretty good. When he came home, the ex-girlfriend was out of the picture, and Tripp had a different kind of construction experience under his belt."

"I'm sure you're aware that Tripp had a relationship with a woman here in Brandywine, Tammie Caballero."

"If that's what you'd call it," Anderson said, a distinctly bitter tinge to his voice.

"What would *you* call it, sir?"

"All I can say is Tripp never had much luck with women. From the time he was young, the ones he liked didn't like him. The ones who liked him—well, Tripp's mother and I never thought any of them really cared for him. Opportunists, you know."

"After him for his money?" Parrott hadn't gotten that impression about Tammie, but he couldn't deny questioning the relationship between the two lovers.

"That's what we think. Raised by a single parent, no college degree, working as a caregiver. We couldn't see what Tripp saw in her."

Parrott took pains to hide his reaction to this comment. Many of the people he grew up with could be described that way. If it hadn't been for football, he would never have made it to college and a professional career. "If you don't mind my asking, could money have been a motive in his death?"

Pausing, as if considering whether to share his son's, or perhaps his own net worth with Parrott, Mr. Anderson folded his arms across his middle. "I don't know if I can answer that question with any accuracy. I've not been privy to my son's bank statements for many years. Guessing he probably has about a million dollars in assets, but he was poised to take over a well-established construction firm. In the next decade he'd probably have been worth five times that. More than he'd have made as a veterinarian, most likely."

Parrott nodded. "Let me change subjects. Tammie told me Tripp was coming back to Brandywine this last time because he had a project to work on, something that might keep him here for a while. Do you have any idea what that project was?"

"Hnh. News to me. I'm sure it wasn't another project with my friend Arnie. Tripp had just finished a strip mall we were doing in Raleigh. He told me he was going to take time off, visit some friends. That was almost three weeks ago." Anderson wiped his eyes, and his voice grew husky. "We didn't want to bother him the first week, but when he didn't come home or call, we started looking for him. None of his friends had seen him, and he wasn't answering his phone or texts. So, we filed a missing person's report."

"Did you try to contact him at Tammie's during that time?"

"Honestly, no. Maybe my wife did, but I never even thought about Tammie. Maybe it was wishful thinking, but I thought the two of them were finished."

Anderson's responses sparked multiple questions in Parrott's mind, but questions meant progress, and progress was good. "I was wondering whether you'd be meeting with Tammie before you leave town."

"Heavens no. I'd have nothing to say to Miss Caballero, and I doubt she'd have anything to say to me."

CHAPTER FORTY-THREE

The arrangement between Claire and Robert to communicate only once a week and under strict conditions, was often frustrating, and today was one of those times. Oh, they had many reasons to keep their relationship under wraps, reasons that dated back to before Scott died and Jacqueline lost her mind. Theirs was a complicated relationship based on mutual interests and values, a strong attraction, and a closely guarded secret that must never come out.

Claire trusted Robert in ways she could never trust anyone else—her children, her granddaughter, or her employees. Robert was brilliant, an eclectic reader and a savvy businessman. He had been the one to introduce Claire to Brock Thornton, and whenever she received investment reports, Robert helped her evaluate them. So far, this arrangement had worked out well. Claire's money was multiplying beyond her wildest dreams, and if Thornton himself had been unavailable whenever she had a question, Robert would always step in and give her the satisfactory answer.

This was Tuesday afternoon. Claire had been trying to contact Thornton for days now, and the financial planner had not returned her calls. Normally, Claire could be patient, but the past week had tested her to the point where she considered switching investors. None of her friends had trouble contacting the people who managed their money. Of course, no one claimed to have increased their holdings the way she had, either. At this point, if she cashed out, she could set up a world-class nature farm in Brandywine Valley and still have enough left over to take care of her heirs.

She wasn't due to talk to Robert for two more days, but she didn't think she should wait. Screwing up her Old English stubbornness, she called the financial planner's number, expecting to have to leave another message. When Thornton's golden-toned voice answered the phone, Claire thought it was the answering machine. "I'm sorry I haven't returned your calls, Mrs. Whitman," he said, before she could even identify herself. Of course, he had caller ID. "I didn't mean to ignore you, ma'am. I've been out of town all week."

"Yes," Claire said. "Well, a lot has happened this week, and I'm in need of money."

"Would you like to make an appointment? I can come to Sweetgrass, and we can talk about your needs." Beneath the syrupy words, Claire could detect a stall when she heard one.

"Actually, why wait? We can talk about it now, over the phone." The more she thought about it, the more she wanted to get started immediately. "I'm sure you remember my bank barn renovation. Because of that project, I reserved a few million dollars from my investment portfolio."

"I remember. I still wish you hadn't done that. Think of the amount that couple of million dollars could have earned in all this time." He paused, as if adding numbers in his head. "But what about the barn?"

"It's burned to a cinder. A meth explosion." Claire held back on mentioning the dead body. For this conversation, Tripp's death seemed unnecessary, and perhaps it was disrespectful to talk about Tripp in the same breath as talking about money.

"Someone had a meth lab in your barn? How terrible."

"I'm surprised you haven't heard about it. It was quite horrible." Knowing how gossip spread in Brandywine faster than the horses ran at Steeplechase, she wondered if the financial planner was pretending not to know.

"I'm sure the barn was well-insured. Have you filed a claim?" Thornton covered the phone and called out to an unknown person. "I'll be there in just a few minutes."

This was not the first time he had rushed her off the phone with this tiresome tactic. Claire wondered how the man had held on to so many wealthy clients if he treated them all like this. "I haven't talked to my agent yet. I've been somewhat preoccupied with firefighters and police. I'm calling because I want to withdraw a large sum of money from my investment portfolio."

Thornton's voice morphed into a warm, compassionate melody, played by a full orchestra. "I understand if you want to rebuild the barn, but before you take out money that's working for you, you should see how much your insurance company will cover. That's the prudent thing to do."

"If I were planning to rebuild the barn, I would wait, but I have no intention of doing that. I have other ideas, some personal projects to enhance the land here at Sweetgrass. How soon can I get my hands on my money?"

"How much are you thinking you'll need?"

Claire hated the feeling that she was a child, asking her father for her allowance. The money was hers. She could find another way to invest whatever portion she didn't use for the nature preserve. And, with Tripp's death, she had some other ideas, as well. "My last statement from you, the bottom line was over twenty-two million. I want to take it all back."

"Argh. You've got to be kidding. That would be a very foolish move. The market's been exceptional this year. Also, you should consider the taxes you'd incur. I'd strongly advise against it."

"Why? Isn't this my money to do with as I see fit?"

"Listen, Mrs. Whitman. I have to hang up now. My wife needs me to help her with something. Why don't I call you back? Maybe we can meet with your daughter, Jessica. We can work out something less drastic that won't cause you to shoot yourself in the foot financially."

Brock Thornton could have said many things that wouldn't have angered Claire as much as threatening to involve Jessica. Claire prided herself on her independence. For as many years as she had left, she would grip the reins of her own destiny. No one was going to tell her what she could and couldn't do with her own money.

Her face burned, and the hand holding the phone shook as she replied. "Today is Tuesday. How long will it take you to sell out my holdings? And if you breathe a word to either of my daughters, I will sue you for breach of fiduciary duties, breach of privacy, or both."

Claire wanted the last word, and she got it, because the next thing she knew, a dial tone buzzed in her ear.

CHAPTER FORTY-FOUR

When Parrott finished interviewing Tucker Anderson at the coroner's office, he found a text from Wilcox of the Wilmington Police. *You've been cleared to see Wyatt Wukitsch. He's in isolation but wants to talk.* Delaware Rehab was a shorter drive from Chesco than from the station, so Parrott jumped on I-95, delighted with the results of his colleague's intervention.

Soon Parrott was in a tiny, but well-appointed room that smelled of pine disinfectant. Everything was spotless, from the sparkling windows facing the afternoon sun to the glossy linoleum floor to the crisp white linens on the hospital bed.

The patient in the bed looked like hell. Long hair was pasted to his head, a day's growth of beard roughened his face, and the hospital gown he wore was stained with something brown. An orange ring of light surrounded the bed on the floor, signaling the patient's confinement to the bed as a fall risk, but, atop the bed, his body twitched, as if tied to a live electrical source. Worst of all, the patient's bloodshot eyes told of torment and exhaustion. Still, when Parrott introduced himself and thanked him for the interview, Wyatt's lips curved into a semblance of a smile.

Wyatt's voice was trembly, weak. "N-not my best day, but maybe not my worst either. As my d-dad says, I'm one step closer to living my best life."

Parrott had seen worse. "Your dad has spoken with me. I interviewed him the day he was rescued from being assaulted and restrained in his home."

Throwing his arm over his eyes, Wyatt said, "Let's cut to the chase. I'm the one who tied up my dad. I'm totally ashamed about it, but I need to own up to it and face the consequences."

Glad for the quick confession, Parrott said, "I assume you had a reason for doing this to your dad."

"Yeah. The same reasons I've done every bad thing in my life—money and drugs." Wyatt groaned and rolled over onto the side facing the wall.

Unruffled, Parrott planned his next question. He didn't care whether Wyatt made eye contact, as long as he kept talking. "You saying someone paid you to rough up your father?"

"Yeah, yeah. I needed cash bad. In-between jobs, and I owed a lot of money. This seemed like a perfect answer. I didn't have to hurt him. I just had to make it look like I hurt him."

"Who hired you?"

'No idea. To start with, somebody put a note on my windshield outside the hole where I live in South Philly. Told me if I wanted to earn some quick cash to hang a dollar bill on my rearview mirror. After that, a couple more notes—instructions, date, time—that kinda stuff. Paid me a thousand ahead of time. Stuck under the floor mat of my back seat. Another thou the day after."

"You still have those notes?"

"Nah. I dunno what happened to them. I was strung out."

"You know the dates?"

"Not exactly, but it warn't much more'n a week between the first and the last."

"You have the money?" It was a longshot, but Parrott could dust the bills for fingerprints.

"Long gone. I needed it to pay off debts."

"What about your car? I'd like to check it out for evidence."

"Sure. Talk to my dad. He's got the car and keys. I doubt you'll find anything, though."

"So, an anonymous person paid you two thousand dollars to terrorize your father. You have any thoughts about who that person might've been?"

"I dunno--been thinking. Whoever it is knows where I live, what car I drive, who my dad is. Pretty scary."

Parrott found it fascinating to hear what would frighten a person who has already succumbed to the scariest nightmare of illegal drug addiction, one of the ironies among criminals. "Yes, and the timing—just before a barn where your dad lives and works blows up. Probably not a coincidence."

"Yeah. Was I being set up as a patsy for blowing up the barn? Or was I just there to keep my dad away? Maybe I'll never find out."

"You ever cook meth?"

"Nah. That stuff's dangerous. And even if I did, I wouldn't cook it in a nice lady's barn. I know you suspect me. I don't have a lot of cred with cops, but all's I did was mess up my dad and take his keys. He can tell you I've given them back to him now."

"Where were you when the barn blew?"

"I left Dad's and went straight home. I wanted to stop somewhere and call in an anonymous tip to the police, so Dad wouldn't have to lie there so long, but I was afraid. I had no idea about the barn until Dad called me." Wyatt's speech had grown faint, and his head flopped against the pillow.

Pleased with the information so far, Parrott didn't want to push his luck. He took down Wyatt's address and the make and model of his car. "Your dad knew it was you, tying him up at the time?" He was pretty sure of the answer, but if Wyatt answered in the affirmative, he would peg his dad for withholding evidence.

"I didn't tell him, but he prob'ly figured it out. Radar didn't bark much. Anybody else would've hurt him more. I was careful." Wyatt's legs shot around under the covers as if seeking refuge from the worst kind of torture.

"You've given me some good information, Wyatt, and I appreciate your help. Just wondering why you've decided to come clean. Why detox? Why talk to the police?"

"Oh, man. You really mess up when you got it so bad, you commit a crime on the one person who's always been there for you. I gotta get clean for good this time—for my dad's sake and mine. All's I can say is I feel like shit."

CHAPTER FORTY-FIVE

B y the time Parrott left Delaware Rehab, the sun was chasing the horizon, dragging her petticoats behind her. He checked his voicemails and found one from Herman. The man's naturally loud voice came across as exuberant.

"Hey, Ollie. I've set up a meeting for you and Tonya, your mother, and me with Brock Thornton. Tomorrow morning at ten at my office in Exton. I expected it to take weeks, months even, to get an audience with this guy—hard to see as the Pope—but he seemed very interested in working with our little group. I hope Tonya's free and you can get the time off from work. Your mom has cleared her calendar. Call me if there's a problem. Otherwise, see you there."

The satisfaction of placing another piece into the jigsaw puzzle caused Parrott to hum a little tune. He jumped into his car and called the Chief, before heading northwest toward home.

"Parrott? You in the car? Me, too. Got some news?" The chief was decidedly in a loquacious mood.

"Sounds like *you've* got something. You go first."

"Okay. Sylvester came through with some great stuff. His report's in your inbox. Lots of detailed info on all the characters—Thornton, Caballero, Anderson, Wukitsch, and Pennington. No surprise, but the common denominator looks to be Claire Whitman. But Pennington's a common denominator, too—at least for Thornton and Caballero."

Parrott's skin tingled as he pulled around an eighteen-wheeler going ten miles under the speed limit. "We know Pennington is the biological father of Tammie Caballero, but how does he connect with Thornton?"

"Evidently, when Thornton moved to Brandywine, Pennington was the first to sign on with the investment company. Pennington introduced Thornton around. Many of Pennington's friends became clients, too." The click of the paper clip in Schrik's mouth caused Parrott to smile. The odd habit had kept the chief cigarette-free for several years. "Pennington's credibility is impeccable, and that helped Thornton build his business—which is quite lucrative. Last year he reported personal income of over twenty million."

Parrott, of all people, understood that money was round—it could roll away from you just as suddenly as it rolled toward you. But something about Brock Thornton's success in Brandywine raised his suspicions. "What did Thornton do before he came to Brandywine, and where?"

"There you go, asking the perfect question again. Sylvester couldn't find anything at all about Brock Thornton prior to his coming here. Nothing. A blank slate."

Prickles ran up and down Parrott's spine. If Sylvester couldn't find something, that meant there was nothing to be found. "Brock Thornton never existed before coming to Brandywine."

"That's right. His wife, either. There are stories floating out there about being from the East coast, families that came over on the Mayflower, vast experience on Wall Street, but nothing verifiable."

Parrott thought of Herman and his confidence in Thornton's abilities. "If that's right, lots of smart people may have been taken in."

Parrott stopped for a red light and admired the Old English sheepdog being walked across the street on a leash. "Exactly. Now, what've *you* got for *me*?"

"Two things. Interviewed Wyatt Wukitsch, Charlie's son, over at Delaware Rehab. The guy's in deep detox withdrawal, but wants to come clean. He alleges he was paid to rough up his father. Took the job because he was desperate for money. All contact with the mastermind was anonymous. Notes left on and in Wyatt's automobile."

"You believe him?"

"I do. I'm going to check out the neighborhood, see if there are any cameras on that street. See if there are prints on the car.

The story smacks of an amateur, but, if it turns out to be true, it indicates pre-meditation by whoever killed Anderson and blew up the barn."

"That's right, Parrott. What's the second thing?"

The irony of his upcoming meeting with Brock Thornton after hearing about Sylvester's findings caused Parrott to chuckle. "You won't believe this, Chief. I've got a meeting tomorrow morning at ten to discuss investing with Thornton. Tonya, my mother, my mother's significant other, and me. Requesting time off."

"Hah, I take it you aren't serious about investing. Especially now."

"The rest of the group is serious, but I only agreed to the meeting because I wanted to meet the elusive financial planner, get a bead on how he operates. Just kidding about the time off. I'll be working the case the whole time."

"That's brilliant. Thornton is notorious for dealing only with Brandywine's wealthy elite. You're the only detective I know who'd qualify."

Uncomfortable with the comment, Parrott disconnected and pulled onto his street. He had a strange thought. *Finally, there's a practical use for all this money.*

CHAPTER FORTY-SIX

The next morning, Parrott climbed out of bed early. He took care of Horace's needs and let the cockatiel play with his toys in the family room, while Parrott cooked breakfast for Tonya and himself. He wanted to make the most of being able to stay home until mid-morning.

Last night when he'd told Tonya about the meeting with Brock Thornton, she'd balked. "I'm not ready to change our investment strategy right now, Ollie. My priority is a new house."

Parrott didn't want to burden his wife with the truth, that the meeting would be a ruse. "I'm not overly excited about investing with this guy either, but I think we should hear what he has to say. We owe that much to Ma and Herman, too."

"Okay, but I'm warning you ahead of time. I'm suspicious of anyone who makes a lot of promises or seems too eager."

Parrott turned his back on Tonya's last comment, devoting his attention to the eggs he was whipping for omelets. What was the comment the crime writer, Andrea Baker, had made? Something about Brock Thornton's not wanting people to come to him, that he sought out his clients. Why had it been so easy for Herman to set up an appointment with the most successful money manager in Brandywine Valley? Or to use Tonya's words, why did he seem so eager?

Last night he'd pored over the information the chief had given him from Sylvester. The fact that there was no information about Thornton prior to coming to Brandywine wasn't in and of itself damning. It seemed fishy, but maybe there was a legitimate reason for him to have scrubbed his profile. A better question was what had made M. Robert Pennington sponsor the new financial planner? People in Brandywine Valley weren't all that welcoming to outsiders. Parrott knew that from experience.

While he sautéed the vegetables, added the beaten eggs to the pan, pulled the cooked edges from sides, and let the liquid fill up the spaces, Parrott couldn't stop thinking this was going to be a very interesting morning.

The office of Powell Construction Company in Exton was not luxurious, but still impressive, with two full walls of shelves full of tile, paint, flooring, cabinet, and countertop samples. Herman ushered Parrott and Tonya into a large conference room, where Cora already sat, hands folded on the table before her.

The chrome and glass table gleamed in the sunbeams streaming from the east-facing windows. The room smelled of lemon and ammonia. Dressed in casual attire, khakis, sport shirts, and blazers for the men; pants, silk shirts, and pumps for the ladies, the four potential investors looked from one to the other.

The modern clock struck ten. "Wonder when this guy Thornton's going to show up," Herman said, his face drawn into a scowl.

Always the first to give people the benefit of the doubt, Cora said, "I'm sure he'll be here soon. Maybe he's caught in traffic."

"What traffic?" Tonya threw back her head and laughed. "I'm just glad none of us Black folks are late."

The comment was no sooner out of her mouth than Herman's assistant appeared at the door to announce Thornton's arrival, less than one minute late. Framed by the doorway, the financial planner was a specimen of sartorial excellence. Blond, broad-shouldered, and wearing a navy pinstripe suit and a starched white shirt, open at the neck, he had a casual glamour that transcended his somewhat ordinary looks. He posed in the doorframe for a moment, then strode right up to the table, giving a firm handshake to each person and making eye contact with his deep-set watery-blue eyes. The guy knew how to make a first impression. Parrott had to give him that.

Herman played host and offered a chair, some coffee. Thornton declined both. He dug into his leather briefcase for a folder, an iPad, and what looked to be a fancy pen. Then he set the briefcase on the floor next to him.

"Thank you for meeting with us this morning," Herman said. He offered a brief introduction of Cora, Parrott, and Tonya, leaving out what each of them did for a living. Parrott was glad for that, although he thought it odd, considering that the financial planner would surely want to know that detail if he were to handle their money. Maybe Herman didn't want to drive the guy away right off the bat by saying they were a caterer, a police detective, and a retired military pensioner.

"A pleasure to meet you all." Thornton shot his cuffs and ran his hands through wavy, blond hair. "I understand from Mr. Powell here that you are interested in investing with BMT Financial Services. I have a short video to introduce you to our products and services." His eyes scanned the room. "Do you have a projector?"

Herman shook his head. "Sorry."

"No problem. I'll just use my iPad." Thornton turned up the volume, set the iPad on a tiny stand retrieved from his briefcase, and touched the iMovie icon. A professional-sounding woman's voice welcomed them to BMT Financial Services, while soft, melodious music played in the background., and stark black, white, gray, and green graphics attested to the cutting-edge techniques practiced there.

Words like "grow," "skyrocket," "multiply," "reliable," whizzed past Parrott's ears, while he paid more attention to Thornton's facial expressions, body language, and demeanor. From the top of his perfectly coiffed hair to the buff on his soft leather loafers, he exuded the impression of confidence and success.

After the presentation, Thornton invited whatever questions the group might have. "That's one of the hallmarks of our service. We are transparent and ready to guide your financial decisions at a moment's notice."

"Well, I have a question," Herman said. "You claim to provide a higher return on investment than any of your competitors. Can you explain how you do that?"

"Sure." Thornton flashed a dazzling smile that seemed to Parrott to be both condescending and practiced. "That's probably our number one most frequently asked question." He pulled a stack of brochures from his folder and passed them around, so everyone had one. "Investments work just like any other industry. The greater the volume, the better the deals. Because all my clients are heavy hitters—like you folks—I'm able to put their money into dividend-paying investments with low risk and high performance." He paused to pat his iPad. "My volume of business is so high that I'm able to operate with a higher profit margin, and I pass this along to my clients by taking a lower percent in commission. Most of my clients are investing for the long-term, so they're happy to watch their money grow each quarter, knowing it's being nurtured by a knowledgeable and trained professional."

Cora, who apparently had hung on every word, asked, "Your video stresses 'personalized' service. What does that mean, exactly?"

"Good question. BMT is a one-man operation. You won't be bombarded with calls or visits from different agents who don't know you or your history. You will deal with me and me alone, and I will be there for you whenever you need me. I treat every one of my clients with the respect and care that he or she deserves, and I treat your money as if it were my own."

Thornton looked from one to another of the group for another question. He was unhurried, unruffled. Tonya's posture and toe-tapping on the carpeted floor signaled to Parrott that it was his turn.

"Mr. Thornton, do you encourage your clients to diversify? In other words, do most of them maintain holdings in real estate or other assets besides what they have invested with you?" Parrott tilted his chair back and pretended to stare at the ceiling, while he scrutinized his subject through peripheral vision.

Thornton stood at his place, bestowing a beneficent smile upon the group. "That would be entirely up to the client, or in this case, clients. Mr. Powell told me you would be interested in investing as a group. Perfectly fine. I'd be honored to have your business."

Sensing that the sales pitch was drawing to a close, Parrott asked, "Would you mind if we contacted some of your current clients as references?"

A flicker passed over Thornton's eyes There are anonymous testimonials from clients in the brochure. I must protect the privacy and security of my clients, for obvious reasons. You probably wouldn't like me giving out your financial information to other people, so I hope you understand."

"I'm sure you are very discreet, Mr. Thornton. Still, this is a lot of money we're talking about investing with you. I think my family and I would like to verify with at least one or two of your clients that they are satisfied with your work."

"Fair enough. There is one client who has given me permission to share his contact information with prospective clients. His name is M. Robert Pennington. Why don't you have a chat with Mr. Pennington and get back to me? The sooner, the better. Every day that goes by, your money could be growing exponentially."

As Thornton shook hands and made his exit, Parrott congratulated himself on allowing Herman to set up the meeting. If Parrott had truly been interested in investing, he would have asked way more specific questions. As it was, Parrott had given the appearance of being a potential investor, and that was good enough. *This is going to work out even better than I thought.*

CHAPTER FORTY-SEVEN

arrott left Herman's office and headed to South Philly, where Wyatt Wukitsch's apartment was located. The thirty-minute drive gave him a chance to reconsider the details coalescing in his mind. At this point, any one of them might break open the case. Parrott had to become the kaleidoscope. He had to roll the details around, look at them from every aspect, and push them together into patterns that made sense.

Wyatt had given him an address on Tenth Street, an old neighborhood populated with mixed residential and commercial entities. If Wukitsch's story about someone's using his car as a drop were true, somebody on the street might have seen something. There had been at least four contact events—when the first note was left on the windshield, when the subsequent note was placed on the windshield, and twice when the money was placed in the back seat of the car. The final payment was last Wednesday or Thursday, after the explosion, so Parrott was looking at the time frame of the week before that.

Parrott's GPS took him to a corner grocery store, Liberty Foods, a two-tone brick building with a sign in front that said, "United We Stand.". On either side of the store were walkup apartment buildings, and across the street was a liquor store, The Hob-Nob. Parrott checked the address to make sure the grocery store was the address Wyatt had given him.

Parrott opened the screen door and pushed against the inner one, greeted by the smell of chickens, cooking on rotisserie spits beyond the front counter. The store was small, but neat. A long wall of colorful refrigerated and frozen items stared him in the face. A dark-skinned man with pock-marked cheeks and a name tag that said Ankush presided over the counter, ringing up a handful of customers. When the last in line had paid, Parrott sidled up to the counter.

"I'm a police detective from West Brandywine P.D." He showed his badge. "A man named Wyatt Wukitsch gave me this address. Said he lives here."

The clerk grunted and pointed. "Upstairs. They's four apartments. Wukitsch lives in the first one."

"You the owner?"

The man nodded, as his eyes scanned the store. Maybe he didn't want the customers to know he was anything more than a cashier. Keeping his voice low, he asked, "You got a warrant to see?"

Parrott shook his head. "Not this time. You know Wukitsch's car?"

"Yeah, an old Ford Escort. Dark blue." Parrott nodded. Wyatt had said the same, plus he'd given Parrott the license plate number.

"He parks it on the street here?"

"This street's busy. Traffic every day. Night-time, peoples park who live here."

"You have a security camera outside the store?"

The man nodded and pointed to one aimed at the cash register. "Inside *and* outside. Part of business these days, eh? You go across the street. You hear the same story. The cameras, they may be a pain in the ass, but we got them."

"How long do you keep the videos?"

"They get uploaded to the computer every night, you know? I don't do nothing with them unless I need to. They sit there forever."

Hope rose in Parrott's throat. Depending on where Wyatt's car had been parked, he had a possible four chances to find someone, putting notes on the windshield or opening the back door. "You mind if I look?"

"Sure. Give me to ring up this customer. Then I take you into the back room over here."

A few minutes later, Parrott sat at a metal kitchen table with a fake marble top, whizzing through videos from the past three weeks. The camera angle showed a slice of the front of the store, and a broad expanse of the west side of Tenth Street. Dates and times were given at the bottom of the screen.

Ankush was right. Tenth was a busy street with both car and foot traffic. Cars pulled in and out of parking spots. People went in and out of the camera's view, most likely shoppers at Liberty Foods or residents of the apartments on that side of the street.

Parrott scanned the videos, looking for a dark blue Ford escort. He didn't see it. What he did see, though, sent ripples through his stomach. On Wednesday, the week before Claire's barn had exploded, someone was walking down the street, placing flyers under the windshield wipers on every car. No one paid any attention. The stocky figure in a greenish workout suit with an Eagles cap strolled between cars and plopped down flyers with an unremarkable rhythm. The man or woman—he couldn't tell—moved with speed and efficiency.

How easy it would be to place a fake notice on every car, except one, and for that one, to substitute an invitation for mayhem. Parrott waited for a quiet moment in the store and asked Ankush to view the video in question. "Do you recognize this person? Might he or she have been a customer?"

Ankush shook his head. "Many of my customers wear these clothes."

"How about the flyers? How usual is it that someone puts flyers on cars here?"

"Ah, flyers are more uncommon, but occasionally a restaurant or store puts out coupons." He scratched his head. "Typically, these are more colorful. Looks like the flyers in this video are white or light-colored."

Parrott had noticed that, too, a detail that might help people remember the flyer or the messenger. "Do you have any idea what this light-colored flyer might have advertised?"

"No. Sorry. You can maybe ask the residents or the customers."

Thanking Ankush for his time, Parrott stressed the importance of keeping the security videos available for re-viewing. He crossed the street and entered the Hob-Nob Liquor Store, which was surprisingly busy for this early in the day. If Hob-Nob had security cameras, they would show the east side of the street, and, if lucky, Wyatt's car.

Parrott waited until the customers had been served before approaching the clerk at the counter. Introducing himself and showing his badge, he cut to the chase this time.

"Yeah, we've got security cameras. Gotta today. Everyone grabs and goes."

"I'm interested in seeing videos from the last three weeks."

The middle-aged clerk's eyes narrowed into slits. "Something happen I don't know about?"

"This is related to a case in West Brandywine."

"Why should I help you? You got a warrant?"

Parrott hated dealing with guys like this, but sometimes he had to. "No warrant, but I'll tell you what. I'll call a Philadelphia police officer to come babysit you in this store for ten hours to make sure you don't touch those videos. When I come back with a warrant, you and he should be very good friends."

"All right, all right. You made your point. You got an hour to spare—I'll set you up. M'name's Mike, by the way."

Mike took Parrott into a back room, nearly identical to the one at Liberty Foods. The computer was already on, and current views of the street showed in thumbnails. Mike took the video back to the given date and pointed to the chair in front of the computer. "You do what you have to do."

This time Parrott knew what date and time the flyer-guy would appear. He was tempted to fast-forward the video to one-thirty-two on that day, but he decided to start at noon. He wanted to get a feel for the other side of the street, the comings and goings of people and cars, and especially whether he could spot Wyatt's car.

This time, he could see people going into and coming out of Liberty Foods, as well as walking further down the block. Cars came and went, too, and dogs. The east side of the street was just as lively as the west, if not more.

Around twelve-fifteen, a white panel truck vacated its parking spot about six cars down in the frame. The previously-hidden seventh car looked like a dark blue Escort, possibly Wyatt's. Parrott froze the video, enlarging it to see whether the license plate was visible.

Unable to view the plate number, no matter how he edited the view, he decided to let the video proceed, while he kept his eye on the car and the time flashing at the bottom of the screen. As the time advanced, other vehicles moved in or out of the scene, but "Wyatt's" car remained in place. At one-fifty-five, sure enough, the person with the flyers showed up, apparently having finished the west side of the street.

The angle from this camera provided a slightly better view of the person, but Parrott was unable to determine gender. A glimpse of the face showed dark sunglasses, perched over a medical mask. No hair was visible. Eyeballing the body against the height of the vehicles, Parrott guessed the height at about five-eight or nine, weight at about one-eighty. But padding and bulky clothes could make that estimate iffy.

The flyers came from a bag, slung over the shoulder, similar to ones he'd seen newspaper deliverers use. One-by-one, Parrott watched the person slap the white flyer onto the windshield, secure it with the wiper blade, and move on to the next car. Six cars, approximately eight steps between cars, reach into the bag, remove a flyer, place on car.

Parrott held his breath as the person approached the seventh car. Eight steps, reach into the bag—no. This time the person reached into a pants pocket, unfolded a white piece of paper, and placed it on the car. Parrott's heart raced. He made a note of the date and time on his cell phone.

He wanted to burst into the liquor store and ask Mike for a copy of the video, right now, but before he acted on impulse, he wanted to see if there would be a similar nugget later, when Wyatt's car supposedly had a dollar bill hanging from the rearview mirror, or when someone put something on the back seat floor. It took another half hour to examine the videos, but he never found anything else to substantiate Wyatt's description or any other suspicious person on the east side of the street.

Disappointed, but overall, elated with the video he did have, Parrott asked Mike if he could copy it onto the stick he carried in his pocket.

"Sure. I got no problem w'that. You gotta do what you gotta do."

Like Ankush, Mike had no idea who the "guy" in the Eagles hat was, no idea what the flyers said. Parrott didn't really mind. He was so excited by what he'd witnessed on the video. This was the first piece of real evidence that he could tie to the chain of events leading to a young man's death and an older woman's property being damaged.

CHAPTER FORTY-EIGHT

On Tammie's days off, Claire hated to bother the young woman with phone calls or text messages. Tammie was entitled to a life beyond Sweetgrass.

Claire thought of her own life when she was thirty. She'd been plucked out of Brandywine Valley by Robert Pennington and ModCom, given an opportunity of a lifetime. A celebrity with her own television show and an elegant apartment in New York, where she stayed during the week, she had been on everyone's A-list for parties and other social events. Nothing had tied her down—not Scott, not her daughters, not Sweetgrass. Of course, there had been plenty of servants there—nannies, cooks, housekeepers, a chauffeur, even a butler. Many more employees than she had now, with only one person's needs to tend to. On the weekends, she'd come home and try to make up for lost time with her family.

Having been caught up in the glamourous whirlwind of that life, she hadn't had time to think about the costs borne by her family. She had rationalized her choices. She earned a lot of money. The celebrity status she achieved would benefit her daughters. As a working mother, she was a role model.

Still, when she was honest with herself, she had led a rather selfish life. She'd caused Scott to limit his legal career, so that he could be the stable parent while she gallivanted about New York City. She wondered how things might have turned out had she not spent those years in the spotlight as "America's Sweetheart Hostess." Maybe today Jessica wouldn't be divorced and Rebecca childless. Maybe Scott would still be alive and able to enjoy the golden years with her. And Robert—well, Robert would probably still be the same, wealthy, debonair, charming, and devoted to Jacqueline and his children.

Now, Claire would like to make up for having lived an indulged life. The explosion in her barn and learning about the death of Tammie's boyfriend had awakened her to the fact that time was passing by, and she may not have that much left. She wanted to show her affection to and provide for her daughters. She wanted to leave a mark on her beloved Brandywine Valley by dedicating land to the conservancy and creating a nature biome. She wanted to take care of her employees—Charlie and Aiko, and especially Tammie, who was as dear to her as family.

Brock Thornton had not returned her call, and she suspected he would drag his feet when it came to cashing out her investments, all of which had come from her personal earnings. The longer he took to get back to her, the more determined she was to terminate her relationship with BMT Financials.

In the meantime, Claire was not without other resources. She still had money with Scott's financial advisor, and that included a hefty sum from life insurance and Scott's IRA accounts. On top of that, there was family money she had never touched, conservatively invested in Philadelphia banks. Nobody, especially Brock Thornton, knew about any of these. They were nobody's business.

Claire decided today would be a good day to inventory her holdings, but to do that, she needed to make a trip to the safety deposit box at the First Bank of Brandywine. As soon as Aiko cleared her lunch dishes, Claire began searching for the key to the safety deposit box. Normally, she kept everything in file folders in her desk drawer, but this key she had hidden in a less obvious place. The problem was, she couldn't remember where.

Her jewelry boxes, her lingerie drawer, under the mattress—none of these yielded the key. Claire examined every shelf and drawer in her closet and in the closet that had been Scott's, and she still found nothing.

When was the last time I used the key? She was pretty sure it was pre-pandemic, when she had taken some of her mother's jewelry out to wear to a party and put it back the following day.

Claire rifled through the drawers of her bathroom vanity, finding nothing, and then her cell phone rang. "Tammie, my dear. I'm so happy you've called."

"Why? Is there something you need?" Tammie's voice sounded less melodious than usual, as if she'd been crying. And that was understandable.

"I've been looking all over for my safety deposit key. Do you remember where I've hidden it?"

"Did you look in the bar? I believe it's taped to the bottom of the bottle of Hennessy's. You figured no one but you would ever think to look there."

"Ha. Even *I* wouldn't ever think to look there. Thank you. You saved me from tearing the rest of the house apart this afternoon." Claire was relieved, but still concerned about Tammie. She sounded so forlorn. "Now tell me why *you* called."

Tammie sniffed. "I've spent the whole morning going through stuff at my place, too. I can't believe Tripp is gone. I've been sorting through the clothes and personal items he left in my apartment." Somewhere in the background, a dog howled. "I've been going over what Tripp said—that he was coming back on a new project, something that would keep him here a long time."

"Was it a construction project?" Claire asked.

"I didn't think so. If it had been, he probably would have been more specific. He just said *project*. And I never saw him after that. I keep thinking of questions—who did Tripp come to see? Why? Who would have had a motive to kill him?"

"You shouldn't torture yourself with these questions, Tammie. Let the police handle those things. They can be more objective."

Tammie sighed. "The police didn't know Tripp the way I did. For all they know, *I* killed Tripp."

Claire didn't know where this conversation was going, but she sensed Tammie's angst. "How can I help you, dear?"

"I was thinking of the party you hosted when Tripp and the construction guys started the bank barn project. Do you still have the pictures the photographer took there?"

Claire wondered where she had put those pictures. They were more than four years old now. "I'm sure I do, though I'm not sure where."

"If you still have them, I know where they are—in the right cabinet under the bookshelves in the living room. I think there's a picture there of a group of guys, with Tripp in the middle. I remember Tripp that evening, saying, 'These are my people.' I want to know who is in that photograph."

"Can it wait until tomorrow, when you're here, or would you like me to go look now?"

Tammie blew her nose and said, "I'd like to know now. Tripp didn't have any 'people' here in Brandywine, but me. I want to know who he was calling his people."

Claire agreed to find the photograph and call Tammie back. She went downstairs, first stopping at the bar to retrieve the safety deposit box key, then locating the photo album Tammie referred to. She flipped through the pictures, many of them showing food, drink, and décor. Others were candid photos of people talking, even dancing. There was a quite flattering one of Tammie and Claire, chatting with the architect, Richard Buchanan. Finally, she came to two photos of Tripp with a group of guys. The first photo caused Claire to gasp. The four men had their arms around each other's shoulders and were leaning forward, as if singing an old school song. Youthful and good-looking, they could have been cousins, co-workers, teammates, or fraternity brothers, having a good time. In order, from left to right, they were Tripp Anderson, Ray Plummer, Wyatt Wukitsch, and Brock Thornton.

CHAPTER FORTY-NINE

P arrott marched into the police station, after his discoveries in South Philly, like a victorious gladiator, brandishing the flash drive that held both stores' security videos. His plan was to log the flash drive into the case file and place it in the evidence room for safekeeping. Then he'd call M. Robert Pennington and try to set up a meeting.

Before he could get that far, he bumped into Chief Schrik in the hallway outside of Parrott's office. "You just missed a visit from our friend, Dave Simmons."

"The Democratic Zone Leader? What did he want?" Parrott didn't care to get into the politician's complaints or interference in the case. He had better things to do.

"Status report, he called it. Wanted to know where we are with the bank barn case."

"I hope you told him to buzz off." Parrott tried to tamp down the impatience rising in his throat. "Just because the guy has a title doesn't mean he can jerk the police department around."

"Relax, Parrott. I sent him away empty-handed, but no sense getting into a spat with Democrats, Republicans, or anybody in-between. That's the beauty of Brandywine Valley. We're supposed to be above all that."

Parrott motioned his boss into his office. "I'm trying, but sometimes it's hard, Meanwhile, I had a productive day."

The two men sat opposite each other, and Parrott filled Schrik in on the meeting with Brock Thornton. "He's slick—comes off like a mover and shaker, but I'm not feelin' the hype, and he's too eager. More about that later, but here's the big news."

Parrott brought Schrik up to speed on his visit with Wyatt Wukitsch and the search of security videos. He held up the flash drives like objects for "show and tell." Schrik's eyebrows nearly popped off his face. "And you've got this flyer guy on video? Sweet."

"Thought you'd be pleased. Even if we don't know the *who*, we know the *how*. Somebody paid Wyatt Wukitsch to get his father out of the way of the bank barn."

Schrik slapped the arms of his chair and ambled to the door. "Good work, Parrott. Now I'm going to get out of your way, 'cause I don't want to impede your progress."

Parrott wasted no time. His watch said a quarter to five. He found the unlisted telephone number of M. Robert Pennington and called, using his private cell phone. After going toe-to-toe with a male servant, Parrott dropped the name, Brock Thornton, and a magic door slid open.

When Pennington came to the phone, Parrott introduced himself as a potential client of Brock Thornton's. "Mr. Thornton gave me your name as a reference, and I'd like to come by to talk with you this evening."

"Uh, well, I—" Pennington said, "I don't see a need. I can tell you over the phone I'm very satisfied with Mr. Thornton's handling of my money. My holdings have outperformed those of any of my friends or colleagues. You'd be lucky indeed to be part of BMT's network." The ModCom magnate ended his last sentence with a finality that hinted at dismissal.

Talking fast, Parrott took the crapshoot. "I appreciate your recommendation, Mr. Pennington, but in an effort at full disclosure, I have a double reason to meet with you in person. I'm a detective with the West Brandywine Police Department. I'm sure you're aware of the meth explosion in your neighbor's barn. I'd planned to interview you even before Mr. Thornton gave me your name. I'd like to come over this evening and talk to you about both matters."

"I—I don't understand," Pennington said. Parrott was sure Pennington couldn't reconcile the salary of a police detective with the kind of money needed to invest with BMT.

"I'm sure it's confusing. I assure you it's legitimate, however. My wife and I came into a substantial sum of money last year, and we're interested in growing it. May I come to your home this evening to talk about this?"

"I—I suppose so, but let's make it early. I'm not in the habit of staying up late anymore. Shall we say six-thirty?"

The early time was great for Parrott. Driving out there in the dark with no streetlights and plenty of deer wasn't his favorite summertime sport. "That'll be perfect."

Parrott hated mixing his personal finances with police investigations, but now the money he'd received from Elle came in handy. He justified it by thinking Elle would approve of its being used to find and apprehend a murderer.

The Pennington estate, ModCom Way, reminded him of Jay Gatsby's house in the Leonardo di Caprio movie. A butler ushered him into a living room the size of the Wells Fargo Center. Soft classical music filled the room with an elegance far different from the occasion.

Pennington kept him waiting only a few minutes. He sauntered into the room, wearing a maroon silk jacket, black pants, and leather slippers, and carrying a brandy snifter filled with amber liquid. Parrott thought he'd stepped into an old Hitchcock movie.

"May I offer you a drink?" Sitting, Pennington looked from Parrott to the butler and back.

"I wouldn't mind a cup of black coffee, if it isn't too much trouble." Parrott sat where his host pointed. Facing the television mogul, Parrott couldn't help being impressed. For a man of eighty-seven, the silver-haired gentleman still had remarkable posture, piercing blue eyes, and a photogenic face.

Nodding at his butler, Pennington said, "Really? Coffee at this time of day? Oh, to be young again." He swirled his glass and took a whiff. "Now, how can I help you?"

Parrott sat back and rested his elbows on the arms of the chair, aiming for a casual pose. He was gratified when Pennington did the same. "Why don't we start off with BMT Financials. How long have you been investing with Brock Thornton?"

"Oh, three, four, five years. Since Thornton first came to Brandywine and started the business. I might have been his first client."

"How did the two of you meet? Did you know each other before?"

Pennington's mouth curved into a broad crescent, showing perfect teeth. "You know that song that goes, 'I met him at the candy store,'—that's literally how I met Brock and Mavis. They were shopping at Govatos Chocolates in Wilmington. The rest is history."

"How do you feel he has done with your invested money? Is it true you get a huge return on your investment?"

"Oh, yes. Exceeding expectations. He's practically a magician when it comes to money."

The butler walked in with Parrott's steaming coffee, served on a tray with condiments, despite his having asked for it black. Parrott paused to accept the cup and saucer, express thanks, and take a swig. "How do you suppose he does that magic?"

Pennington grinned and winked. "Can't give away trade secrets, you know. Brock would never tell anyone, but all you have to do is listen to his clients. Nobody has a bad thing to say about how his portfolio is performing. That's a real accomplishment, I'd say." Pennington swirled his brandy again. "By the way, that's impressive that you've come into substantial money. Unusual for a police officer. I'm surprised you've stayed in the job."

Happy for the segue, he said, "A lot of satisfaction in serving the community. The job's never boring, and I have the chance to meet a lot of important people, present company included."

"Don't you worry about the dangers? You must deal with some rough characters."

Parrott glanced sideways at Pennington. Many times, that kind of statement was code for something racial. "There are rough characters in every walk of life, Mr. Pennington. Some of the roughest I've met were right here in Brandywine Valley."

"If you say so," Pennington said, raising an eyebrow. "You said you wanted to talk about a case?"

Parrott nodded. "Your neighbor, Claire Whitman. I'm sure you're aware her bank barn burned in a meth explosion last week. A man's body was found in the rubble."

Pennington's expression remained the same. He was neither shocked nor fascinated. "I heard about the fire, of course. I assume the body was that of the meth cooker."

Watching for tells, Parrott said, "Actually, that is not the case. We've identified the body as Tucker Anderson, III, the construction supervisor when the barn was renovated a few years ago."

Pennington stared at Parrott, sipping his brandy and remaining quiet. If he wanted to play the strong, silent type, Parrott could try a different tack.

"Mr. Pennington, it's come to our attention that you are the biological father of Tammie Caballero, the personal assistant to Mrs. Whitman. Can you verify that, sir?"

Pennington's eyebrow rose again, and he gave Parrott a hard stare. "Why, yes, that's true. What does that have to do with the meth explosion, however?"

"Maybe nothing, but Tripp Anderson was Ms. Caballero's significant other. Were you aware of that?"

Now he nearly choked on a sip of brandy, and his eyes took on a hard squint. "Aargh. I'm sorry to hear that. I'm fond of Ms. Caballero, and I don't wish her any heartache, particularly the grief of losing an important person in her life. I'm not, however, involved in Ms. Caballero's life. Aside from sending child support payments to her mother for many years."

"You wouldn't say that you and Ms. Caballero have a close relationship, then?"

"Not at all. If our paths cross, we are certainly cordial to one another, but aside from making a biological contribution to Ms. Caballero's existence, I have not been a part of her life. Nor has she been a part of mine."

"Are you at all familiar with Tucker Anderson?"

"Why would I be?"

"Well, he worked at Sweetgrass for two years. He lived with your daughter. I believe they had a serious relationship."

"Again, I'm not involved with Tammie Caballero or her romances. I wish her no ill, but I can't comment on the death of this young man."

Not willing to let his host off the hook, Parrott persisted. "How friendly are you with Claire Whitman?"

Pennington's crystal blue eyes glazed over, and he stared into his brandy. "I've known Ms. Whitman since we were children, but it's rare that we communicate. You know how it is out here—you can live on the farm next door and still never see or hear what goes on. My wife and I keep pretty much to ourselves."

Parrott set his coffee cup down. "Speaking of your wife, where is Mrs. Pennington now?"

"As I said," Pennington said, clenching his jaw, "we are private people, detective."

Something told Parrott that the ModCom magnate might be many things to many people. One of those things was a liar.

CHAPTER FIFTY

All day Thursday, Claire had trouble concentrating. This evening she would see Robert, and she wanted to be prepared. After brunch, Claire had sat at her computer with a legal pad and pen, taking notes from websites about how to set up a nature preserve. She was amazed at how much information was out there, both scientific and financial. Apparently, she had stumbled upon a cause young millennials had embraced, and here she was, headed into her mid-eighties.

She studied about nest boxes for birds, bees, and bats. Some conservationists had even installed close-circuit television around the nesting areas, so they could monitor how the animals fared in the habitats.

A habitat in the English countryside had over six thousand visitors per year. That place hosted popular events such as wildflower exploring, moth-watching, and pond-dipping. The thought of turning Sweetgrass into a delightful venue where people could enjoy the gifts of nature caused a pleasurable warmth to surge through her veins. She would be the visionary, and her money would be the agency to make the dream come true.

Another site explained the differences between a profit or non-profit nature reserve and how to set up each. Claire couldn't remember being this excited about anything since she'd started her *Entertaining with Elegance* show. This project had the potential to leave a much bigger impact on the world.

Annoyed that she hadn't heard back from Brock Thornton, she re-dialed his number. When his voicemail kicked in, she left the briefest message she could think of. "Claire Whitman, waiting to hear from you. Call me now."

While waiting for the return phone call that might not come, Claire made a list of to-do items related to the project.

Claire was aware that someone of her age might not be taken seriously, but she was determined to take this project to completion. Her parents had taught her to pursue her dreams, and she'd had to overcome obstacles in the past to accomplish her goals. She wasn't about to stop now.

By the time she'd committed her thoughts to paper, it was time to get ready for her date with Robert. As usual, she wouldn't meet with him until after Tammie had come on duty. Tammie was the only person Claire trusted with the secret of these trysts. Neither of Claire's daughters would approve. Claire had met with Robert almost every Thursday evening since Scott had died, and Tammie had not only facilitated the meetings, but helped to keep them under wraps. Though Claire and Tammie had never spoken in detail about the arrangement, Claire had the sense Tammie enjoyed knowing about the clandestine relationship between her father and her employer.

Where the lovers met varied somewhat, depending on circumstances in each of their households at any given time. Claire's house and grounds were used much more often, because Jacqueline's presence and the larger number of servants at ModCom Way made it difficult to meet there. Robert had a lovely outdoor garden, though, with a swimming pool and a fire pit, shielded from his house by an arbor. On beautiful summer evenings, that was a favorite place.

Claire was eager to go there this evening. As soon as Tammie replaced Aiko at five-thirty, Claire would hop on her golf cart and drive across the fields separating her estate from Robert's. Surrounded by the sweet chirpings and aromas of nature, she would luxuriate in the arms of the man she loved and tell him her burning thoughts. Robert would know what to do about BMT. He would help her with the nature center. She had another important issue to discuss with Robert, as well.

The weather was perfect. July evenings were outrageously lovely with pastel blue skies and soft breezes that tousled the hair and caressed the face. Tammie arrived on time, and Aiko took off for a family reunion. She wouldn't be back until Monday morning.

Claire wore a light salmon-colored pant suit with matching flats. Her hair was fluffed and held behind her ears on each side with a comb. A touch of eye shadow and mascara on each lid, two dots of blush, and an application of coral lipstick, and she was as ready for "showtime" as she'd ever been for her television show.

"I'll be back around eight," she said to Tammie, snickering inside at the irony of such an early curfew and such a young "parent" watching over her comings and goings.

Tammie nodded. It was lovely to have someone non-judgmental, who cared, but never interfered. Tammie brought the golf cart around to the front of the house and turned the driver's seat over to Claire.

Claire checked the battery gauge, as usual. She kept an extra battery in her garage, in case she needed a replacement at an inopportune time. As she drove across her property, she imagined the layout of the nature reserve. Fifty acres was a lot of land. She would have to hire a knowledgeable landscape architect. She also wanted to maintain the horseback riding trails. Even though she wasn't riding anymore, the community was full of equestrians who enjoyed riding or fox hunting through her acreage. She'd never do anything to block that.

She was approaching one of the most popular trails now, and the sound of oncoming hooves caused her to speed up. She wanted to cross the trail before anyone saw her in her golf cart. It wouldn't do to raise questions about what a silver-haired lady was doing on a golf cart out in the middle of nowhere.

As she crossed the path, she looked back. A man on a single dark horse was bearing down on the trail, fast. Claire's backward glance was good enough to give her an estimate of the horse's speed, about fifteen miles per hour, but too poor to give her a view of the rider.

Not wanting to be seen, she accelerated and cleared the trail as fast as possible. In all her trips across the land to Robert's, she had only encountered people a handful of times. Her heart pumped double-time and her face grew hot. This was the price of being "the other woman" in Robert's life.

She drove over the bumpy land, inhaling the fragrant air as it whooshed past her in the open cart. Nearing Robert's, she veered into a thicket of bushes that offered three-sided cover for her cart. She climbed down and walked the fifty feet or so to the edge of Robert's pool area. The pool, the garden, and the fire pit were all surrounded by gray-green slate, so attractively laid out. It looked like MGM had designed it for a blockbuster movie. As she crept closer, her hand over her eyes in the weakening sun, a tall, striking figure emerged from the shadows of the structure beyond, a bath house with a bedroom, bathroom, den, and kitchen. She had spent many hours there.

Robert held his arms out to her, and she rushed into them, as eager for his embrace as a young girl with her first love. For several moments they kissed and held each other in the summer evening.

When they separated, the words couldn't come fast enough. "I saw someone riding a dark-colored horse on the trail. Don't know if he saw me or not, but he might have."

"I wouldn't worry about it." Robert led Claire to a pair of chaise lounges and a glass end table, where a couple of high ball glasses filled with Cape Codders sat. Robert handed a glass to Claire before picking up his own. "Here's to Thursdays. I can't tell you how much I look forward to these evenings."

Claire sipped her cranberry juice and vodka before sitting back and stretching her legs out on the long chair. "You know I do, too."

Robert sat on the edge of his chair, staring at his drink, as if pondering how to deliver some news, good or bad. He reached for Claire's hand, placed it on his knee, and patted it.

"What's the matter, Robert? Are you feeling all right?" Claire had never been one to imagine the worst, but so many bad things had happened this week. She braced herself for another problem.

"Nothing really. Feelings of mortality. This has been a hard week to be apart. I've wanted to help you deal with the barn, filing your claim. I had a visit from a detective. He asked me about Brock, also about Tammie. I have this awful sense of foreboding. You're the only person I can talk to."

It was rare that Robert showed vulnerability. Claire wanted to wrap her arms around him and comfort him like a baby. Instead, she put down her drink and walked behind him, massaging his neck and shoulders. "We'll get through this together, as we've done before."

Robert took her hands, and she bent forward for a kiss. "Come sit," he said, patting the chaise beside him. "Times like this I wish—"

Instead of sitting, she paced. "—I know. You don't have to say it. I've been saving up things to talk to you about all week, too." There was no point in rehashing old conversations about divorce, about living together. They had made their decisions, and now it was too late to change anything. Every time they were together, it could be the last. "We need to make the best of the time we do have together."

She recounted the plans she had for the nature reserve. "I can use the insurance money from the bank barn, add the money I've invested with BMT, and that should be enough to get the place started as a non-profit. After a while, the attraction should draw visitors who keep it going. What do you think?"

"What about your family? Your home? Sweetgrass has been in your family for many generations."

"True, but my girls don't need or want it. Rebecca loves Chicago, and Jessica has her own big house to take care of. The house could be converted into lecture rooms and exhibit space. Perhaps the manager of the nature reserve could have a portion of it to live in for free. That would all have to be worked out."

Robert shook his head. "From an investment standpoint, this seems unwise, Claire. But you appear quite determined."

"Yes. The barn is insured for a million dollars, and BMT has another twenty-two million I've ordered closed out. I'd like to have that money ready as soon as possible, but Thornton hasn't returned my calls." She picked up her drink and sipped. "I also want to talk to you about Tammie."

"What about her? I told you the detective was asking questions."

"I'm concerned about her. You know, the man who was found dead in the barn was Tammie's boyfriend. She's taking it hard, of course, and I've got doubts about her future, now that he's gone. I won't be around forever to keep her employed."

"That's nice of you, Claire, but what do you expect me to do?"

"Maybe, if she's interested, she can be the manager of the nature reserve. She can live at Sweetgrass. I'd love to see that. But whether that happens or not, I think we should join forces to secure Tammie's financial future. We owe her that much."

"How can we do that without creating an uproar in both our families? Jacqueline won't be a problem, of course, but my children would have many questions. I could see that leading to lawsuits down the road."

Claire wanted to raise her voice to the darkening sky, but she lowered it instead. "Have you ever thought that there might be lawsuits if we don't provide for Tammie? These days with DNA matches, it's hard to keep secrets. Even if the truth doesn't come out in our lifetimes, I would feel much more content knowing that Tammie will receive her rightful share from our estates."

"I'll have to think about it. My estate planning is tighter than this wedding band on my finger. Bobby is the executor, and he might balk."

Claire grabbed her lover by both hands and clutched them. "All the more reason we need to do something while we're alive. Promise me you'll take care of this. If not for Tammie's sake, then for mine."

Robert held her so close that his heartbeat merged with hers. "You know I can't say no to you when you are so passionate about something." His warm lips on hers sealed the deal.

An hour later, Claire climbed into her golf cart and turned on the ignition and headlights. The sun hadn't set, but dusk was knocking on the door of the landscape, and without streetlights or roads, Claire was eager to get home.

She waved goodbye to Robert, satisfied her issues had been aired and heard. Sometimes being the other woman in Robert's life was as good as wearing a crown and carrying a scepter.

Claire had traveled about four minutes across the bumpy landscape, far enough that she could see neither Robert's pool nor her long wraparound porch. She passed a cluster of bushes when her cart came to an abrupt, jolting stop, causing her heart to pound. This had never happened before. There she was, just before dark, in the middle of nowhere.

CHAPTER FIFTY-ONE

E arlier that Thursday, Parrott was taken out of the office, investigating tips about drug houses and meth labs in Brandywine Valley. The article in the Unionville *Times* had struck fear in the minds of residents, and all it took was a single rolling stone to create an avalanche. *Thank you, Dave Simmons.*

The chief had been apologetic. He hated to stop the momentum on the Whitman case, but, putting it in terms that Parrott would understand, "Think of this as taking a sack and living to see another play. All we have is you and Officer Barton, and I can't put all this on him. We don't follow up, and some other crisis happens, we're in big trouble." As he handed over the printout of the tips, he'd winked.

Parrott wanted to argue. His discovery of the videos of the person putting flyers on Wyatt's car had given him the footing he needed in the investigation, and he hated to take a single minute away. But there was no point in arguing. As public servants, the police department had to accede to public pressure sometimes. A fact, as his grandmother would say, "As sure as a dog has fleas and a cat has lives."

The seclusion of homes and the distance between residences made it hard for people to snoop on their neighbors, or even, in Claire Whitman's case, to know what was happening in an outbuilding on her own property. On the other hand, equestrians rode on trails through neighboring property, and artists often set up easels outdoors, so nature offered opportunities to break through the illusion of privacy.

As Parrott scanned over the list of suspicious activity, he shook his head. Suspected marijuana plants, fumes, regular late-night car traffic in an otherwise-sleepy neighborhood, various and sundry rumors—all difficult to investigate in the country setting. But when he saw the list of names, a surge of excitement passed through him. One of the suspected sites was an outbuilding on the property of M. Robert Pennington. So that's why Schrik had winked when giving Parrott the assignment. Now he'd have another reason to visit with Mr. Pennington and have a look around his property, assuming Pennington cooperated. Maybe this unwanted assignment would work out fine, after all.

Parrott and Officer Barton met in Parrott's office to brainstorm how they would handle this assignment. Parrott brought the coffee. Barton brought breakfast burritos. The two sat at the desk, eating and dishing over their mutual frustration.

"If we were on a police force in a city, we'd never be pulled from an important case to chase bunny rabbits. That's what this is," Barton said. "I guess the jewelry theft at the Henrys will have to take a back seat for a couple days."

"Hmmph, city cops think we have it so easy—all we have to do is collect a paycheck. They don't realize how everything, big or little, falls on the two of us." Parrott thumped the sheet of information handed to him earlier by Schrik. "Even this stuff. If we were in a city, we could conduct surveillance from the street, interview neighbors and landlords, without being concerned about trespassing on private property. Here, everything depends on a cooperative estate owner or a warrant."

"Not to mention the rich folks who pay taxes to support our salaries. They don't take kindly to our poking around in their business."

"That's true anywhere," Parrott said. He didn't like painting all rich people with the same brush, especially now that he was one of them. "Might as well get started," he said between bites. "We're going to have to follow up on all of these, even if in a cursory way."

"Hahhh, how're we supposed to approach somebody based on fumes? Unless there's an explosion like yours at Sweetgrass, ain't nobody gonna smell fumes from one fifty-acre estate to the next."

Parrott grabbed a legal pad and pen from his desk and made notes. There were seven allegations, but only five addresses. Parrott and Barton ran through each of them, deciding how they would sniff around enough to determine whether a crime was being committed. They would spend the rest of the day in the field, separately, knocking on doors, talking to colleagues in nearby departments, as well as some drug offenders-turned-informants who had helped them before.

The tip about Pennington's property intrigued Parrott the most. He told Barton he would check that one out, himself. Because Pennington's acreage bordered on Claire's, and because his interview with Pennington about Brock Thornton had left him suspicious, he couldn't wait to use these drug tips to dive deeper into the television magnate's business.

At five o'clock, Barton and Parrott met up at the station to debrief. Parrott had slung his jacket over his desk chair and opened his collar. Barton resembled a wilted tomato plant, needing water.

"Make yourself comfortable," Parrott said. "I'll get us some cold drinks from the break room." He returned with two ice-cold cans of lemonade from the pop machine, and he broke out two power bars from his stash.

Barton popped the tab and guzzled the lemonade. "Beastly day out there today. Glad I don't have to pound the pavement like this every day."

"You find anything?" Parrott bit off a giant piece of the power bar and chewed. "Nobody *I* talked to knew anything."

"Same here. I wish people wouldn't get so skittish every time there's an op-ed in the paper. Nobody I talked to has heard anything about a meth lab or drug dealing. Most I got outta any of 'em was that Old Man Hatteras is a frequent user of CBD products."

"Registered user?" Parrott asked.

"Yeah. Uses it for pain."

"Using and growing are two different things, especially in a conservative state like Pennsylvania."

"I doubt he's growing. He's about eighty years old, and not well. I can't see him messing with marijuana plants. Meth either."

Parrott finished his power bar and drained the can of lemonade. "Most of the people on this list are in their eighties. Claire and Pennington are. But younger people work for them, and they could be the ones planting dope. I think we need to keep our feelers active for a few more days. If we don't learn anything, we can tell the chief we came up with scratch."

"What about this guy, Pennington? You want help with that?"

"Nah, I've got an idea about checking his estate out after dark, see if there's any traffic out there. I might make a visit to the Whitman house, too. Let's touch base tomorrow and see where we're at."

As Barton was leaving, Parrott's cell phone rang. Herman's name flashed on the caller ID, and an inexplicable clammy sensation shot through Parrott's arteries. It had been a long, frustrating day, and whatever Herman wanted, Parrott wasn't interested. He walked to the window and stared out at the vacant playground before answering.

"Hey, Ollie. Can we meet for a quick bite of dinner? I want to talk about this deal with Brock Thornton."

"What deal? I'm not ready to decide about investing right now. Besides, I'm going to be working late tonight. I can't afford the time to go out for dinner."

"I can bring something over to the station. An Italian hoagie from Wawa? I don't want to pressure you, but Thornton has called me fifty times today. He says this is the perfect time to invest in the market, before it makes a correction. He doesn't want us to miss out. I've talked to your mother, and she's ready to go."

All the goodwill he'd felt toward Herman at Portabella's was turning sour now. "Why don't you go on ahead without us? Tonya wants a house, and I'm too busy right now. If we miss out on the good timing, so be it. At least we won't be standing in your way."

"No, no, no. Thornton was clear that this is an all or nothing deal. He won't take our money unless we have the whole group. Ten million, minimum."

Parrott sank into his desk chair and leaned back. "Sorry to be the party pooper, but Tonya and I are not going to be pressured into something we're not sure of. Thanks for offering to bring food, but I can't stop to eat or to visit. I've got to go now."

As soon as Parrott hung up, his stomach demanded food, and the thought of a hoagie from Wawa made his mouth water. He called Tonya to catch up on her day of work at Elle's and tell her he wouldn't be home for dinner. "I'll grab a sandwich and get some work done. Call you on my way home." As an afterthought, he told her about the conversation with Herman. "You don't want me to call him back and say we've changed our minds, do you?"

"You know how I feel, Ollie. I'm even more distrustful than you are."

"Okay. Hope we don't regret this, but I don't think we will. See you in a few hours."

Parrott disconnected the call and straightened up his desk. He had no intention of coming back to the office to do paperwork. He headed out to purchase a hoagie and then he was going to make an unexpected visit to Claire Whitman at Sweetgrass.

The sky had dropped its veil over the landscape, but the streetlights had not yet come on. Parrott bought his sandwich and a cold root beer. He drove into Unionville and parked his car on the side of the road. A doe and two fawns crossed the road ahead of him, and he wondered where the stag was.

The hoagie was warm and spicy, chock-full of cheese, ham, salami, sweet peppers, and swimming in oil, vinegar, and oregano. Not as good as one of Tonya's home-cooked meals, but it was delicious.

When he finished eating, he wiped his hands and face and pointed his car toward Sweetgrass. He had a lot of new questions for Tammie and Claire.

CHAPTER FIFTY-TWO

When Parrott rang Claire's doorbell, it was a quarter past eight. Sunset was imminent, and the air had that soft thickness that ushered in the night-time sounds and smells of country living. A full minute or two passed before someone turned on the porch light and a muffled voice asked who was there.

Parrott identified himself, and the door flew open, revealing an agitated Tammie. Her bob hairdo was standing out in several directions, as if she'd pulled on it. Her eyebrows were drawn into furrows, and her blue eyes shifted from side to side. Whatever he'd interrupted, it wasn't happy.

"Is something the matter?" Parrott asked, making no move to gain entrance.

Tammie barked a reply. "No, nothing. That is, what can I do for you?"

"I'd like to speak with Mrs. Whitman if she's available."

Shifting her weight from one leg to another, Tammie appeared to make up her mind how to answer. Finally, she said, "Come on in." She walked Parrott into the kitchen, a room he'd not seen before. A long counter separated cooking space from eating space. A table and six chairs occupied the eating space, where Tammie sat in front of a cell phone, what looked to be an address book, and a coffee mug.

Parrott sat next to Tammie, hoping she'd tell him why she was clutching her elbows in a death grip. He held back on questions. There was no sign of Claire, no television sounds, no dinner dishes. A clock over the kitchen sink ticked.

After what seemed like an hour of silence, Tammie jumped up, wringing her hands. "You might as well know. Maybe you can help." Her normally melodious voice had become shrill. She dashed to the kitchen window and peered out into the darkening landscape. "Mrs. Whitman isn't here. She's never been late like this before. I don't know what's happened to her."

"Where did she go?" Parrott asked. "How did she get there?"

Choking back a sob, Tammie returned to the table. She checked her cell phone. "She's in her golf cart. She's always back before eight, and it's almost eight-thirty. She's not answering her phone. I'm worried."

Parrott repeated in his calmest voice, even though alarms were ringing in his head. It wasn't cool for a woman in her eighties to be out after dark in a golf cart, even in bucolic Unionville. "Where did she go?"

The struggle between confiding in Parrott or maintaining loyalty to her employer played out on Tammie's face. Finally, she choked out some words. "She went to the next farm over—Mr. Pennington's."

Sparks flew inside Parrott's brain. He had also planned to go to Pennington's this evening. "Why don't we call there, see why she's delayed?"

"It's not that simple." Tammie stared at the table. "No one is supposed to know about this meeting. I wouldn't have told you, except that I'm so worried—"

Parrott ignored the image of Claire and Robert Pennington, huddled in a corner, smoking pot or doing some other clandestine activity. "You said, 'She's *always* back before eight.' What does that mean? Is this meeting with Pennington a regular event?"

Tammie covered her face and sobbed. "Yes. She meets him every Thursday. Here or somewhere on the grounds of his estate—not at his house."

"Can I assume that's because of Mrs. Pennington?"

"More because of the servants. Mrs. Pennington is so out of it, she probably wouldn't care."

Parrott glanced out the window at the growing darkness. He needed to act fast to find Claire. In a half hour, the task would be a hundred times harder. "What were you doing with this address book before I got here?"

"Debating about calling Mr. Pennington. His private cellphone number's here." She opened the book to the P's and pointed. "But I hate to blow the cover.."

"Never mind that," Parrott said, grabbing the address book and punching the private number into his phone.

When Pennington answered, there were voices in the background, probably from the television. Parrott identified himself in a rushed voice.

"How did you get this number?" Pennington's tone was packed with arrogance and perhaps a tinge of fear.

"That's not important," Parrott said. "Are you alone right now?"

"N-No-o-o. What seems to be the problem?" Now he had Pennington's attention.

"Tell me when you are positive that no one else can hear me."

The television voices grew fainter, and a door closed. "All right, detective. What's going on?"

"Two things. Claire Whitman has not returned home from your meeting. She's not answering her cellphone."

"My God. What could have happened to her? She was fine a few minutes ago. I can't—"

"You have a vehicle that we could use to search for her in the fields, correct?"

"Yes, a golf cart, but I—"

"Don't worry. You will tell your servants the West Brandywine police department is investigating a complaint about marijuana plants on your property. Grumble to your servants about having to cooperate, especially this time of the evening. Tell them I'm five minutes away. Get ready to accompany me in your cart."

Parrott disconnected and rushed toward the front door.

Tammie trotted behind him. "Did Mr. Pennington sound upset that you knew about their meeting?"

Parrott replied over his shoulder. "No. Just that Claire was missing."

"He loves her. That's why."

CHAPTER FIFTY-THREE

Robert Pennington sat shotgun on his four-seater golf cart, while Parrott drove into the tepid air, darkness hovering about them like a blindfold, almost fastened from behind. The headlights cast two broad stripes ahead, but these provided little comfort. Unless this cart were following the exact same path as Claire's, they could miss her.

Thus, Parrott steered the vehicle to the right and left, sending light in zigzags across the land.

Flies and an occasional sudden movement in the brush were the only sights at first. Chirps of insects punctuated the tension. "You need to keep me going in the right direction," Parrott said to his co-pilot, whose tight posture was almost palpable. Despite Parrott's pressing the accelerator hard, the cart was only moving at about ten miles per hour.

"I will. If something's happened to Claire, I'll never—"

"We'll find her. How long does it usually take to get between the two farms?"

"Twenty minutes, maybe a little more at night." The cart plugged along. "How did you come up with that cover story?"

"Not a cover. Real complaints about cannabis on your property. We can talk about that after we find Ms. Whitman."

"Hah. What kind of frivolous charge is that? As if I'd be interested in growing marijuana at my age and stage in life."

"Might not be you. Maybe a farm hand or neighbor. Probably frivolous, but tonight it comes in handy." Parrott had been driving at least five minutes with not even a hint of Claire or her golf cart. "I wish there were tire tracks or footprints, something to let us know we're on the right path."

"Might have been some in the daylight, but when the sun sets in God's country, anybody could get away with anything." Pennington laughed or coughed. Parrott couldn't tell which. "When I was a kid, I took plenty advantage of that fact."

"Who else knows about your Thursday night trysts?" Parrott asked.

"Besides Tammie, you mean? Nobody." Pennington touched Parrott's arm. "You don't think someone knew and ambushed her, do you?"

"I don't know what to think just yet. Let's find her first."

The headlights caught some movement behind a copse of bushes, and Parrott veered in that direction, arriving in time to see a stag leaping across a creek. Maybe he belonged to the doe and fawn Parrott had seen earlier.

Now they were three or four minutes into the distance between the two farms. "Would it hurt anything if we made some noise out here?"

"Nah," Pennington said. "Nobody's out here but the animals."

The two men yelled Claire's name, pausing for a response, then raising their voices again. The zigzag driving was giving Parrott a headache. "You sure we're headed in the right direction?"

Pennington huffed. "There's no doubt. I'm usually the one driving to Claire's. The cart knows the route by heart. We're about two-thirds of the way now."

Stars and the three-quarters moon had made their presence known, and Parrott was beginning to worry. He shouted, "Claire, Claire." His voice was scratchy.

At that moment, an empty golf cart appeared in their path about twenty feet ahead, and a faint sound coming from beyond that on the left caught Parrott's ear. He slammed on the brake.

"Here! Oh, here."

Parrott accelerated again, steering to the left of the empty golf cart, lighting up a patch of tall grass. A lump in pastel fabric rolled about on the ground.

Pennington jumped out of the cart faster than Parrott could have imagined, considering the man's age. "Claire, my dear. Are you all right?" He hurried to the place where Claire was lying, and he fell to his knees next to her in the grass.

The headlights illuminated Claire's face as she looked from Parrott to Pennington with reddened eyes. "I'll be fine," she said, her jaw clenched. "My cart broke down. Don't know what's wrong with it. Tried to call Tammie, but my cellphone wouldn't work. I decided to walk the rest of the way, but I turned my ankle and fell. I think I may have broken it."

CHAPTER FIFTY-FOUR

Parrott lifted Claire onto the golf cart, seating her between Pennington and himself on the wide bench. He drove her home, where Tammie flew into action, wrapping the ankle in ice packs and making Claire comfortable on the sofa in the office, with the leg elevated.

"Do you want me to take you to the emergency room?" she asked.

"So I can wait all night for an x-ray? I'd rather take Tylenol and call the doctor in the morning." She turned to Robert, who had pulled up a chair next to her and was holding her hand. "Much as I appreciate your comforting me, you need to get back home before anyone starts to suspect something. You and the detective wouldn't be driving around in the dark, looking for marijuana plants."

"She's right," Parrott said. "Let's get you home. We'll say it got too dark, and we'll go out again tomorrow morning. I'll need to figure out a way to get Claire's cart back, too."

"That won't be a problem," Claire said, flapping her hand. "The cart can stay out overnight. We have an extra battery in the garage, and we can move it tomorrow morning."

Parrott flashed on the lithium battery he'd seen in the garage, chagrined for suspecting its possible connection to the meth explosion.

"I checked out the golf cart this afternoon, as usual," Tammie said. She was carrying a tray with a bowl of consommé, a plate of cheese straw pastries, and a highball glass filled with Dewar's on the rocks. "Nothing unusual then." She placed a linen bib around Claire's neck. "Anyway, top priority tomorrow morning is getting you to a doctor."

"Fine. We can have Charlie take care of the cart. He's back from Delaware."

Parrott had moved toward the doorway, eager to return Pennington and his golf cart to ModCom Way, but he returned to the sofa. "Don't involve Charlie. My investigator and I will take care of bringing your golf cart back. I don't want anyone touching it until we've had a chance to process it."

Somebody sabotaged Claire's golf cart, someone who watched her and/or knew her habits. Someone wanted to harm her, even if only temporarily. Figuring out who and why was Parrott's next step, but he didn't share these thoughts with Claire or Pennington.

He had plenty to worry about, too. On the way to dropping Pennington and his golf cart off, Parrott asked about the timing and location of the rendezvous and where Claire had parked her golf cart. Then he hopped in his car and swung by the station to make notes. This evening had put a new slant on the meth lab explosion and Tripp Anderson's death. Whoever committed those crimes was a schemer and a planner. He or she knew the way around Brandywine Valley, taking a risk to enlist Wyatt Wukitsch's assistance, and, if Parrott was correct, taking another to follow an eighty-two-year-old woman and sabotage her golf cart.

Pressure mushroomed on Parrott now, sitting like a boulder between his shoulder blades. Unless he was mistaken, Claire Whitman was in a good deal of danger.

CHAPTER FIFTY-FIVE

The next morning, Parrott and Officer Barton met at the Whitman estate. Parrott had left a voicemail for Tammie. When she called back, Parrott explained his plans to retrieve the golf cart.

"Are you sure? I've got that extra battery in the garage, and it's no problem for Charlie or me to take care of that."

"I have my reasons," Parrott replied. "You should focus on getting Ms. Whitman safely to the doctor."

"Well, at least stop by the garage to pick up the battery. The orthopedist is going to work us in before his first appointment, so if all goes well, we should be back around ten. Aiko's coming in and can let you into the garage if I'm not here."

Parrott stopped short of telling Tammie to take extra precautions. He wanted to confirm his hunches before he sounded alarms. Tammie seemed like a responsible young woman, certainly devoted to Claire, but he also remembered Jessica's distrust of Tammie.

By eight-thirty, Parrott and Barton, dressed in jeans and nondescript t-shirts, pulled up to Sweetgrass in Parrott's Toyota. In case anyone was watching, they appeared to be two workmen on a mission to bring back a disabled vehicle.

Parrott wore a backpack and a carryall with tools, and Barton carried the lithium battery. The day was only beginning to heat up, and a light breeze made the hike pleasant. Within fifteen minutes they located the cart. The ground there was uneven. Easy to understand how an eighty-two-year-old woman might have turned her ankle in the dark.

Both officers donned plastic gloves. Parrott took photos of the cart, before removing the fingerprint kit from his backpack and sprinkling the cart with powder. There were lots of prints, most likely belonging to Claire or Tammie, but there was always a chance, if someone had disabled the cart, he or she hadn't worn gloves.

After Parrott took detailed photos of the prints, Barton lifted the seat to examine the engine. "Oh, cripes. Here's the problem—take a look at this battery."

Parrott bent to peer into the compartment. "Couldn't be more obvious." The bolts securing the battery terminals had been loosened, and gray corrosive material surrounded the points of connection. When Claire drove the cart, the heat had caused them to melt.

"This was no accident. Ms. Whitman's personal assistant said she checked out the cart before its last use. Even if she wasn't an expert, she would have noticed this." Parrott took numerous photographs of the battery.

Barton wiped the sweat from his forehead. "Okay. Let's change this battery out. Good thing we have the proper tools."

"You know how to do this?"

"Yep," Barton said. "I help my dad. He works on cars in his spare time."

"Glad to watch and learn. When you're done, let's take this baby for a spin. I want to check out the spot where it was parked last night."

A few minutes later, the two officers drove across the farmland, the corroded battery sitting between them on the floorboard. They parked the cart near Pennington's pool pavilion. Barton whistled. "Nice set-up."

From this distance, the early morning sun sent sparkles onto the surface of the pool, and the aromas from an adjacent herb garden teased the senses. The garden of Eden couldn't have been more colorful or fragrant. For a second, Parrott pictured Tonya and himself, enjoying a leisurely swim in a pool like this.

Robert had described the bushes that provided a three-sided parking spot for Claire's golf cart. Discreetly placed, the bushes offered a convenient camouflage for the vehicle, about fifty feet from the pavilion. Pennington had gone to some trouble and expense to create this hiding place, more evidence that his relationship with Claire was not frivolous. Or maybe Claire wasn't the only secret visitor.

"This is where the cart was parked last night." Parrott braked a few feet from the area and cut off the motor.

"Plenty of space here for someone to tamper with the battery." Barton climbed out of the cart and walked the short distance to the parking spot.

"And plenty of cover to keep from being seen or heard," Parrott said, joining Barton in the partial enclosure.

"Loosening the battery bolts would be quick and quiet. The perp knew how little time it would take to break down the cart," Barton said.

Parrott wondered who would have known about Claire's secret meeting. "Whoever it was knew she'd be able to start up the motor and get part-way home, right?"

"Exactly. The saboteur knew how quickly lithium batteries corrode, too."

The officers drove the cart back to Sweetgrass in silence. Parrott's mind, however, was full of questions. *Who followed Claire's cart to the hiding spot? Who tampered with her battery? Who wanted to do harm to an eighty-two-year-old lady?* Then there was the most important question of all—*why?*

CHAPTER FIFTY-SIX

When Parrott and Barton returned Claire's golf cart to her open garage, Parrott checked the backdoor to make sure it was locked. It was, but that was small comfort. At this point he watched for anything that might be hazardous to Claire.

Barton left for ModCom Way, where he would finish examining the grounds for marijuana. Claire wouldn't be back for another hour or more, so Parrott drove to the groundskeeper's house, hoping to find Charlie.

Radar dashed to Parrott with exuberant leaps as he drove up to the house and exited the car. The dog had been sitting outside in the shade of a sycamore tree. Three bowls of water and a rubber chicken kept him company.

"Where's your daddy, Radar?" Parrott asked, as he petted the dog on his shiny black head. Parrott strode to the cottage, the dog keeping in step with him. Knocking on the door brought no response.

Disappointed, Parrott started back to his car, but the faint roar of a farm machine in the distance drew him to the back of Charlie's house. A green and yellow farm vehicle was mowing the field. Parrott could make out the driver, a blur of blue with a wide-brimmed hat.

Parrott yelled and waved his arms, trying to get the man's attention. Radar joined in with a gruff staccato melody. After what seemed like ten minutes, the tractor made a curve and drove in their direction. It was Charlie. The motor filled the air with smoke and a raucous, grinding noise, but Charlie cut off the engine and pulled plugs from his ears, stuffing them in a pocket.

The hat shaded his face as he patted Radar's head and turned to Parrott. "What can I do for you, detective?"

"Can we talk a few minutes?" Parrott pointed toward the house's back patio, where two Adirondack chairs sat. He needed more than a stand-up interview.

"Sure." Charlie trudged up the incline toward the patio, Radar glued to his side. "Wyatt told me you visited him."

"Yes, I did. Now I need to follow up with you."

"Is Wyatt a suspect, then?" Lines on Charlie's forehead deepened, and his head bowed a little.

"At this stage of the investigation, there are many components and many people. Everyone is suspect until we can determine with certainty who did what. For example, Wyatt has admitted to tying you up."

"You aren't planning to arrest him for that, are you? If I don't press charges?" Charlie's voice had the whine of a man at the end of his rope.

Parrott reached out, stopping short of touching Charlie's arm. His fingers grazed Radar's back instead. "This isn't about arresting Wyatt or anybody else. I'm gathering facts. When did you know that Wyatt was your attacker, Charlie?"

Charlie rubbed his face. "I didn't know ahead of time, if that's what you're getting at. Everything happened just as I told you last time—the blindfold, the chair, all of it—except that when he was roughing me up, Wyatt shouted at me to cooperate, and I wouldn't get hurt. I recognized his voice and said, 'Wyatt?'

"He didn't answer me, but he sobbed, and I knew it was him, though I didn't want to believe it. Wyatt came to see me a few days ago. He was in bad shape, worse than I'd ever seen him. He told me he wanted to go back to rehab. That's when he confessed to tying me up."

"I know Wyatt has a long history of drug use. What can you tell me about any other problems he's had?"

Charlie sighed. "Wyatt's had a rough go. His mother and I thought he had so much potential when he was young. He always made honor roll, made friends easily. He was a happy kid."

"He grew up here at Sweetgrass, correct?"

"Mostly. He moved away with his mom when we divorced, but he continued to spend weekends, holidays, and summers here. He loves the farm, the land, the animals—he's a nature guy."

"He never thought of working on a farm like you do?"

"Nah. There was a girl he wanted to impress. He had bigger aspirations. Too big, it turned out. He couldn't find his place in any high-paying positions. Pretty soon he quit trying."

"Who was the girl?" Parrott pulled on this unlikely thread, just to keep Charlie talking.

A joyless grin spread across Charlie's face. "Don't know why you need to know that, but I'll tell you anyway. It was Bonnie Abramson, Claire's granddaughter. I think he still carries the torch for her."

Parrott thought of Bonnie's blonde curly hair, her office at the college, her young son, and the adoring look she had for the scruffy-looking man in the photograph on Claire's desk. She was probably unaware of Wyatt's passion for her, and if she knew, she probably wouldn't care.

"Does Wyatt still have contact with Bonnie or her mother, or Claire?"

"He sees all of them from time to time, when he comes to visit me. Less so during Covid. They're all very nice to him. They remember the little boy he used to be, and they treat him like they treat me—like family."

"So, can you think of any reason Wyatt might want to hurt any of them?"

"Not at all, detective. Wyatt's not that kind of person. He may be messed up from the drugs, but he doesn't have a mean bone in his body."

Parrott sat back in his chair and gave Charlie a searching look. "Okay, but tell me this. You've been around Ms. Whitman and Sweetgrass longer than almost anyone. Who, do you think, might want to cause harm to her property or to her?"

"I can't think of a soul. The only people who come around here regularly are Jessica and Bonnie, Aiko and Tammie. There's a group of ladies who are friends, mostly widows, but I can't see any of them wishing her harm. Ms. Whitman gets along with all her neighbors. Quite a few people out here live on family estates like she does. They grew up together."

Parrott hadn't expected Charlie to serve up the name of the person responsible for Tripp's death and the barn explosion, but he'd hoped for more than a catalogue of people who loved Claire. "And, of course, there's you."

Charlie's mouth formed an "O," and his eyes squinted. "You don't think I'd ever do anything to hurt Ms. Whitman, do you? I'm shocked that you'd even suggest that. She and her family have been nothin' but grand to me. I'd never intentionally harm a hair on her head. Mrs. Whitman is an absolute angel."

CHAPTER FIFTY-SEVEN

P arrott ended the interview with Charlie and ambled back toward the car, thinking about all the nice things Charlie had said about Claire Whitman. Nobody, in Parrott's experience, was an absolute angel. Human beings, regardless of whether rich or poor, old or young, had flaws and made mistakes.

Charlie didn't mention anything about the relationship between Claire and Robert Pennington. Maybe he didn't know, or maybe he was holding back.

Wyatt's infatuation with Claire's granddaughter might be important. Parrott had known instances where unrequited love between people from different social classes, had resulted in tragedy. If it had been Bonnie's boyfriend, instead of Tammie's, who'd been killed, Parrott might have had to ratchet up his suspicions of Wyatt Wukitsch. As it was, he couldn't eliminate either Wyatt or Charlie from his suspect list.

Parrott sat in his car, preparing to head back to Claire's. Maybe she would be back home from the doctor by now. Before starting the engine, he checked his cellphone for messages. There were two—one from Tonya, and one from Herman.

Tonya's was first. "Ollie, I've been house hunting in West Chester, and I found a real gem. Five bedrooms, three bathrooms, thirty-six hundred square feet. Beautiful kitchen, gym, outdoor pool, fire pit. They even have a volleyball court on the property. Under a million dollars and in move-in condition. Your mom called, and I asked her if she wanted to go with me to look at it again, but she said she couldn't."

Tonya paused to slurp something, and Horace chirped, "She couldn't," in the background. "Evidently Herman injured himself last night at one of his construction projects. He may have sprained an ankle, so your mom is taking him to the doctor today." Another slurp. "Sorry, I'm drinking a smoothie for breakfast. I hope you can go with me to see the house, either tonight or tomorrow morning. The agent said this one will go fast, so we might need to forget about Herman's offer to inspect it before we put in a bid. Anyway, call me when you can. Love you."

Parrott let the news about Herman's sprained ankle simmer in his mind. What work would Herman have had at a construction site at night in the dark? Was it coincidence that both he and Claire had ankle injuries? What connection might there be between Herman and Claire, beyond his unsuccessful bid to renovate her bank barn, and his knowledge of Brock Thornton? Might Herman have been the one lurking in the acreage between the two country estates as twilight set in last night?

He'd call Tonya back in a few minutes, but right now he wanted to return Herman's call. Hopefully, the man wouldn't pressure him again to invest with BMT. Parrott wanted to find out more about this ankle injury, including exactly where Herman had been last night.

Parrott punched in Herman's cellphone number and waited. Within two rings, Herman answered. "Hey, Ollie. Thanks for returning my call. I can only talk a minute now, because I'm in the exam room at the ER with your mother."

Parrott decided not to let on that he knew about Herman's ankle. "What's the matter with Ma?"

"Hah. Nothing. Your mother is perfect in every way. I've hurt my ankle—can barely walk on it."

Parrott kept his voice even. "Sorry to hear. How'd you do that?"

"Stepped too hard and fast coming down a staircase. It happened last night. I came home, iced it, elevated it—thought it'd be better this morning, but no."

"Hope it's not broken," Parrott said. "Anyway, I'm returning your call. You weren't going to lean on me again to invest with Brock Thornton, were you? 'Cause Tonya's found a house she likes."

"Oh, you'll have to tell me about the house. No, I wasn't calling you about investing. Quite the opposite. I got a phone call from Brock Thornton telling me that the investment opportunity was closed."

"Closed? What does that mean?" Parrott couldn't believe Thornton would pass up the chance to get ten million dollars, especially after he'd been pushing them to invest.

"Exactly what I said. We couldn't invest with BMT now, even if we wanted to."

CHAPTER FIFTY-EIGHT

Parrott called Tonya before driving to Claire's. He surprised himself by saying he was also excited about the prospect of finding a new house. Perhaps part of his change of attitude came from having the stress of a multi-million-dollar house off his plate. "I'm sorry I can't free myself to look at the house with you, but if you love it so much, I probably will, too."

"That's okay. Elle's going to go with me this afternoon. That way you can hear the plusses of the house from two of us."

Parrott disconnected but held the phone to his chest for several seconds afterward. Tonya's voice hadn't sounded so full of vitality in a long time. He hoped this signaled a turned corner in her PTSD treatment, though, more likely, the cheeriness would be temporary.

On the way back to Claire's Parrott drove to the area where the bank barn had been. He parked his car next to the remains of a stone wall. Before going back to work at Sweetgrass, he needed to change out of his jeans and t-shirt and into the pants, shirt, and sport jacket he kept in the trunk. Maybe it wouldn't have mattered to Claire—or Tammie—that he was dressed like a farm hand, but Parrott believed clothes made a huge difference in people's attitudes, including the attitude of the wearer.

First, he walked through the rubble again. The meth smell had subsided, but the odor of burned flesh still hovered, and, as Parrott walked, he kicked up a vile-smelling dust. He returned to the spot where Tripp Anderson's body had been found.

He put on gloves and squatted there, sifting debris through his fingers. The heart of this case was Tripp Anderson. Someone went to great extremes to poison him, to keep Charlie Wukitsch away, and to blow up this barn. Someone with the means, motive, and opportunity.

The list of people in Brandywine Valley who had the means to commit this crime was extensive. The poison, the meth ingredients, a vehicle to transport the body—these weren't expensive for someone who lived or worked here. The opportunity might have been trickier, but once Wyatt tied Charlie up, the killer would have free reign. Keys to the barn had apparently been available to Claire, Charlie, Wyatt, Tammie, Bonnie's boyfriend Ray, and Brock Thornton.

That left motive. Parrott stood and paced around the rubble, poking at pieces of unidentifiable objects with his shoes. Who could have had it in for Tripp Anderson, and why? Coming from out of town, Anderson's only significant connection appeared to be with Tammie. Did someone want to prevent the two of them from getting married?

Tripp's father had thought the relationship was over, and he was admittedly happy about that. He didn't seem to know anything about the "project" that Tammie said was bringing Tripp back to Brandywine.

Parrott chided himself for letting himself be caught up in so many possibilities. This case had way too many pieces to it—like a mosaic crowded with too many tiles. To solve the case, he was going to have to ignore the distractions and prioritize. He needed to know more about Tripp Anderson, and he needed to know it quickly.

Hopefully, Claire and Tammie were back from the doctor now. He changed his clothes and headed to the house to question them both about Tripp Anderson. He wouldn't leave until he had some answers.

CHAPTER FIFTY-NINE

P arrott rang the doorbell at Sweetgrass at a quarter to twelve and was greeted by Aiko. "Is Mrs. Whitman back from the doctor? I'd like to speak with her." Parrott expected to be told to wait at the doorstep, while Aiko announced him to her employer. He shifted his weight from one foot to the other and watched as a bumblebee darted in and out of the flowers on either side of the door.

"You can step in, detective. Ms. Whitman told me you might come by. She wants to see you." Aiko held the door open and moved aside to admit Parrott. "She and Tammie are in the study. I believe you know the way."

In all the visits Parrott had made to homes in Brandywine Valley, he'd never been allowed to walk himself to an interior room. Then again, he'd never been in the home of an octogenarian with an ankle injury. He thanked Aiko and headed for the study, where he found Claire, propped up on the sofa with a foot-to-knee cast resting on a pile of pillows. Her complexion was sallow, but her turquoise eyes were sharp as ever.

"Detective, I owe you a debt of gratitude for last night, and again for this morning. I understand you found my golf cart." Claire held out her hand to clasp Parrott's. "Aiko's preparing lunch. I hope you'll join us."

Tammie chimed in from where she sat at Claire's desk, pen in hand. "Ms. Whitman rarely invites people to lunch. You should be complimented."

"I'm honored," Parrott said. "And glad to be of service. The cart's being processed at the lab. I can't stay for lunch, but I do need to talk with both of you." He sat in one of the chairs opposite the sofa and motioned for Tammie to sit in the other one. "Before anything else, what did the doctor say about your ankle?"

"It's going to be fine in no time," Claire said. "All I need is a little rest and TLC."

Tammie joined the group, addressing Claire, but looking at Parrott. "That's not quite the whole story. Your *sprained* ankle will need at least six weeks of TLC, followed by weeks of physical therapy. The good news is that yoga has kept you in better shape than most people your age who get injured."

Claire pressed her hands together and whispered. "Namaste."

"Also, hairline fractures may show up several days after an injury, so Dr. Smith can't be sure it's not broken."

"Let's not look for trouble," Claire said. "And don't think I'm going to be idle during this convalescence. I'm planning to use this time to work on my plans for a nature reserve at Sweetgrass."

"I'd like to hear about those plans," Parrott said. "But first—"

"—Yes, first. You probably have questions for me, and I have questions for you. Shall I begin?" Claire waved her hand, as if giving herself permission to go first. "How did you happen to ring the doorbell last night at the most opportune time?"

Parrott explained he was in the neighborhood on police business. "I wanted to ask you the same questions I have for you today. I stopped by on my way to another house in the valley."

Claire exchanged looks with Tammie. "Hm, I appreciate your discretion in not revealing anything about the other police business. Can I count on you to be equally discreet about what you've learned about my relationship with Mr. Pennington?"

Parrott gave what he hoped was his most ingratiating smile. Claire might be more concerned about preserving her secrets than learning about the "accident" that had caused her sprained ankle. "Discretion is part of my oath of office. I will never share anything of a private nature unless I need to do so for the safety and well-being of a human being."

Claire pressed her lips together. "All right then. How are things coming along with your case? Are you any closer to finding out who killed poor Tripp Anderson and destroyed my barn?"

Parrott glanced at Tammie before answering. Normally he would ask a second party to leave the room before he launched into talk about the case. Though not high on the list, Tammie could be considered a suspect. At this moment, however, Parrott wanted Tammie to stay right where she was. That way he could assess her body language and facial expressions while he questioned Claire. He had some questions for Tammie, and he wouldn't mind watching Claire's reactions, as well.

"We're making progress," Parrott said. "But we need your help. I want to know everything you can tell me about Tripp—who his friends were, if he had any enemies, what kind of work ethic he had, what his attitudes were toward money, anything you can think of that might suggest a motive for killing him."

Claire stared at Tammie, her mouth forming an "O," and her hand on her chest. "Goodness, that's a tall order. I'm not sure I'm the one to fill it. All I know about poor Tripp is that he was awfully sweet to Tammie."

Tammie brushed tears from her eyelashes. "I'm sure I've answered those questions before. I can't tell you anything new."

"Why don't you show Detective Parrott the photograph from the pre-construction party I hosted? The one we talked about the other day. It's in my left-hand drawer." Claire pointed.

Tammie crossed the room to the desk and opened the center drawer. "Here it is." Tammie gazed at the photo for a few seconds before taking it to Parrott. "I trust you know who all four of these guys are—Tripp, Ray Plummer, Brock Thornton, and Wyatt Wukitsch."

Parrott studied the photo, the arms around the shoulders, the expressions on the faces. If there were audio, they'd surely burst into raucous song. Four good-looking young guys in the prime of life, feeling good and enjoying each other's company. The date at the bottom of the photograph was four years earlier. Who would've guessed that one of the four would be dead so soon, and another in drug rehab?

Looking from one to the other, Parrott said, "Tell me about the people in this photo. I know who they are, but I want to know how they're connected, what relationships they have with each other."

Claire spoke first. "I'm not sure that they are connected, really, except that they were of similar ages, having fun together at a party. What do you think, Tammie?"

"Isn't Bonnie's boyfriend Ray friends with Brock Thornton somehow? I think Ray happened to be in town when you had this party, and he was staying with Thornton at the time. After the remodel wasn't it Thornton's idea that Ray stay in the bank barn whenever he came to town?"

Claire nodded. "That's right. I'd forgotten."

Tammie leaned toward Parrott to look at the picture again. "Bonnie was at the party too. Wyatt came with Charlie. Everyone was looking forward to the barn renovation project." A brief smile passed over Tammie's lips. "You always give the best parties, and everyone was jolly and happy. That was the night Tripp and I met."

"Did Tripp appear to know any of these young men beyond having just met them at the party?" Parrott needed to move on beyond the nostalgia of the photograph. "Or did he come to know any of them better through his work here?"

Tammie hesitated. "I can't say for sure. Tripp didn't hang out with the guys much when he was here. When he was working, he supervised other guys. He didn't think supervising and socializing mixed well. When he was with me, he didn't talk about his friends. He must've had some, but he didn't say so. He was kind of quiet."

Parrott watched her face. "Have you had any more thoughts about Tripp's new project? Specifically, who else might be involved?"

"I wish I could tell you more." Tammie closed her eyes and pressed on her forehead. "All I can say is Tripp was a person of integrity. He fought with his father about the palimony suit. He insisted on settling, rather than challenging his ex in court. Tripp cared about money as much as the next guy, but he was generous and fair."

"Was there bad blood between Tripp and his father?" Parrott wondered whether Tammie would show resentment against Tucker Anderson, as he had shown toward her.

"Not really. Tripp and his father disagreed about some things, but Tripp respected his father's business acumen, and he generally did whatever his father suggested. That's why he took the job with J.W. Sterling and came here. And that's why he accepted his role in his family business."

Parrott looked at Claire, whose eyes had glazed over. She was likely on painkillers, and he wouldn't blame her for nodding off during these questions about Tripp. He had one more question for Tammie, though. "How do *you* feel about Tripp's father?"

"I'm not a fan. I think Tripp was a better man than his dad, but I don't think he'd ever intentionally hurt his son. I'm sure both of Tripp's parents are distraught."

Soft clucks came from Claire, who had shifted her position. "Of course, Tripp's parents are distraught. I can't imagine anything worse than losing a child—or any worse way than through violence."

Taking the comment as a cue, Parrott directed his attention to Claire. "Speaking of violence, we need to talk about what happened to you last night."

Claire sat up straighter, adjusting her leg on the pillows. "What do you mean, violence? I turned my ankle on the uneven ground."

"I'm not talking about your ankle, exactly. Someone intentionally and maliciously disabled your golf cart. Whoever it was ensured that you would break down before you got home."

"What? How do you know this?" Claire pushed back against the end of the sofa and stood, prompting Tammie to fuss over her.

While she and Tammie thrashed out whether it was okay to stand, Parrott pulled up the cellphone photos of the disabled battery. Standing next to Claire, who said she would damn well stand whenever she felt like it, Parrott demonstrated how the battery cables had been disconnected, causing her to stall.

Claire made Parrott flip through the photos twice, before she plopped back onto the sofa, head in her hands. "So, you think someone knew I was at Robert's. Someone followed me there and tampered with the bolts on my battery while I was with Robert." Raising her head with a sigh, she said, "Whoever that someone is wanted to do harm to me. I was targeted."

"I'm afraid so, and that means you need to be extra careful from now on." Parrott retrieved and pocketed his phone. "I need you to help me find out who might have a grudge against you, who might want to hurt you."

Before Claire could answer, Aiko arrived at the doorway to the study with a large rectangular tray. "May I interrupt you for lunch? There's plenty for everyone."

Tammie crossed the room to assist in unloading the tray and placing the homemade sushi rolls, iced tea, and luscious-looking iced cookies onto the coffee table, along with the linen napkins and hand-painted cocktail plates for three.

"You'd think I'd have no appetite after hearing what you've just told me, detective, but Aiko's sushi makes my mouth water, no matter what. Please join us. You'll never have better sushi anywhere. Thank you for reading my mind, Aiko."

After a testimonial like that, how could Parrott refuse? He'd learned from previous cases that sometimes it was best to accept offers of food. Besides, the sushi smelled so fresh and the wasabi so pungent. His mouth watered, too.

Parrott was about to accept a plate and napkin from Tammie when Claire called out to the retreating Aiko. "Where did these pretty cookies come from? They don't look like any I've seen before."

Aiko returned to the group. "Someone left them in a bakery box on the back doorstep this morning. Maybe your friend Myrtle, the one who brings eggs from her hens?"

"Can't be Myrtle. She's out of town for a family reunion in Colorado. She won't be back until the end of the month."

Parrott shot out of his chair and grabbed the plate of cookies. "Sorry to spoil the party, but no one's going to eat these cookies. Aiko, do you still have the box they came in? I'm taking the cookies to the lab to test for poison."

CHAPTER SIXTY

While driving the decorated cookies to the lab at Chesco, Parrott reviewed the status of the case. He'd been dissatisfied with the pace of progress thus far. But now, with likely threats to Claire's life in the mix, an urgent drumbeat throbbed in his temples. He needed to act.

There was so little information to go on about Tripp Anderson. No computer, no cellphone, no known friends, or enemies. The guy took privacy to an extreme—unless Tammie and/or Tucker Anderson had been hiding information. Parrott wished he could subpoena Anderson's phone records, but with ample case law affirming the right to privacy, even for the dead, he wouldn't have a prayer.

Officer Barton had already taken Claire's golf cart to the crime lab. If that, or the cookies, revealed information about who had tried to harm Claire Whitman, this would constitute a major break, but why would the killer of Tripp Anderson have it in for Claire? These could be two unrelated cases, though Parrott didn't think so. At any rate, it might take several days to get answers from the lab.

Meanwhile, Parrott could think of only two new avenues for probing the barn victim's social life, the woman who sued him for palimony, and the Sigma Alpha Epsilon fraternity. Both might be pulling at straws, but he had to try.

Traffic was light on the highway this time of day. Parrott had cracked his windows to let the warm air whip across the top of his head in a cross-breeze. Somehow that helped him think.

The photo of Tripp Anderson with Wukitsch, Thornton, and Plummer replayed in Parrott's mind like an old country song. Factoring out Plummer, whose music engineering kept him out of the country most of the time, Parrott fixated on the others. A world of difference separated Wukitsch from Thornton— one was an unprivileged drug-addict, the other a polished, wealthy businessman. If Wukitsch carried the torch for Claire's granddaughter Bonnie, that might explain his going after Plummer, but not Anderson. After meeting Thornton in person, Parrott couldn't picture the financial planner being caught dead with his hands or his luxurious suit dirty, but Thornton's non-existent internet presence created a red flag.

Exiting the highway, Parrott followed a shiny, red Lamborghini that reminded him of Preston Phillips, the former treasury secretary and victim in Parrott's first murder case. That case had been equally convoluted, but he had managed to piece things together, and he would do it again.

In some ways, Pennington reminded Parrott of Preston Phillips. Both men had wealth, power, and, apparently, sex appeal. There were differences, too. Phillips had been almost two decades younger when he died of unnatural causes. Pennington was not a victim, but Parrott could categorize him as a person of interest. Pennington's support of Brock Thornton was suspicious. Did Brock Thornton have some hold over Pennington that would cause him to steer his closest friends and colleagues into investing with Thornton? How would that translate into killing a construction worker who also was engaged to Pennington's biological daughter? If Pennington had learned that Tripp Anderson was breaking with Tammie, would he kill Anderson out of revenge? While this seemed far-fetched, Parrott knew of murders committed for less provocation.

Tying Pennington to a plot to disable Claire's golf cart or to poison her with cookies was even less plausible. Pennington loved Claire, to quote Tammie, and his behavior and actions after the golf cart incident supported that. But what if the weekly meetings with Claire—or his duty to Tammie—had become an albatross. Poisoned cookies from an unknown stranger could be a convenient way to free himself of both obligations.

Parrott parked in the lot at Chesco and retrieved the bakery box of cookies from the trunk of his car. As he carried the potential evidence into the building, he paused his ruminations. One other suspect nagged at his attention like a torn cuticle. He would have to think about Herman Powell later.

CHAPTER SIXTY-ONE

laire's emotions had flown into turmoil at the suggestion that the delicious-looking cookies might be poisoned. "That's impossible. Why would anyone want to poison me?" She railed on at Parrott for jumping to conclusions, being overly cautious, treating her like a baby. Nevertheless, Parrott insisted on returning the cookies to the bakery box they came in, wrapping it in plastic, and loading it into his car to take to the lab for testing.

When Parrott returned to the study to say goodbye and to warn Claire and Tammie to keep all doors and windows locked and not to accept anything from strangers, Tammie joined in the fray. "Detective, you don't understand. People in Brandywine Valley leave little gifts on doorsteps all the time. It's the community vibe. We leave canned peaches, packets of potpourri, things like that on neighbors' porches throughout the year, and at Christmas, we deliver pizzelle cookies. Everyone knows they come from us."

Grateful for Tammie's explanation, Claire said, "So why don't you put back the cookies and have some lunch?"

"Let me ask you this," Parrott said, his penetrating eyes making Claire feel uncomfortable. "Which of your neighbors has given you decorated cookies before?"

Claire and Tammie exchanged looks, and Claire clutched her hand to her chest. "I can't remember any, but—"

"No buts. You need to trust me. I'm trying to protect you." Parrott reminded Claire of the sabotage to her golf cart. "Someone is trying to hurt you, and you can't take any chances." He hurried toward the door. "I'll be in touch, but I mean it. No unlocked doors—not even the garage door." Parrott made Tammie promise to call him if she or Claire needed anything at all.

Parrott's foreboding and sudden departure stripped Claire of her appetite and left her ankle throbbing. Turning to Tammie, she said, "Why don't you help yourself to sushi and take the rest into the kitchen. I'd like another pain pill and a nap."

"Time for an anti-inflammatory, too." Tammie handed both pills to Claire with a glass of iced tea. "I'll let you rest now. Glad I'll be here all weekend."

Claire swallowed the pills and nodded, watching Tammie close the drapes and turn off the lights. Claire would have loved nothing more than to fall asleep. She relaxed into the downy pillows and closed her eyes.

But sleep eluded her. Parrott had rattled her more than she wanted to admit. If he was right—if someone wanted to hurt her—there was little she could do, an elderly lady with a sprained ankle in a huge house with only two young ladies to watch out for her. Once Jessica found out—and she would—she would whisk Claire off to an assisted living place within a day. The thought of all she would lose—visits with Robert, Tammie, her independence—brought a wetness to her eyes that even the pain of her ankle hadn't.

She couldn't let that happen. She needed to think. What if the meth explosion in her bank barn hadn't been arbitrary? What if, instead of targeting Tripp, someone had been targeting her? And when that didn't change anything, the person followed her to Robert's and disabled her golf cart? And then dropped off poisoned cookies?

Why would anyone have anything against her? What did the person want from her? Her thoughts rolled back to before the conversion of the bank barn, when her husband Scott was still alive. Scott had been convinced the renovation would be a good investment.

Shortly after she'd agreed to the project, Scott had died. The bidding and awarding of contract to J.W. Sterling had been a blur. She'd been aware of other contractors who'd submitted competitive bids, but Robert had stepped in to advise her, recommending she change financial advisers and accept the Sterling bid. Had she been wrong to trust Robert these past several years?

The barn had turned out great, but now it was cinders and stone, detracting from the value of her property. Brock Thornton had made her a lot of money. According to the quarterly statements she received, the money she'd invested with him out-earned any of her other investments by far. Of course, she hadn't seen the actual earnings, except on paper, because she'd agreed to roll dividends into principal, another suggestion of Robert's.

She really needed to straighten out her finances now, especially since she wanted to build this nature reserve at Sweetgrass. Soon she might be too old and infirm to handle such a big project. Maybe she should stop relying on Robert, who was even older than she. She could ask her daughter Rebecca's husband Matt to help her sort things out, but that might compromise the secret that she and Robert had so carefully protected.

She was no closer to figuring out who might want to cause her harm, but the pills she'd taken were starting to kick in. Her last thought before she fell into a drugged sleep was, *Why does everything have to be so complicated?*

CHAPTER SIXTY-TWO

After dropping off the cookies at the lab at Chesco, Parrott was eager to get back to his office, but there was one big piece he needed to fill in before he sat down to organize his thoughts.

He detoured back to Unionville to pay another visit to Pennington. A few cars were parked in the driveway, and the afternoon sun above the trees dappled the stone walkway to the front door. The butler who answered the door rolled his eyes. Voices from inside indicated more activity than at Claire's, but Parrott imagined Pennington's wife required more care.

With no enthusiasm in his voice, the butler requested that Parrott wait on the doorstep while Mr. Pennington could be informed of his visit. Parrott didn't mind. He used the time to prepare for the interview, which could be tricky.

Pennington, himself, came to the door. His eyes were blearier, and the lines in his face deeper than last night. "Things are a bit dicey here. My wife isn't feeling well, and we're trying to locate her physician. How can I help you?"

"An emergency?" Parrott didn't want to come back later, but he would if need be. The voices from inside had increased in pitch and volume.

"No. Jacqueline takes a panoply of drugs for a variety of ailments. Sometimes the drugs interact and cause distressing reactions. That's what this is, I'm sure."

The words *distressing reactions* caused Parrott to jump out of his skin. "Have you called 911?" He motioned to gain entry to the house, and Pennington stepped aside.

"Calm down, detective. There's no need to call 911 yet."

Parrott was down the hall and into the large family room adjacent to the kitchen. The stench of sweat permeated the air. A wild-eyed woman threading gnarled hands through her reddish-brown hair writhed in a wheelchair, crying out in bursts of distress. "Ohhh, hot." An aide held a cloth to the woman's forehead, which was drenched in perspiration.

Parrott turned away from the sight, toward the coffee table where a wooden tray contained a used napkin, an empty teacup, and a plate half-full of decorated cookies.

By this time, Pennington had followed Parrott into the room and was standing nearby. Parrott waved his cellphone to get the man's attention. "I'm calling 911 immediately. I'll explain later."

As soon as Parrott was sure help was on the way, he fired off questions to Pennington and the two aides in the room. "Did anyone, besides Mrs. Pennington, eat the cookies on this tray?" "When did she eat them?" "Where did the cookies come from?"

Possibly because they were still in denial, the aides and Robert Pennington exchanged bewildered looks, but Parrott's urgency loosened their tongues. The consensus was that only Mrs. Pennington had eaten the cookies, just moments before Parrott's arrival. The cookies had been a gift, left on the back porch by a neighbor this morning.

Jacqueline continued to cry out and twist in her chair. Her face was contorted into an unnatural grimace.

Parrott demanded to see the box the cookies had come in, and one of the aides took him to the garbage can, where a white bakery box had been disassembled and thrown away. Parrott donned gloves and asked for a large plastic bag. "Don't anyone touch this box or the remaining cookies. I suspect poison."

"Poison?" Robert Pennington sat at the kitchen table, his face paler than the honeydew-colored walls. "What the hell's going on?"

Parrott examined the expressions on the faces of Robert and the person helping Parrott collect the evidence and preserve it in plastic. Genuine shock drew both faces into frowns, and the assistant's hands shook as he handed Parrott two gallon-sized zippered bags.

As Parrott eased the box and cookies into separate bags, the doorbell rang. Parrott darted to the door. He wanted to be the first to give information to the emergency crew.

"Detective Parrott?" the female paramedic recognized him from another case months earlier.

He glanced at her name tag, grateful not to have to take precious seconds to introduce himself. "Beth, I have reason to suspect Mrs. Pennington ingested poisoned cookies about fifteen minutes ago. If I had to guess, the poison is plant-based, monkshood." Tripp's poisoning by monkshood made this logical. "If you act quickly, maybe you can save her." Parrott grabbed Pennington, who had followed him into the entry hall. "Let's get out of their way."

"I won't interfere, but I need to be in the room. If Jacqueline dies—"

Parrott steered Pennington to a desk chair ten feet from where the two paramedics administered to Jacqueline. Parrott leaned against the desk, where he could speak directly to Pennington and view what was going on at the same time.

"How—how did you know that Jacqueline was poisoned? You hadn't even seen her." Pennington wrung his hands so hard the knuckles bulged. This man might love Claire Whitman, but he had strong feelings for his wife, too.

Choosing his words carefully, Parrott replied in a whisper. "I'll answer your question, but I have questions to ask you, also. Let's stay focused on your wife right now. Once she's out of danger, we can talk."

Pennington bowed his head, as if in prayer, while the retching sounds and smells continued. "What are they doing to her?" he asked.

Craning his neck, Parrott saw Beth ripping open a packet of black powder. "They took her vitals. Now it looks like they're administering a treatment."

"W-what kind of treatment?"

"My guess is activated charcoal. It can keep the poison from leaving the stomach and traveling through the bloodstream." Parrott took a deep breath. He said a silent prayer of thanks for being at Claire's before the cookies were consumed. He hoped Jacqueline would be saved, too.

After a half hour of monitoring, Jacqueline's cries softened, and the EMS workers moved away from her chair. Beth walked over to Parrott and Pennington, a curve in her lips and a dimple showing on one side. "I think we're in time. Blood pressure's high normal. Temperature's low, but not dangerously so. She needs to go to the hospital to be checked further. They'll probably keep her overnight."

"Should we take her in our van?" Pennington asked. "She won't understand being strapped to a gurney. That would frighten her."

"Our van accommodates wheelchairs," Beth said. "You can ride in the back with her if you want."

"Which hospital are we going to? Brandywine's closed. You aren't taking her all the way into Philadelphia, are you?"

Beth smiled. "Chester County's the closest. About twenty-five minutes away. Is that okay with you?"

Parrott clasped Pennington on the shoulder. "Tell you what. You ride in the ambulance with your wife, and I'll meet you at Chester. Once she's situated, we can talk, and if you're ready to come home, I'll give you a ride." Parrott hoped he wouldn't regret offering. Settling Jacqueline in a hospital room might take longer than Parrott wanted to stay. On the other hand, having extended, uninterrupted time with Pennington might reap huge benefits in solving the case.

Pennington's voice cracked. "How can I ever thank you? I hate to think of what might've happened if you hadn't rung the doorbell when you did."

"No need to thank me," Parrott said, putting a smile on his face. Of all the possible advantages a detective could have when working on a difficult case, having a grateful suspect was right at the top.

CHAPTER SIXTY-THREE

On the way to the hospital, Parrott stopped at Chesco to drop off the second bakery box and cookies. "Whatsa matter?" the desk clerk asked. "You gotta cookie monster out there?"

"Maybe so." Parrott thought of the furry blue cookie gobbler from his favorite childhood television program and wished this case could be that simple. "This time the person who ate the cookie is being hospitalized. Please put a rush on these."

"Will do, detective. The first batch is already in the queue. Look for a text with the results on both."

By the time Parrott strode into the emergency room entrance at Chester Hospital, Beth had completed the paperwork and was ready to take off. She waved to Parrott. "They're in a cubicle in the ER. Probably not for long. Patient's convulsing now."

Parrott thanked her and headed for the ER waiting room desk. He showed his badge, and the nurse assistant got a message to Pennington. A few moments later, she returned. "Mr. Pennington asked if you could wait a few minutes. They're about to take Mrs. Pennington to intensive care, and he doesn't want to leave her."

"Intensive care? Is her survival in jeopardy?"

"Not necessarily. The doctors want to give her the best supportive care possible to give her body time to recover from the insult. Intensive care is the best place to manage the types of support she needs."

"Okay. Thanks for your help." Parrott pointed to an empty vinyl love seat behind a low coffee table. "I'll be over there."

While he waited, he looked up monkshood on his phone. He'd read about it before, when he saw it in Tripp's autopsy report, but this time there was a living victim. *High in toxicity, the alkaloid plant can poison both the cardiological and neurological systems. There is no known antidote. Treatment options include minimizing the amount of toxin that reaches the bloodstream, monitoring for infection, and treating the symptoms.*

If Jacqueline had started convulsing, Parrott imagined there was still toxicity in her body. Pennington would likely not be allowed in intensive care except a few minutes a few times per day. The man would naturally be distressed, but Parrott needed him to talk, and none of them had the luxury of waiting. A potential serial killer was lurking in Brandywine Valley. The crimes were piling up. Something had spurred the killer into decisive, risk-taking action. Parrott was determined to bring this to a stop.

A few minutes later, a woman in scrubs summoned Parrott to the double doors, leading to the hallway. "We're taking Mrs. Pennington to ICU now. Mr. Pennington asked me to bring you. Poor man. He can really use the company."

Parrott followed the nurse to the spot where Jacqueline was being wheeled into the hallway. Pennington stood against the wall, a weary soldier before the real battle had even started. Parrott thought of how he would feel if Tonya were the patient. Not knowing whether she would live or die would be excruciating.

Touching Pennington's elbow in a gesture of support, Parrott gazed at the gurney. The woman was hooked up to IV fluids. Her pale green complexion contrasted with her reddish hair, and a sheen of perspiration covered her face. It was hard to tell whether she was breathing.

"Let's go, Pennington." The cart was already being pushed down the hall. "Your wife's in good hands. Let's stick with her and keep the positive energy flowing."

At the door to ICU, the transporter pointed Parrott and Pennington to the waiting room. Pennington would be relegated there until visiting time, a few hours away.

The waiting room was stale-smelling and almost empty this time of the afternoon. A woman and a young boy had staked out a corner, where toys and picture books were strewn about. The boy sat in his mother's lap, sleepy-eyed, listening to a story. The trash cans were full of used coffee cups and food wrappers, souvenirs from other worried relatives throughout the day. A television with no sound streamed the CNN banner across the bottom.

Pennington selected a spot near a window, where two upholstered chairs pushed up to a small table. "Let's sit over there." Outside, puffy clouds gave glimpses of blue that seemed at once ordinary and ethereal.

Before he sat, Parrott spied a small refrigerator with bottles of water. He pulled out two and carried them to the table. "Nothing like H-two-O to refresh your spirit."

Pennington opened his bottle and swigged. "Thanks. I really need this. I hope Jacqueline will be okay. They're giving her some heavy-duty drugs. If her oxygenation goes down any further, they're going to have to put her on a ventilator. I'm really frightened." He wiped his face with his hands. "I can't even think about what would have happened if you hadn't been there. I'm in your debt, Parrott."

"Glad I was there, too. Don't think of it as a debt, but I would like to ask you the questions I came to your house to ask, if you don't mind."

"Go ahead. Probably a good distraction." Pennington leaned his elbows on the table and made eye contact. "I'll do my best to help you."

"Okay. My first line of inquiry is about your relationship with Brock Thornton." A small flinch gave Parrott hope. "Other witnesses have told me when Thornton settled in Brandywine, you mentored him in establishing BMT. You referred clients to him. You helped spread the word about his services. You also invested a sizable amount of money with him, as well. Is that true?"

"I'd have to say that's accurate."

"I'm curious about that, Mr. Pennington. A successful businessman like you, entrusting not just money, but your reputation, your friends and neighbors, with a young guy—basically a stranger—why did you do that?"

Pennington stared at his hands on the table. "I'm an old man, detective. As you say, a successful one. Men don't arrive at this age and station in life without fetters—or secrets. Do you understand me?"

Parrott thought for a moment. He hadn't known many successful men, growing up, but many of the older men he'd encountered in the last several years—Elle's partner, Blake Allmond, for one—had borne complicated and painful secrets. "I know that secrets can break hearts and ruin lives. I've seen that happen. And right now, we're faced with murder and attempted murder. We don't have time for secrets."

The old man cringed. "I know. I'll tell you, but not without a good deal of shame. I hope this is for your ears only."

Parrott gave the standard assurance that he would not reveal anything unless he had to. Each time he uttered these words, he was struck by the enormity of the promise. The trust of a witness was sacred to him, even when the witness turned out to be a bad guy.

"When I was a young man, I had a buddy who practically grew up in my house. His father worked on one of the farms, so there was a big difference between our lifestyles and social status. Despite this, my parents encouraged the friendship. I suppose they felt Harvey's parents were good people, and they wanted me to have age-appropriate company.

"I won't bore you with the long and close history of our friendship, but to understand the rest, you need to know that I'd have given Harvey the shirt off my back, and vice versa. When we were seniors in high school, I was accepted to Yale, and Harvey was planning on going into the Marines. I felt sorry that Harvey wasn't going to college, but he wasn't envious. He often expressed pride in the fact that I was smart enough to be accepted to an Ivy League school."

Parrott couldn't see where this tale was headed, but he was impatient for Pennington to fast forward to present times. He couldn't sit here the rest of the evening with a killer out there.

As if reading Parrott's mind, Pennington skipped to the heart of the matter. "One night in August, two weeks before we would go our separate ways, Harvey and I decided to go into Philly and enjoy the night life together—no dates, no other buddies—just us.

We got pretty liquored up, and when it came time to drive home, we flipped a coin. The loser would have to drive."

Pennington's hands began to shake, whether from nerves or an ailment, Parrott couldn't tell. "Were you the loser?"

Pennington nodded. "It was late. We were both what my great-grandson would call wasted. Coming off I-95, I didn't see a guy changing his flat tire." He groaned, as if witnessing the tragedy all over again. "I was going fast. The impact was deadly."

This was a story Parrott had heard many times before, but the pain of telling was always the same—devastating. He responded in a whisper. "Did you stop to render aid?"

"We stopped. The man was clearly gone, but we stayed there until someone could summon the police. That was way before cellphones, so it took some time." Pennington clenched his jaw. "Hitting the man and his car sobered us up fast. Harvey always had more common sense than I did. I stood on the pavement, doubled over and screaming. He shook me by the shoulders and said, 'Listen. *I* was the one driving the car. You hear me? *I* lost the coin toss, *I* got stuck driving, and *I* caused the collision.'

"I couldn't understand why he was shouting at me, why he wanted to lie. But then he said, 'You've got a brilliant future ahead of you. I don't. Whatever the consequences, I'll be able to handle them.'" Tears rolled down the grooves in Pennington's wrinkled cheeks, and his breathing was heavy.

"I don't know why I let him take the rap for me. I've hated myself every day since. Harvey did jail time for manslaughter, and I went to Yale and became a rich and famous television magnate."

Parrott imagined what a burden this secret had been. "Did you keep in touch with Harvey?"

"I tried, but he wanted nothing to do with me. His family was crushed. They left Brandywine. Eventually I lost track of Harvey completely."

Trying to put this story into the context of the question he'd asked, Parrott asked, "So, what was Harvey's last name?"

The hoarse reply came quickly. "Harvey's last name was Thornton. Brock Thornton is his grandson."

CHAPTER SIXTY-FOUR

"That's it," Pennington said, after spilling his story about Harvey Thornton. "Now you know the secret I've been sitting on for almost seventy years. Nobody knows—not my wife, not my kids, not even Claire."

"Knowing it could make a difference in solving this case before someone else dies," Parrott said. "But I'm glad you mentioned Claire, because I need to ask you some questions about your connection with her."

Pennington crossed his arms and shuddered, but before he could reply, an attendant came to get him. "Mr. Pennington, you can come visit your wife for twenty minutes now."

The old man's knees popped when he stood, and he took a moment to steady himself. "You can ask Claire about our connection. I think I've told you enough secrets for one day." He started for the doorway to ICU and turned back. "No need for you to stay here, detective. I'll call my chauffeur to come get me. More important for you to go back to work and save people's lives."

Parrott was itching to go back to the office, but what happened to Mrs. Pennington had raised the stakes, and he worried about Claire and anyone else who might have received cookies. He checked for a text from the crime lab—nothing yet. Pennington's words, "You can ask Claire about our connection," echoed in his ears. His car almost drove itself back to Sweetgrass.

When he arrived, he found Claire sitting at the desk in her study, her leg propped on an ottoman, poring over spreadsheets and printouts.

"I didn't expect to see you working," he said. "How's the ankle?"

Claire removed the half-glasses from her nose and set them on the desk. "It is what it is, detective. I can't let a sprained ankle keep me from what I must do. I'm going to convert my property into a nature reserve. Others have done similar things, working with the Brandywine Conservancy." She pointed to the chair opposite her. "Please sit."

"Sounds ambitious," Parrott said, easing himself into the chair. He was at once impressed by Claire's chosen goal and her ability to achieve it. He hadn't met many octogenarians who were that smart and capable.

"Don't know about ambitious, but it is complicated. Since I'm grounded with a bum ankle, I might as well take advantage of 'desk time.' I've sent Tammie upstairs. That poor girl needs more rest than I do. She's taken on too much responsibility for me. Blames herself for what happened."

"She seems very fond of you."

"And I am quite fond of her." Claire brushed her palms against one another, as if to signal a change of subject. "Personally, I think both you and she have over-reacted. Golf carts break down sometimes." She frowned. "What about the cookies?"

She didn't know about Jacqueline. Parrott didn't typically share information, but at this point he gave in to the urgency pressing against his temples. Claire needed to know how serious a threat she might be faced with. "No lab report yet, but you should know that Jacqueline Pennington ate cookies from a similar box, found on her doorstep, and she's in ICU right now."

Claire stared at Parrott and blinked. "You aren't kidding."

"No, I'm not. I've just come from the Chester County Hospital. Mr. Pennington is still there. Hopefully they'll be able to save her."

"Could've been me. I would've eaten a cookie, too, if you hadn't swept them away." Her hands flew to her temples, rubbing them slowly. "Poor Robert. I should contact him later."

"I think he'll be tied up at the hospital for quite a while." Parrott leaned forward, elbows on his thighs. "In fact, I was questioning Mr. Pennington before they called him in to see his wife. I asked him about the relationship between the two of you, how you happened to become so close."

Claire's lips curved into a smile that was at once coquettish and shy. "What did he say?"

"He told me to ask you." Parrott watched as Claire's face hardened. "I wouldn't ask if I didn't think it was important."

"I don't see how—"

"Look," Parrott said, raising his voice more than he'd intended. "We're dealing with a murderer. I'm not here to play games with you or anybody else. The relationship between you and Mr. Pennington could be central to this person's motive. Whoever disabled your golf cart knows that you were at Pennington's."

The sharp look from Claire's crystal blue-green eyes could have slit open wounds. "Robert and I have known each other all our lives. We grew up as neighbors, and we grew old as neighbors. *Entertaining with Elegance* was a ModCom television show. I never would have had that opportunity had it not been for Robert. Anything else is nobody's business, yours included. I'm already regretting that you know about our weekly meetings."

Parrott could understand Claire's reluctance to take him further into her confidence. Brandywine was a small, close community, and there were those who would judge the two lovers for their adulterous relationship, regardless of the circumstances. "I assure you, as I assured Mr. Pennington, I will not reveal anything that I learn about your relationship, including what I already know, unless I absolutely have to. All I'm interested in is serving and protecting this community."

Claire sat perfectly still, her arms folded across her chest. She appeared to be thinking, and Parrott gave her time. Finally, she leaned forward and whispered. "I don't know what you're thinking about Robert and me. We aren't bad people. We haven't done anything wrong. That's all I'm prepared to say."

As much as Parrott liked Claire Whitman, he was becoming exasperated with her cat and mouse game. He'd had enough. "Listen. I've promised you I'll be discreet. I've explained why I need to know. If you won't tell me whatever secrets you and Robert Pennington are hiding, I'll leave here and go see Judge Manetti. I'll get a subpoena, and you'll have to tell me in front of the Grand Jury. One way or another, I need to find out. And I need to find out soon, because yours and his and Jacqueline's lives are at risk." Parrott stood and pounded the desk with his knuckles. "What'll it be? Tell me now or tell me later, but you *will* tell me."

Claire shrunk into her chair, all shoulders and elbows and elevated foot. Her eyes and upper lip glistened with moisture. She pushed away from the desk in a clumsy attempt to stand. "If I could, I would stand up and run away from you, detective. I know you're doing your job, but you've put me in an intolerable position. Certain things—if I tell you—could hurt people I love, people Robert loves. You give me no choice but to trust you with an age-old secret that nobody knows, except Robert and me. Scotty knew, too. He's the one who impressed upon us never to tell."

The crack in the armor encouraged Parrott. "Go on."

"Close the door. I wouldn't want Aiko to overhear a word."

Parrott padded to the door and closed it as soundlessly as possible. When he returned to Claire's desk, she motioned him to pull his chair closer. Parrott prepared to hear another secret, marveling at how cases unfolded in their own time—sometimes going days or weeks without significant progress, sometimes revealing big clues one after another. An hour ago, he'd learned about Pennington's support of Brock Thornton. Now he would learn another of Pennington's secrets.

Claire leaned forward, so far that her upper body appeared to graze the top of the desk, and her chin rose to point at Parrott's face. The effect was that of a witch, ready to share the recipe for her magic brew. "This year," she said, "my personal assistant, Tammie, will turn thirty-five. Tripp Anderson was the love of her life. They had planned to marry."

This was not a revelation for Parrott, and, unsure how Tammie's age and relationship to the murder victim played into Claire's relationship with Robert, he nodded. He reminded himself that Pennington was Tammie's biological father.

"Anderson's death has been a terrible shock for Tammie, but also a tremendous disappointment to Robert and me. We had hoped that Tammie would marry and start a family. Tripp Anderson was Tammie's first serious romantic attachment. I fear it may have been her last."

"All the more reason to bring Tripp's killer to justice," Parrott said. "To give Tammie and Tripp's parents some closure." Even as he said the words, Parrott realized how simplistic they were. Whoever killed Anderson and burned the barn had also, most likely, paid Wyatt to disable Charlie. The same person may have sabotaged Claire's golf cart, causing her to sprain her ankle. And delivered poisoned cookies to Sweetgrass and ModCom Way. Was Tammie's lost romance germane to all this? "I know Mr. Pennington is Tammie's biological father."

"Did Robert tell you that? He freely admits having had a brief relationship with Tammie's mother. He provided child support for the first eighteen years of Tammie's life."

"I believe I heard it first from your daughter Jessica. I'm sure Tammie's life has been enriched, knowing her parentage and being supported by her successful father."

Claire's features drew inward, part squint, part pout. "Jessica has always been jealous of Tammie. Her jealousy is, in my opinion, unfounded and irrational. Nevertheless, Jessica is one of the reasons we've had to keep quiet about Tammie."

"I don't understand," Parrott said. "Why would Jessica mind that Robert Pennington lent support to his biological daughter?"

Claire drew a breath and exhaled with a sigh. "Because— Tammie is not actually Robert's biological daughter."

"Now I'm really confused."

"Robert claimed paternity to protect Tammie's real father—"

"—Who is?"

Claire clasped her hands together so tightly that the joints creaked. "Tammie's real father is Robert's son, Bobby. No one knows this—not Tammie, not Bobby, not Jacqueline, nobody."

"But if Bobby had an affair with Tammie's mother, surely—"

"The mother Tammie lives with, grew up with, is not Tammie's biological mother. Tammie was given up for adoption to Maya Caballero. Bobby has no idea that his father's so-called 'love child' is actually Bobby's own offspring."

Parrott couldn't imagine why Pennington would damage his own reputation to cover for his son's wild oats. Wouldn't it have been simpler to give the baby up for adoption, perhaps in another state, then seal the records of her parentage? Thirty-five years ago, that was done all the time. "Why—?"

"Bobby was only sixteen and never knew he'd impregnated Tammie's mother. Robert didn't want to chance having Bobby's future compromised. Robert has always had a lot of influence. Maya was only too willing to raise Tammie as her daughter. She was paid handsomely and raised her with love. No one was any the wiser that Tammie was Robert's granddaughter, instead of his daughter."

Parrott digested the story for a moment. Combined with the story about Pennington's connection to Brock Thornton's grandfather, and his clandestine relationship with Claire, Pennington had woven an intricate web of lies in his lifetime. "What about Tammie's biological mother?"

Claire uttered a soft cry. "Ah, detective. That is the hardest question to answer. Tammie's mother is my daughter. Rebecca gave birth to Tammie at the age of fifteen. So, you see, Tammie is *my* granddaughter, too."

CHAPTER SIXTY-FIVE

B y the time Parrott returned to his office, all was quiet.
Chief Schrik was long gone, and the cleaning crew had
left his office smelling sweetly antiseptic. This was
Parrott's favorite time to organize his thoughts. While he made a
pot of coffee in the break room, he reviewed what Pennington had
told him about Brock Thornton. Originally, he'd said he met him
at a candy store, obviously a cover story.

Then there was the cover story that Pennington had fathered
Tammie Caballero, when really his son Bobby had been the father.
Parrott wondered whether being rich and famous had forced
Pennington to craft falsehoods, or the other way around. Either
way, both Pennington and Claire would have complicated issues
when it came to writing their wills. Substantial bequests to Tammie
would likely raise questions among the legitimate heirs. Parrott
was glad he and Tonya wouldn't have such problems, although a
twinge ran through his gut at the thought of their having no family,
except a cockatiel, to inherit their money.

Carrying his thermos of strong coffee, Parrott returned to his
desk. He pulled a brand-new legal pad from the bottom drawer.
He drew a circle in the center of the page and wrote, "Tripp
Anderson" inside. Beneath the name he made notes—palimony,
fraternity tattoo, construction, new project. He drew a vertical
line below the circle. He would list any positive relationships of
Tripp's on the left, any negatives on the right. He listed Tammie
and Tripp's father on the left. He couldn't think of anyone who
had a grudge against Tripp to list on the right, except for Tripp's
former girlfriend, but, according to Tammie, Tripp had paid her off.

While he pondered how a young man with no enemies could have met with such a violent and malicious end, Parrott's cellphone rang. "CC Forensic Lab" came up on the caller ID.

"Detective Parrott? Juan at the lab. Your cookies were tainted with poison, both sets."

Parrott sucked in a deep breath. "Sorry to hear that, but no surprise. Was it monkshood?"

"Yeah. Aconite. You said someone ate one?"

"She's in ICU now." Parrott wanted to scream with frustration. Tripp's death and the meth explosion had been bad enough, but two boxes of poisoned cookies had elevated this case beyond a single murder and arson. Not to mention the tampering with the battery of Claire's golf cart. "Let me call over there and tell them."

"Okay. I'll send you the report by email. The cookies will be held in evidence."

Now that the poison was confirmed, Parrott hoped for prints on the bakery boxes and/or golf cart. He disconnected and called the hospital. He went through three people before reaching a nurse's station in ICU, where he checked on Jacqueline's condition, very grave, and left a message for the doctors that, as suspected, the patient had ingested aconite.

Back to his legal pad, Parrott drew a circle and wrote Claire's name inside. For notes, he wrote, "Mother, grandmother, employer, hostess, lover, landowner." *What was it Claire had been working on at her desk? Turning her property into a nature reserve?* He wrote, "Nature reserve."

Sophomore year in high school, Parrott's English teacher had shown the class how to use graphic organizers to clarify thinking. Parrott had excelled in designing the best depiction for every task, and those skills had carried over into his work. Parrott always drafted his organizers using pencil and paper. The tactile-kinesthetic activity surged from his hand to his brain in a fluid, visceral motion that he couldn't explain in words or numbers. For many of his cases, the Venn diagram had worked to provide insights into the connections among people, both victims and suspects.

Now, the Venn wasn't working. Tripp had too few connections, and Claire had too many. Parrott flipped to the next page and started a standard graph with names of suspects on the rows and the topics: means, opportunity, and motive on the columns. The people he listed were: Claire, Tammie, Robert, Charlie, Wyatt, Brock. Then he added Jessica, Bonnie, Bonnie's boyfriend Ray, Tucker Anderson II, and Herman.

Before filling in any of the spaces, he scanned the page into his computer and printed three copies. He then titled each of the four pages with a crime/intended victim—poisoning of Tripp/Tripp, explosion of barn/Tripp or Claire, disabling of golf cart/Claire, and poisoned cookies/Claire, Tammie, Robert, Jacqueline. He spent the next hour plugging in whatever information or evidence he had against each person in each of the crimes.

When he had completed the task, he was able to eliminate several people from his suspect list. For example, Tripp's father may have disliked Tammie, and he may have been disappointed in his son's choice of Tammie as a partner, but he had no reasonable motive to harm anyone, and he had been in North Carolina when each of the incidents occurred. Bonnie's boyfriend Ray had stayed in the barn whenever he came to town, so why would he have wanted to destroy it? Also, he had been out of the country at the times of these crimes.

Gulping the hot coffee, Parrott examined the rest of the rows. Bonnie's columns had very little information of importance. As Claire's granddaughter, she might share her mother's suspicion of or animosity toward Tammie, but Parrott hadn't picked up on that in his interactions with her, and he couldn't see her harming her grandmother.

Jessica, Bonnie's mother, was a different story, mainly because of the letter she'd delivered to the police station about Tammie. Even if Jessica didn't know that Tammie was her niece, and might dilute her inheritance, she apparently blamed Tammie for Scott Abramson's death and suspected her of manipulating Claire. Jessica might have done harm to Tammie, but Parrott couldn't imagine she would want to harm her own mother—unless she wanted to hasten her inheritance. He wondered whether Jessica and Rebecca knew about Claire's plans to turn Sweetgrass into a nature reserve. Parrott left her on the list of suspects, but not very high.

Next, he studied the columns next to Herman's name. Parrott's stomach turned at the thought of Herman's being a suspect in a murder case. What would that mean for his mother? While he didn't want to suspect Herman, the man did know his way around Brandywine Valley. He was industrious enough to figure out how to poison someone, how to create a meth explosion, and how to disable a golf cart. His motive was thin, but maybe he wanted revenge against Claire for not accepting his bid to renovate the barn. What made Herman most suspicious was his steadfast support of Brock Thornton.

Keeping Herman on the list of suspects, Parrott turned to the financial advisor. Why had Brock Thornton pushed so hard to get Parrott to invest with him, and then closed the option without warning? Maybe he'd discovered Parrott's occupation and backed off. Why was there no history of Brock Thornton? Could he be dodging his family background because of his grandfather's prison time? Based on the photo from the construction party at Claire's, Thornton at least had met Tripp Anderson, and he lived near all the crimes.

The others: Claire, Tammie, Robert, Charlie, and Wyatt all were heavy on means and opportunity, light on motive. Wyatt was an obvious suspect for the meth explosion because of his drug addiction, as well as his role in tying his father up. On the other hand, Wyatt's story about being hired to do that by an anonymous person had been supported by the videos. Parrott reviewed the names on the list with the memory of the size and shape of that hooded and masked figure. Possibles were Tammie, Charlie, Brock, Jessica, and Herman. It was hard to imagine Claire as a murderer or arsonist, but what if she and Pennington had conjured a plan to poison Jacqueline? What better way to deflect suspicion than to have them delivered to herself, as well as to the Penningtons? She and Robert would have known not to eat the cookies.

Parrott finished his coffee and slid his charts into a folder, which he locked in his bottom desk drawer. The exercise had been helpful in suggesting next steps. He still had missing information to fill in, and he'd need to act fast to find it. He had a hunch Tripp's killer was panicking, ready to kill again. Parrott had to make sure that didn't happen.

CHAPTER SIXTY-SIX

Even in the heat of summer, Parrott loved driving with his car windows down. Growing up, he'd always thought of that as the poor man's convertible. Now he could afford the real thing, but why pay for a new car, when the wind slapping his face through the open windows was pure delight?

Lightning bugs dotted the yards of the neighborhoods he passed on his way home. The time he'd spent sorting out his suspect list had gone past the dinner hour, and he was eager to get home to Tonya and Horace.

First, he needed to make a phone call, hoping his mother hadn't already gone to bed. He raised the windows and turned on the air conditioner in his Toyota. He used the car's voice command to call without taking hands off the steering wheel. He hoped Herman wouldn't be with her.

"Ollie. Herman and I were just talking about you. We've been watching *All Rise*, and Herman thinks J. Alex Brinson favors you. He's from Philadelphia, you know." Parrott had to admit, his mother's voice had a genuine lilt to it ever since Herman had come into the picture. "By the way, you're on speaker."

Herman's voice boomed in the background. "Tell Ollie he should think about a career in Hollywood when he retires from detective work. He'd be a natural for these legal dramas."

Parrott apologized to himself for the lie he was about to tell. "Thanks for the compliment, both of you. But, hey, were you guys together last night from, say, five-thirty till about eight?"

"We sure were, son. We were helping with the Thursday night potluck at church. Why?"

Relieved that Herman had an alibi for the time when Claire's golf cart had been disabled, Parrott breathed easier. "I tried to call you off-and-on that whole time. Kept getting, 'Your call cannot be completed as dialed.' Maybe something wrong on my end."

"Hm. I didn't get no missed calls. Why were you calling?"

"Mainly to tell you Tonya's looking at a house in West Chester. She was going to check it out today with Elle."

"That would be wonderful, son. Did she like what she saw?"

"I don't know yet. On my way home now."

"Well, let us know. I'd love to see you two settled in a larger house, and—well, someday—"

Parrott could complete the sentence, but he didn't want to. As long as Tonya was struggling with PTSD, having children was a taboo topic. "I gotta go now. I'm almost home."

Herman shouted in the background, "Don't forget, I'm available to check out any house you kids are interested in."

Tonya was on the phone with her therapist when Parrott walked in. She gave him a quick hug, pointed toward the stove, and scurried toward the bedroom. "Sorry, Alice. My husband just came in.... No, I'm going into another room."

This late, and Tonya's having a therapy session? Something either very good or very bad must have happened. A flapping of wings and squawks of, "Mwah, mwah," caused Parrott to grin. Horace, at least, was ecstatic to see him.

Parrott dashed to the cage to let the frenetic bird out. The little guy flew around the room twice, finally landing on Parrott's shoulder. "I missed you, too, buddy. Let's see what's here to eat." He sauntered to the stove, careful not to dislodge Horace, who was now rubbing his head against Parrott's cheek. A dinner plate sat on the stovetop, covered by a napkin. He peeked under it to find a slab of meat loaf, a mound of macaroni and cheese, and a pile of green beans. The aroma of homemade comfort food caused Parrott to salivate. All that thinking had made him ravenous.

He walked Horace to his plush toys and told him to play. The bird flew from Parrott's shoulder onto a swing, singing, "Oh, boy," as he launched into an impressive gliding arc.

After heating up his dinner in the microwave and grabbing a cold beer, Parrott sat at the table, alone, but not lonely. Tonya's voice carried through the walls in unintelligible murmurs. Whatever she was sharing with Alice, Parrott believed some good would come of it. Compared to a year ago, Tonya had made progress, even if slow. Parrott was grateful that the VA hospital provided such a quality therapist. There weren't many who would conduct sessions by phone this late on a Friday.

Horace did his tricks while Parrott chowed down. Not wanting to bother Tonya, who was still talking in the other room, Parrott picked up his cellphone and called Claire.

She answered in a groggy voice. Other voices in the background suggested the television was on.

"Hope I'm not waking you," Parrott said.

"Of course not. I'm not part of the dinner-at-five, bed-by-nine set yet. What can I do for you, detective?"

"Call it a wellness check. All the doors and windows locked?"

"That's standard operating procedure here, Parrott. But why? Has something happened that I don't know about?"

"Only that the cookies tested positive for poison, the same poison that killed Tripp Anderson." Parrott let his voice linger on the last syllable, hoping Claire would draw the right conclusion without his having to spell it out.

"Oh, no. Poor Jacqueline. Has anyone heard how she's doing?"

"Last I heard she's alive, but still very ill. Aconite is a deadly poison. She'll have a rough recovery, assuming she does." He paused. "The point is, you need to be very careful. Don't let anyone in and be careful about what you bring into the house. Do you have this number on your contacts list?"

Claire's voice was groggy no more. "I'm sure I do. I'll double check when we get off."

"Good. Keep your phone next to you at all times and call me if you have the slightest concern about anything, day or night. I don't mean to scare you, but if you call me, I'll drop everything and come." Horace chose that moment to shriek, "Mwah, mwah."

"What was that?" Claire asked, laughing. "Sounds like kissing."

"Just my bird, Horace. He's an affectionate fellow."

"Haha. Parrott has a parrot!" Claire's laughter apparently drew attention, because Claire said, "It's Detective Parrott."

Annoyed that Horace had undermined what he'd intended to be a serious phone call, Parrott said, "If that's Tammie, be sure to tell her what I said—lock up, be on guard, and call me."

"All right, I'll tell her." Her voice still exuded mirth. "Don't worry. I'm taking your instructions seriously, and I appreciate your trying to protect me, Detective Parrott with a parrot."

Tonya emerged from the bedroom, holding a box of tissues in one hand and a ball of used ones in the other.

Parrott spoke into the phone. "I have to go now. Hope you have a good night's sleep. Oh, and by the way, he's not a parrot. He's a cockatiel."

"Who was that?" Tonya asked, sniffling. She set the tissues down on the kitchen counter. She nuzzled into Parrott's arms.

"The woman whose barn blew up, Claire Whitman." He squeezed his arms around his wife's waist, then pulled back. "Never mind that. Do you want to tell me what's going on with you?"

Tonya took Parrott's hand and led him to the sofa. They sat in the usual positions for when they had something important to discuss, Parrott in the corner, Tonya next to him, but seated at an angle, so she could look into his eyes. The warmth of her bent knee and calf against the side of his thigh was reassuring.

Taking a deep breath and exhaling with a sigh, Tonya said, "This morning Elle and I went to that house I told you about in West Chester. It was stunning, every bit as pretty as the one in Malvern, but not so expensive. Five bedrooms, four baths, a gym in the basement, and an outdoor pool. Hope to go back with you tomorrow or Sunday."

Parrott remained silent, but he took Tonya's hand in his. There would be much more to this story.

"The realtor was excellent, not pushy at all. When he was showing us the bedrooms, he made the comment this would be a perfect home for a family with young children. The schools are excellent, beautiful parks nearby—you know. I didn't reply, but I wondered why he would say those things to me, when he knows we don't have kids.

"Afterwards, Elle and I went out for lunch, and that comment was still sticking in my craw. I asked Elle how she felt, living in a huge mansion basically just her and LeRoi."

Parrott nodded. "Elle is a good person to ask. What did she say?"

"You know Elle. She sees through me. She said, 'I know why you're asking. The agent's mention of children.' She reached across the table for my hand and said, 'I'll answer your question, but first I want to say your situation is a lot different from mine. You're young and healthy, and you have a good marriage.'"

Parrott squeezed his wife's hand. He was beginning to see how this conversation could set her off.

"Elle said, 'I never expected to have children. That was one of the sacrifices I made when I entered the convent. By the time I met Blake and left, I was past child-bearing years. So, I never considered motherhood in the traditional sense. As for being alone in the house with LeRoi, I'm totally fine with it. I'm surrounded there by art and history and memories, and I enjoy sharing the property with house guests and the special people of Don Guanella. A home can be a home with or without children. You must decide for yourself.'"

Parrott and Tonya had never talked seriously about having children before. Part of him was elated that the subject had come up without his prompting, but the other part dreaded what might come of it. Secretly, he'd always hoped to have a family. "So that set you to thinking?"

"Uh-huh, thoughts I didn't want to be thinking. Remember when we first married, how I had nightmares almost every night? And I told you something bad happened in Afghanistan that I could never talk about?"

Parrott stared at Tonya's hand. He drew imaginary circles in the palm, hoping to release the pain inside his wife's heart. He would never press her on that.

"The trauma from that incident has kept me from even thinking about having kids. I never wanted to disappoint you—or your mother, but—" Tonya's eyes shone with incipient tears.

"You aren't a disappointment, honey. Don't ever think that."

"Well, the point is, I came home and put in a call to Alice. I planned to schedule an appointment to talk about all this. She called me back after hours, and when I told her about the house, the comment about kids, and how this incident was hindering me from dealing with the idea of having kids, she insisted on talking it through tonight, on the phone."

"I hope it was helpful," Parrott said.

"When you came in, I was telling Alice what happened that night in Afghanistan. I've never been able to put it into words, but I suddenly realized talking about it might break the spell. The incident has held power over me for too long. Can you understand?"

Parrott hugged his wife and stroked her between the shoulder blades, where tension had formed a tight knot. "Of course, I understand. We all have our demons."

Tonya pressed her cheek against Parrott's chest and clutched him around the waist with both arms. "Well, now I want to tell you what happened that night. Alice asked me if I could trust you with it, and I know I can. Just hold me like this and let me talk."

Horace had flown back into his cage, and the whole house was still as Tonya began her story. She told of a special operation in which she was the only female. The leader of an Arab terrorist group, Rakan al-Gamdhi, had been located. He was in hiding with his wife and two daughters. Intel said he was preparing to escape that night. Transport to Kabul and then to Pakistan was already in place. The Navy had paid dearly for this tip, and they had to act fast, or he would elude them as he had before.

"There were six of us in a helicopter, and I was co-pilot. Five guys and me. We landed in the pitch black about a mile from where a terror cell was supposed to be. We moved as quickly and quietly as we could, and we surrounded the place. It was little more than a hut pushed up against the side of a mountain. It was supposed to be a peaceful grab—surprise the target, cuff him, and take him back for 'treatment.'

"It all went surprisingly well. No screaming, no fuss. The target looked scared but resigned to being caught. The problem, though, happened before we took him away."

"What happened?"

"The guy's family. Wife and daughters. Two pretty, young girls, maybe twelve and thirteen. They were curled up on mats on the ground, two peas in a pod. They were just lying there—"

A sob flew from Tonya's lips like a speeding train from a tunnel, low and long. "Al-Gamdhi turned his back to bid farewell to his wife and daughters."

"As he hugged them, he slid a sharp knife deep into each of their throats. They died without a cry." Tears flowed from Tonya's eyes now, yet she was oddly composed. "He tried to kill himself with the same knife, but two of the SEALs stopped him. The mission was a success. We were praised for our bravery.

"But I've never felt brave, or proud, not a single day since. I watched two innocent girls being slaughtered like chickens. I don't know how a parent who creates a life can take that same life and destroy it.

"I'm ashamed of my weakness, my inability to handle this. Many people doubt a woman's capacity for serving in these types of situations, and I never thought I'd succumb. But the girls on their mats, so sweet and peaceful in their last moments of life, have haunted me ever since."

Parrott brushed his lips against the top of Tonya's head. "I'm glad you've shared this with me. Maybe I can help you carry the weight."

Tonya pulled her head back to gaze into her husband's eyes. "That's what Alice told me. She's wanted me to tell her and you for a long time. Now I've done it." She sighed, and the sound carried the weight of the burden. "Do you understand, Ollie? This is why I'm afraid to have kids. Whenever I look at our babies, I'm afraid I'll see the faces of those dead little girls."

CHAPTER SIXTY-SEVEN

Parrott soothed Tonya as best he could. As a police officer, he'd been trained in techniques for calming angry or distraught people, but none of the protocols applied to this personal situation. He was winging it, but Tonya did respond to his drawing her a hot bath with infusions of chamomile and lavender. He sat on the side of the tub and washed her back.

When she emerged from the tub, he wrapped her in the soft, oversized bath sheet she had given him when they were dating. "This is to comfort you after a hard day," she'd said. Parrott decided this day would qualify.

"I'm really exhausted," Tonya said in a murmur from inside the velvety towel. "Would you mind going to bed now?"

Parrott was exhausted, himself. "I can't think of anything I'd rather do." He took care of Horace's needs, turned off the lights, and joined his wife in bed. Within minutes, Tonya was asleep, and Parrott lay next to her, inhaling her goodness and matching her breathing with his own.

Tonya didn't stir when Parrott's cellphone rang in the next room. He sprang out of bed and darted to the counter to answer before it woke her. The kitchen clock said eleven-ten.

"Detective, I hope I'm not waking you." Tammie's distinctive musical voice had lost some of its lilt, but Parrott recognized it all the same, and the edginess told him something was up.

"No worries. What can I do for you, Tammie? Is Claire okay?"

"She's fine. Sleeping on the sofa. She's had a hard day. You asked me to call you if I learned anything important. I think I might have. Can you come over? There's something I need to show you."

Parrott rubbed his eyes. He considered asking Tammie to tell him over the phone, but she had said, "Show you," and that could mean evidence. This case merited in-person responses, and Parrott didn't want to take shortcuts based on his own convenience. "I'll be there in about fifteen, twenty minutes."

He dressed and left a note for Tonya, though he doubted she would wake anytime soon. At the last minute before leaving the house, he strapped a back-up pistol on his ankle. He slipped out the door and into his car.

The middle-of-the-night drive to Sweetgrass with the windows down reminded him of the first one, when the bank barn was burning. That drive had started the case, and perhaps this one would end it. His pulse pounded with his thoughts about what Tammie might have found.

When he drew near to the front of the house, he detoured onto the path leading to Charlie's cottage. He parked on the side of the road past a curve and next to a small hillock covered with vegetation. He hiked back to Claire's front door, hoping these precautions would amount to overzealousness on his part. As prearranged, he knocked on the front door four times, and Tammie let him in quickly, locking the door behind him.

Tammie was wearing the same jeans and denim shirt she'd worn earlier. A headband held her hair back, revealing a resemblance to Claire in the forehead and eyes. Or maybe the privileged knowledge about Tammie's parentage had colored Parrott's perception.

"Let's go to the kitchen. I've set everything up for you there, and I don't want to disturb Ms. Whitman's sleep."

As before, when Claire had gone missing in her golf cart, Tammie's cellphone sat on the kitchen table. Next to it were several packages of photos and a magnifying glass. Parrott sat catercorner from Tammie and waited.

Tammie turned on her phone and tapped on the texts. "I've turned myself inside out, trying to think of something Tripp might have said, anything about his 'new project' might have been." She scrolled through, looking for a particular date. "I asked him, but he never explained. I went through all his text messages from the

last few months. Here's what I found on the first day of June." She
handed the phone over.

Parrott peered at the messages:

Can't wait to spend more time together.

How long of a project?

Depends. Frateri ad infinitum.

What?

*Nothing. I've been in touch with an old friend. Could be
anywhere from a week to months. Maybe you can come back with
me after.*

Maybe.

Nothing jumped out at Parrott, except the Latin phrase.
Brothers to infinity. He let that roll around in his mind, while he
kept scrolling.

"That's the only part I wanted to show you. Seemed odd.
Tripp never talked like that."

"Nevertheless, I'd like to borrow your phone. I might find
something else meaningful."

Tammie nodded. "Keep it. I'll use Ms. Whitman's. Looks like
she's going to need me every day for a while."

Parrott pocketed the phone and asked, "What's next?"

Before she could answer, a scraping sound coming from
outside the kitchen window startled them both. Parrott's hand flew
to his ankle before he rushed to look out the window. "Did you
hear that?"

Tammie had jumped from her seat and rushed to the back
door, making sure it was double-locked. "It might have been an
animal—a bird or a racoon. Sometimes they hit against windows
when they're hunting for food."

Parrott looked out onto the shrubbery and landscape. Seeing
nothing, he asked Tammie to turn off the outside light and lock
the kitchen door behind him, while he conducted a safety check
outdoors. He pulled his pistol and crouched behind the hydrangea
plants, listening for footsteps or cars. All he heard after fifteen
minutes were the chirpings of insects and a faraway whinny of a
horse.

He gave the four-part knock, and Tammie let him back in, her eyes as round as the full moon over the Whitman farm. "You don't think someone was trying to get in, do you?"

"I don't, but that's why I need you and Claire to be extremely careful. The closer we get to finding the murderer, the bolder he or she might become. Poisoned cookies didn't work, so he might try something else." Parrott put away his pistol and returned to the table. "You said you had something else?"

"These," she said, sitting next to him and opening the packs of photos. She dealt them out on the table like an open poker hand. "When I went to put the photo of Tripp and the three other guys back in the cabinet, I found more photos from the party. I think you'll be very interested in some of them." Her hands shook, and Parrott wondered whether she might cry again.

The photos were more candid shots of what looked like the same pre-construction party. The buffet table, the bar, the flowers. Some guests stood with drinks or plates of food in their hands. There were a few small tables, where people sat, apparently in conversation. All told, Parrott estimated a crowd of twenty or so. One photo showed a Black man from an angle, holding a drink to his lips. Could that be Herman? Parrott couldn't tell.

The second package of photos revealed a more raucous impression of the party. Still shots of people in motion, perhaps singing and dancing. "Look at these," Tammie said, her voice an octave higher. She pointed to a series of photos of what looked like limbo dancing. Five or six people were standing in line, while one approached a string of colorful, tied-together scarves, being held by two women.

"The limbo?" Parrott asked.

"Yes. After everyone was tanked up, someone had the bright idea. I didn't limbo, but that's me holding one end of the scarf."

All Parrott could see of Tammie from the angle of the photo was hair, torso, arm, and leg. "Who's the woman at the other end?"

"Wife of the financial guy. The limbo was her idea. Anyway, that's not why I called you. Look at these limbo pics." She slid a few of the photos toward Parrott. "Here, this is the first one." She held the photo in mid-air, in front of Parrott's nose.

Parrott recognized the limbo dancer as Brock Thornton. The scarves were about two and a half feet above the floor, so Thornton had to bend his back pretty far. His shirt tail had come loose from his pants, and it rose up, showing a gap of skin.

"Do you see it?" Tammie almost shouted, then lowered her voice. "Here, you'll see it better on the next one." She handed over the next photo, still showing Thornton, but this time halfway through the silk marker and shot from a different angle, almost bird's-eye.

This time his shirt showed a little more skin, and the ink of a tattoo was visible. "May I use this magnifying glass?" he asked, certain that Tammie had set it out on the table for this very reason. Holding the photo in one hand and the glass in the other, he peered at the section of Brock Thornton's torso.

What he saw took his breath away. "Is this tattoo what I think it is?"

"Exactly. What you're seeing is a part of the Greek letters, sigma alpha epsilon. I'm pretty sure it's the same tattoo that was on Tripp's stomach."

CHAPTER SIXTY-EIGHT

Saturday morning, Tonya left for an extra appointment with Alice, and Parrott drove into the station to get some work done at his office. When he arrived, the clerk on duty handed him a message from the coroner. "Maria Rodriguez called to say they're sending Tripp Anderson's body to North Carolina this afternoon."

"I know, but thanks for taking the message."

After brewing his coffee and settling into his chair, Parrott called the SAE office in Chicago. He didn't expect anyone to answer on the weekend, but he left an urgent message and followed up with an email. No names appeared on the website, so that would be a dead end until they got back to him. Next, he called Tripp's father.

After preliminaries, Parrott asked, "Are you aware of whether Tripp had college yearbooks or fraternity composite photos from his years at Chapel Hill?"

"Yes, as a matter of fact, my wife and I have all of them here, at our house. We were just going through the things in Tripp's room, and we found them on his nightstand. We wondered why, since he's been out of college so long. Why? Do you think they're pertinent to his murder?"

"They could be. Can you please send them to me by FedEx Priority Overnight? I'll reimburse you for the cost. You can send them to me at home to speed things up."

"I can do better than that," Anderson said. "I'm coming back to Philadelphia this afternoon. The coroner has finally released Tripp's body, and my wife and I want to fly on the same plane with him. Probably sounds strange."

"Not at all. I'm sure I'd feel the same way. How about if I meet you at the airport, and you can bring me the yearbooks, composites—anything at all related to Tripp's college years involving names or photographs."

"Sure thing. Glad you caught us before we left home." Anderson gave Parrott information about where and when to find him.

Grateful for the way fate had shortened the time to acquire these items, Parrott took a chance to garner another bit of information. "By the way, did you ever hear Tripp talk about someone named Brock Thornton?"

"Brock Thornton? Not that I can remember. Was he a college friend?"

"That's what we want to find out. Mention the name to Mrs. Anderson, and if it rings a bell, she can tell me when I meet you both at the airport."

After he disconnected, Parrott drank his coffee and did a search in the court archives for Commonwealth v. Thornton. Not that he doubted Pennington, but it never hurt to verify, especially since Pennington still had one foot on the suspect list. After some digging around, he found the case. Harvey Thornton had been convicted of involuntary manslaughter and remanded to the state correctional facility at Rockview. He served three out of a four-year sentence and was released.

Whatever happened to Thornton after he left Rockview, he never had another arrest or conviction. He never served in the military. Claire had said Brock Thornton came Newport. There were no Rhode Island drivers' licenses issued currently under the name of Harvey Thornton, but who knew if the man was still alive, still driving, or if he still used his real name. For now, it was enough to know that Pennington's story about the involuntary manslaughter was true.

As long as he had the criminal database open, Parrott did quick searches for Herman Powell and Brock Thornton.. Neither came up dirty, but he didn't expect them to. Searching technology behind Sylvester's deep dive was like picking bones after a heavy feast.

He had four hours before meeting the Andersons at the airport. He called Tonya, who was leaving Alice's office. "Hey, honey. How was your appointment?"

"Good. Alice applauded me for telling you. She says that was a huge positive step."

A bubble of hope rose in Parrott's throat, and his jaw relaxed. He hadn't realized until now how tightly he'd been clenching. "I've got a proposition for you, if you can arrange a spur-of-the-moment house tour. I have to be at the airport at four-thirty. That should give us time to check out the house, right?"

Tonya's response had a new lightness. "Oh, Ollie. I'm sure the agent would be *glad* to meet us there. He knows about your erratic schedule and told me I could call him anytime that was good for you." She gave Parrott the address and told him that, unless she called him back, she would meet him there right away.

His coffee was long gone by the time he shut down the computer. He called the hospital to check on Jacqueline Pennington. Introducing himself and giving his badge number to the clerk at the patient information desk, he learned that Jacqueline's condition had been upgraded to "serious, but stable." The news made him cautiously optimistic. When he caught the poisoner, maybe he'd only have to charge him with attempted murder.

With next steps planted in his mind, Parrott neatened his desk and left the office. Who knew? Maybe today would be the day he bought a new house.

CHAPTER SIXTY-NINE

Claire was already tired of being laid up with her ankle. She had always thought the key to an active life was living one, and spending all day reclining on a sofa was getting to her. Tammie had ordered her a knee scooter on Amazon, but it hadn't arrived yet.

Tammie had insisted Claire tell her daughters about the accident. Claire had pushed back with a million excuses, but Tammie wouldn't relent. "Think of how bad it would be if they heard about this from somebody else. They'd never trust you again."

Finally, Claire agreed to tell them what had happened, but she left out the part about driving the golf cart to Robert's. She let them think she'd been driving to Charlie's cottage.

Early this morning, Jessica brought over a pot of chicken soup, her cure for everything. Claire pretended to be delighted, although hot soup in the summer was not her idea of a treat. A fleeting thought of Parrott's warning not to eat anything brought in from outside passed through Claire's mind, but she dismissed it. Jessica would never think of poisoning her—just bossing her around a bit.

"While you're here," Claire said, "I want to talk to you about something important."

Jessica moved her neon green glasses down on her nose and stared at her mother. "Okay, what is it?"

"I'm determined to set up Sweetgrass as a nature reserve. I plan to work with the conservancy. There will be a high startup expense, but once established, the visitors' fees will keep the place going. Think about Longwood Gardens, only on a much smaller scale." She paused to assess Jessica's reaction so far—a hmm, a nod, a shoulder shrug. "You and your sister don't seem interested in moving here when I'm gone, and I hate to think that this estate might fall into the hands of strangers who won't care about preserving the natural beauty."

"I'm fine with it, Mom, and I'm sure Rebecca will be, too. We've talked about what would happen to Sweetgrass when you're not living here, and we feel the same way you do."

A warmth spread through Claire that had nothing to do with the temperature. She was proud to have raised two unselfish daughters who cherished the land the way she did, although more credit belonged to Scott for involving them in community issues at a young age. "You understand I'll be using a substantial amount of money to establish this entity. That's money that you and Rebecca will not inherit."

Jessica removed her glasses altogether and smiled. "Check with Rebecca to be sure, but I'm okay with it. After all, it's *your* money to do with as you wish. The only thing I'd caution you about it to get good, solid legal and financial advice. I know that's the first thing Dad would tell you."

"I will. I'll call Rebecca this afternoon and ask to consult with Matt. Even though he doesn't practice in Pennsylvania, he'll be able to guide me and maybe recommend a local attorney experienced in conservancy issues." Claire straightened her posture, trying not to flinch from the shot of pain in her ankle. "Now, tell me what's new in your world. How are Bonnie and Scotty doing?"

"Bonnie's off to New York next weekend. Ray's got a job at Madison Square Garden, and I'll babysit Scotty. Maybe we'll come swimming if that's okay. That way we can both see you." Jessica picked at a thread on her linen pants. "Seems like Bonnie and Ray are getting way more serious. I don't know what that will mean if they get married and Ray keeps traveling all over the world."

Claire reached for her daughter's hand. "I know how you feel, but if Ray is the one who makes Bonnie happy—"

After Jessica left, Claire called Rebecca and left a message. Then she decided to pester Brock Thornton for her money. His lack of responsiveness was starting to needle her, and she wanted to get going on the conservancy project.

She pressed his number on her cellphone, fully expecting to have to leave another message that he probably wouldn't return.

When Thornton answered on the third ring, Claire nearly fell off the chair, not a good thing for her bad ankle. "Good afternoon, Mrs. Whitman," he said in his clipped Eastern accent. "I was just leaving my office for the day, but when I saw your name pop up, I wanted to answer. I'm sorry it's taken me so long to get back to you."

Unimpressed by his politeness, Claire got to the point. "Yes, I expected you to contact me sooner. When will I have my money?"

"Perhaps you don't understand. These things take more than a phone call to accomplish. Your money is tied up in secure stocks and bonds. I will need time to draft sell orders and obtain your signatures. Meanwhile, I'd like you to rethink—"

"I'm not rethinking. How soon can you draft the sell orders? Why haven't you already done so?"

The financial advisor's tone switched from polite to sarcastic. "Look, I know you're upset about your barn and all, but you aren't my only client, and I can't put myself at your beck and call. If I wanted to work for prima donnas, I would have become a Hollywood agent."

Heat rushed to Claire's face. She couldn't believe her ears. "That remark does not speak well for a man in your position, Mr. Thornton. So many of us have entrusted you with large sums of money, and you could at least show some respect." Taking a deep breath, she tamped down her anger. It wouldn't accomplish much to antagonize. She'd save her comments for *after* she got her money back.

"It's true, the loss of my barn has been a blow, but nothing compared to the fact that a person I cared about has lost his life there. I'm happy to say Detective Parrott has been working hard to solve the case, and I'm confident that he will soon discover the perpetrator of these crimes." She tapped a fingernail against the cellphone, thinking of what to say next. "Nevertheless, the barn and the death have nothing to do with my desire to cash out my account with you. I've already committed the money to another cause. When can I sign the orders?"

"How about I bring them to your house this evening? Would seven o'clock be a good time?"

Somewhat mollified, Claire said, "That would be fine. And how soon after I sign will I have my money?"

"I'll be able to provide you with a cashier's check within seven days of my submitting your orders. That would be no later than a week from Monday. I promise."

Claire disconnected but continued to hold the phone to her chest. No matter how conciliatory Brock Thornton sounded, she simply couldn't trust him. She wondered why Robert had ever recommended she do business with such a slimeball.

CHAPTER SEVENTY

Parrott scooted out of the house in West Chester to head for the airport. The house was exactly as Tonya had billed it— large, well-appointed, and well-situated for people in their circumstances. He'd taken Tonya aside and whispered the terms they would want in a bid. They agreed she'd take care of it with the new real estate agent.

Now he entered the airport, donned a mask, and headed to the American Airlines terminal, where the Andersons were to disembark. He'd allowed plenty of time to badge his way into the gate area, a fairly elaborate process, since he was carrying a firearm. He managed to get through in time to see Mr. Anderson shuffle through the jetway from the plane to the terminal. The woman next to him was pretty in a Meryl Streep kind of way— hair swept back from her face, classic cheekbones, a faraway look in the eyes. Parrott couldn't imagine the grief she carried behind that stoic expression.

Tripp's father carried a black zippered travel bag with the word, "Hawaii," scribbled all over it in pink and white letters. When he saw Parrott, he blinked in recognition and walked a little faster.

They met at the edge of the gate area and shook hands. Parrott expressed sympathy to Mrs. Anderson, who bit her lips together as if to keep the plug in the dike of her emotions. Because they had arranged their return flight to be on the same airplane as Tripp's body and casket, they had no time to chat. Their return flight would leave shortly.

"Here's the stuff you requested," Anderson said. "We'd like it all back when you're finished."

Parrott took the bag by the sturdy handles, surprised by the weight. "I'll return everything to you as soon as possible." He considered how he might show his gratitude. A hug would be too personal, another handshake perfunctory, a pat on the back inappropriate. Finally, he settled for a nod and meaningful eye contact with each of Tripp's parents.

"If you'll excuse us, detective, we need to leave you. Our instructions from Terry Funeral Home are to watch from the window while our son is loaded onto the plane's cargo section. Please forgive us."

"Of course. I'll be in touch," Parrott said, turning to go. The bag swung against his knee as he strode down the hallway of the terminal. The rhythmic swinging and hitting seemed to say, "Tick-tock, tick-tock." Parrott picked up his pace.

He'd intended to wait until he arrived back at the station before going through the bag, but when he reached his car, the urge to peek was too great to resist. He unzipped the Hawaii bag and pulled out one yearbook, entitled, Yackety Yack. Finding the index of students at the back of the book, he searched for Brock Thornton's name. There was nothing.

He shoved that yearbook back into the bag and tried another. Same result. Disappointed, he checked the other two yearbooks. Perhaps Thornton was a bit older or a bit younger than Tripp. Nothing showed up, however. Possibly, this was another dead end in a case full of dead ends, but Parrott wouldn't give up.

Driving to the station, Parrott pondered why all his searches for Brock Thornton had come up dry. Thornton failed to exist on Google, and now the hunch about the fraternity connection that had seemed the most promising was petering out.

Parrott parked near the playground where families were swinging and sliding and running around. He hoisted the Hawaii bag over his shoulder. In his office, he removed the contents and spread them out on his desk—four yearbooks, four SAE composite photos, taken by a photographer, and a plastic bag with a stack of casual photos.

Too fired up to stop for coffee, Parrott opened the yearbooks to the index pages again. Perhaps he had missed Thornton's name the first time. He used a ruler to isolate each name in the six-point print. When he couldn't find anything, he shifted to the fraternity composites. He paid no attention to the photos. At a glance, they were all the same, white, healthy, and good-looking. Right now, all Parrott cared about were the names beneath the photos.

Brock Thornton's name didn't appear on any of them. Parrott leaned back in his chair and sighed. *Damn, I was so sure this would pan out. The tattoo on the stomach—it had to be more than a coincidence.*

Parrott pulled a magnifying glass from his desk drawer and went back to one of the yearbooks, this time looking at the fraternity section. A page for SAE showed several group photos, some with captions, some without. Parrott looked for Tripp Anderson's name and found it beneath a photo of a large group of guys forming a cheerleading pyramid. Tripp was on the bottom right, blond hair hanging over his eyes, a toothy smile. The magnifying glass teased out a few other details—a strong chin, dimples.

He examined the faces of the other guys in the photo. Could one of them be Brock Thornton, even though his name didn't appear in the caption? Parrott was practiced in distinguishing facial features and expressions. Nuances, such as eyebrow shape, hairline, tooth alignment, and ear features, came under scrutiny beneath the magnifier. Still, the fraternity brothers looked remarkably similar. Also, the Brock Thornton of today, whom Parrott had only seen in person that one time at Herman's office, would have been about twenty years younger in these photos.

One face stood out as a possible, though. The guy at the top of the pyramid gazed directly into the camera with a surly expression. The forehead, cheekbones, and mouth reminded Parrott a lot of the financial manager, but something was off. Parrott closed his eyes, trying to recreate the image of Thornton's face. After several seconds, the memory of Thornton coalesced before him, and he was able to compare it with the young man's image in the photo. The younger man had straight hair, while Thornton's was wavy. More importantly, the grin on the young man's face under the magnifying glass, showed an overlapping of front teeth. The smile was different.

Parrott checked the caption for the name of the guy at the top of the pyramid. It was Ethan Pryor. Then Parrott used the index to find Ethan Pryor elsewhere in the yearbook. On page seventy-seven, a bigger and closer photo of Ethan Pryor gazed out with a tooth-revealing smile. Excited, Parrott sped through the other three yearbooks, looking for and finding Ethan Pryor. More and more convinced, he checked out the composites, where Ethan Pryor appeared, as well.

Hair and teeth could be changed almost as seamlessly as a name, and Parrott grew more certain that he had found Thornton's real identity. And if *he* had found it, then it was likely that Tripp would have recognized him, too.

Parrott searched in his police database for a criminal record for a man named Ethan Pryor, and what he found caused cymbals to crash in his head and a major piece of the puzzle to fall into place.

CHAPTER SEVENTY-ONE

arrott stood at the window in his office, overlooking the playground, where the afternoon sun had cast geometrical shadows onto the rubber pellets covering the ground. If Chief Schrik had walked in, he might have thought the detective to be considering what to have for dinner or where to go for entertainment on this Saturday evening. But beneath the casual pose, Parrott's heart was pounding double-time.

Detective work knew no schedules, no regular hours, no weekends. Parrott's heart and mind were on fire with the new knowledge about Ethan Pryor, and he knew he had to act fast. He pulled up the list of names and addresses Sylvester had given him and memorized the one for Mavis Thornton. Sylvester had made a note saying there was no home or office address available for Brock. Parrott plugged the address into Google Maps, noting how close it was to Claire's and Pennington's.

Parrott checked the ammunition in his pistol and stuffed the firearm in his shoulder holster. He strapped a second pistol on with the ankle holster, and then, for good measure, threw a small pepper spray canister in his other pocket. "Brock Thornton" may or may not speak to him without a warrant, but Parrott wanted to be prepared for anything.

Not wanting to take the time for a phone call, he texted Tonya to tell her he'd be late. Even with the excitement of their bid on the house, she would understand. Working late on a Saturday night meant crunch time.

He texted Chief Schrik, as well. *Brock Thornton really Ethan Pryor. Going to his house to shake things loose. If things get ugly, may need backup.*

Soon, Parrott arrived on the doorstep of a massive country mansion, set a quarter mile from the road. To get there, he had passed a stable, a paddock, and more than a dozen horses, grazing in the evening air. He supposed the care of the horses fell to hired hands, since the Thorntons were purportedly out of town so much of the time.

It was six-thirty, Parrott's Toyota was the only vehicle in sight. A row of peonies flanked the front porch and door, and was bookended by flowering dogwood trees, gave the exterior of the house the polished look of a magazine spread. The gray flagstone porch matched the facing of the house, and a large brass door knocker in the shape of a horse's head completed the rustic look. The average Brandywine visitor would never have noticed the discreet security cameras tucked into the porch lintel and aiming at Parrott.

When he lifted the door knocker, a four-note melody sounded, and a PA system activated from within the house. Parrott scraped his shoes against the welcome mat, while he waited. After what seemed like ten minutes, Parrott turned to leave, but a tinny female voice stopped him.

"Who's there?"

Expecting a servant to open the door, Parrott hesitated. "Detective Parrott, West Brandywine Police. May I please speak with Mr. Thornton?"

"Mr. Thornton isn't here now. May I give him a message?" Something tipped Parrott off that this was not a servant, and maybe "Mr. Thornton" was indeed inside, trying to avoid a confrontation with a police officer.

"Is Mrs. Thornton there? I'd like to speak with her then." Parrott shifted his weight from foot to foot. He would have to change his approach

The voice took on a curious lilt. "Can you tell me what this is about?" Even without seeing her, Parrott knew this was Mavis Thornton, not a servant. Could it be that the Thorntons had no servants, or was this just a Saturday night thing?

"I'm investigating a case in Brandywine Valley, and I'm going door-to-door to caution residents about some possible scenarios. I think you'd want to know about them."

A long pause and some rustling. "All right. I'll be right down. But you'll have to show me your badge before I'll let you in."

Andrea Baker had told Parrott that Mavis Thornton was blonde and heavily made up, but the woman who answered the door looked nothing like Parrott expected. The petite woman had on a waffle-embossed bathrobe, long and tied at the waist with a sash. Most of her hair was pulled back in a ponytail, but stray hairs had escaped the elastic band in the back and on both sides of her face. Worst of all, streaks of mascara had laid tracks down her face, and her eyes and nose were red.

Parrott couldn't help suspecting abuse, although experience told him not to jump to conclusions. He showed his badge and asked to come in. The silence in the house created an awkwardness. No husband, no pets, no servants—just Parrott and a woman in a bathrobe.

As if she had read his mind, Mavis Thornton said, "Why don't you make yourself comfortable in the living room? I'm going to put on some better clothes. Be right back."

Her absence gave Parrott a chance to look around, but he needed to stay alert. The floor plan of the house was like others in Unionville. The décor had a totally different vibe, though. Parrott tried to analyze the difference, and all he could come up with was a sense of temporariness. There were no pictures anywhere—no family photos, no paintings. The furniture, window coverings, carpeting, and wall color were color-coordinated and looked expensive, but they reminded him of a fancy dollhouse, all for show. He wondered whether the sofa had ever been sat on.

These observations took less than a minute. Parrott was too keyed up to dwell on interior design right now. The culmination of facts in this case had led him to this house and this moment, but the person he wanted appeared not to be there.

True to her word, Mavis returned soon, wearing jeans and a t-shirt. Her ponytail had been released from its band, and her hair framed her face with bangs and a shoulder-length flip. The mascara tracks were gone, but she had made no attempt to cover her sad expression.

She perched on the edge of the chair across from Parrott, her posture as precise as a statue's.

"You said Mr. Thornton is not at home?" Parrott asked. "When do you expect him?" As much as Parrott wanted to talk to the husband, he also saw an opportunity to elicit information from the wife.

"I don't know." She pushed a strand of hair behind her ear. "Brock never tells me where he's going or when he'll be back. You'd think I'd know more about his habits by now. We've been married four years, living here in Unionville for three." She stared at her lap, clasping and unclasping her hands. "My husband is an important man. He's got many wealthy clients who don't want him to talk about their business, even to me."

"Anyway," she said, meeting Parrott's eyes for the first time, "you wanted to warn me about something?"

"Yes," Parrott said. "Two homes in this neighborhood have had poisonous food delivered anonymously to their doorsteps. I wanted to caution you not to eat anything suspicious, anything that comes from an unknown source."

"Omigod, that's terrible." Mavis' eyes opened wider. "I don't know our neighbors that well, but people out here—well, we all drop things off on doorsteps all the time. I just took jars of homemade pasta sauce to ten different households."

Parrott watched for a tell that she was hiding something, but her facial expression and body language spoke of genuine surprise. "I suggest you suspend this neighborly practice for the foreseeable future. I can't give any names, but one of your neighbors is in the hospital, in ICU. I suggest you keep your doors and windows locked and call me if you see or hear anything suspicious, especially if you receive any food from someone you don't know or trust."

"You're very kind," she said, picking at a spot on her chair.

Parrott withdrew a card from his breast pocket and handed it to Mavis.

She stared at the card. "What was the food that poisoned the neighbor?"

Parrott watched closely as he responded. "Decorated cookies. They were delivered in a white bakery box."

A whoosh accompanied Mavis' intake of breath. The woman wobbled in her chair, as if she might fall forward in a faint.

Parrott jumped out of his seat and bent to hold onto the woman's shoulders. "I'll get you some water," he said.

"N-no, I'll be okay. For a moment I thought I might throw up, but it's passed now."

"Was it the mention of the decorated cookies? Did you receive some, too?"

Mavis averted her eyes and shook her head. "N-no—"

Before she could answer any further, a ping came in on Parrott's phone. He glanced at the caller ID and saw Tammie's name. "Excuse me a second," he said. He opened the text and read the two words: *Come now.*

CHAPTER SEVENTY-TWO

P arrott bolted out of Mavis Thornton's house and sped to Sweetgrass, only three farms down the road. A new model Ferrari sat in the circular drive. Instead of ringing the doorbell, Parrott ran around the circumference of the mansion, peering into windows and checking to see if any were unlocked. He couldn't take Tammie's call for help lightly. Something was going on inside, and, if he could, he wanted to use the element of surprise.

Now he wished he hadn't been so insistent that Tammie lock the doors and windows and keep the garage door down. The garage door was closed, but the garage also had a window. Parrott tested the window, but it, too, was locked. The pane of this window, however, was a single piece of glass, easy to cut out and remove.

Whenever Parrott had removed glass panes before, he had used masking tape and a tarp, neither of which he had available, and his pounding heart reminded him that time was scarce. Using the butt of his pistol, he smashed the glass repeatedly until no shards were visible. Reaching through the opening, he unlocked the mechanism and lifted the frame. Climbing through what might be a forty-inch-wide window might be difficult for a six-four-four-inch, two hundred-twenty-pound man, but he had no choice.

He peered in. A utility table with a toolbox and other items sat beneath the window, covered with broken glass. Parrott removed his sport jacket and tossed it through the window. Maybe it would save him from a few cuts. He hoisted himself on the window frame, high enough to duck his head through the opening, but not enough to get a knee up. The thought of Claire and Tammie in peril spurred him to exert more force. Elbows and knees working to full capacity, he leveraged himself through the window and onto the table. The jacket had helped, but tiny bits of glass clung to his hands and knees, and he had no time to pick them out. He donned his jacket, brushed himself off, patted the places where his weapons were concealed, and prayed the door from the garage to the house was unlocked.

He remembered this door led to the laundry room and into the kitchen. Not knowing what he would find if the door opened, he grasped the knob and turned it, a bit at a time. It worked. Thankful he'd found an entry point into the house, he paused inside the doorway to listen, his hand on the pistol in his right pocket.

He tiptoed toward Claire's study, where muffled cries caused sparks of fear to burst into flame in Parrott's gut. He peered through the doorframe, ready to spring into action, no matter what was happening. What *was* happening, however, gave him a start. Facing him were Claire and Tammie, both gagged and tied to chairs.

Both women reacted to seeing Parrott at the doorway, but he held a finger to his lips. A man stood with his back to Parrott, chattering in an excited voice, as if bragging about his invention at an awards ceremony. "Nothing personal, you understand," he said. "I have nothing against old ladies or their caregivers. I tried to get you to back off, but even after I caused your accident, you pushed me to return the money." He waved a handgun at each of their faces. "I simply can't cash out your investments. You never should have asked me."

Even before the man headed for Claire's desk, where a stack of papers sat next to a large leather briefcase, Parrott recognized Brock Thornton. His voice had slipped away from the cultivated Eastern accent he'd used at Herman's office, but his build and wavy blond hair were the same. His shape also matched that of the man in the security videos who'd put the flyers on Wyatt Wukitsch's car.

Still not seeing Parrott, the man strutted. He lifted the briefcase and carried it back to where the two women could see what he was doing. He was an actor on a stage, and the play was a horrifying drama. "Don't worry. You won't feel a thing. I'll make sure of that," he said, as he set down his pistol and yanked objects from the briefcase with both hands, putting them on the floor.

The objects barely registered in Parrott's brain at first. The fact that Thornton had set down his gun caused Parrott to spring into action. "Put your hands up, Thornton, or should I say, Pryor?" Parrott was a much larger man, and, holding a pistol, he had the advantage. He rushed at Thornton, only realizing as he made contact that the items being removed from the briefcase were the ingredients for making meth.

Thornton spun around and squirted a liquid into Parrott's face, causing him to drop his pistol and fall to the ground in pain. Parrott recognized the bottle of nasal spray with a yellow and white label. It was fentanyl. Articles had been popping up about policemen who had been overcome by fentanyl sprays, a few of them dying from the overdosed exposure.

Parrott fought to hold onto consciousness, while Thornton stood over him, taunting him for his weakness. "Did I hear you say, 'Pryor,' detective? How brilliant of you. I don't know how you found out about me and my ingenious plan. Once I learned my buddy Steve Thornton's grandfather went to jail for Robert Pennington, I was golden. All I had to do was kill and impersonate Steve Thornton, changing his name to Brock. A nice touch, don't you think? Too bad you won't get to use that information, though. And neither could that douchebag, Anderson. According to my research, this fentanyl will kill you within the next ten minutes."

Thornton turned to Claire and Tammie. "Don't worry, ladies. I have more fentanyl for you. By the time I've finished with you, none of you will even notice when this whole house blows up from meth."

CHAPTER SEVENTY-THREE

Parrott lay on the floor, overcome with dizziness and confusion. His breath was coming in slow, shallow puffs, hardly enough to sustain him. Thornton was babbling about how he'd come too far to lose his multi-million-dollar investment empire. Parrott only half-heard what Thornton was saying. In his semi-conscious state, Parrott gritted his teeth, struggling to hold onto muscle control.

Reaching for his pistol was hopeless. He was more disabled than if he'd been hog-tied. He concentrated on clenching his right hand. If only he could grab the ankle pistol and fire. Then he remembered the pepper spray in his left pocket. The canister was much lighter than a pistol, and small enough to be concealed within his large palm.

Guttural sounds came from the direction where Claire and Tammie sat, bound and gagged, but fully conscious of Thornton's movements. Parrott was their only chance of surviving, and he didn't have much time—or strength—left.

Thornton kept a running patter as he went to work. Parrott paid less attention to the gloating words. His left hand had worked its way to within a few inches of his left pocket, but the dizziness was increasing, and his eyes blurred so badly that he could barely see. Unless he received medical attention soon, the fentanyl would slow his respiration and heart to a stop, but he couldn't give up. If he disabled Thornton before he sprayed Claire and Tammie with fentanyl or blew up the house, he might be able to save them.

A fleeting thought of Tonya and the house and the babies they would now never have passed through his mind, causing him to push harder. At last, his left hand closed itself over the pepper spray canister, and he drew it out of his pocket.

Humming sounds came from above Parrott, who could no longer see anything but dark shapes. Thornton hovered over Parrott's body, singing, "We Are the Champions." As he sang, droplets of spit landed onto Parrott's face, and Parrott curled into a ball, then uncurled in a move he'd learned in training. With his left hand, he unleashed the pepper spray, right into Thornton's eyes.

"You sonofabitch." Thornton yelled at the top of his lungs. "My eyes are on fire."

A surge of elation caused Parrott to smile, at least inside. Brock Thornton would be out of commission for an hour, hopefully long enough to prevent him from completing his plan to kill Claire and Tammie and destroy Sweetgrass. The chief would read Parrott's text and know that Thornton was Ethan Pryor, a loser drug dealer from North Carolina, who had served time for blowing up a liquor store and killing the owner—a man named Steve Thornton.

Parrott's breathing slowed to the point where only wisps of air entered and exited his lungs. He stopped listening to the thrashes and moans of Ethan Pryor. His last thought before he lost consciousness was of Tonya. She deserved to heal and be happy.

In the next minute, Officer Randy Barton burst through the door to Claire's study, followed by Chief Schrik. Within seconds they assessed the situation—the women tied and gagged, Parrott lying motionless on the floor, and Ethan Pryor, blind and crying out for help.

Barton rushed at Pryor, throwing his weight on the blind man's shoulders, pinning him to the ground, and cuffing his hands behind him.

Schrik called 911 and screamed into the phone to hurry. "Fentanyl overdose. My best officer's down," he said, not thinking about whether his words would offend Barton. Schrik cut the bonds and tore the gags from Claire and then Tammie, who both talked at once, explaining what had happened. He hustled them outside, instructing them to sit separately and not converse until further notice. Then he called Chesco to get evidence techs out to the scene.

Barton jerked the blind and handcuffed Pryor outside and into the squad car's back seat and shackled his ankles together. Leaving him in the thick summer night, he returned to photograph and bag the evidence of Pryor's foiled plans.

When the paramedics arrived, they took Parrott's vitals immediately. "He's got a pulse. Weak, but present. Let's get some naloxone in him right away." An intramuscular injection caused Parrott to stir, but the paramedic warned Schrik not to get his hopes up. "Gotta transport him to the hospital ASAP. Naloxone wears off, and he's gonna need more treatment." They started an IV in his hand and loaded him onto a stretcher.

"I'll call Tonya to meet you at the hospital," Schrik said. As the stretcher was rushed out the door, Claire called out from the porch, "Thank you for saving our lives, Detective Parrott. Now God bless you and save yours."

Twenty-four hours later, Parrott awoke in his hospital room. The only lights came from the television and the wall sconce aimed at the ceiling. Tonya sat in the recliner next to his bed, holding his hand, and snoring softly. Delighted he could move, he lifted her hand and brushed it against his lips.

Tonya's eyes flew open, and she jumped out of her chair. "Ollie? You're awake." Several hugs later, she called the nursing station. The night nurse came in with an armload of goodies, including a fresh pitcher of water, a handful of graham crackers, and a warm blanket.

"You had us plenty worried, Mr. Parrott," she said, as she typed information into the computer. "Don't be thinking you're all well, though. You're gonna need to stay right here in this bed for a few more days, while you get your strength back."

After the nurse left, Tonya squeezed his hand. "You want company? I wouldn't mind sharing that warm blanket with you." She crawled onto the bed and lay on her side, propped on her elbow, careful of the various tubes.

"You want to talk?" she asked, after a while.

Parrott nodded. "Tell me what happened. Last thing I remember is spraying Ethan Pryor with capsaicin. How'd I get to the hospital?"

Tonya explained how Schrik and Barton had arrived at the scene and called 911. "You were pretty bad off."

"How'd Schrik and Barton know to come to Sweetgrass?"

"You might not believe this, but Brock Thornton's wife, Mavis, called them. She said you'd saved her life, and she wanted to save yours."

Parrott had trouble processing how he'd saved Mavis' life. He must have looked perplexed, because Tonya explained further. "Evidently, things had been rocky between Mr. and Mrs. Thornton, and Mavis had mentioned divorce. Brock flew into a fury and left the house for several hours. When he returned, he tried to make up. He'd brought her a gift from the bakery—a box of decorated cookies."

Parrott chuckled. "So, when I told her about the poisoned cookies, she realized that her husband was a killer."

"Yeah. She said she might have eaten a cookie if you hadn't warned her off. When you flew out of the house after receiving a text, she called the police station and left a message for the chief."

"What happened to Thornton? His real name is Pryor, you know."

"He's in jail. Chief Schrik talked to the DA. Case will go to the Grand Jury tomorrow, charging him with murder, arson, and a bunch of other things—they've thrown the book at him. He's had quite the Ponzi scheme going for the past few years. Aren't you glad we didn't invest with him?"

"We never would have gotten that far, and I wouldn't have let Ma and Herman, either. Once Pryor realized I was a cop, he pulled back. He didn't want me anywhere near him or his operation."

"He blew up Claire Whitman's bank barn, didn't he?"

"Yes. He'd killed the boyfriend of Claire's personal assistant, Tammie. He burned the barn to cover Tripp Anderson's death."

Tonya patted Parrott's forearm. "So why did he kill Anderson?"

"You know, you should be a detective. You ask all the right questions." Parrott touched his wife's cheek, so grateful to be alive. "Tripp and Ethan Pryor were fraternity brothers at Chapel Hill. They both tattooed their stomachs with the letters Sigma Alpha Epsilon. Later, Pryor changed his name, had plastic surgery, and reinvented himself as Brock Thornton. He came to Brandywine with a story that convinced Robert Pennington to sponsor him as a financial advisor." Parrott pointed to the pitcher of water. "May I have a drink?"

Tonya climbed out of the bed and poured two cups of water, one for her husband and one for herself. "Here's to us," she said, touching one cup to the other.

Parrott took a long drink and continued to talk. "Anderson didn't recognize Pryor at first. Years had passed since college, and Pryor's disguise was successful. But at some point, Anderson must have seen the tattoo and put two and two together. He told Tammie he was coming back to town for a project. I think he threatened to expose Pryor, and the guy went ballistic. He had to kill Anderson, or he'd lose everything he'd worked so hard to build up."

"He tried to kill Claire, too," Tonya said. "Claire and Tammie were here this morning to check on you. Claire said she'd demanded the return of her money."

Parrott nodded. "He couldn't return her money. He'd already used it to pay dividends to other clients. His whole scheme had started to unravel, and he was desperate to control the damage. He's the one who disabled her golf cart, which led to her sprained ankle."

Tonya gazed at her husband. "Exactly. He confessed to all that while you've been in here sleeping. But how did you know?"

Parrott tapped his forehead and laughed. "I have my ways. I guess you didn't know your husband was clairvoyant."

Tonya leaned over and gave the clairvoyant a big kiss. "Well, in that case, Mr. Detective, tell me what I'm thinking right now."

Parrott held a hand to his forehead and closed his eyes for a few seconds. When he opened them again, he said, "That's easy. You're thinking about how to tell me that we're going to be the proud owners of a fabulous house in West Chester."

A look of disbelief crossed Tonya's face, and she burst into giggles. "Yes, Ollie. That's exactly what I was thinking. And we're going to fill that house with every happy moment that you and Horace and I can imagine. And while you're recovering, Mr. Clairvoyant, you can help me figure out how to decorate the nursery."

ACKNOWLEDGEMENTS

The writing of *Crystal Blue Murder* has been a treasured journey, enriched by the many knowledgeable, experienced, and generous people who have shared of themselves to authenticate details in the book. My deep appreciation to Richard D. Buchanan of Archer & Buchanan Architecture; Peggy Hart Earle; Missy Schaffer and Ben Barnett; and Scott Richard and Mamie Duff of Brandywine Valley. Their explanations and tours of bank barns and Brandywine Conservancy land gave substance to Claire's renovated barn and her plans for Sweetgrass.

Tim Brainard provided hundreds of details about meth and other drugs, as well as information about Wyatt Wukitch's struggles. Holly Gross gave me details about real estate, pertinent to Tonya's home search. Sheila Lowe shared her handwriting expertise, and Dr. Ike Silverman assisted with medical procedures used by EMTs and hospital personnel. Bette Berns, Camille Downes, Glen McGlothin, and Minette Lauren helped "feed" Detective Parrott.

I'm gratified that the Galveston Elks Lodge, including Asta Timm and Karen Crummett Sawyer, honored this book and *Bad Blood Sisters* by hosting a charitable event benefitting the Texas Elks Children's Services, and I'm especially pleased that Tammie Caballero contributed so generously to that worthy cause.

I'm eternally grateful to Lieutenant Destin Sims for his invaluable assistance and support in fleshing out the details of Parrott's investigation. Destin knows Parrott almost as well as I do, and he's always willing to listen to my scenarios and supply insightful suggestions. Dan Royse, formerly of the Tennessee Federal Bureau of Investigation, also assisted with procedural information.

Last, but not least, are three more debts of gratitude. My two author critique groups have helped me in huge and tiny ways to bring clarity to the story. I'm so fortunate to have a husband who encourages my passion for writing and helps with everything, including, but not limited to, brainstorming, legal advice, alpha-reading, revising, business decisions, events, and more. He also puts up with all the hours I am holed up writing or on zooms, when I could be doing something he wants us to do together. Thank you, Ed Richard.

Finally, a book doesn't live until it's read and enjoyed, so I thank you for reading *Crystal Blue Murder*. I hope you will leave an honest reader review, and I invite you to subscribe to my monthly newsletter at http://www.saralynrichard.com so you can join the fun adventures that comprise the reading-and-writing life.

ABOUT THE AUTHOR

Saralyn Richard writes award-winning mysteries that pull back the curtain on people in settings as diverse as elite country mansions and disadvantaged urban high schools. An active member of International Thriller Writers and Mystery Writers of America, Saralyn teaches creative writing and literature. Her favorite part of being an author is connecting with readers. Please subscribe to her monthly newsletter at the website, www.saralynrichard.com.

Photo by Jennifer Reynolds